...ARFIST

"This is state-of-the-art military science fiction."
—*Publishers Weekly* (starred review)

"Caution! Any book written by Dan Cragg and David Sherman is bound to be addictive. The authors have a deep firsthand knowledge of warfare, an enthralling vision of the future, and the skill of veteran writers. Fans of military fiction, science fiction, and suspense will all get their money's worth. These novels are fast, realistic, moral, and hard to put down. Sherman and Cragg are a great team!"

—RALPH PETERS,
New York Times bestselling author of *Red Army*

"[*Flashfire*] continues with a vivid depiction of ground combat worthy of ranking with Heinlein's classic *Starship Troopers*."
—*Booklist*

"Fans of military SF who appreciate down-and-dirty ground action will enjoy Sherman and Cragg's hyperrealistic look at the infantry combat of the future."
—*Publishers Weekly*

"A faced-paced tale of military heroics and personal courage."
—*Library Journal*

"Vivid characters, amazing but believable technology, and explosive action combine in a riveting adventure. Military fiction of any age or type simply does not get any better than this."
—MICHAEL LEE LANNING,
author of *Inside Force Recon: Recon Marines in Vietnam*
and *Inside the Crosshairs: Snipers in Vietnam*

WINGS OF HELL

STARFIST

DAVID SHERMAN AND DAN CRAGG

BALLANTINE BOOKS • NEW YORK

2009 Del Rey Books Mass Market Edition

Copyright © 2008 by David Sherman and Dan Cragg
Excerpt from *Starfist: Double Jeopardy* copyright © 2009 by David Sherman and Dan Cragg

Published in the United States by Del Rey, an imprint of The Random House Publishing Group, a division of Random House, Inc., New York.

DEL REY is a registered trademark and the Del Rey colophon is a trademark of Random House, Inc.

Originally published in hardcover in the United States by Del Rey Books, an imprint of The Random House Publishing Group, a division of Random House, Inc., in 2008.

This book contains an excerpt from the forthcoming book *Starfist: Double Jeopardy* by David Sherman and Dan Cragg. This excerpt has been set for this edition only and may not reflect the final content of the forthcoming edition.

ISBN 978-0-345-50100-4

Printed in the United States of America

www.delreybooks.com

9 8 7 6 5 4 3 2 1

To: PO3 Stuart Goldman, USN
USS *New Jersey* (BB-62)
RVN, South China Sea, 1968–69

PROLOGUE

The Grand Master sat at state on a raised dais in his hall. Idly, he watched as a diminutive female knelt before the low, lacquered table sitting at his side in convenient reach of his hand. The female poured hot liquid from a delicate pot into a small cup on the table next to a slender vase that held a lone, long-stemmed flower—the only ornament on the table. He continued to watch as she placed the pot on the table on the other side of the vase; then she picked up the small cup and delicately drank it down. Drinking complete, the diminutive female replaced the cup, sat back on her heels, folded her hands on her thighs, and waited as impassively as the four Large Ones who stood to the rear of the Grand Master, swords ready in their hands to protect their lord from attack. Only then did the Grand Master look away from her and raise a languid hand in signal.

In response, a column of diminutive females appeared from a side entrance to the hall, each bearing a pot of steaming liquid, and went in precise order around the hall, kneeling next to small, lacquered tables that sat between the pairs of Great Masters and Over Masters who knelt in ranks before the Grand Master. Each table held two small cups flanking a slender vase with a single, long-stemmed flower. The females poured steaming liquid into the cups, then placed the pots on iron trivets that lay behind the tables on the reed mats that covered the floor. The Great Masters and Over Masters were the senior staff of the Grand Master's corps, and the commanders of his major combat elements and their seconds.

Once all the Great Masters and Over Masters had been served, the Grand Master returned his attention to the female who had served him. When he detected no sign of distress in her countenance or posture, he nodded. She poured a fresh cup of liquid for the Grand Master. The Grand Master took the cup from her hands when she offered it to him, faced the assembled Great Masters and Over Masters, and raised the cup in salute.

He waited a beat or two for the assembled upper-rank Masters to raise their cups in return, then spoke: "To our coming great victory!" He quaffed the steaming beverage then held out the cup for the female to take and refill. The Grand Master's voice was rugged and raspy; as with nearly all Masters of the Emperor's army who attained such high rank, he had not exercised his gills in so long that they had atrophied, allowing air from under his arms, as well as from his lungs, to exit through his larynx, and affect his voice.

When the Grand Master offered his toast, the assembled staff and major combat unit commanders replied in kind and quaffed.

"The Master, Leaders, and Fighters who attacked the Earthman Marines in their own lair did not survive their mission," the Grand Master rasped. "But they killed or wounded many of the enemy. The survivors will have already sent a report on the encounter to their headquarters. The report will surely tell the Marine commanders that we are here, on this Earthman mud ball, and they will send more Marines for us to fight and kill." He grinned, exposing pointed incisors. "We shall soon complete plans for the coming fight, and we will rehearse them until both our staffs and our fighting forces execute them flawlessly.

"This time, as never before, we *shall* defeat the Earthman Marines!"

Finished speaking, the Grand Master extended his hand for the female kneeling near his side to hand him his refilled cup. He raised the cup in another salute and roared, "Victory!"

The hall reverberated with cries of "Victory!" from his staff and senior commanders.

* * *

Lieutenant General Pradesh Cumberland, Confederation Army, Deputy Commander of Task Force Aguinaldo, less formally known as "the Skink Force," stood in the doorway of General Anders Aguinaldo, late Commandant of the Confederation Marine Corps, and cleared his throat.

Without looking up from his console, Aguinaldo said, "Come on in, Pradesh."

Cumberland did so, shaking his head, wondering not for the first time how the Marine knew he was at the door. *Or am I the only one who clears his throat instead of knocking?* He closed the door behind himself.

"I've been going over the most recent personnel reports," Aguinaldo said as he finally looked up and waved his deputy to take a seat. He smiled wryly. "Ever since I sent that war warning to the commanders of Confederation forces, I've been inundated with requests—make that demands—from planetary presidents, prime ministers, dictators, and oligarchs, that I immediately return to their control the forces they committed to the Skink Force, to defend their home worlds." He snorted. "I even have demands from the senators from each of those worlds insisting that the units be returned."

"But we—you—can't do that!" Cumberland said.

"And I won't," Aguinaldo agreed. "We'll need every one of those units by the time this is over. Besides, several of them are already in transit to Haulover." He shook his head. "So much for the distribution limits I put on that message."

"You knew the limits would be ignored."

"I did, indeed." He leveled a look at his deputy. "I think my war warning woke them up as much as the President's public announcement of the Skinks' existence."

"A wake-up call they likely needed."

"So long as it doesn't cause a panic. I'm letting the President deal with that." Aguinaldo turned his console around so Cumberland could see it. "A fresh communication from what I've dubbed 'Confederation Forces Haulover (Provisional).' "

Cumberland quickly read the message:

TO: CG, TF AGUINALDO, ARSENAULT
FROM: BHIMBETKA, ALADDIN, LTCMDR, CPT. CNSS *BROWARD COUNTY*
RE: UPDATE OF ENEMY ORDER OF BATTLE, HAULOVER

SIR:
FOLLOWING DETAILED ANALYSIS OF STRING-OF-PEARLS MAP-PING OF HUMAN WORLD HAULOVER, DETERMINATION HAS BEEN MADE THAT ENEMY FORCE IS PROBABLE 50,000. PER-HAPS NOT ALL ARE COMBATANT. MAP WITH LOCATIONS OF SIGHTINGS OF ENEMY, INCLUDING ESTIMATED TYPES OF UNITS AND NUMBERS, IS ATTACHED.
RESPECTFULLY SUBMITTED,
BHIMBETKA, *BROWARD COUNTY*

"A probable force of fifty thousand," Cumberland murmured.

"Which number probably doesn't include support troops. So I'm staying with my earlier estimate of one hundred thousand enemy."

"It could be more."

"Indeed it could. That's why I'm standing up the XXX Corps in addition to the XVIII Corps. If we need them, they'll be ready to go on a few days' notice."

Cumberland tipped his head back for a moment, thinking. He nodded sharply. "Andy, there was an American general in the late twentieth century, name of Powell. He established what came to be called 'the Powell Doctrine.' It essentially said that you should never enter a war unless you have overwhelming force on your side."

Aguinaldo mentally rifled through his memories and quickly found the Powell Doctrine. "And it only held for a few years before someone with more faith in machines than in men scrap-heaped it." He thought for another moment, then added, "As I recall it, Powell won his war against a huge army in a matter of days."

"And the man who didn't want to use enough soldiers made a war that threw his country and a large part of the rest of the world into a turmoil that lasted far too many years."

"Your point is taken, Pradesh. You're a good thinker; that's why you're my deputy. I will issue orders for XXX Corps to deploy to Haulover as soon as shipping is available for it."

"Overwhelming force, sir?"

"Overwhelming force."

(*The incidents referred to above are detailed in* Starfist: Force Recon: Recoil.)

CHAPTER
ONE

Captain Lew Conorado, the commander of Company L of the infantry battalion of Thirty-fourth Fleet Initial Strike Team, settled into the chair behind the desk in his office and sighed. A thought crossed his mind: his wife, Marta. He shrugged it off. Let him finish the little bit of work he still had to do, then he could think of Marta. Better, he could go home to her.

He was at *his* desk, in *his* office. It felt like a long time since he'd last been there. And it *had* been a long time, as deployments go. In a normal forty-year career, a Marine might have a couple of dozen deployments, many involving combat. But only one or two of them would be actual *wars*. He thought back to the war on Diamunde, which had been his first war. It hadn't lasted as long as the later war on Kingdom, his second war. And now he was back from his *third* war, which was even longer than the one on Kingdom.

Three wars in less than ten years. He couldn't help but think that if Thirty-fourth Fleet Initial Strike Team hadn't been quarantined, he would have long since been transferred to a different posting and wouldn't have gone to either Kingdom or Ravenette. Maybe. Maybe there would have been other wars he would have gone to. He was sure there had to have been other operations involving Marines and army units acting together during that time, operations that counted as *wars*. He might have lost as many of his Marines on those operations as he had on the ones he'd actually fought in.

That's what was bothering him, what made sitting at *his* desk in *his* office in Marine Corps Base, Camp Major Pete Ellis, on Thorsfinni's World, feel so good. For the foreseeable future, he wasn't going to lose any more Marines.

He shook himself, because that kind of thinking could turn morbid in a hurry. It was better to think of what he still had to do before he could leave his office to go home, to where Marta waited for him, and begin the five days' liberty on which he'd already released his Marines.

The Marines had been debriefed on the voyage home from Ravenette, and Brigadier Sturgeon had already had his end-of-mission commanders' call, at which the FIST commander informed his unit commanders that the Confederation Ministry of Defense was striking a medal for the just-completed mission against the rebellious Coalition—which was only to be expected. He smiled to himself; Ensign Charlie Bass hadn't been informed yet, but the brigadier had told Conorado privately that at the awards ceremony following the liberty, Bass was going to be promoted to lieutenant. Nothing morbid in *that* thought. And Conorado liked the idea of not notifying Bass in advance.

The only thing he saw that couldn't wait a few days was Lance Corporal Francisco Ymenez, who had come in from Whiskey Company as a replacement when Lance Corporal MacIlargie was wounded on Ravenette and was still with the platoon as a temporary replacement. Ymenez wanted to stay with the platoon when MacIlargie returned to duty, and Bass wanted to keep him. But when MacIlargie and Lance Corporal Longfellow, the two men still recovering from wounds, returned there wouldn't be any open slots in the platoon for Ymenez to fill. It would be unconscionable for Conorado to leave the lance corporal dangling. He looked at the company roster.

And found he couldn't think straight. Marta was too much on his mind to allow him cogent thought. Anyway, personnel shuffling was the first sergeant's job. Figuring out how to shuffle people to allow Bass to keep Ymenez could wait a few days.

On the off chance that Ymenez was still on base, Conorado checked the location of his men. Ymenez was still in the barracks, almost the only one who hadn't yet taken off on liberty. Conorado told Corporal Palmer, the company chief clerk, who also hadn't yet left on liberty, to summon Ymenez.

Ymenez must have run from third platoon's squadbay, because less than a minute later Palmer announced him.

"Enter," Conorado commanded.

"Sir, Lance Corporal Ymenez reporting as ordered!" Ymenez said, as he stepped up to Conorado's desk and stood at rigid attention.

"At ease, Lance Corporal."

Ymenez shifted to parade rest.

"Ensign Bass tells me you want to stay in his platoon, that you'd rather not go back to Whiskey Company. Is that so?"

"Yes, sir. I'd like to stay with third platoon, sir."

"Why?"

"Sir? B-because third platoon is a damn fine platoon. And Ensign Bass is just about the best officer I've ever served under. Sir."

Conorado nodded. "Ensign Bass thinks you're an asset to the platoon. No promises, but I'll see what I can do. If possible, you'll get your wish. Now, Lance Corporal, liberty call has been sounded. Why are you still in the barracks?" He gave Ymenez a quick once-over. "Your garrison utilities are clean and your insignia is on right, head for Bronnys and enjoy yourself with the rest of the platoon." *And let me get home to Marta.*

A grin splashed across Ymenez's face as he snapped back to attention. "Aye aye, sir! Thank you, sir!" He executed a sharp about-face and marched out of the company commander's office. He was running by the time he hit the corridor outside the company office.

"Palmer, what are you still doing here?" Conorado demanded, leaving his office.

"Waiting to make sure there's nothing I have to do before I head for liberty, sir."

"Everything's done. Now get out of here so I can leave; my wife is waiting for me."

"Aye aye, sir." Palmer grinned. He locked his comp and preceded Conorado out of the office.

Most of the enlisted men of Company L, like the Marines of the rest of Thirty-fourth FIST, had headed just outside Camp Ellis's main gate, to Bronnoysund, for their five-day liberty. Most of the Marines of third platoon headed straight for Big Barb's, the combination ship's chandlery, hotel, bar, and bordello where every one of them could be found at one hour or another on any given day (or night) of shore liberty.

They were, as usual, greeted with boisterous enthusiasm when they entered Big Barb's. And a lot of joyful squeals from Big Barb's girls.

"Te-em!" The synchronized squeal wasn't the first, but it certainly cut through the others. Two lovely young women, one as dark as the other was fair, burst through the others crowding the Marines and hurtled onto Sergeant Tim Kerr, the second squad leader.

Unlike the last time Thirty-fourth FIST had returned from a deployment, when Frida and Gotta had almost knocked him off his feet with their greeting, Kerr was ready for them and braced himself for the onslaught.

Other young women threw themselves at the Marines:

The one called Erika cried, "Raoul!" and jumped off the lap of the farmer she'd been sweet-talking and encouraging to drink up; she ran to Corporal Raoul Pasquin, abandoning her farmer.

Carlala, long-haired and almost painfully thin, was coming down the stairs from the private rooms when the Marines came through the door. She nearly jumped over the banister in her haste to reach Corporal Joe Dean.

Corporal Dornhofer was blindsided when a voluptuous young woman named Klauda darted up behind and jumped on his back without crying out his name.

Corporal Chan saw statuesque Sigfreid barreling through the room, and ran to meet her head-on, acting on the theory that if he had enough momentum going when they collided, she wouldn't knock him to the floor. Considering how much bigger she was than he, that could be a serious issue.

Svelte Hildegard hadn't paired off with any particular one of the Marines in the past. She sashayed into the crowd and pressed herself against Lance Corporal Isadore Godenov. "Come here often?" she purred into his ear, then laughed so hard she almost doubled over. When she was able to stand straight, she managed so say, "That's such a dumb line, but I can't help it; I've wanted to say it for so long." Then she was laughing hard again. When she regained control she asked, "Seriously, Izzy, would you like some companionship?" Godenov looked at Hildegard's still-red face with tears on her cheeks. He was straining to hold back his own laughter, so he merely nodded. She took his hand and led him to a large table where some of the other third platoon Marines were already congregating with their girls.

Sergeant Ratliff, first squad leader, turned with a sharp retort on his tongue when a voice said into his ear, "Buy a girl a drink, sailor?" He swallowed the retort; it was Kona. Kona wasn't one of Big Barb's girls, she was a young widow from the village of Hryggurandlit who had come to the big party thrown for the Marines on their return from the war on Kingdom. She hadn't gone to the party looking to do anything in particular, and certainly she hadn't been looking for a man. But during the course of events she had found herself paired off with Sergeant Lupo Ratliff. And subsequently found that she actually liked him. She said, "I heard the FIST was back. Thought I'd like to see you again." She cocked her head. "And I hoped you'd like to see me again."

Ratliff gave her an exaggerated stern look. "I ain't no squid, lady. You take that back, and yes, I'd love to buy you a drink."

She reached out a hand and caressed his cheek. "I'd love to have a drink with you, Marine."

"Vat's goink on here!" All eyes turned to the booming voice. It was Big Barb Banak herself, the owner of Big Barb's, plowing her way through the crowded common room like an icebreaker through pack ice, heading unerringly toward the men of third platoon.

"Timmy," she roared when she reached the table, "you still beink greedy, you godda hab *two* girls?"

Before Kerr could answer, Gotta stuck her tongue out at Big Barb, and Frida shouted, "You gave him to us, and we are keeping him. So there!"

Big Barb snorted. Then she saw the sergeant's stripes on Kerr's shirt collars. "Who got kilt?" she gasped, searching the faces of the Marines of third platoon, looking for who wasn't there. "Vhere's Rat?"

Kerr shook his head. "Sergeant Linsman was killed."

"Ant you vas bromoted to tage his blace?"

Kerr nodded.

Big Barb continued searching the faces. "Vot aboud Billy?"

Corporal Orest Kindrachuck thumbed the chevrons on his collars. "I was promoted to replace him," he said in a thick voice.

"Glaypoole, Volfman, Longfeller, dey det too?"

Ratliff, as senior man present, answered her. "Claypoole's fine, he went off on his own. MacIlargie and Longfellow are in the hospital, but they'll be back with us soon." He paused, then continued, "They were too new. I don't think you had a chance to get to know them. PFC Smedley and PFC Delagarza were also killed."

"Ach min Gud," Big Barb muttered. She vaguely remembered Smedley, but the name Delagarza meant nothing to her. "Too many, too many det young men. Alla time, too many." She shook herself—and when Big Barb shook her hundreds of kilos it was something to see—and stood erect. "Vell, you're back. Enchoy yourselfs." She gave the Marines another look, and blinked. "Vat you doink here?" she squawked at a pretty young girl called Stulka, who was sitting on the lap of PFC John Three McGinty.

Stulka jumped, and whipped her arms from around McGinty's neck to her lap. "I'm, I'm just, I'm helping the other girls."

Stulka was the youngest of Big Barb's girls, and mostly waited tables and helped out in the kitchen.

"You don' godda do dat, you know."

"But the other girls are always saying how much fun they have with third platoon. I just want to have fun."

Big Barb gave Stulka a penetrating look. "Hokay," she finally agreed. *Vhy nod,* she thought as she waddled away. *Da girl mags more money for me dat vay.*

Einna Orafem spun about to snap at her staff when the normal clatter of the kitchen at Big Barb's suddenly went silent. But whatever she'd been about to say was forgotten the instant she saw the reason her staff had abruptly gone still and quiet; she stood gaping open-mouthed at Lance Corporal Dave "Hammer" Schultz, who stood just inside the kitchen doors, looking at her. To everyone in the kitchen except her, Schultz's expression was a glower that promised sudden, violent death. To Einna Orafem, Schultz's look was one of tender passion and love.

She slowly closed her mouth, and her lips moved in the shape of his name, though she didn't have the breath to speak it.

The big Marine lifted a hand and pointed a crooked finger at her. That broke her paralysis, and she screamed and ran to him, flinging herself into his arms and throwing her legs around his waist with enough force to stagger even the big man.

The Big Barb's kitchen staff ogled their tyrannical boss and exchanged disbelieving glances at the way she rained wet kisses all over Schultz's face, emitting squeaks and squeals as she did. Schultz did the manly thing, stoically accepting the kisses and clasping his hands under her buttocks to hold her up. There was no way of telling how long Einna Orafem would have continued blubbering over Schultz if she hadn't been interrupted when Big Barb herself burst through the door.

"Vat's goink on in here?" Big Barb bellowed in a voice that could stampede a herd of kwangduks, and did rattle crockery. "Dis is a *vork*blace! I don' hear no sounts of *vork*! You!"—she smacked Schultz on the seat of his pants with a crack that echoed off the kitchen walls—"Unhant dat voman! She's my *cook,* she's got *vork* to do!"

Einna Orafem wrapped her arms tightly around Schultz's neck and pressed her cheek into his, glaring at her employer. She snarled at Big Barb in the same tone she'd been about to use on her staff before she lost her voice, "My Hammer's back from war. I'm off duty!"

"Sez who?" Big Barb demanded, stepping close to shove her face at her chief cook. "You tink you can get anodder chob easy?"

"Go ahead, fire me! I'll get a job cooking in the mess hall at Camp Ellis. Then see what happens to your business when the Marines decide to eat there instead of here!"

The two women glared at each other for a long moment before Big Barb reared back and roared out a laugh that would have stampeded a distant herd of kwangduks, and did knock a few pots off stoves.

She beamed at Einna Orafem and patted her on the cheek. "You got spirit, girl. I like dat in a voman." She stepped around to face Schultz and wagged a sausagelike finger in his face. "Don' you hurd her. An I vant her back in time for domorrow's dinner. You unnerstan?"

Schultz rumbled something that Big Barb took to mean, "I promise not to hurt her, and I'll have her back in time for tomorrow's dinner."

"Gut. Now da two a' you gid outta here, you distracting da res' a' da peoples." She spun about, glaring at the kitchen staff. "Who tol' you ta stop *vorkink*? You god meals ta cook, hungry peoples ta feed. Gid back to *vork*!"

Later, after they'd sated themselves and given each other as much pleasure as they could, while Schultz slept, Einna Orafem cried over the fresh scars on his back, scars from the wound he'd suffered on Ravenette.

Corporal Rachman Claypoole looked around nervously. Near the southern horizon, he could just about make out the village of Brystholde. To the west, beyond cultivated fields, was forest. Snow dusted the fields to the north. Where they gave way to scrubland, reindeer grazed. Low mountains rose beyond the fields to the east; farm buildings were visible in the distance. Claypoole saw no people in the fields, only the various farm machines going about their business. Claypoole was a city boy born and bred; he had no idea what the huge machines were doing in the fields, only that whatever it was, they did it without close human supervision. Sheep and hogs, descended from animals long ago imported from Earth, occupied pens just far enough away that their strong scent wasn't a stench.

He started at a feminine giggle.

"What's the matter, is my big, strong Marine afraid to take a bath?"

Claypoole looked to where Jente Konegard stood a few meters away, next to a huge washtub. She'd already removed her blouse, pants, and boots, and stood, cock-hipped, in very utilitarian underwear. He blushed.

"N-no," he stammered.

"Then why don't you get undressed and join me?" She shucked off her undergarments and stepped into the tub. Submerged almost to her shoulders, she tipped her head. "Or don't you like girls anymore?"

"Oh, I do, I do!" Claypoole gave one last, searching look around, then stripped and darted to join Jente, facing her, in the tub. It may have been winter, but the tub and its immediate surroundings sat in a pool of warm air. They'd have to run to get from the tub to the house, though, because the generated warmth didn't extend very far.

Jente sat with her legs crossed and her arms folded across her breasts. She stretched forward and lightly kissed Claypoole's forehead, then leaned back against the end of the tub and unfolded her arms to lay them along the tub's rim. "Don't you feel better now that you're in the water? With me?"

Claypoole scooted forward, sending waves sloshing up her chest and splashing against the tub's sides. "Much better," he croaked, and reached for her.

She fended him off with a laugh. "Not until you're clean, mister!"

"I'm clean!" he protested. "I showered this morning."

"Uh-huh. And just *where* did you shower?"

"On the *Lance Corporal Keith Lopez,* just an hour or—"

"Uh-huh, that's what I thought," she cut him off. "On board ship, washing in recycled bath and toilet water." She leaned forward and made a face at him, shaking her head. "You aren't touching me until you've been bathed in water I *know* is fit for human use."

"B-but navy ships do a good job of recycling—"

"That might be good enough for you, but it's not good enough for me. Now turn around."

Reluctantly, looking as pained as he felt, Claypoole shuffled himself around to show Jente his back. She bathed his back, shoulders, and arms and felt all around them with her bare hands. "Turn around," she ordered. When he was facing her again she bathed his face, neck, chest, and belly—again carefully feeling where she washed. "Turn around and kneel," she commanded when she was through. He did, and she bathed his hips, front, sides, and back, and his legs to his knees. Then, "Stand up," and she washed his lower legs and feet. Finally she finished and took a deep breath.

"You didn't get wounded," she whispered, and hugged him.

"I told you I didn't get hurt," he said. He turned in response to the pressure of her hands on his hips. And had the expected physiological reaction.

"Down," she said softly.

"I can't help—"

"That's not what I meant. I meant sit down."

"Sit. Right." He bent over to kiss the top of her head and saw the water she sat in was as clear and clean as when he first got in the tub. "The water's still clean," he said as he sat.

She cocked her head. "What, do you think that just because I live on a farm I don't have any of the modern conveniences?"

"Well—ah, no, I—"

"But of course, I have a self-cleaning tub. I wouldn't take a bath with you if it meant I had to sit in water that was used to clean the recycled bath and toilet water off of my big, strong Marine." She grasped his hands where they were at his ankles and leaned close to kiss him on the lips.

"Does this mean I'm clean enough to touch you now?"

She lifted his hands to her breasts.

CHAPTER TWO

No combat arms officer worth his pay wants a desk job, not even in peacetime. But competition for combat commands is always fierce, even though an officer's career can be ruined if he gets a troop command but makes mistakes, even unavoidable ones. Many an up-and-coming young officer with stars or novas written clearly in his future has retired at a much lower grade because Lady Luck did not smile on him—or because at a critical moment he screwed up.

Nobody understood that better than General Alistair Cazombi, Chairman of the Combined Chiefs. He made every effort he could to give Task Force Aguinaldo the very best commanders available, even if that meant going to the President and requesting authority to recall retired officers. General officers are *never* retired, they are subject to recall for whatever purpose—to return to active duty, to head up a special commission, to fill a cabinet post, etc.—until they are beyond this life, and even then their names are often invoked to inspire other soldiers to emulate their deeds. With the assistance of his service chiefs, Cazombi very carefully went down the retired and active lists, selecting commanders for the units assigned to Task Force Aguinaldo. Some units were already commanded by fine officers and they stayed; those who were found lacking in any respect were replaced. General Aguinaldo had final say, of course, but the two thought so much alike that there was little disagreement between them. When they were finished, the army's XVIII Corps had a new commander, Lieutenant General Patrice Carano, called back from retirement.

"This may result in a small shit storm," Cazombi remarked to the Army Chief of Staff, "but Pat's the best man for this job." The "storm" he was referring to would be those three-star generals yearning for a corps command and those two-stars who'd kill for a third star and a corps command. "So, 'Under the authority invested in me by the President and the Minister of War' and all that crap, issue the orders. Pat can handle any fallout."

Lieutenant General Patrice Carano was short and stocky. His friends called him "Fireball" because wherever he went, whatever group he was with, he virtually sizzled with energy and determination. As a cadet at the Confederation Military Academy, he naturally attracted the unwanted attention of many upperclassmen. This was due in part to the fact that he stood out in ranks next to the taller cadets, and from his first day there he was dubbed "Short Round." Henceforth "Mr. Short Round" was the unfortunate subject of marathon harassment sessions at the hands of his upperclassmen, not because he was deficient in any of the areas of military knowledge and deportment, but because he stubbornly bore up under their hazing without complaint. Their treatment was clearly against academy regulations and Carano would have been well within his rights to complain about it. But he never did. They were infuriated that he bore up under torture so well. Eventually, most of them gave up on Carano and focused their attention elsewhere.

But one in particular, whom we shall call Cadet Z, developed a personal dislike for Cadet Carano, on whom he lavished the most fiendish punishments, the least of which consisted of making Carano clean latrine floors with his own toothbrush. At a morning inspection after Carano had been up much of the night cleaning latrines, this particular cadet officer examined Carano's toothbrush. "Mr. Carano," he hissed, thrusting the brush under Carano's nose, "is this hideous instrument your toothbrush?"

"Yes, *sir*!" Carano, standing at rigid attention, shoulders braced, shouted.

"You must not be using it, Mr. Carano," Cadet Z smiled

deceptively, "not judging by the smell of your foul breath. Don't you know proper dental hygiene is essential to being a good officer?"

"Yes, *sir*! The cadet knows that, *sir*!"

"Then why don't you use this to brush your teeth?" Cadet Z screamed, his face turning red, the veins in his face standing out like sewer pipes.

Carano replied in a deep baritone:

"Last time I went to the toilet
Shit all over the flooooooor
Cleaned it up with my toothbrush
Don't brush my teeth much anymooooooore."

Everyone in the room burst out laughing. But not Cadet Z. Cadet Carano subsequently stood six all-night guard tours outside the post chapel, that in addition, of course, to a heavy class schedule. But the subject of the toothbrush never came up again. And for the rest of the time he was at the academy, Cadet Z left him alone. Carano graduated second in his class of 243 cadet officers.

Years later, Brigadier General Carano commanded an infantry brigade when former Cadet Z was assigned to his staff as a major in charge of logistics. Neither officer ever mentioned their time together at the academy and Major Z proved to be a conscientious and efficient logistics officer. General Carano gave him outstanding officer efficiency reports and eventually his former nemesis earned his own star.

And that was the hallmark of General Patrice Carano's career: He never allowed personal feelings to get in the way of his mission.

Anders Aguinaldo and Patrice Carano hit it off at their very first meeting. There is something about a soldier, something in the way he carries himself, the way he talks, the way he shakes hands, the way he smiles, the way his eyes light up when talking shop, that tells other soldiers far more about him than even how he wears his uniform or the medals on his chest. Professionals develop a sixth sense for the nuances. No one was more adept at reading men than Anders Aguinaldo and what he "read" about Pat Carano was all good.

When the two sat down together to review the organization of the force being formed to go to Haulover, Carano smiled briefly when the name of a division commander came up. Aguinaldo caught this slight indication of recognition. "You know this guy, Pat?" he asked.

"Yes, sir," Carano answered, "we were at the academy together and he served under me as my brigade S4, many years ago. He's an efficient officer."

"That's good, Pat." Aguinaldo nodded and passed on down the list. In Aguinaldo's opinion, commanders who knew one another cooperated smoothly when the shooting started.

But that was not true of everyone in the XVIII Corps.

The predeployment briefing had just been completed. Generals Aguinaldo and Carano had both presided. The force being sent to Haulover was impressive: The army's Fifteenth Armored Division, Twenty-fourth Infantry Division, Twenty-seventh Medium Infantry Division, and the Eighty-seventh Heavy Infantry Division (Reinforced), together with the Marine Corps's Twenty-sixth and Thirty-fourth FISTs. The Navy's Vice Admiral Geoffrey Chandler would command the fleet, thirty-five amphibious landing ships with armed escort, including an aircraft carrier with the Eighth and Fourteenth Air Wings, each comprising ninety-six Raptors.

Major General Donnie ("Doc") McKillan, XVIII Corps Chief of Staff, blew on his coffee carefully before raising it to his lips. Major General Reginald ("Rocky") Kocks, commanding the Eighty-seventh Heavy Infantry Division (Reinforced), rolled an Avo Uvezian thoughtfully in his fingers before putting it into his mouth and lighting it. "How do you get along with old Carano?" Kocks asked.

McKillan leaned forward and put his coffee cup on the edge of his desk. He took a cigar out of the humidor, clipped it carefully, ran his tongue over the leaf, and lit it. "Almost a Davidoff," he sighed, expelling a blue-white cloud of tobacco smoke. He fished a tiny piece of tobacco off his lip. "Best officer I ever served under, Rocky," he said.

Kocks said nothing, just bit his lip.

"Yeah, I know." McKillan nodded. "I'm in line for a third star, just like you. In fact, I have about a year date-of-rank on you." He grinned; all officers knew where they stood in line for promotion based on seniority. "At first I was, well . . ." He shifted his weight in his chair. ". . . a little pissed that I'd been passed over for command of this corps. But . . ." He shrugged.

"Well, Doc, it's the chief of staff who really runs a corps—"

"Not *this* corps," McKillan answered wryly. "Old Fireball runs *this* corps; I just help him. But tell you what, Rocky, you do your job, he gets to trust you, and he lets you alone, he's not one of those insecure micromanagers we've all known."

"Yeah, I know. I served under Carano, too," Kocks admitted.

"You *did*? When?" McKillan raised his eyebrows. This was something he'd missed. Kocks had not commanded the Eighty-seventh Division that long. He was also one of Cazombi's hand-picked officers, so that spoke highly of his ability. But there was something in the way he'd said "I know" that spoke between the lines. "You two weren't at the academy together, were you?" McKillan remembered they'd both been there about the same time.

"Yes. I graduated before he did," Kocks sighed. "But we served together a long time ago and far away." He smiled. "Say, this is damned good coffee, Doc." He regarded his cigar. "And a damned fine cigar, too, I might add."

Major General Reginald Kocks had been the "Cadet Z" previously referred to, the upperclassman who'd treated Carano so vilely at the Military Academy. Kocks had never forgiven Carano for not holding that against him.

* * *

"Fucker!" Major General Reginald Kocks shouted, and then uttered a string of expletives of which the first was the least derogatory. "The sumbitch is brought out of retirement— *retirement!*—to command this corps! Left us hangin' like a bunch of grapes while that superannuated old shit gets the command. Not right! Not fair! Goddamn!"

"Well, Reggie," Brigadier General Alfred Small, the Eighty-seventh Division Chief of Staff, protested mildly, "he was hand-selected by Cazombi himself." He was referring to Lieutenant General Carano.

"Yeah! Just like the booger he is!" Kocks exclaimed. He reached for the half-empty bottle of Scotch and poured himself another finger. "Cazombi," he sneered, "goddamned shitbag."

General Small glanced apprehensively at his commander. The Old Man had drunk most of the bottle so far that night and was feeling no pain. Small was very embarrassed that his division commander hated the corps commander so intensely that he'd talk this way about him. He could see nothing wrong with General Carano, thought him a fine officer, in fact. So what if he'd been called out of retirement? Carano's recall to active duty and elevation to corps command had been decided far above his pay grade—and General Kocks's as well.

"Well, he's seen some service," Small protested mildly.

"Service my ass!" Kocks yelled. "Service," he snorted. "I knew the little shit at the academy, Al." Kocks shook his head. "I was his upperclassman. Miserable little snot then, miserable high-ranking snot now. All's there is to it." He waved one hand drunkenly to make his point.

"Sir, maybe we'd better call it quits for tonight? Assumption of command ceremony in the morning," Small said with a glance at his watch. It was three hours; formation at six-thirty hours. They'd all have to look sharp and stand tall on Hurlburt Field in a little more than three hours and his division commander was drunk. "What do you say, sir? A little shuteye?"

"Fuckeye!" Kocks mumbled. "You go to bed, Al. 'Assumption of command!'" He snorted derisively. "Ass-umption, you ask me. I'm sleepin' in. You go in my place, Al."

General Small got to his feet, "Well, good night, then, sir." Shaking his head, he turned to go.

Behind him Kocks poured more Scotch into his glass and grimaced. "Don't brush my teeth much anymore," he mumbled. General Small had no idea what his commander meant by that remark.

Five-thirty hours came early the next morning. As General Small was dressing in his trailer, General Kocks's aide knocked on the door and announced, "Sir, I can't get the general out of his bed."

"That's all right, Captain. I'm representing him at the assumption of command," Small answered.

"Fine, sir, uh, just is . . ."

"Yes?"

"Well, sir, the general, he's—"

"He's indisposed, Captain. You stay back here and look after him. Tell the division sergeant major to join me in ten minutes."

More than 110,000 men, the infantry and Marines along with representatives from the navy air wings, stood assembled on Hurlburt Field that morning. The formation had been called at an early hour so the men could be off the field before the heat and humidity began to rise.

"Where's General Kocks?" Lieutenant General Carano asked when he saw Brigadier General Small and the Eighty-seventh Division's sergeant major.

"He's not well, sir."

"Oh? Nothing serious, I hope?"

"Oh, no, sir, it'll pass."

"Fine. But Al, when the ceremony's over I'll just stop by and make sure there isn't anything I can do for him. You and Top come with me." He nodded at the division sergeant major.

"Oh," Brigadier General Small said quickly, "he'll be just fine, sir." He smiled lopsidedly.

"Well, Kocks and I go back a long, long way, Al. Least I can do for him." Carano smiled and took his place before the corps.

The sergeant major raised an eyebrow and General Small thought to himself, *Uh-oh*.

The ceremony went off without a hitch. As the units assembled, the bands played old military airs, "Bold Sojer Boy," "Garryowen," "The Rock O' Silvasia," and others. Then General Aguinaldo formally presented General Carano with the XVIII Corps guidon. The bands struck up the Confederation Anthem, and all colors dipped as 110,000 men snapped to attention and saluted. General Carano passed the guidon to the corps sergeant major and, together with General Aguinaldo, conducted a motorized review of the troops, passing down the division fronts slowly, as honors were rendered. An artillery piece slowly fired fifteen rounds, the traditional salute for an arriving army lieutenant general, while with three ruffles and flourishes, each divisional band struck up "The General's March" as the inspection vehicle drew abreast of its front. And then it was all over.

General Carano visibly recoiled upon entering General Kocks's trailer. "Smells like a distillery in here," he muttered. Kocks's aide gestured helplessly at Brigadier Small. "I couldn't get him up," he whispered.

"Reggie? Reggie?" General Carano touched Kocks's shoulder and shook him gently.

Kocks mumbled, then rolled over. "Whaaa?" he gasped, staring up at his corps commander, eyes red-rimmed and bleary. He blinked. "Carano. Fuck you, asshole!" he mumbled, and rolled back over.

Carano stepped back quickly. "General, you are *drunk*," Carano said. "Is this what you meant when you said he was indisposed, Al?" he asked Brigadier General Small.

"Well, hungover, sir, actually, is what I meant," Small answered. "Rather badly hungover, sir."

"I can see that, and smell it," Carano answered. "Outside," he nodded toward the door. "Brigadier General Small," he said formally once they were outside, and Small snapped to attention, "you are now in command of the Eighty-seventh Division. I am going to have General Kocks's reassignment orders cut immediately. I want him out of here as soon as you receive them, in fifteen minutes, in an hour, whenever. I'll square this away with General Aguinaldo personally. I'm going to ask personnel to expedite his orders. So, get him up, clean him up, get his things packed, and stand by to take him to the space port.

"Very well, gentlemen." Carano came to attention and saluted the small group of officers. "Carry on." He did a smart about-face and marched off.

Some people just do not know how to handle forgiveness.

CHAPTER
THREE

"Our Certificate of Intention to Wed." Cynthia Suelee Chang-Sturdevant held up the flimsiplast document. She carefully put it to one side and took up two more sheets. "Our medical clearance certificates. You," she said, nodding at Marcus Berentus, "are a mature, healthy Caucasian male citizen of the Confederation of Human Worlds, and I am a likewise mature, healthy female citizen of mixed Caucasian-Asian descent. We are certified sound in body and mind."

"Better double-check that last one, Suelee," Berentus chuckled.

"Speak for yourself, Marcus." She placed the health certificates on the Certificate of Intention, carefully straightening the three sheets into a neat stack. "Next, we have our tax withholding statements since henceforth we shall be filing our taxes jointly. Next, our proof of domicile and employment certifying that we are neither homeless nor unemployed and therefore can sustain the obligations of married life." She placed the certificate on the growing pile. She held out another flimsiplast document. "Here is certification that neither of us is presently married to anyone else and that any previous relationships we may have entered into with anyone else are hereby declared null and void."

"If anyone here now objects to this union let him speak out or forever hold his peace," Berentus intoned solemnly.

Chang-Sturdevant looked about the room questioningly. "No response, so I guess we're okay on that score, then." She laughed, placing the certificate on the pile. "Next, our background che proving that neither of us is wanted by the police or is a fugitive from justice. Finally, we have our registration with the Ministry of Vital Statistics certifying that on this date it has been duly and officially recorded that Marcus Aurelius Berentus and Cynthia Suelee Chang-Sturdevant, in the city of Fargo, planet Earth, Confederation of Human Worlds, blah-blah-blah, have entered into the state of matrimony and are hereby husband and wife with all the obligations and privileges appertaining thereunto. It is digitally signed by us and witnessing officials and carries the Ministry of Health and Education's official seal. We are now officially husband and wife."

"So that's it?"

"That is *it*. As far as our government is concerned, we're married, Marcus."

"Funny, I don't feel a bit different. When did this marriage take place?"

Chang-Sturdevant shrugged. "When they put the seal on the registration document, I guess."

"No bridal shower, no bachelor party, no preacher, no ceremony, no rings, no reception, none of that stuff?"

"Ain't required by law," Chang-Sturdevant said.

"If it's so easy to get hitched, how hard is it to get unhitched?"

"That's not easy, Marcus. It requires at least six high-priced lawyers. And twenty-three million credits later you're a free man once more." She laughed again.

"I always suspected this marriage stuff was all a plot hatched by lawyers!"

"Well, at least we're not living in sin anymore." Chang-Sturdevant chuckled.

"You don't want a formal church ceremony, then, you know, before God and all that?"

"God is supposed to know everything already, so why bother Him/Her/It with our vows, Marcus? Besides, after our experience with Jimmy Jasper and his Tabernacle Rock of Ages True Light Christian Church or what the hell ever it was called, I'm turned off on preachers." Jimmy Jasper's preaching had almost single-handedly derailed the war against the Skinks until it was discovered he'd been brainwashed by the Skinks while their prisoner and sent to Earth as their agent.

Berentus nodded. He'd been afraid for a while that Jasper had actually managed to influence Suelee, so powerful was the man's charisma. Jasper had been swept away by a tornado that struck downtown Fargo and his body never recovered. But his ministry had been exposed and ruined. "The Finger of God, Suelee, that's what some are calling that tornado. There are still some hangers-on who believe he was translated to heaven by the Finger of God and will return someday to resume his ministry. Fortunately they are few and impotent. But once we pound the piss out of the Skinks it won't matter if the bastard comes back."

"The 'Fickle Finger of Fate' is what it was, Marcus. It sure didn't bother sinners like us."

"Well, if what we did together is sin, bring it on! But you know the biggest disappointment? We don't get any presents!" He snapped his fingers. "And you know what else? No goddamn wedding cake!"

"Only each other."

"And these." He produced a small box and flipped it open. Inside reposed two rings, one sized for a man, the other for Chang-Sturdevant's finger. The small stones sparkled in their settings.

Chang-Sturdevant smiled. "They're beautiful, Marcus. Putting them on will seal the deal." She held out her left hand and Berentus slipped the beautiful ring on her finger; she did the same for him. She held her hand out at arm's length and admired the ring.

"And now, the obligatory smooch." They embraced. "Well, come on, Mrs. Chang-Sturdevant Berentus, over to the bar! This deed is not done until we wet these rings down with some of that fine old Scotch you keep on hand."

"Lagavulin it is! And while we sip we'll smoke Davidoffs to further speed our slide into this madcap fling called marriage. If my parents were alive, they'd be shocked their daughter married an ex-flyboy and a political appointee. They wanted me to marry a doctor."

"They'd be proud to know you are their president, Suelee."

"A politician? *That* would've shocked them even more! They were decent people, you know."

Berentus poured two healthy dollops of Scotch and selected two Anniversario Number Three Turbos from Chang-Sturdevant's humidor. "Ah, fifteen centimeters of delight!" he enthused, clipping the cigars. He held his up, examining it. " 'Rich, characterful tobacco blends.' " He sighed. "Like us, Suelee, rich and characterful." He lit them both. They smoked and sipped in silence, enjoying the moment.

The best moments the two had ever had together were like that, standing close but relaxed, neither saying anything, just comfortable in each other's presence, thinking their own thoughts. Each knew instinctively when those thoughts involved the other and expressed that awareness with a smile, a touch of the hand. It was an intoxicating sensation, their wordless communication, two people absorbed in each other, silently melding into one.

When a young man, Marcus had thought women were only good for keeping house and sex. He said then that the ideal woman stood one meter high and had a flat head, so you had somewhere to set your beer as she was giving you a blow job. When another man said a woman was his friend, he couldn't understand that. Men had male friends, but who could be friends with a woman? But as he matured, Marcus began to see women as individuals with brains and aspirations and hopes just like men, people with more to them than what might lie between their legs. He became comfortable in the presence of women and started listening to them and taking them seriously. In time he found he could admire women for a lot more than their physical charms, and gradually those charms became secondary to his evaluation, and that was when he himself became most attractive to women.

But no woman had ever had the effect on Marcus that Cynthia Chang-Sturdevant did. Gradually it dawned on him that what he felt for her must be love: not the simpering infatuation that bad poets write about, but the deep and lasting realization that without her he could never be whole.

"Suelee, what about honeymoon plans?" Berentus asked suddenly.

Chang-Sturdevant shook her head. "No time for that, luv. I've got a reelection campaign to run. We can honeymoon when I lose."

"Well, don't be so negative, my dear." Berentus put down his drink and cigar. "You will now make time for a brief respite on that couch over there."

Chang-Sturdevant kicked off her shoes. "Think you can handle that?"

"Yup." He guided her toward the couch. "There'll be a sensation when the media finds out we're married."

"That ain't nuttin', Marcus. Wait'll they find out I'm pregnant."

Every capital city has its seamier side, usually in an industrial part of town where few people choose to live permanently. At night the streets there are deserted and working stiffs getting off late shifts frequent sleazy bars to deaden the dreary humdrum before trudging home. The Green Lizard was such a place in that part of Fargo. While the great and powerful, even the ordinary citizens lived in comfort elsewhere in the city, the Lizard hosted the working derelicts of society. The late-night barflies clustered there that night did not recognize the two men who crept into in a back room and would not have cared had they known who they were. The barkeeper knew them, but he had been paid to keep their identities to himself.

"The goddamned old whore *married* him." Haggel Kutmoi, senior member of the Senate Armed Services Committee, shook his head in disbelief. The news had been announced earlier in the day and that had been the occasion for the late-night meeting at the Green Lizard. Across the table sat Sanguinious Cheatham of Feargut & Cheatham, one of the most prestigious law firms in Human Space. The two were not strangers to the Green Lizard. They had met there before, during the General Billie fiasco. It provided the kind of anonymous privacy that made safe the hatching of plots.

"We might be able to use that," Sanguinious mused. "Nepotism, retaining a family member in a high government office." He was referring to Marcus Berentus, the Confederation Minister of War, and now President Chang-Sturdevant's husband. "I think we can force his resignation as a result of his marriage to the President."

"We should force *her* resignation." Kutmoi grimaced. "That'd sure simplify things."

"Sorry, old man, you won't get rid of her that easily. No, you'll have to beat her by running against her on the Independent Party's ticket. But she's vulnerable. All you have to do is exploit those vulnerabilities."

"Yeah? Like we 'exploited' the Billie fiasco?" Kutmoi sneered. He was referring to the testimony of General Jason Billie, formerly commander of the army in the war against the Secessionist Coalition on Ravenette. Billie had been summarily relieved by a Chang-Sturdevant favorite, General Alistair Cazombi. Kutmoi thought he had Chang-Sturdevant over that until she appeared before the Congress wearing that goddamned commendation medal she'd won on active service years ago, and announced the presence of the Skinks. And then Billie had gone off and shot himself.

"Well, old man, it wasn't as much her as it was Cazombi, remember? He came before your committee and presented himself as the plain old soldier, no bullshit, and just told the truth. In effect, he told your committee to go screw itself. On the heels of Billie's 'Old Soldiers Never Die' performance, Cazombi came across as Horatius at the bridge and Billie like the windbag he was. He did everyone a favor by shooting himself. Remember, I told you, politics is theater. And," he said as he held up a finger, "nothing succeeds like success."

"I'm going down tomorrow and throw my hat in the ring,

Sanguinious. I'm going to challenge Chang-Sturdevant in the upcoming election. I want you to run my campaign for me."

Cheatham was silent for a moment, drawing circles on the tabletop with a finger. "You promised me a seat on the Supreme Court if the Billie fiasco worked out. I presume that will be my reward if I help get you elected?"

"Yes. When I am elected president of the Confederation, I will appoint you to the Supreme Court. The first vacancy that occurs; they're all doddering old wrecks, so one should occur very soon. I'll appoint you. Don't go out and get fitted for your robes just now, but in time you'll be chief justice yourself. Until that time you manage my campaign and, until I can get you on the Court, you'll be my chief of staff or a special advisor or something of that sort."

"Done." Cheatham reached across the table and shook Kutmoi's hand. "Now, if I'm going to run your campaign, you'll have to do it my way, Senator. Do you agree?"

"Yes."

"Good. You must come out fighting, hit her hard and fast, and never let up the pressure. Use every weapon at your disposal. Lie if you have to, cheat if you must, but you cannot let up on her, not for a second."

"Lying and cheating come naturally to senators—and lawyers," Kutmoi said with a grin. "Continue."

"Her marriage to Berentus can be exploited. Possibly we can get him to resign his post. I'll have to research the precedents. But by getting him out of the Ministry of War we will win a tiny psychological victory over Chang-Sturdevant, deprive her of one of her closest advisors. Oh, Berentus as her husband will become her advisor ex officio, but causing his resignation will chip away at her self-confidence."

"She's got all those generals behind her," Kutmoi complained.

"Don't fuck with the generals! And for God's sake, even if you don't believe in God, never screw with the enlisted personnel! That little medal she wore during that speech to both houses, some doodad she won for meritorious service, when the vets, their wives, their children, all the people who love the military services saw that—*bingo!*—public opinion swung right behind her! Nothing counts for more in politics than a good military service record, especially in wartime. Shows everyone you've been down in the shit with the ordinary man. You don't have any military service, do you, old boy?"

"No." In fact, Kutmoi had done everything he could to avoid military service as a young man. Bulon, his home world, had universal military training in effect when he was of draft age, but to avoid military service he'd used every deferment and excuse he could muster, including bribes to draft boards administered by his wealthy parents. He knew that would come out during the campaign. But somehow he would finesse his way out of any embarrassment that might cause; it had never hurt him during his election campaigns at home. Surely there were precedents, politicians throughout history who'd been elected to high office despite their draft dodging. He would look into that.

"So stay away from criticizing the military men. Blame Billie's suicide on Chang-Sturdevant, not on Cazombi. Most of our generals are apolitical creatures; they follow their orders. Go after the one who *gives* the orders, the *president,* the commander in chief. The fact that Cazombi, on his own initiative, had to seize the moment on Ravenette, relieve the incompetent whom Chang-Sturdevant appointed to that command, is worth a trillion votes. Play that up big.

"The people at home are not happy about this so-called war on the Skinks. They're afraid that if the threat is real, their defenses have been stripped to reinforce this Task Force Aguinaldo. Aguinaldo," he said sneering, "another Chink."

"Actually, I believe his ancestry is Filipino, but yes, play on that. Remember, she knew about the Skinks long, long before their existence was officially announced. How many of our people died before they were warned, eh? The war on Ravenette, the Secessionist Coalition, none of that would've happened if she'd warned us about the Skinks early on. Those people out there saw the reinforcement of the Ravenette garrison as an oppression, not a defensive measure! How many lives did that cost? Rub that in her face at every opportunity."

"Yes, and then there's Darkside." Kutmoi was becoming excited now. Darkside was the prison world where the worst criminals were confined, but there were big problems with the constitutionality of sentencing without a public trial, which is just what had happened to many of the criminals confined there.

Cheatham smiled. "I will write you a brief that'll singe the hairs off old Cynthia's backside. She announced she was doing away with Darkside, all well and good, but your point should be, Darkside is representative of the secretive way she's run her administration, trampling on the constitutional rights of her citizens. And there's something else, old chap, you may not be aware of. Ever hear of Jorge Liberec Lavager?"

Kutmoi shook his head. "Name sounds familiar but—"

"He was head of the Union of Margelan on a world known as Atlas."

"Oh, yes, yes! An agricultural world, I recall. Something about a crop virus there that ruined the economy."

"The crop virus was introduced accidentally by assassins who were sent there to murder Lavager. Chang-Sturdevant ordered his murder." Cheatham grinned.

"*What! Can we prove* that?" Kutmoi almost shouted.

"No," Cheatham said with a shrug, "but we don't *have* to, old man. In politics and the media, you are guilty until proven innocent. All you have to do is bring it up during the campaign. I'll help you word it so it doesn't sound like an outright accusation. Then let the old bitch explain it away. But whatever she does, the damage will have been done, another nail in her coffin. Besides, with a little digging—and once it becomes a campaign issue, you bet there'll be digging—I think it'll be proved true, or mostly true. Oh, sure, maybe the assassination was based on bad intelligence, maybe loose cannons in her administration set it up, blah, blah, blah. But *she* was in charge and it happened on *her* watch. Case closed.

"Then there's Jimmy Jasper." Cheatham grinned.

"That fake? He was as nutty as a fruitcake. I've seen the Ministry of Justice report. He was brainwashed by the Skinks and sent here to upset the war against them. Best thing ever happened was him getting sucked up by that tornado along with several members of Congress, ones who'd never have supported me. Good riddance to all of them."

Cheatham held up a cautioning finger. "Not quite, old boy, not quite. Don't say that in public, whatever you do. Praise the fool instead; suck up to the religious right. Play to that crowd and they'll vote for you. The average person only knows Jasper was accused by the *government* of being a Skink provocateur. Do you think one person in a million has seen those reports or that one in a hundred million would understand them if they did? No, no, his surviving followers believe he was translated directly to heaven by God Himself and that the allegations against him were trumped up by Chang-Sturdevant because he opposed her war. Yes, *her* war. Play the Jasper card as just another example of how the old bitch has trampled on the rights of citizens—in this case the right to freedom of religion. Remember El Neal, Wanderjahr, Kingdom, Atlas, on and on? All examples of how she used military force, *military force,* to overthrow governments she didn't like. She's used our constitution as toilet paper, old man, and if you play these cards right, you'll flush her right down the drain with them."

"Good God, man," Kutmoi gasped, "you've handed me the election on a platter." He poured a healthy dollop of whiskey into each of their glasses and they toasted their new partnership.

"Let me run your campaign, let me devise your strategy and your platform, old man, and you shall be the next president of the Confederation of Human Worlds." Cheatham lifted his glass again.

They clinked glasses and drank. "We have her by the short hairs!" Kutmoi exulted.

"We have her teats in a wringer!" Cheatham cried.

They laughed and shouted and slammed their fists so hard on

the tabletop that one of the drunks outside woke up and asked if it was raining again.

"I'll tell you what, Mr. Cheatham," Kutmoi vowed, "if I lose this election, why, you can call me—you can call me—" The name of a late-twentieth-century American politician whose inept campaigning had become a textbook example of how to lose a sure thing, suddenly sprang to mind. "Why, you can call me *George Bush*!"

CHAPTER FOUR

The special envoy's smile filled the room, and it was a big room.

President Joen Berg unfolded himself gracefully from his seat and advanced to meet the envoy halfway across the room. "Madam Motlaw, I am pleased and honored by your visit," he said, bowing slightly and kissing the back of the envoy's hand; it was smooth and cool in his, the fingers long and tapered, the fingers of a concert pianist, which she had been, with the Brosigville Symphony Orchestra, before joining Ms. Kuetgens's staff. She was famous among the people of Wanderjahr for her brilliant interpretations of Mozart, Beethoven, and the twenty-third-century composer Hank Scrobbins, particularly his very difficult Etudes in Organdy. "How may I be of assistance to you?" Berg asked as he gestured toward comfortable seats to one side of the room.

"I'm here to deliver a message, Mr. Berg."

"Please, madam, everyone calls me simply J.B." Berg smiled and shrugged. "I am, after all, merely the president of the Stortinget, not the prime minister," he added apologetically as they took seats.

"I am familiar with your parliamentary form of government, J.B." She gave him that glacier-melting smile again. "And, as a mere envoy, a messenger, in fact, I'm really not exactly that high on my own government's totem pole. Call me Sonia."

"Well, Sonia"—Berg's face colored slightly with pleasure at the first-name privilege—"one good thing, since all the bigwigs are out of town right now, we two have the pleasure of meeting. How is his excellency, Ambassador Morelles?" Eduardo Morelles, known to everyone as "Big Ed," was the Wanderjahrian ambassador to Thorsfinni's World.

"I've never met the man. He was away on a ski trip when I arrived. His secretary made the appointment with you for me. I was given to understand that he was vacationing up in the mountains with your prime minister."

Berg chuckled. "Those two? At their age? On a ski trip!" He shook his head. "Oh, excuse me! Refreshments? I have some of our superb Thorsfinni's World coffee, grown from Earth-descended trees. Uh, do you smoke, madam?"

"The occasional thule cigarillo. Coffee would be very welcome, though, J.B. It is very cold in this part of your world." She pretended to shiver and rub her exquisite hands together.

"Ah! It's cold everywhere here, Sonia. But coffee will warm you up—and may I offer you a Davidoff Tatiana Night Cap Miniature? Delightfully exquisite smoke."

They lit up, smoked, and sipped coffee in silence for a few moments. "Delicious coffee. And these cigarillos are magnificent, J.B. Thank you!"

Berg's face colored again with pleasure. "You're entirely welcome. The way you hold that cigarillo gives you a delicious air of mystery and intrigue." They laughed. He regarded Sonia carefully but discreetly so as not to give offense. She was tall, very athletic, almost Berg's height, and she had the most luxurious head of black hair he'd ever seen. It framed her face like a painting by Leonardo da Vinci. "Um, so how may my government help you, Sonia?" he managed to croak at last.

"I would like to visit the Marines stationed here, J.B. I have a message for one of them." She gave him that disarming smile again but it said, very clearly, *don't bother to ask me why.*

"Um, certainly, certainly. I believe the protocol calls for you to pay a visit to the Confederation's ambassador here and then Rear Admiral Blankenboort, who commands the Naval Supply Depot. Camp Major Pete Ellis is where the Marines are stationed.

But Blankenboort is the senior Confederation military representative here. Old 'Blankie,' as I call him, has been here so long we think he'll take out citizenship." He chuckled. "And then, of course, he'll arrange for you to go down the chain of command to, er, to whomever it is you're delivering your message at Camp Ellis. That's right outside the town of Bronnoysund. Delightful little place."

"To Thirty-fourth Fleet Initial Strike Team, actually. I believe Brigadier Theodosius Sturgeon still commands? His Marines assisted my government some years ago, J.B. We are eternally grateful to them for their help at that time. The current Chairman of our Ruling Council, Miss Hway Kuetgens, has commissioned me to deliver a message to them. She was a young woman when the Marines were on our world. Upon her grandmother's death she succeeded to the head of the state of Morgenluft and now she is the Chairman of our Ruling Council."

"I do know something of your world's recent history. The Marines broke the power of the oligarchs, didn't they, and essentially established a democracy in its stead, if memory serves. The chairman is now elected by all the people in the different states that compose your government instead of being appointed from among the oligarchs, who are also elected to their terms. Right?"

"Yes, oligarchs to a six-year term, the chairman to eight years. Miss Kuetgens has two years left on her term of office. Before she retires—she can't be reelected—she wants this private message delivered. Will you make the arrangements for me to meet with that admiral, J.B.?"

"Of course! And Sonia, when your mission is over, perhaps you would like to participate in some of our wonderful winter sport activities. We have beautiful lodges in the mountains. It would be a shame for you to have come all this way and not to experience some of our hospitality."

"Why, thank you, J.B., I may take you up on that very kind offer." And she smiled again, implying that she probably would.

* * *

Christian Mirelles, the first secretary to the Confederation ambassador to Thorsfinni's World, was a gracious gentleman of the old school who greeted Sonia with the utmost cordiality before sending her, reluctantly, on her way.

But Rear Admiral Blankenboort was a different person entirely. If he had as many credits in the bank as he did barnacles on his reputation he'd be a millionaire. "A freaking 'special envoy,' Billy," he remarked to Captain Billy Reems, his executive officer. "Why in the freaking freak is *she* coming freaking down *here*?" He slapped the printout of the message from the Confederation ambassador in New Oslo that Reems had just passed to him. Although marked "Eyes Only," as depot exec, Reems had already read it.

"The ambassador didn't say, sir, but note he 'requests' you extend to her the 'utmost courtesy and assistance in the rapid dispatch of her mission,' whatever that mission might be."

"Damn!" The admiral put a hand wearily to his forehead. "With all the freaking problems I've got running this freaking dump, what the frigging else do we need besides a surprise visit from some frigging diplomatic skirt? Fuck." He shifted an unlit Clinton from the right to the left side of his mouth. He frowned, removed the cigar, and with a stubby forefinger fished from inside his cheek a wad of masticated tobacco, which he flicked onto the floor. He wiped his finger on his trousers. "All right, we'll meet her at the port, bring her here, take her to the mess for drinks, coffee, whatever, and send her on her frigging way as freaking soon as we freaking can. And," he said, waggling his freshly moistened finger at his XO, "I'm going to find out what the skirt wants with us, Billy, 'cause ol' Blankie Blankenboort never draws a blank."

Actually, Admiral Blankenboort enjoyed the various nicknames his men had invented for him over the years, among them "Barnacle Blankie" and his favorite, "Blowtorch Blankie." The longer he missed the promotion lists and the longer he had been kept on Thorsfinni's World without a real command, the more of a curmudgeon he'd become, although he had been born that way to begin with. He'd never made the connection between his natural irascibility, which tended to rub everyone the wrong way, and his exile at the remote naval depot. It had been his heroism at the great naval battle in orbit around Stormont during the Third Silvasian War that had saved him from early retirement.

Sonia was fascinated by the admiral's office. The walls were covered with plaques, certificates, holograms of the admiral in all stages of his career. Every flat surface in the room boasted a model or a naval knickknack of some sort, mostly starships, all of which she assumed Blankenboort had served on or commanded at some time in the past. In fact, there was so much of this personal material cluttering the office that she wondered where he had room to do his work.

"Ma'am," Blankenboort growled after they were seated, "will you be staying with us? I notice you don't have any bags."

"No, Admiral. I plan to catch the twenty-hours shuttle back to New Oslo. It will not take me that long to conclude my business."

What a relief, Blankenboort thought. Then, "Well, it's getting on toward lunchtime. Let's go to the mess. We can talk easier there." Sonia agreed. Sitting in Admiral Blankenboort's office was too much like sitting in a pawn shop.

"So why are you here, Ms. Motlaw?" Admiral Blankenboort asked around his peach cobbler.

Since the admiral was addressing her with his mouth full, Sonia glanced inquiringly at Captain Reems before trying an answer. "My hearing is perfect, Admiral," she answered, thinking he was making a comment about her ear.

"Here! Here! I asked why you're *here*—goddammit!" He slapped a hand to his jaw, "Oh, Jesus freaking Christ, goddamned peach pit! I think I broke a frigging tooth!" He spit a pit onto the table. It bounced off his plate with a ping and dropped to the floor. "Eh, ma'am, excuse me, but gawdam, ma'am, that *hurt.* Ohweee!" He held the hand to his jaw and muttered.

"I'm not at liberty to say, Admiral," Sonia answered, trying hard to suppress a laugh. Her eyes sparkled with good humor as she glanced again at Captain Reems and in that instant the officer's heart was enlisted. "It's entirely confidential, sir, and for the Marines only."

"Ah, hum, tell it to the Marines, eh?" Blankenboort muttered.

"Yes, sir, that is it. Now I must be on my way, Admiral. Thank you for the excellent luncheon. Very sorry about that tooth." She rose from her chair.

"I'll take her, sir," Reems volunteered, jumping to his feet and rushing to help Sonia up. "Just a short drive, ma'am. And Brigadier Sturgeon has been notified you're coming. Uh, that all right with you, Admiral?" Reems was suddenly terrified the admiral would assign someone else to drive Sonia to Camp Ellis.

"Eh? Okay, okay," Blankenboort muttered, still clasping his jaw with one hand. When a steward came to offer the admiral more coffee he said, "I'd have gotten it out of her if that goddamned peach pit hadn't screwed me up! Steward! Take me to the freaking kitchen. I'm going to have somebody's ass over this."

"Well, what do you suppose *she* wants with *us*?" Israel Ramadan, Thirty-fourth FIST's executive officer, asked as he read Blankenboort's message over Sturgeon's shoulder.

"Belated thank-you note from the government of Wanderjahr?" Sturgeon suggested.

"Very belated, Ted. Guess we'll find out when the lady gets here, which"—he checked his chronometer—"should be just about now."

"Come on, then, let's get outside and welcome her aboard."

When the landcar drew up to the headquarters building Sonia opened her own door, jumped lightly to the ground, and came around the vehicle to join Captain Reems. The captain introduced her to Sturgeon: "Sir, may I present Special Envoy from Wanderjahr Ms. Sonia Motlaw."

Sturgeon took Sonia's hand, squeezed it briefly, and introduced Colonel Ramadan. He shook hands with Reems. "Billy, thanks loads for getting us those hydration units in such good time," he said. "Well, shall we get inside out of this freezing wind?"

"Captain, don't wait on me. I don't know how long I might be. I have detained you long enough from your important duties." Sonia laid a hand on Reems's shoulder and kissed him lightly on one cheek.

"I'll have someone drive her back to Mainside, Billy," Sturgeon offered. "Thanks very much for bringing her down here."

"No problem, sir." Reems saluted, climbed very reluctantly back into his vehicle, and drove off.

"We can put you up here in our guest quarters for the night if you wish, madam . . ."

"Sonia." She gave Sturgeon her smile. "Call me Sonia. I apologize for the inconvenience, Brigadier, Colonel." She nodded at Ramadan. "And I promise not to take up very much of your time. Thanks for the offer but I'm catching the twenty-hours shuttle back to New Oslo."

"Well, Sonia, I'm Ted, and Colonel Ramadan is Izzy." Once inside the building they took seats around Sturgeon's desk. "Very Spartan in here, Brigadier." Sonia grinned.

"Well, I don't spend much time in the HQ, Sonia. You know, with comfortable offices, commanders will find too much time to spend in them and that's not how I run this FIST." He smiled. "Coffee or something stronger to drive out the chill?"

"No, thank you, Ted. I'll come straight to the point of my visit. I have a personal message for Joseph Finucane Dean, who I believe is assigned to the third platoon of Company L in your infantry battalion."

Few things in life ever surprised Brigadier Theodosius Sturgeon, but this information did. However, he kept his composure. "Yes, that'd be Corporal Dean; he's in Captain Conorado's company. Colonel Ramadan, would you have Sergeant Major Shiro get Dean up here on the double."

"Excuse me, Brigadier, but I'd much rather go to him. If that's possible and no trouble for you."

"Well, sure, Sonia, but you're the highest-ranking visitor we've had to this place in as long as I can remember and . . ." Sturgeon shrugged.

"Oh, not that high ranking, Brigadier." Sonia smiled. "I'm just a messenger, in fact. Is his residence far from here?"

Colonel Ramadan could hardly suppress a smile. No one, in his memory, had ever referred to an enlisted Marine's barracks as a "residence." "It's a brisk walk, ma'am, and I'd be honored to escort you there."

"That is very kind of you, Colonel."

"Are you sure you can't spend the night with us, Sonia?" Sturgeon asked.

"No, Ted, my business with Dean will not take very long. Besides, I have parsecs to travel before I sleep and promises to keep, as the poet hath said." She laughed and her laughter proved infectious, even bringing a smile to Ramadan's normally grave expression.

"Very well. I'll have Dean meet you in his orderly room where Colonel Ramadan will escort you. Uh, Sonia, one thing, though. Can you tell us what this is all about? Dean is a fine Marine and he'll go far in the Corps. I hope this does not mean trouble for him. As his FIST commander I need to know about such things. You understand."

"Yes, I do, Ted, I do. But this is a purely personal matter, and I am not at liberty to divulge any more than that. I am sorry, truly. This must seem a great imposition to you. But just remember, we Wanderjahrians will never forget what your men did for us. While my message is important to Mister, er, *Corporal* Dean, it in no way reflects unfavorably upon him, this FIST, or the Confederation Marine Corps. I assure you of that."

On the way to the Company L orderly room, Colonel Ramadan made small talk with Sonia Motlaw and he found her a very pleasant, engaging, but thoroughly determined young woman. He admired her for that, her stunning figure aside.

As they walked along Marines saluted the colonel smartly as they passed by. "Good afternoon, sir!" one would announce.

"Good afternoon, Private Wigley," Colonel Ramadan would reply, returning the salute. After about twenty such engagements with different Marines, Sonia turned to Ramadan and asked, "How do you manage to remember the names of *all* these men, Colonel?"

"Well, it's a talent you develop as a Marine officer, ma'am. When I was an ensign, a platoon commander, oh, many years ago now, I forgot the name of one of my men. It just slipped my mind. My company commander gave me an ass reaming, er, excuse me—"

"I have one of those, too, Colonel," Sonia laughed.

"—so bad that I've never forgotten the lesson."

Colonel Ramadan found he really enjoyed talking to the bright young lady. He briefly considered taking her the long way around to the Company L orderly room, to remain in her company a bit longer, but aside from the fact that his right arm was getting tired, he was too old and too much a professional to play that game with such a serious and dedicated lady. She didn't deserve that. He smiled to himself, though. What was beautiful sixty years ago was *still* beautiful. He left her, somewhat reluctantly, in the care of Captain Conorado and made his way back to the headquarters, shaking his head. "Now what the *fuck* did Dean get himself into, back there on Wanderjahr?" he asked aloud. He'd have a word or two with several NCOs in Company L, after Sonia was gone, and he'd find out. You can't keep secrets in the Marine Corps.

CHAPTER
FIVE

Rachman Claypoole woke to the clatter of pots and pans being readied in the kitchen, and smiled. It would have been better to wake up and find Jente in his arms, but having a breakfast specially made by loving hands just for him came in a close second. He got out of bed and went into the head—the bathroom, he corrected himself; he was in Jente's home, not a military installation—and gave himself a quick wash then padded naked to the kitchen. He leaned on the doorjamb and smiled again as he watched Jente preparing breakfast.

"Do you want your eggs over medium?" she asked.

"Sounds delicious."

She turned to look at him, smiling. Her smile widened when she saw his nudity, and she struck a pose. "Like what you see?" she asked.

"I very much like what I see." Jente wasn't what anybody would call classically beautiful. A life spent running a farm had taken much of the softness from her curves, roughened her hands, and darkened her skin where it was constantly exposed to the sun. But everything about her was properly shaped and well proportioned.

"What," she said with a laugh in her voice, "a woman barefoot, naked, and in the kitchen?"

The question startled him. If it hadn't been asked with a smile, it would have offended him. But since Jente had smiled, he came back with "You're not naked, you're wearing an apron."

She laughed lightly. "Bide your time. And come, sit. Breakfast will be ready in a couple of minutes."

Claypoole pushed off from the doorjamb and sat at the table. "I like an eat-in kitchen," he said. "It's so homey."

Jente smiled at him over her shoulder. A moment later, she dished out the food and placed the plates on the table. She whipped off the apron and struck another pose. "There, now you have your barefoot, naked woman in a kitchen." She bent over with a hand on his shoulder, kissed him on the mouth, and danced away from his hands. "Not yet, love. Food first. Then fooling around."

He grinned at her. "Yes, ma'am." And dug in. He enjoyed the meal—and the sight of Jente across the table.

Later, back in bed and sated, Claypoole lay supine with one arm under the pillow behind his head and the other curled around Jente's shoulders, enjoying the feel of her breast on his chest as she lay half on him, toying with his chest hair.

"I love you," she murmured, almost too low for him to hear.

"I li—" He realized exactly what she had said and corrected himself. "I love you, too."

"Do you? Really?" She raised her head to look into his eyes and propped her chin on the hand that had been playing with his chest hair.

He gazed into her eyes and bent his neck to kiss her forehead. "Yes," he whispered.

She looked into his eyes a moment longer then lowered her head and resumed playing with his chest.

He sighed contentedly and gave her shoulders a light squeeze. She snuggled in closer.

Some minutes later she asked, "When will you get promoted to sergeant?"

He barked out a surprised laugh. "Promoted to *sergeant*? Me? I don't know."

When he didn't say anything more, she asked, "Why don't you know?"

"Because . . ." He had to think for a moment. "Because I don't know if the quarantine on Thirty-fourth FIST has been lifted yet. Or if it *will* be lifted."

Again he stopped talking long enough that Jente had to ask another question. "What does the quarantine have to do with you getting promoted?"

He raised his head, but she wasn't looking at him and all he could see was the top of her head. "Because the only way I can get promoted to sergeant is if a squad leader billet opens up. If the quarantine is still on, that means one of the squad leaders has to get killed to open up a position. And even then"—he paused briefly to think of who was ahead of him—"the platoon has three fire team leaders who are senior to me, who would get the promotion before I would. That means four Marines, men I've lived with and fought alongside for years, have to die or be too severely wounded to return to duty before I can get promoted." He lowered his head and his voice dropped almost to inaudibility. "I hope I never get promoted if that's how it has to happen."

Claypoole didn't notice the strain in Jente's voice when she asked, "And what if the quarantine has been lifted, or is lifted soon?"

Claypoole shrugged with his free shoulder. "I don't know. Most of us are well past our normal rotation dates. For all I know, I could get shipped to a FIST all the way across Human Space, or—*oooph!*"

Jente had doubled her fist and slugged him in the solar plexus as hard as she could.

"What?" he gasped. "Why'd you—"

She jumped out of bed, wrapping a sheet around herself.

"Get out!" she screamed, and pointed at the bedroom door. "Get out of my house! Go away! I never want to see you again!" She twisted around and burst out crying.

"What? What's the matter, honey?" Claypoole asked, getting out of bed and going to hug and try to comfort her.

She slapped at him. "Get away from me. Go away! Leave me alone!"

"But, Jente, I—"

"Go!" she screamed.

"But . . ." he objected, looking around for his clothes.

"Just go." She stormed into the bathroom and slammed the door. "Go away or I'll call the police."

Claypoole continued to entreat her while he pulled on his clothes, but her only response was a demand that he leave or she was going to call the police and have him arrested for breaking in and assaulting her. Thoroughly confused, he left. He used his comm to call for a taxi and took it into Bronnys, and had it let him off at Big Barb's.

When Corporal Claypoole entered Big Barb's he didn't find anybody from third platoon there. Not that he expected to. He knew that any of the Marines from the platoon who were still in the place at mid-morning would be upstairs, sleeping off the previous night's festivities. The rest were elsewhere in and around Bronnoysund, shopping, at an early vid, card playing in the minuscule, not-quite-legal casino, or in the town library. Possibly some were lounging along the fjord's pebbly beach, or bantering with the fishermen. A few might even have gone out as day crew on one or another of the fishing boats. Bronnoysund was more than just Camp Ellis's liberty town; it had been a long-established fishing village before the Confederation put a military presence next to it.

It was fine with Claypoole that none of the other Marines were available in Big Barb's; at the moment, he didn't want the company of his fellow Marines anyway. What he wanted just then was a strong drink—and Reindeer Ale wasn't anywhere near strong enough. He chose a table from which he could see both the door and the stairs leading to the rooms above.

"Hi, Marine. What can I get for you?"

He looked up and didn't recognize the face that went with the voice. Before answering, he gave a quick look around and what he'd seen when he entered finally registered on him; Big Barb's was almost empty. Four serving girls were preparing the common room tables for the lunch crowd and a bartender busied himself with bottles and polishing glasses; Claypoole was the only customer.

He looked up at the girl. "I thought I knew everybody who works here. What's your name?"

"Gina. I'm lunch shift. What's your name?"

He studied her face for a moment: pretty, broad, dark, but the darkness looked more like genes than exposure to the sun. He gave himself a shake. "Call me Rock," he said.

"All right, Marine Rock, what can I get for you?"

"Get me a double, a double . . ." His voice trailed off. He couldn't think of any liquor because he almost always drank beer. "I want something strong. What do you recommend?"

Gina raised an eyebrow at him. "Bad night?"

Claypoole opened his mouth to say, "Yes," but reconsidered. "No, I had a real good night. It's the morning that was bad."

"Umm-hmm. I'll ask Rhon," she said nodding toward the bartender, "what he recommends as forget-it juice."

"Whatever he recommends, I want a double."

"You got it." Gina's hips swayed as she headed for the bar. Claypoole squeezed his eyes closed and turned his head away. After the unexpected and incomprehensible way Jente had kicked him out, he really didn't want to even look at another woman. What on earth had set her off? Had he said something wrong? He ran the conversation through his mind for what must have been the tenth time since he left her farmhouse, and couldn't think of a thing he might have said that was out of line.

Gina was back quickly with a tumbler of something deep amber. "Rhon says it's his own concoction and he hasn't given it a name, but it begins with a base of strong rum and gets stronger from there." When Claypoole went to take the glass from her hand, Gina snatched it back. "Rhon also said to tell you that it's deceptively smooth, so you should take it easy." She placed the glass on the table in front of him, and stepped away, glancing over her shoulder at him.

Claypoole's gaze followed Gina for a moment as she busied

herself preparing other tables, then he turned to the tumbler of deep amber liquid and lifted it to his lips. He took a sip and his eyes widened; the fluid flowed easily over his tongue and down his throat. It barely burned when it hit his stomach. He took a mouthful, swished it around, and swallowed. In a moment a comfortable warmth began to suffuse his body. He smiled for the first time since Jente had slugged him. Relaxed, he sagged back in his chair, and languidly raised the glass in salute to Rhon the bartender, then tipped the glass and drained it in two or three gulps.

Head lolling like a puppet with a broken string, he looked around for Gina, beautiful Gina, Gina who had brought him this wonderful ca-ka-concoction that made him feel so, so—so *good* when he'd felt so, so, so—*bad*! Gina, the marvelous woman who didn't attack a man for no reason out of the blue. Blue? Tha's right, outta the blue. *Gina!* the best damn—*woman* Big Barb ever hired! The fourth time his gaze swung by her, his eyes juddered to a stop, and he recognized her. Grinning broadly, he signaled for a refill.

Gina gave him a dubious look, then glanced at Rhon, who shrugged and began mixing another drink for Claypoole. When Gina went to the bar to get it, Rhon drew her into brief, whispered consultation. She nodded, then picked up the fresh drink and marched it to the wildly grinning Claypoole.

"You're cut off after this one, Marine," she said firmly.

He grinned innocently at her. "Tol' you, call me Rock."

"It doesn't matter what I call you. You're cut off after this one."

"Wha' eber you say, love." He reached for her, but she'd already stepped out of reach, and he had to grab the table with both hands to avoid falling onto the floor. More or less stable, he lifted the glass with both hands and drained half of it without spilling too much down his chin. He barely got the glass back on the table before he began swaying too much to keep a firm grip on it.

With much cautious twisting, turning, and shifting about on the chair, Claypoole propped his elbows on the tabletop and laid the top of his chest against the table's edge. Squinting to focus, he gripped the glass with both hands and lowered his head until his grinning mouth was in contact with the rim of the glass. Gingerly, as though lifting something of immense value and incredible fragility, he raised himself, holding the glass in a three-point grip—both hands and his mouth—tipping his head and the glass back. Before he realized it, he was tipped back far enough that the liquor was flowing into his mouth. He kept tipping backward until he overbalanced and toppled to the floor.

Gina wasn't looking, and jumped at the crash of Claypoole and chair hitting the floor, but she knew instantly what had happened and ran to kneel at his side. Her hands gently probed his head, looking for soft spots and blood. She didn't find any.

That just happened to be when Big Barb came out of her office, located behind the bar. "Vot's goink on here?" she bellowed. Her eyes immediately picked out the source of the noise and she bustled over to see whether she had to worry about liability.

"Glaypoole?" she said when she saw the passed-out Marine. She shot a look at Rhon the bartender. "Dit you gib him von off your con*coctionsh*?"

Rhon shrugged. "He said he wanted something strong."

"That's right, Big Barb," Gina put in. "He said he'd had an awful morning and wanted something to help him forget it."

"Zo you giff him a con*coction*? Dat vasn't enuf to knock him out."

"Two of them," Gina said.

"Doubles," Rhon added.

Big Barb shuddered at the thought of someone drinking two of Rhon's "concoctions." Doubles, no less.

"Gid ober 'ere," she ordered Rhon. "Stan' 'im up. No, no," she said when Rhon grabbed Claypoole under his shoulders. "Put the chair ub, den sid 'im on it. Tha's right, lay his head on his harms. Led 'im sleep it off. We ain' gonna be so busy for a while we'll need the table." She waddled away, shaking her head and muttering under her breath.

Gina watched until Big Barb was far enough away, then adjusted Claypoole's head, arms, and shoulders into a position that would leave him less stiff than the way Rhon had dumped him.

And that's how Sergeant Kerr and Lance Corporal Ymenez found him when they entered Big Barb's a few hours later.

"Mmrph."

"That's not good enough, Marine," Sergeant Kerr said, and shook Claypoole's shoulder again.

"Mmlmpf."

"Is this *really* the image you want your junior man to have of his fire team leader?" Kerr clamped a hand on top of Claypoole's head, lifted, and let go. Claypoole's head *clunked* back onto his folded arms.

"Emmeone." Claypoole feebly shifted his head's position on his arms.

Big Barb bustled over. "Dam drunk Marine," she sputtered, as though she were seeing the passed-out Claypoole for the first time. "Timmy, vhy you led your corporals gid drunk like dat, and zo early inna day?"

As broad as Big Barb was, she didn't look big enough to bowl Kerr over; he was the tallest Marine in third platoon, several centimeters over two meters. He looked down at her from his imposing height.

"Big Barb, I wasn't here when Claypoole got drunk. You were. Why did *you* let him get so drunk?"

Big Barb didn't care that she barely came up to Kerr's chest; she wasn't intimidated by his height. "Dat don' madder," she snorted. "He's *your* man, nod mine! *You* da responzible von!"

Kerr locked glares with Big Barb, and shook Claypoole's shoulder again. The two were so intent on staring each other down that neither noticed when the kitchen doors swung open and Lance Corporal Schultz walked into the common room. For those present who did see Schultz, the big, bronze-skinned Marine didn't appear to look around, or to be in a hurry to get anywhere in particular, but within seconds of entering the room he was at the table where Claypoole was still mumbling demands to be left alone. Schultz kicked the chair out from under his fire team leader, dumping Claypoole quite unceremoniously on the floor.

Kerr and Big Barb broke their stare-down and switched their attention to Claypoole. But before either of them could move, Claypoole bounded to his feet, and came up swinging. He didn't know who had knocked him down, and didn't care, only that somebody was going to pay for it. He swung blindly at the first human form in his sight.

Which happened to be Hammer Schultz.

Schultz was expecting a violent reaction from Claypoole and was ready. His left hand flew up and caught Claypoole's flying right fist like an infielder's glove snagging a line drive. Then his right hand caught Claypoole's left. Schultz held on to both. Claypoole tried, and kept trying, to pull his fists back and throw more punches, but all he accomplished was to give his shoulders a workout. He didn't see who was holding his hands.

Kerr and Schultz looked at each other over Claypoole's bobbing head. They knew that he had planned to spend the entire five-day liberty with his girlfriend and that he had gone straight to her farm when he left Camp Ellis the day before. But they'd found him sleeping off a drunk at Big Barb's. Kerr nodded at Schultz, then stepped close to Claypoole and put his mouth near the corporal's head.

"Attention on deck!" he roared into Claypoole's ear, and jerked back fast enough to avoid being hit when Claypoole snapped to attention.

Claypoole blinked a few times as he gained awareness of his surroundings: Schultz standing in front of him; that new guy who'd replaced MacIlargie when the Wolfman went into the hospital, standing wide-eyed on the other side of the table; Marines and locals at other tables staring at him; some of Big Barb's serving girls frozen in place, staring at him. He turned his head and saw Sergeant Kerr giving him the gimlet eye. He noticed that nobody else had come to attention at the command.

"What the fuck?" he murmured.

"Are you over your fight?" Kerr asked.

Claypoole looked from Kerr to Schultz, realized whom he'd been trying to fight with, and swallowed. "I'm over it."

"Good. Pick up your chair and sit down. When was the last time you ate?"

Claypoole had to think about it. "B-breakfast." His voice broke when he remembered what happened shortly after breakfast.

"That's long enough." Kerr looked at Big Barb. "I think he needs some stew."

Big Barb eyed Claypoole. "I tink you right," she agreed, and signaled for one of the servers. "She take care off it," she said, and waddled away.

"Water for him, no beer," Kerr told the girl when she took the order for stew for Claypoole, reindeer steaks and ale for the others.

Before the food and drink came, Claypoole abruptly leaped to his feet and bolted toward the restroom. He was gone for nearly ten minutes. When he came back his face was obviously scrubbed, and the chest area of his shirt was wet.

"Barf?" Schultz asked when Claypoole sat back down.

Claypoole nodded. "Where's a corpsman when you need one?" he asked.

"You can go without," Kerr told him. "That'll teach you not to get so shitfaced." He saw the look that Schultz gave him, and added, "Or maybe not."

CHAPTER
SIX

Sonia Motlaw, special envoy from Wanderjahr, sat comfortably in the Company L orderly room waiting for Corporal Dean to arrive. She regarded Captain Conorado silently. He had the rugged, athletic look she prized in a man. His office, like that of the FIST commander, was devoid of any personal items save a small hologram of what appeared to be himself and his family, which sat on one corner of his desk.

"I was told not to ask you what you're here for, ma'am," Conorado began. "I was told you would not be staying long."

"Please, 'Sonia.'" She smiled. "Yes, I'm returning to New Oslo tonight. My message for Corporal Dean is personal and my instructions were not to reveal its contents to anyone. But I assure you, Captain—"

"'Lew,' then, if you please." Conorado smiled.

"—Lew, that it in no way constitutes an embarrassment to Dean or your Corps. I don't have to tell you how much we Wanderjahrians appreciate what your Marines did for us during your deployment to our world. I also want to assure you— Ye gods, what in the hell is *that*?" she screamed, rising halfway out of her seat and pointing at the corner of the room. Her face had turned ghastly pale.

Conorado looked up to where she was pointing and he half expected to see an apparition. "Oh, that." He smiled. "That's only Owen. He's a Woo. He perches on the top of that locker when I have strangers in here. He likes to size them up, so to speak, from that vantage point. We Marines believe in seizing the high ground whenever we can."

"Good God, Lew." Sonia laughed nervously, her face turning from pale with fright to red with embarrassment. "I thought it was a ghost, shimmering away up there like that. What is that thing?"

"Woos are native to Diamunde. We deployed there some years ago. Corporal Dean, actually, brought him back here with him and he's become our company mascot. We named him Owen. Ask Dean to tell you how they met. Fascinating story. He almost got us all court-martialed on another occasion when a scientist wanted to take him from us for vivisectioning and Dean threatened to shoot her." He chuckled. "One thing about that lad, Sonia, he's a tough Marine, and he knows what's right—and he isn't afraid to act on it."

"Hello, Owen." Sonia waved at the Woo. "Are they sentient?" she asked.

"No," Conorado replied, *a bit too quickly,* Sonia thought. "Well, nobody knows, actually. They can sense moods in humans and express their own moods by changing colors, like chameleons. I think he likes you."

Someone knocked twice on the door. "That should be our man. Come," Conorado responded.

Dean strode into the room, came to attention, and saluted. "Sir, Corporal Dean—"

"No need for that, Corporal. Come over here and meet this lady."

Sonia rose smoothly, walked over to Dean, who was still at rigid attention, and held out her hand to him. "Corporal Dean, my name is Sonia Motlaw. I'm a special envoy from Wanderjahr. I've come a long way to see you. I have a message for you from Hway Kuetgens." She smiled that enchanting smile.

"Hway?" Dean glanced at Captain Conorado, who just nodded silently. "Hway?" he repeated, swallowing hard. "How is she?" The question sounded very awkward to Dean as his mind raced back to their parting, he to return to duty, she to take over

the government of Morgenluft, their short, passionate relationship ending almost before it had begun. "My brave Marine," he
remembered her saying to him as she gave him a parting kiss.
It seemed like only yesterday, but they had parted, what, six or
seven years ago now? He'd thought of her often since then
through all the lonely and hellish days and nights the men of
Thirty-fourth FIST had endured. Now he found himself overwhelmed by a flood of emotion.

"She is fine. Corporal, what do your friends call you?"

"Uh, Joseph?" He glanced again at Conorado, who nodded.

"May I call you Joseph? You may call me Sonia." She laid a
hand on Dean's shoulder and smiled.

"Yes, ma'am, sure."

"Good. Captain, I'd like to talk to Corporal Dean privately.
Can you let him drive me back to Mainside? I can deliver my
message on the way."

"I'll have the first sergeant make the company landcar available. Be back in time for reveille," Conorado said with a wink.
Dean's face flushed.

"He'll be back very soon," Sonia said as if to reassure Conorado, but totally missing the joke.

"Whew," Lew Conorado sighed, after the pair had departed.
"What do you make of all that, Owen?"

"I like the lady, and if I'm not mistaken, Lewis, our Joseph
Finucane Dean's message has something to do with another
lady."

"Yes, a matter of honor, I take it. You're getting to know us
humans rather well in your old age."

"You aren't hard to understand, once someone gets to know
you." Owen leaped gracefully onto the corner of Conorado's
desk and stood there wobbling, regarding him intently with his
huge eyes.

"How are you feeling, Owen?" The Woo was showing his
age. He was not as agile as he once was and he'd often reminded Conorado that he was nearing the end of his life span.

"Tolerable, skipper, tolerable. That envoy lady, she's some special dish, ain't she?"

Conorado scowled. "Owen, where'd you pick that up? You've been spending far too much time in the goddamned barracks."

Once seated in the landcar, Sonia turned to Dean. "Take your time driving me back to the port, Joseph. What I have to tell you may take a while. Is there someplace along the way you can pull off and we can talk?"

"Yes, ma'am."

"Please, Joseph, call me Sonia! That 'ma'am' stuff makes me feel so old." She laughed. To Dean she appeared very young, certainly under forty.

"Well, it just is . . . you're some kind of ambassador and I'm just a Marine corporal, ma'am, so I feel really awkward calling you anything but ma'am." Dean shrugged. "It's the way we're brought up in the Corps, I guess. Anyway, would you call me 'Joe'? Joseph is what my mom used to call me all the time."

"Where do your parents live, Joe?"

"They're dead. My dad died a long time ago and my mom just after I enlisted in the Corps. I was an only child, so I guess the Corps is my family now. How about you?"

"My particulars are of no importance in this," she replied. Then she asked, "Do you have a sweetheart?"

Dean glanced hard at Sonia sitting muffled in a huge parka, her breath steaming in the cold. "Well . . . Are you cold? The heat'll be up in a minute. Sometimes it gets so hot in these cars it blasts you right out—"

"A handsome man like you should have someone, Joe."

"Well, over in Bronnys, that's where we go for liberty, Bronnoysund, there are some nice girls, but you know, we Marines are off on deployments so much . . ." He left the sentence unfinished in the hope that she would change the subject. He wasn't about to tell this sophisticated lady anything about Big Barb's and what went on there. Not that he felt guilty about it, but he sensed that a place like Big Barb's was totally alien to a person like Sonia Motlaw.

They pulled into a roadside park. It was at least a meter deep in snow but the landcar plowed easily through it into the empty parking lot. "This is a nice place when there isn't any snow," Dean offered. He put the car into park but left the engine running.

Sonia turned in her seat to face Dean directly. "Joe, you do have someone and she is Hway Kuetgens. Here." She opened her bag and handed him a portable reader. "Look at what's on the screen."

In the reader's screen appeared a smiling boy perhaps seven or eight years old. Dean's heart skipped a beat. The child was holding Hway's hand. Suddenly the memory of her rushed back upon him, the smell of her hair, her breath against his neck, the warmth of her cheek against his, the rich odor of the earth in that tomato patch back on Wanderjahr where they'd made love in the dust between the rows of plants. "Ah," he sighed.

"That boy is your son."

At first Dean couldn't say a word. Gradually the import of what Sonia had just told him sunk in, causing him to catch his breath. "I—I—"

"You didn't know." Sonia nodded. "Hway wanted it that way. She had her mission, you had yours. You had to go your separate ways." She told Dean all that had happened to Hway Kuetgens in the intervening years, including her assumption of the leadership of the Morgenluft government and her election to the Chair of the Ruling Council.

"Wh-what is the boy's name?"

"Dean." Sonia took the reader back, glanced at the hologram image, and smiled. "He looks just like you, doesn't he?" She handed the reader back. "Keep this, Joe. It's the reason I've come all this way to see you. Joe, in two years we're having an election. Ms. Kuetgens cannot run for another term as chair and she plans to retire to Morgenluft. Your son asks after you often. It's time he met his father. How much longer do you have on your enlistment?"

"Uh, two years, ma'am."

"Well." Sonia scratched her chin. "That really is the message."

"That's it?"

"Yes. Well, if you were to take your discharge and come back to Wanderjahr, if only for a visit, that would make your son very happy. I know what kind of Marine you are, Joe, and he would be thrilled to have such a brave man as his father. And of course if you wanted to stay with us"—she brushed the side of Dean's face with her hand—"you would be welcome."

"Quit the Corps?"

Sonia did not reply. She rubbed her hands together. "It's warming up in here."

"Yes," Dean replied absently. "Am I at liberty to tell anyone else about my—Dean?"

Sonia shrugged. "You may tell whomever you wish, Joe."

"You see, ma'am," he said, "although on the books I have two years left on my enlistment, we're all in this actually for the duration, until the alien threat is finally eliminated, and that could be a *long* time. The best I can promise anybody is, if there's a lull, a drawdown on deployment, maybe I could get some leave. Hell, I've got a lot of unused leave in my account. Sooner or later, the Corps has to give it to me. But this is a bad time to take leave. We can be deployed at any time, so I can't even think of requesting leave."

"I know. The alien threat hangs over all of us, Joe, and you Marines are on the cutting edge of the war. I understand and so does Hway and so will Dean, when he's older. Do you have any message for your son that I can take back with me?"

"Yes, ma'am, tell him—tell him—tell his mother—I'll see them, soon." He thought for a moment, staring at the swirling snow outside the car. "I have something I want you to take back to my son," he said at last.

At their parting Sonia held Dean tightly, just the way his

mother had when he left home to join the Corps. "Joseph," she whispered, "any woman would be proud to have you as her companion."

Once back in New Oslo, Sonia decided not to take Mr. Berg up on his offer to go skiing: Ambassador Morelles, she heard, had broken both legs on one of the slopes. They said he was calmly smoking a Davidoff during the medevac flight to the hospital.

Dean had been called up to the orderly room just as he was getting ready for liberty in Bronnys. Now, of course, that was the furthest thing from his mind. But when finally he got back to his room in the barracks, he was all alone. He needed the privacy. He lay on his rack, the tiny reader in one hand, studying the images. He was a father. It was hard to believe.

"Mind if I join you, Marine?"

It was Charlie Bass. Startled, Dean made to get off his bunk.

"Keep your place. This is not an official visit." Bass pulled up a chair and sat facing Dean. "Busy day, I hear."

Dean grinned. "Yes, sir."

"For this conversation, you call me Charlie. Word's all over Ellis about this ambassador lady who came all the way from Wanderjahr to have a private chitchat with Corporal Dean." He grinned. "Everyone wants to know why but it's all a big secret."

"Well, I can tell you—"

Bass waved a hand. "No, you don't have to, Dean. I already know what it was all about. You and Claypoole had quite a time back there on Wanderjahr, on detached duty with Commander Peters, didn't you? Claypoole talks a lot. Said you were pretty hot on this oligarch's granddaughter. Now she's head of their planetary council and you get a visit from a special envoy of her government. You going to go back there when your enlistment is up?"

Dean's face twisted with emotion. "I-I don't know, sir."

"Son, let me tell you something. You are responsible for other people. As a corporal in this Corps you're responsible for the men under you and around you. As a man you're responsible for what you do with other people, whether they're other Marines or the girls down at Big Barb's. Some men screw their way all across Human Space and never think twice about it. I don't think you're like that, Dean. Are you?"

"Well, sir—"

"I didn't think so. Those women take a piece of your heart away with them, don't they? And maybe you left one of them with a piece of yourself. It happens. Maybe you have a decision to make. Now, speaking as your platoon commander, I'd hate to lose you. But we get used to that in the Corps. I want you to do three things, Dean. One, as long as you're a corporal in this outfit I want your mind focused on your duty. Two, I want you to keep faith with the people who've kept faith with you, whoever they may be, and three, be true to yourself." He got up. "Well, that's it. Shift into your civvies and take the next liberty bus into Bronnys. Do what any man facing a big decision would do: Get drunk with your buddies." Bass extended his hand. "You're a damn fine Marine and when the time comes you'll make a damn fine daddy."

On his way back to his quarters Bass reflected on the little speech he'd just delivered to Dean. A fine advisor he was. He fingered the flimsiplast letter he'd just gotten from Comfort Brattle back on Kingdom. She'd named his own son Charles. Damn! He hated that name.

CHAPTER
SEVEN

Ensign Charlie Bass walked slowly back to his quarters. *Dean,* he thought, and smiled to himself. The lad had gotten that girl pregnant back on Wanderjahr. Where the hell had he ever found the time to do that? He laughed out loud. Give a Marine a chance . . . He shook his head.

What am I laughing about? he thought. *What have I gotten myself into?* He'd promised back on Kingdom before he left that he'd marry Comfort if she'd join him on Thorsfinni's World and he had meant it. But then time passed and he had come to consider that promise something made on the spur of the moment, that Comfort would find a man from her own world who could be with her, help her raise their children in the proper manner, in a family environment, not gallivant all over Human Space, leaving her to languish in government quarters with a brood of screaming brats while he was away for extended periods. What kind of marriage would that be?

And then there was Katie Katyana. Charlie Bass was no welsher, but here he was, promised in marriage to *two* women. Love is not something you dish out in dribs and drabs; it's an all-or-nothing proposition and it's entirely possible to love equally more than one person at a time. And Charlie Bass really did love both Katie and Comfort, two completely different women, maybe not even compatible personalities.

And to complicate the problem further, he had his own illegitimate child to think about now. He'd already been to Personnel and designated Comfort Brattle the sole beneficiary of his insurance policies. That would take care of her and the boy if anything were to happen to him, and it was likely something would since Thirty-fourth FIST had been alerted only that morning for another deployment.

Well, Bass thought, *if I make it through this one I'll figure something out.* But right now he had to clear his mind, get ready to do his duty.

Back in his quarters Bass shook off his cold-weather gear, rubbed his hands together vigorously, and opened his tiny liquor cabinet. Time for some bourbon, and he still had some of those Montecristo cigars in his humidor. Might as well relax and enjoy the comforts of home while he could, since soon they'd be off to another deployment.

Someone knocked on the door. It turned out to be a red-faced yeoman from Mainside. "Ensign Bass, sir?"

"Yeah, first class, what is it?"

"Special letter, sir, just came through in this evening's dispatches."

"Little late for mail call, isn't it?"

"Sir, the chief told me to deliver it in person. It's marked 'High Priority' and 'Deliver Upon Receipt.' Please sign for it here." He held out a digital clipboard. Bass swiped it with his ID bracelet and accepted the envelope. The yeoman saluted and left.

The flimsiplast envelope was stamped "Kingdom" and had been mailed ten days earlier. It was from Zechariah Brattle, the patriarch of the Brattle family. *Well, here it is,* Bass thought. *Either I'm a beloved son-in-law or a vile seducer who betrayed Zechariah's trust.* In fact he was a bit surprised Zechariah hadn't written him much sooner since Comfort's baby had been born some months ago. Charlie Bass was not the type of man to hesitate facing bad news, if bad news it was, but before he read the letter he was going to be prepared. He poured a generous dollop of Old Snort into a glass, clipped one of his Montecristos, and lit up. He sipped the whiskey, letting it slide slowly down to explode in a fiery ball deep inside his stomach. When there was a tiny white ash on the end of his cigar he felt ready for anything and tore the envelope open.

He read only as far as the first paragraph and exclaimed aloud, *"Holeeee shit!"*

"Dear Charles," the letter began. Bass shook his head. Zechariah would just *never* learn to call him Charlie. "Some time ago the boys found a Skink, as you call the creatures that devastated our homes, a baby, evidently left behind when they evacuated Kingdom . . ." At that point Bass got back into his cold-weather gear and took the letter to Captain Conorado.

"Holy shit!" Conorado exclaimed, and the pair walked over to Commander van Winkle's quarters.

"Holy shit," Commander van Winkle sighed after he'd read Zechariah's letter. "Let's go see the brigadier about this!"

Brigadier Ted Sturgeon was still at FIST headquarters despite the lateness of the hour. He read the letter in silence. "Get Colonel Ramadan and Sergeant Major Shiro," he said. They waited in silence until those two notables joined them. He handed Ramadan the flimsiplast. "Read this and pay particular attention to the concluding paragraph."

"Buddha's balls," Ramadan exclaimed, and passed the letter to Sergeant Major Shiro.

Sergeant Major Shiro read the last paragraph aloud:

"We gave Moses up to the two 'scientists,' this Joseph Gobels and Pensy Fogel, because at the time we were convinced he would be of use to humankind in its war with the aliens. I am convinced now these men are charlatans and took the boy for their own purposes, not back to Universal Labs in Fargo on Earth. I believe this is so because they seem to have fallen completely out of Human Space; they never returned to Fargo, far as I have been able to find out. Charles, you are the only person I know who has the contacts that might be able to find Moses; the authorities here are not interested in tracking these two men down. I'm only sorry I didn't say something about Moses much earlier, but Hannah and the boys, well, they love the little thing,

Charles, and I just couldn't. But finding Moses is of the utmost importance to us all. What he can tell us about his species would be invaluable in our war against the Skinks. But bear this in mind, during the time he lived with us, became a member of our family in fact, we came to realize these creatures are much more like us humans than anyone ever realized."

Silence enveloped the six Marines. "A live Skink that speaks Standard English and has adopted human ways," Commander van Winkle mused aloud at last, "would be a great asset infiltrating those damned caves they like to hide in."

"He could tell us what makes them tick," Sergeant Major Shiro offered. The others nodded their agreement.

Sturgeon said nothing, just drummed his fingers on his desk. Then he said, "Charlie, you know this Brattle. He doesn't sound like a kook."

"No, sir, he is not, *definitely* not. If Zechariah says all this happened, it did."

Sturgeon fell silent for another long moment. "This exobiologist, Gobels, he's kidnapped the damned thing to get himself a Nobel Prize, you can bet on that." He slammed a fist on the desktop.

"We've run across his type before," Captain Conorado said. "That crazy bitch on Avionia Station who wanted to dissect Owen." Conorado's defiance of the scientist had gotten him in a lot of trouble, but he'd have come out all right, even if the lady scientist hadn't up and died suddenly. But ever since, he'd harbored a profound distrust of the "pure scientist," which this Gobels appeared to be another example of. He'd also felt guilty because he'd kept the fact that Owen was a sentient being to himself all this time. He'd done it because he didn't want someone like this Gobels taking him away to study him. He understood fully how the Brattles felt about the Skink whom they'd named Moses. Now, in view of what had happened to this Moses creature, Conorado knew he'd been right to keep quiet about Owen.

"How is that little bugger?" van Winkle asked. "That Owen

of yours. He's Thirty-fourth FIST's unofficial mascot, so we should know how he's doing."

"Very interested in Skink physiology." Conorado grinned, glad no one in the room was telepathic. But he didn't like the way Bass glanced up at him, a half smile on his lips. Rumors had begun to spread in Lima Company that their CO had been talking to himself in his office at night. Everyone knew he wasn't *that* far around the bend.

The remark broke the tension and Sturgeon laughed. "I'm going to jump channels with this. I'm going straight to General Cazombi, info copy to General Aguinaldo. If we go through fleet with this it'll only get delayed. I'm classifying this information Ultra Secret and you know what that means about keeping this under your covers. I'm going to send it off tonight. We have too much to do to get ready for this deployment to waste time screwing around. Who's staff duty officer tonight?" he asked Colonel Ramadan.

"Lieutenant Hamish, I believe, sir."

"Have him stand by with a driver. I'll write up the back channel and he'll take it over to the navy at Mainside. I want it hand-delivered to the sparkheads. Now, gentlemen, kindly leave me alone while I put this thing together. Oh, Charlie, good work! This Zechariah Brattle, he took good care of you while you were on R & R on Kingdom, didn't he?" They all laughed. Bass's experience on Kingdom, where he'd been captured by Skinks and then left for dead, had become legend in Thirty-fourth FIST. His fellow Marines often referred jokingly to the ordeal as his period of authorized "rest and relaxation," although he'd managed almost single-handedly to survive captivity, and overthrow a ruthless dictator. All in a day's work. But of his personal victory over Comfort Brattle's heart, only he knew of that.

Back in the company office Conorado slumped tiredly into his chair. Owen sat perched comfortably on top of the bookcase, digesting some rocks. "When do you move out, Skipper?" the Woo asked.

"Couple of days. Owen, can you keep a secret?"

"I guess so, since there's nobody I can tell it to except you, Skipper."

Conorado told him about Moses. "What do you think of all this, Owen?"

Owen wobbled precariously on the edge of the bookcase, his bulbous eyes regarding Conorado steadily. "All I know about those Skinks is what I've heard you Marines say. They're tough customers. This baby could tell you much about them you need to know. Where did they come up with a name for him like 'Moses'?"

"It's from their scriptures. Moses as a baby was taken in by some people who found him floating down by a river."

"An extraordinary baby, no doubt."

"Yes, extraordinary indeed. And so is this Skink Moses, Owen. We have to find him, rescue him from this renegade scientist, and put him to work for us."

"That's not what you let them do to me, is it, Skipper."

That made Conorado pause for a moment. "Well, you're different, Owen."

"How? I'm not dangerous? You know very well your exobiologists would cream their jeans if they could get their hands on me. You've been denying them their shot at that Nobel Prize I hear you talking about sometimes."

Conorado had to laugh at how expertly the Woo had learned Marine slang. "Cream their jeans!" Of all the expressions an alien entity would pick up! "Well, fuck them. And yes, Owen, you are *not* dangerous but if anyone's to discover the potential of you Woos for the good of humanity, well, it'll have to be someone else, not me. But there's another reason, more important, why I'm not telling anyone about you."

"And what would that be, Skipper?"

"Because you're one of my Marines."

"If I can't find the sonofabitch, he don't exist!" Huygens Long exclaimed, jumping to his feet and smashing a fist into his palm. "I mean, Madam President, that's one thing we do very well, we find people like this—this Gobels guy!"

President Chang-Sturdevant smiled. She appreciated her attorney general's direct manner and plain speech. "Sit down, AG. Take a load off." She gestured that he should resume his seat. "What can you tell us about this Dr. Joseph Gobbles at this point?"

"Where have I heard that name before?" General Alistair Cazombi asked. He'd called for the meeting as soon as he'd received Brigadier Sturgeon's back channel recommending that the attorney general also be present: Finding Gobels and the missing Skink named Moses was a civilian law enforcement matter now, not a military operation.

" 'Gobels,' madam," Long began. "Alistair asked me to do a check on him before we came over here"—he nodded at Cazombi—"so I had his name run through the system. He's one of the chief scientists at Universal Labs right here in Fargo. He was sent to Kingdom along with a lot of other people to survey the survivors of the Skink war and find out what he could about the enemy. As far as the people at Universal Labs are concerned, he's still there, still surveying. But this Brattle guy says neither he nor his assistant, this Pensy Fogel guy, are anywhere to be found on Kingdom."

"What about his background?"

"Well, Madam President, nothing unusual there. His curriculum vitae is public knowledge. He held the Chair of Exobiology at Miskatonic University for a number of years; has led or participated in as chief scientist some expeditions to newly settled worlds to investigate the native life forms; written a string of papers, usual academic shit. When we contracted with Universal Labs to do this survey on Kingdom they contacted him and he jumped right on the wagon with the rest of the scientific community." Long shrugged.

"Where do you think he is now?" Cazombi asked.

Long shrugged again. "Anyone's guess, Alistair."

"What's *your* guess, AG?"

Long hesitated before answering the President. "He's here on Earth somewhere. The reason I think so is, he's got to have someplace private and quiet where he can take that Skink and work him over. He doesn't have the resources to set up a lab somewhere light-years away. The bastard's got the scientific find of the centuries! A live, sentient alien life form that's at war with us but about which we don't know squat. That's a Nobel Prize just waiting to be opened. No, he'll do his work here, somewhere. All I've got to do is start interviewing people who know this guy and his sidekick. We'll find him." He rapped his knuckles on the tabletop for emphasis.

"Very good, AG. Alistair, thank you for bringing this to my attention. Please assure Brigadier Sturgeon and General Aguinaldo we're on it." She turned back to Long. "AG, time is of the essence, I think. When can you get started?"

Long smiled. "I already have, Madam President, I already have."

Linney Liggons, Gooden Ashcake, and Adner Shackelford sat, as they usually did, around the trid in Tanner Hastings's Hardware and General Store, talking about the jobs they hadn't had over the past twenty years or so. Steady employment among the 653 (give or take) residents of Wellfordsville, in the southwestern portion of what used to be the state of Virginia, was as rare as a full set of teeth.

"Wisht I'd stayed in the army," Linney remarked. He leaned over and expectorated a stream of tobacco juice into a No. 10 can sitting on the floor. "I'da been retired now 'n livin' on a big guvmint check."

"What you complainin' about, Linney?" Gooden Ashcake cackled. "They give you three hots 'n a cot 'n taught you how to wear shoes. Ain't that enuff guvmint assistance fer one lifetime?"

"You boys gonna watch this trid or not?" Adner Shackelford asked.

"We seen it six hundert times, Adner," Linney said. "Next scene ol' John Wayne, he—

"Hey! Tanner!" Linney Liggons shouted across the store. "Yew got enny deliveries I could make fer ya today?" Tanner, busy with an inventory, shook his head. "Damn. He give me a load o' stuff to take out to ol' Treemonisha's place a week or two ago. I tell you 'bout that?"

"Sixty-seven times," Adner said. " 'N-nobody believes that old woman's had a baby." He laughed.

"Well, I dunno, I said th' kid was hers, but he shore looked like one o' them Giddings, yew know, wif a face like a rat."

"Hell's bells, Linney." Gooden Ashcake laughed. "Sounds like you. You sure you didn't climb up on't ol' girl n' pump 'er up some?"

"Gawdamn you, Gooden! That ol' woman's th' queen of rattlesnakes! I'd ruther fuck a shit-assed cow than her!"

"Some folks around here sez as that's jist what you bin doin', Linney," Adner said with a laugh, then shifting his chair to avoid the blow Linney directed at him.

"Aw, thet thar kid's probably one of 'er great-grandchirren," Gooden volunteered. "Yew know how thet Giddin's clan bin intermarryin' fer generations. Hell, they ain't no different than most other folks around here." He laughed.

"Well, lass time I wuz out there ol' Treemonisha, she come out wif that ol' goddamn shotgun o' hers. She mighty nervous 'bout sumptin'. I figure it got to do wif that kid's living wif her, no matter whose side of the fambly he come from."

"I'll tell you boys sumptin'," Adner began, leaning forward confidentially and speaking in a near whisper. "Lass time I delivered some stuff to those two doctors, yew know, yew seen 'em plenty o' times down to Verne Driscoll's tavern—"

"Them's th' ones livin' out by Jack's Shop?" Gooden interjected.

"Yup, them's th' ones. Anyways, they tipped me might generous like—"

"I remember! Yew got drunk thet night down at Driscoll's on the tip!" Linney shouted, slapping his knee and licking his lips in memory. "It shore got drunk out thet night!"

"Will you jist shut up? But they wouldn't let me inside that barn or whatever it is they's livin' in. But most strange of all, they kep' askin' me all sorts o' questions about ol' Treemonisha! Now, why you 'spose them fellers would wanta know about thet ol' hag for?"

"Sheeyit, boy," Linney shouted. "Them city boys ain't a-gonna shack up wif enny o' the wimmen in *this* here town! Hell, compared to them, Treemonisha's a beauty queen!"

"Hey!" Tanner Hastings shouted from the counter. "Yew boys cain't talk decent over thar, git on outside! I got wimmenfolk comin' in here to trade 'n I don' want enny o' thet barnyard talk in here! 'N yew jist forget about Treemonisha Giddings. She kin take keer o' herself."

Huygens Long's agents began their search by contacting Dr. Gobels's colleagues at Miskatonic University and his neighbors in the upscale neighborhood where he lived alone in Fargo. They wanted to know if he'd been seen recently or if he owned any remote property where he could sequester himself. If any of those people knew anything, they weren't talking. None of his colleagues at Universal Labs, and that included the administrative staff, knew him well enough to contribute anything helpful. A search of his home in Fargo revealed nothing, either. Neither did anything come up on his assistant, Pensy Fogel. The agents gave their contact information to everyone they interviewed with the admonition that if anything was to come up, please call immediately.

Then one afternoon a lab tech at Universal called the lead investigator, Special Agent Don Rittenhouse. "I remember he asked us to do some lab work," she said.

Rittenhouse shot bolt upright in his chair. *"Where did the request come from?"* he almost shouted.

"A post office box in a place called Wellfordsville, in Old Virginia."

"Ummmm-*waaaa!* I'm throwing you a kiss, young lady," Rittenhouse exclaimed. "I'm on my way over and I'll recommend to your supervisor he give you the rest of the week off! You are a darling!" He turned to his assistant, Trace Keen. "Mr. Keen, we've got a trace on the bastard! Grab your toothbrush, we're off to Old Virginny! Hope they got a good hotel down there."

Wellfordsville hadn't had a decent hotel since Uriah Shamhat's place burned down in 2236.

CHAPTER EIGHT

Einna Orafem came out of the kitchen to personally oversee the serving of the meal for Lance Corporal Schultz and his party. She stood, hands clasped between her breasts, close enough behind Schultz's right shoulder that her hip brushed his upper arm, and eagle-eyed every placement of dish, every movement of the servers. Satisfied that the staff had done justice to her man, she bent at the hips to touch her lips to the crown of his head, then marched, head held high, back to the kitchen.

The room was silent as the kitchen doors swung closed behind Einna Orafem, and all eyes were on Schultz. Schultz gave no sign that he was aware of the silence, or the attention. Other than the expression on his face. On anybody else, that expression would have rightly been called "smug." But this was Hammer Schultz, and the Hammer was too tough to ever look *smug*.

Schultz picked up his knife and fork and proceeded to eat. In moments, the normal dinner hour noises resumed and everybody's attention returned to what they'd been doing before the appearance of Big Barb's chef at Schultz's table.

Only a few bites into the meal, Corporal Claypoole looked at Sergeant Kerr and asked, "What's he doing here?" He poked his spoon in the direction of Lance Corporal Ymenez.

"He's in your fire team. What do you think?"

"He's a temporary replacement, until Wolfman comes back."

"He wants to stay with the platoon, and Ensign Bass wants to keep him."

Claypoole nodded and dropped the subject. Even with some

nourishment entering his system, he didn't feel up to pursuing anything.

During the rest of the meal, the four of them talked—and Kerr made sure Ymenez was included in the conversation—about the usual things military people talk about when on liberty: places they've served; good places to pull liberty or go on leave; men they'd served with; mutual acquaintances and friends from other duty assignments; odd things they'd seen or done; lessons learned from various deployments. Everything, in fact, with one glaring exception—women. It's virtually impossible for four un-married enlisted men to converse for more than five or ten min-utes without the topic of conversation shifting to women. But Kerr and Schultz knew that something must have gone very wrong between Claypoole and Jente, and Ymenez followed their example.

So they waited until the dishes had been cleared, and Kerr, Schultz, and Ymenez were on their third mugs of Reindeer Ale—Claypoole was still drinking water—before Kerr asked:

"What the hell happened with your girlfriend?"

At first Claypoole denied that anything had happened, saying that he'd spent the night with Jente, then she had work to do on the farm today, so he came to Bronnoysund, to Big Barb's, to be with other members of third platoon.

"Right, nothing happened," Kerr said dryly. "And the first thing you did when you got here was get passed-out drunk. What's next? You have an instantaneous interstellar matter transmitter you want to sell me?"

Instead of answering, Claypoole looked around. "Where's a corpsman? I need a corpsman." He rubbed his temples.

Kerr reached into his shirt pocket and withdrew a med packet. "You don't need a corpsman. I've got what you need right here."

"Gimme!" Claypoole reached across the table to take the packet of hangover pills, but Kerr snatched it out of the corpo-ral's reach.

"I'll give you one when you start talking," Kerr said.

Claypoole started to get up, to go after the pills.

"Talk," Schultz growled.

Claypoole froze, slowly turned his face toward the big man, and eased himself back onto his chair.

"Well." Claypoole stopped to clear his throat. "Everything was fine this morning until"—and it all came tumbling out. He paused only once, to swallow a hangover pill when Kerr passed one over.

". . . and that's why I came to Big Barb's, to get drunk and forget her." He shook his head. "But I can't figure out what got into her, why she went crazy like that and kicked me out. Things were going *so* well between us up to then." He looked at the tumbler of water clutched in his hands. "I need something stronger than this."

"Marriage," Schultz rumbled.

"What?" Claypoole yelped. "I can't marry her—I can't marry *anybody*! And she knows it."

Kerr leaned back and thought for a moment before asking, "This wasn't the first time she asked when you were going to get promoted, was it?"

Claypoole had to think about it before he could answer. "No, she's asked once or twice before."

"Did she ever mention marriage?"

Claypoole shrugged. "Maybe. I don't know. I can't get married, so I don't even think about it."

Kerr leaned across the table and put a hand on Claypoole's shoulder. "Jente's a single woman, Rock. She thinks about marriage."

"Babies," Schultz added.

"Babies?" Claypoole squeaked. He tried to imagine himself as a father, taking care of a tiny, squalling *thing* that stank when its diaper needed changing, and he shuddered. "But she knows that the Marines don't allow anyone below staff sergeant to get married. I'm only a corporal, so how can she be thinking of me marrying her?"

"She's a woman," Kerr said.

Schultz nodded. "Woman," he agreed.

"Yeah?" Claypoole turned on Schultz. "What about, about—" He jerked his thumb at the kitchen.

Schultz shrugged. "She knows" was all he said.

Kerr was satisfied he'd gotten the entire story out of Claypoole, and looked around for a serving girl. When he caught one's eye he ordered a large pitcher of ale for the table.

"Drink your water," Kerr told Claypoole when the pitcher arrived and the corporal looked at it longingly. "I think you're over your hangover and well enough nourished, and by Mordred's Mom, you've earned the right to do some serious drinking. But"—he pointed at Claypoole's tumbler—"you have to drink it out of that, to remind you of what happens when you overdo it." He stood. "Now it's time I joined the grown-ups. You two, make sure he doesn't do anything too stupid tonight."

Schultz grunted.

Ymenez gaped at Kerr and said, "Aye aye, Sergeant," and wondered what he was supposed to do if his fire team leader *did* decide to do something "too stupid."

Kerr headed for another table, where Ratliff and Kelly, third platoon's other two sergeants, who had come in while Claypoole was telling his tale of woe, were just digging into their own dinners.

The three of them spent the rest of the evening talking and drinking and even eating more, though Claypoole did most of the talking and drinking. Occasionally a couple of Big Barb's girls came to the table and flirted with Claypoole and Ymenez. They ignored Schultz because he belonged to Einna Orafem and none of them wanted to get in trouble with the chef. After all, she cooked their meals as well. When the kitchen closed, Schultz stood with a grunt and went into it, to leave with Einna.

Claypoole got blind drunk again. The next morning he woke in one of the upstairs rooms. A hangover pill and a glass of water were waiting for him on the nightstand. He gratefully drank the pill down and let it work its magic. Only then did he look around the room. From the condition of the bed, he surmised that he hadn't spent the night alone, but had no idea who might have been with him. He checked the time and saw it was late enough that Big Barb's was probably open. He gave himself a quick washup, dressed, and headed downstairs to get something to eat.

That evening, Gunnery Sergeant Thatcher came through the front door of Big Barb's and looked around. When he saw most of third platoon present, along with a number of other Marines from the FIST and from base personnel, he filled his lungs and called out:

"Listen up, Marines!" He waited a few seconds until even the civilians had quieted and turned their attention to him, then announced, "The fast frigate HM3 *Gordon* arrived in orbit a few hours ago. She brought news that will be officially announced at a FIST formation in three days. But Brigadier Sturgeon thought the news was too good to hold back, so the word is being passed now. Unofficially, of course.

"By presidential order, the quarantine of the Marines on Thorsfinni's World has been lifted! Now maybe we can all get back to normal careers.

"That is all." He turned and exited Big Barb's before anybody could shout questions at him, questions he probably wouldn't have been able to answer anyway.

The lifting of the quarantine that had frozen all changes of duty station, retirements, and ends of active service for the Marines of Thirty-fourth FIST and Camp Major Pete Ellis was *the* topic of discussion and speculation among the Marines for the rest of the evening. Most of them were well past their normal rotation dates—Thorsfinni's World normally being a two-year-duty station—and many were past their nominal end-of-active-service or retirement dates. Were they going to be processed out of the Corps? Were the remaining Marines to be rotated en masse to duties on other worlds? Nobody had answers, but that didn't stop the speculation—or the plans some began making for what they were going to do in a few weeks when they returned to civilian life.

Corporal Claypoole even stopped thinking about Schultz's

claim that Jente got mad at him because she wanted to marry him.

On the morning of the fourth day of the five-day liberty, Corporal Claypoole again woke in an upstairs room at Big Barb's. He'd drunk heavily the night before, but not as heavily as the previous night and didn't really need the hangover pill Sergeant Kerr had left with him. But he took it anyway. And he didn't have to wonder who he'd spent the night with; she was still in bed with him. She woke while he was taking the pill, smiled at him, and held out her arms. He smiled back and went to her arms. And soon after, into other parts of her.

She wasn't Jente, but, well, Jente didn't want him anymore, so . . . If the one you love doesn't want you anymore, then accept the one who does want you. Even if it *is* mostly a commercial relationship for her.

She cleaned up and left afterward. He hadn't asked if she was the woman who'd spent the previous night with him. If she wasn't, he didn't want to know that.

Word of the lifting of the quarantine spread through the civilian community like wildfire. By the morning of the fourth day of Thirty-fourth FIST's liberty, it even reached tiny Brystholde, and Jente on her farm not more than a few minutes after that.

Since she'd driven Rachman Claypoole from her bed and her home, Jente Konegard had spent most of the time crying. Yes, she loved him, loved him with all her heart. And she wanted to marry him. Desperately, almost. He was the kindest, sweetest, most considerate and loving man she'd ever gotten anywhere near close to. And she was positive he loved her in return. But marriage—he made marriage so *difficult*! She understood that he couldn't get married, not to her or to anybody else, until he'd been promoted two more times. Or until he got out of the Marines, and he couldn't do that as long as the Marines on Thorsfinni's World were quarantined. But his response when she asked what would happen if the quarantine was lifted? Why, it sounded as if he didn't *care* what happened to them.

And now, the quarantine *had* been lifted. Of course, she told herself, it was only a rumor, but still . . . She had to know, she had to find out. If it was true, what was he going to do? She knew he'd been in the Marines long enough to get out if he wanted to. Would he get out and return to civilian life? And if he did, would he want to stay on Thorsfinni's World? Would he want to stay with her? Would he want to take her with him to, to—where was he from? She couldn't remember him ever talking about his home world. Would he want to take her to that home world with him, make her give up the farm that had been hers for her entire adult life? Would she give up the farm to go with him? Or if he chose to stay in the Marines, would he be transferred someplace else and would he want to take her with him?

So many questions, too many questions. And she needed answers.

She reprogrammed the farm machines to return to the barn on their own after they completed their day's work, and made sure the animals had sufficient food and water for a couple of days, then changed into her town clothes and got into her landcar.

She found him in that Big Barb's place, where he was just finishing a late lunch.

Since he was alone, with no one to watch his back, Corporal Claypoole sat where he could see both the entrance and the stairs. Not that he expected an attack, just that he liked to know if someone was coming toward him. So he saw Jente enter Big Barb's before her eyes adjusted to the light enough to see him. His heart jumped with joy at first sight of her, then he remembered how she had acted a couple of days earlier when she kicked him out of her bed, her house, and her life, and he wished he were wearing his chameleons so she couldn't see him. He did *not* want a repeat performance.

But he wasn't wearing chameleons. She quickly spotted him

and rushed to his table. He groaned, and pointlessly sank down in his chair.

Jente threw herself into the chair to Claypoole's left, grabbed his left hand in both of hers, and leaned close to kiss him. He turned his head just enough that her lips caught the corner of his mouth instead of full front.

I guess I deserved that, she told herself; out loud she said, "Oh, Rock, I'm so sorry I was so bad to you. I've missed you. Forgive me! Please say you forgive me!" She raised his hand and kissed it; he felt wetness on the back of his hand, and slowly turned to face her. Tears oozed from her eyes and dribbled down her cheeks. Her eyes were rimmed with red, and it was obvious she'd done a lot of crying recently. His heart went out to her.

Aphrodite's tits, she's been crying, and I've been fucking other women? How many women did I take to bed while she's been crying? He shuddered at the thought of his unfaithfulness, but then he remembered how she'd thrown him out, how she said she never wanted to see him again, how she said she'd call the police if he didn't leave, and he decided he wasn't to blame for getting drunk and taking solace in other women's arms.

With that thought, he said coldly, "Why should I forgive you?"

Jente hung her head, and her shoulders shook with the effort to not burst out bawling. Her voice was strained as she said, "Because I love you. Because I was angry, and I was wrong."

Shit, shit, triple shit! Claypoole swore. He couldn't stand to see a woman crying, especially not the woman he loved—no matter how badly she'd treated him. He freed his hand from her grasp and put his arm around her shoulders to draw her to himself. He caressed her head and patted her back with his right hand. He said comforting things; not words, just soft verbal noises. She sobbed into his shoulder, soaking his shirt.

After a few moments, she pushed lightly on his chest and sat up. She drew a cloth from a skirt pocket and dabbed at her eyes and cheeks. He held a disposable napkin to her nose. She nodded and took it from him to blow into.

"Thank you," she said meekly. She sat slumped, with her hands limp in her lap and asked, "Forgive me?"

Many thoughts shot through Claypoole's mind, but none stayed long enough to become coherent. He looked at her for a long moment, then solemnly nodded.

"Thank you," Jente said in a tiny voice. She then looked around. The common room of Big Barb's looked like a restaurant with a bar, not like the anteroom of a whorehouse, and the women waiting on tables and cleaning up looked like waitresses rather than prostitutes. But she knew women's bodies were for sale there, even if many of the women seemed to have relationships with the Marines of third platoon that went beyond that of a whore to a john, had relationships that looked much more like girlfriend-boyfriend. She felt an uncomfortable ambiguity in Big Barb's—particularly when she was trying to mend things with the man she wanted to marry.

"Can, can we go someplace else?" she asked. "Someplace where we can have more privacy?"

He gave her an odd look. "You mean you want to . . . ?"

She shook her head. "No, not that—I mean not right now. I mean someplace where we can talk, and maybe snuggle a bit. And not be interrupted by your Marine friends. Oh!" A hand flew to her mouth. "I didn't mean that like it sounded. It's not, I'm not objecting to your Marine friends, I just mean—"

He nodded. "I know what you mean. Let me settle my tab, then we can walk down by the beach or something." While he signaled for his bill, she excused herself to go to the powder room and fix her face.

Claypoole wondered why it was that women always said "fix my face" when what they meant was "have to pee," but when Jente came back he saw that she had indeed "fixed her face." Most of the redness that had rimmed her eyes was gone, and her cheeks and lips had a healthy blush. There was also a bounce to her step that hadn't been there before.

They were hand in hand when they walked out of Big Barb's.

*   *   *

Bronnoysund's beach wasn't much to speak of. The town was on a fjord, and the beach was more glacial gravel than it was sand. The walls of the fjord were high enough and close enough that the beach only had direct sunlight for a few hours each day—clouds allowing—which didn't encourage a great deal of sunbathing. And the water was cold, which tended to discourage swimming. As a result, the beach was seldom crowded, so not many people were there when Claypoole and Jente reached it. On top of that, it was winter, so the beach was even more deserted than at other times of the year. They didn't have to look very hard to find a place where a jumble of boulders created a small, sand-floored alcove where they could lounge safe from the wind and prying eyes.

They lay against the broad boulder at the back of the alcove. They talked, about the fjord, the cliffs opposite them, the few people on the beach so late in the day, about where they might have dinner and what they might eat. They talked of many things, but not about what had happened two days earlier. At first their only physical contact was where the narrowness of the alcove made them lie hip to hip. After a time Jente sagged onto Claypoole's side and laid her head on his shoulder, and he wrapped an arm around her shoulders, though neither could have said which of them made the first move. They watched the rippling of the water and the changing shadows on the far cliffs, then he turned his face down and she raised hers, and they gently kissed, once, twice, then faced forward once more. Some moments passed, and they kissed again, but more passionately. Again, with unspoken agreement, they looked at the water and the cliffs. After some more moments passed, they slid down off the backrest boulder and their bodies turned toward each other, and they embraced passionately.

Jente abruptly sat up, flipping her fingers through her mussed hair and adjusting her disheveled coat. "Let's find a room," she said hoarsely.

"I can get one right away at Big Barb's," Claypoole said, standing up to adjust his own clothes.

She shook her head. "Not there. Someplace where they don't know us."

Claypoole cut off a snort. Bronnoysund was small enough, and he'd been there long enough, that he didn't think there was any commercial establishment of any sort in the town that didn't know him. He helped her up and said, "Let's see what we can find."

Near the downstream end of the beach they found a small set of rental cabins that catered to tourists who came north for the fishing. The owner recognized Claypoole's face, but didn't remember his name. He didn't know Jente at all. He hid his smirk when he noticed their lack of luggage.

They tore off their clothes almost before they got the cabin door closed. The first time they let out all the frustration, sorrow, anger, and pain they'd felt since she had driven him away, and both ended with a few bruises to show for it. A short time later, they went at it again, but more slowly and gently and lovingly.

Later, when they were lying naked, side by side, he remembered what Schultz and Kerr had said about Jente wanting to marry him. He swallowed before he began talking.

"You asked when I'm going to get promoted to sergeant."

"Yes."

"You've asked me that before."

"Yes."

"And I remember that one time you asked when I will get promoted to staff sergeant."

"Yes."

"You know that Marines below the rank of staff sergeant can't get married, don't you?"

In a very small voice: "Yes."

Claypoole raised himself on an elbow so he could lean over and look into Jente's eyes. "Are you saying you want to marry me?" His voice broke halfway through the question.

In an even smaller voice: "Yes."

He fell back down. "Buddha's blue balls, who would have

guessed?" he whispered. He shook himself. "Damn, the Hammer was right."

"Who would have guessed?" Jente shrilled, suddenly sitting up and clutching the sheet to her chest. "*Who would have guessed? Do you mean to lie there and tell me that you never considered marriage when you seduced me? Did you think I was one of Big Barb's whores?*"

He popped up to sit. "*What?* No, no, no! I know you're not one of Big Barb's girls. You're one of the women Top Myer warned us about."

"Top Myer *warned* you about me?" Her voice dropped and became cold.

Claypoole grimaced and hit himself on the side of his head. "No—no, that's not what I meant!"

"Then what did you mean?" Jente demanded icily. "I know what you *said,* and you said you were *warned* about me. What does that mean if it doesn't mean you were *warned*?"

"Ple-please, Jente, please. Let me explain."

"I'm listening." If her tone was cold before, her voice now could shatter ice.

"Top Myer warned us that there were *good* girls coming to that party." He caught a steely glint in her eye. "*Women* who weren't like Big Barb's girls. And we should treat them like we'd want our own sisters to be treated. *That's* what the warning was about."

"So you'd want your sister to be seduced by a man who just wanted someone to fuck," in a dead flat voice.

"Jente!" Claypoole gaped; where did she get the idea that he only wanted someone to fuck? "It's not like that at all." He reached to take her hands, but she twitched them away from his grasp while keeping the sheet firmly covering her breasts.

Claypoole sat up, back against the headboard, drew in a deep breath, and huffed it out. "Jente, I can't get married until I make staff sergeant. Or until I get out of the Marines. Whichever comes first. So, no, I didn't think about doing something that I *can't* do."

Jente sniffed and looked away from him. "So when were you going to tell me the quarantine's been lifted? And what are you going to do about it?"

"I didn't know about it when I went to your farm the other day. We just got the word yesterday, and it's unofficial. I won't know what it will mean to me until we get the official word the day after tomorrow." He paused, then added, "And I might not even know then."

Jente glared at him. "I don't hear you saying anything about us." She hopped off the bed and dressed.

Claypoole didn't say anything; he didn't try to talk to her. This was too much like what had happened two days before. After Jente slammed the door behind herself, he stared at it for a long moment before saying, "I seduced you? The way I remember it, *you* came after *me*."

CHAPTER
NINE

In a virtually unheard-of fit of appreciation for the fighting men of the military, the Senate of the Confederation of Human Worlds approved a design for the War of Secession Campaign Medal even before the fighting was over and distributed the design to every military command and world from which units were deployed to fight the war on and around Ravenette, including the navy vessels that participated in the blockades of the various worlds of the Coalition.

That meant that Joen Berg, the president of the Stortinget, Thorsfinni's World's legislative body, knew what the medal looked like before anyone from Thirty-fourth FIST did. In appreciation for the Marines and what they meant to the economy of Thorsfinni's World, Berg pushed through a bill to strike a medal in the exact design of the official Confederation medal so the Marines could wear one until the official medals arrived from Earth. President Berg and Stor Edval, the mayor of Bronnoysund, presented the medals to Thirty-fourth FIST commander Brigadier Theodosius Sturgeon shortly after the Marines returned from battle—actually, in the middle of the five-day liberty. As it happened, Sturgeon was taking advantage of the liberty call himself, and the two dignitaries, after looking for him at Camp Ellis and Bronnoysund, finally tracked him down at Bjorn's, a night club in New Oslo, where he was just about to have dinner on the second of two nights he was allowing himself away from his command.

"Brigadier Sturgeon," Berg said with a stiff bow, "I am most pleased to see you again."

"Velcome back, Ted," Edval said, sticking his hand out to shake Sturgeon's. "How come you here in da fancy town, 'stead of in good ol' Bronnoysund?"

"Gentlemen," Sturgeon said, rising, returning Berg's bow, and shaking hands with Edval, "so good to see you. Please, sit." He signaled for a waiter to bring chairs for his unexpected guests. "Can I get you something to drink?"

"Gif me a Reindeer Ale if you got it," Edval told the waiter.

"A nice Thorvall red for the table," Berg said to the waiter. "This meal and drinks are courtesy of the Stortinget. I'll sign for it." He turned to Sturgeon. "We've gotten reports from Ravenette, Thirty-fourth FIST performed magnificently."

"Thank you, Mr. President, for your compliment—and for picking up the tab. But we're Marines; the way we see it, we merely did our job on Ravenette."

"Such modesty, dese Marines," Edval said, nudging Berg in the ribs with an elbow. "Dey got a reputation for beink high on demselves, but dey really very modest."

The waiter returned quickly with Edval's Reindeer Ale and the wine Berg had ordered for the table. When Berg had tasted and approved the wine, the waiter asked, "Would you gentlemen like to see menus?"

"You got a reindeer steak?" Edval asked. "Two-inch tick, medium rare. Bake potato, big von, lots a butter—*reindeer* butter, not dat inferior moo-cow stuff. And something green."

Berg maintained a diplomat's straight expression during Edval's order then said, "A pâté and cracker appetizer will be enough, thank you."

"Would you like me to hold your order and serve it with the others, sir?" the waiter asked Sturgeon. He said he would appreciate that very much.

The waiter bowed away and was back with their food sooner than expected.

They made small talk during the meal, but as soon as the

dishes were cleared away, Berg ordered "a bottle of your finest cognac." He couldn't hold back a grimace when Edval asked for a Reindeer Ale chaser.

Berg waited until they'd had a moment to savor the aroma and taste of the cognac before reaching into his pocket and withdrawing a presentation case of polished, imported, blond oak and handed it over. Edval bounced with joyful anticipation.

"Brigadier, I took the liberty of having enough of these struck for every man in your command."

"It's a beauty, dat's for sure! Open it, open it," Edval exclaimed.

"Thank you," Sturgeon said, turning the box over in his hands and feeling the polished grain of the wood. He turned it upright and lifted the hinged lid. "Buddha's blue balls! Is that an accurate facsimile?"

"It is indeed. I know how the Confederation is. It'll be months before the official campaign medal reaches you. I thought you and your Marines should have it sooner. I'm sure you can get away with using this as a placeholder until the official medals reach Camp Ellis."

Sturgeon looked at Berg. "Mr. President, I believe I will wear this one even after the official medals come. I'm very touched. It is an honor to receive this medal from you."

Berg beamed almost as brightly as Edval did.

As soon as the extended liberty was over, Brigadier Sturgeon had an officer's call. Every officer and senior noncommissioned officer in the FIST attended. There, Sturgeon gave final orders for the following day's awards and promotions ceremony and gave every company commander and higher enough of the campaign medals that President Berg had struck so that each of his men could receive one. He gave additional medals to the commanders of his major subordinate units to send to the families of the Marines who had died on Ravenette.

After that, each company commander and higher held a formation for his unit, at which the medals were distributed. "You *will* wear these on your dress reds at tomorrow's FIST formation," the commanders told their men—needlessly, since all the Marines were thrilled with the unofficial medals that had been struck by an appreciative local government.

There weren't many personal decorations given out; as Brigadier Sturgeon had told President Berg, the Marines had merely done their jobs on Ravenette. While collectively what they did might have been heroic, the ancient descriptor "Uncommon valor was a common virtue" held true. On the other hand, General Cazombi had decided to award Thirty-fourth FIST the army's Distinguished Unit Citation, the equivalent of every man in the FIST being awarded a Silver Nebula. Brigadier Sturgeon pinned that ribbon on the chests of one Marine from each of his major subordinate units as symbolic of the entire FIST receiving it. The ribbons for everybody else, along with the printed citations, would be distributed at company formations following the FIST formation.

The FIST had suffered casualties on Ravenette, and many of those casualties had necessitated the movement of Marines into positions of higher rank. Most of those Marines had been promoted on Ravenette or, at worst, aboard ship during the journey back to Thorsfinni's World. Still, there were a few additional promotions to be given out, meritorious promotions to Marines whose positions didn't require a specific rank but could be held by Marines of a range of ranks. Only the promotees' superiors had been informed in advance of the promotions, so they were a surprise to almost everyone. Those promotions were given out in order of rank, from lowest to highest, in the FIST formation after the symbolic pinning on of the campaign medal. Four enlisted men were called to the reviewing stand, one each promoted to corporal, sergeant, staff sergeant, and master sergeant. The final promotion was of significance to Company L, and of particular significance to third platoon.

"Ensign Charles H. Bass, front and center!" Colonel Ramadan called out.

Charlie Bass was startled to hear his name called but stepped forward and marched to the reviewing stand on which Ramadan and Brigadier Sturgeon stood along with the FIST staff officers and FIST Sergeant Major Parant. Rear Admiral Blankenboort, as the highest-ranking Confederation military officer on Thorsfinni's World, was also on the reviewing stand.

Bass climbed the stairs to the reviewing stand, stood in front of Sturgeon, saluted, and said in a firm voice, "Sir, Ensign Bass reporting as ordered!" In his peripheral vision, he saw Katie Katyana mount the reviewing stand from its side and take position next to Ramadan.

Sturgeon returned Bass's salute and said in an amplified voice that carried clearly, "Ensign Charles H. Bass, in recognition of your years of exemplary service as a platoon commander in Company L of the infantry battalion of Thirty-fourth Fleet Initial Strike Team, both as a senior noncommissioned officer and as an ensign, and by the authority granted me via an executive order from Confederation of Human Worlds President Cynthia Chang-Sturdevant, I hereby grant you a commission as a lieutenant in the Confederation Marine Corps." He turned to Ramadan and nodded.

Colonel Ramadan handed a small case containing the paired silver orbs of a lieutenant to Katie, who in turn stepped up to Brigadier Sturgeon and held the case out to him. Sturgeon exchanged a smile with her and took one of the paired orbs from the case. He waited while Katie took the other and dropped the case into her purse, then the two of them faced the obviously stunned Charlie Bass, removed his ensign's insignia, and replaced them with the lieutenant's.

"I told you I could do this, Charlie," Sturgeon said without amplification. His voice was low enough that it didn't even carry to everybody on the reviewing stand. Then sotto voce, "Kiss the man, Katie."

Katie placed her hands on Bass's shoulders and lifted her face to kiss his lips. "Congratulations, Charlie," she whispered. "We'll celebrate later."

"After the officers celebrate with him, my dear," Sturgeon whispered.

Katie stepped back, winked at Bass, and said to Sturgeon out of the corner of her mouth, "We'll see about that, Brigadier. And you better not get him drunk."

At a signal from Ramadan, Bass exchanged salutes with Sturgeon, about-faced, and marched back to his position at the head of third platoon. Katie returned to her place in the bleachers.

"I have one last announcement to make," Brigadier Sturgeon said when Bass had resumed his place in front of third platoon. "I imagine that by now all of you have heard the rumor that the quarantine that has kept Thirty-fourth FIST under wraps has been lifted. It's not a rumor, it's true, we're no longer quarantined. However—" He had to stop because of the spontaneous cheering that broke out.

"However," he said when the volume of the cheering dropped, "everyone in the FISTs that have come into contact with the Skinks has been involuntarily extended for the duration. That means no releases at the end of active service, and no retirements. Furthermore, we will remain together as a unit, as Thirty-fourth and Twenty-sixth FISTs have been declared to be the best counter-Skink units."

He paused to let that sink in, then continued: "Basically, all the lifting of the quarantine means is we are no longer under a Darkside penalty for talking about the Skinks with people who don't have the clearance to already know about them.

"That is all."

"FIST!" Colonel Ramadan commanded in an amplified voice, "Pass in review!"

The Marines on the parade ground came to attention as one, and company by company, led by the FIST headquarters company and the infantry battalion, began the march that would bring all of them past the reviewing stand.

At the end of the short parade, Company L marched back to the barracks, where Captain Conorado held a brief ceremony to distribute the ribbons and certificates for the army Distinguished Unit Citation. He then dismissed the company and sounded liberty call. Third platoon charged en masse to where Lieutenant Bass stood in line with the company's other officers behind the company commander. Everyone soundly congratulated him on his promotion.

"Sir, does this mean we're going to lose En—, I mean Lieutenant Bass?" several of them asked Conorado.

"As far as I know, Brigadier Sturgeon is going to leave him right where he is," Conorado said. Most of them thought Charlie Bass was the best platoon commander any Marine could have.

After a few minutes of celebration, First Sergeant Myer and Gunnery Sergeant Thatcher, the company's two most senior enlisted men, moved in to break it up and let the other officers take Bass away to a reception at FIST headquarters.

Thirty-fourth FIST quickly settled into a training routine. Some days were spent in the classroom, some in the virtual-reality training facility, more days in the field. Classroom and VR days always included substantial physical fitness and hand-to-hand combat sessions. And on the weekends, liberty. There was a full measure of grumbling about the involuntary extension for the duration, and the lack of normal rotations. The officers had their celebration of Charlie Bass's promotion before Charlie and Katie had theirs, but when they did, Charlie agreed that Katie's celebration was a whole lot more fun than the officers' had been. Jente continued to refuse to talk to Corporal Claypoole, cutting the connection every time he contacted her on his comm. He didn't bother going to her farm; he decided that would be an exercise in pointlessness, and he didn't feel like dealing with that level of frustration. Instead he drowned himself on liberty in drink and women. Lance Corporal Schultz spent every night he could get off base with Einna Orafem—and never talked about it afterward. Lance Corporals MacIlargie and Longfellow were released from the hospital and returned to duty with Company L. Lance Corporal Beycee Harvey, who had replaced Longfellow when he was evacuated on Ravenette, returned to Whiskey Company. MacIlargie was put on light duty as an assistant clerk in the company office. "So I can keep an eye on him and make sure he stays out of trouble," Top Myer said. That left Lance Corporal Ymenez in Claypoole's fire team, where he was feeling more and more comfortable with the Marines of third platoon.

And that's how it went for almost three weeks, until Brigadier Sturgeon had a company commanders' call, after which the company commanders returned to their units and held formations to pass the word.

Captain Conorado looked grim and didn't waste any time in getting to the point.

"Vacation's over," he began. "The Skinks are back, and Thirty-fourth FIST is joining a task force that's going after them." The company's other officers stood in a rank behind him. Even First Sergeant Myer and the company clerks, none of whom normally attended company formations, were there.

"Most of you will remember the CNSS *Grandar Bay;* she's the starship we went to Kingdom on. You've probably heard she was lost in Beam Space. Not so. The *Grandar Bay* has been in quarantine, the same as Thirty-fourth FIST. She's on her way to Thorsfinni's World; she's already in Space Three on final approach and will arrive in orbit in a few days. When she gets here, she'll reprovision; her crew will be given a couple of days of shore liberty. Then we will board and head for a world called Haulover.

"An element of Fourth Force Recon Company was dispatched to Haulover more than a month ago to investigate the hostile destructions of remote homesteads and the deaths and disappearances of the people on those homesteads. The Force Recon Marines had rather a surprise when they encountered the Skinks," he commented drily. He got a restrained chuckle from the members of the company who had faced the Skinks on previous occasions.

"FIST HQ is putting together a package detailing what Force Recon discovered about Skink strength and order of battle on Haulover, along with data about the world, and everything currently known or suspected about the aliens. As soon as it is ready—that should be in a couple of days—it will be presented to you.

"That is all." Conorado turned his head toward Gunnery Sergeant Thatcher. "Company Gunnery Sergeant, front and center."

Gunny Thatcher broke from his position at the head of the company and marched to the company commander. They exchanged salutes.

"Gunnery Sergeant, the company is yours."

"The company is mine. Aye aye, sir!"

Conorado about-faced and led the other officers back into the barracks.

Thatcher stood at attention facing the barracks until the officers and clerks were inside, then turned and faced the company. He looked as grim as the company commander had.

"You heard the man," he said in a growl that carried to everyone in the formation. "It's the Skinks again. Most of you know what that means. Start teaching the Marines who haven't faced the Skinks about them. Teach them everything you can so they stand a better chance to live through first contact than you did the first time you faced those Hades-damned beasts."

He looked the company over from one end to the other, seeming to look every Marine in the eye, then bellowed, "Platoon sergeants, dismiss your platoons!" He about-faced and marched into the barracks.

The Marines spent the next few days making sure all of their weapons and equipment were fully functional and combat-ready while preparing everything they weren't taking with them for storage in the company supply room. And they pulled as much liberty as they could manage—they knew they probably wouldn't have any opportunity for civilian dining, drink, or women until they returned to Thorsfinni's World. And some of them knew this was the last chance they would *ever* have. Some of them may have gotten somewhat carried away.

Einna Orafem called in sick one day. That same day, Lance Corporal Schultz called the Company L office to say he'd be back the next day, so Captain Conorado could go ahead and prepare an Article 15 for his return.

When Jente Konegard wouldn't accept his calls, Corporal Claypoole went to her farm. She wouldn't come to the door.

Lieutenant Charlie Bass obliquely approached the subject of marriage with Katie Katyana but couldn't quite bring himself to propose to her. She seemed amused and let him founder. They had a good time together anyway.

One morning, Frida and Gotta delivered Sergeant Kerr to the barracks. Kerr was so drunk he thought they were Valkyries delivering him to Valhalla. He kept protesting that he was still alive, no matter how much it might appear otherwise.

Lance Corporal MacIlargie tried to get Lance Corporal Ymenez drunk enough to miss reporting in, so he'd get an Article 15 for Unauthorized Absence and get some brig time, so MacIlargie could return to his position in third platoon. Ymenez could handle alcohol much better than MacIlargie had expected and nearly drank the other lance corporal under the table. Either that or Ymenez poured his Reindeer Ale into a nearby potted plant when MacIlargie wasn't looking.

Most of first squad got embroiled in a brawl with the crew of several fishing trawlers that happened to be in port. Several men on each side had to be treated for injuries, but nobody other than a couple of the fishermen was held in the hospital even overnight.

As it happened, nobody got married. Nobody even was hit with an Article 15. Nobody suffered any injuries that would keep them from performing their duties.

Finally the day arrived for Thirty-fourth FIST to board the *Grandar Bay*. Trucks and buses delivered the Marines to Boynton Field, Camp Ellis's landing field. The Marines dismounted and formed up in FIST formation, facing a long row of Essays. A thin group of people in civilian garb lined the edge of the field behind the formation. They were almost exclusively the families of the married officers and senior NCOs. Not all of the families were there; some found watching their men going off to war too painful to endure. Only a few of the civilians were friends of the Marines, or girlfriends of the unmarried men. They weren't actively discouraged from attending, but the Marines generally hinted that they shouldn't. The people on the sidelines watched as the FIST's Dragons trundled onto the field and lined up between the Marines and the Essays. More Dragons, these belonging to the *Grandar Bay,* rolled down the ramps of some Essays and joined the others.

The Marines had their Dragon assignments, so when the command was given to mount up, the units moved smoothly to the Dragons they would ride inside Essays to the *Grandar Bay* in orbit. That was when something never before seen by any member of Thirty-fourth FIST happened.

A woman burst from the sidelines, racing toward one group of Marines heading to the Dragon that they'd ride to orbit. Three different MPs attempted to intercept her. She dodged the first two, and when the third managed to grab her, she kneed him and he dropped to the ground, clutching his injured groin. She reached the group of twenty Marines she was headed for and crashed through their ranks until she reached the one she wanted.

"Rock!" she screamed as she leaped at Corporal Claypoole and wrapped her arms and legs around him, staggering him. She pelted his face with kisses, burbling, "I'm sorry, I'm so sorry for how I treated you!"

"J-Jente?" Claypoole gasped, struggling to maintain his balance and not drop his weapons, gear, or the woman riding him.

"I'm sorry, Rock, please forgive me, Rock!"

"Jente, I have to go now," he said, shifting his grip on his blaster and other gear to free a hand to stroke her.

Strong arms grabbed Jente, pried her off Claypoole, and handed her to the MPs who had finally caught up with her.

"Rock, come back to me. Please promise you'll come back to me!" she shrilled as the MPs hauled her away.

"I will, Jente, I promise," he called back to her. Then he faced front and continued his movement onto the Dragon. His face was almost scarlet and he tried to ignore the hoots and catcalls from other Marines.

Claypoole hoped the trip to Haulover would be quick; he knew he wouldn't hear the last of the incident until third platoon was so heavily engaged in combat that nobody had any energy left to razz him about the scene his girlfriend made at Boynton Field.

CHAPTER
TEN

"You are a bastard." The statement was delivered not as an insult or a challenge, but just a plain statement of fact. "Your father never married your mother, so that makes you a bastard. You can look it up in the dictionary."

Dean Kuetgens regarded Heine Kurtz closely and considered whether he should punch him for using that word. None of the other boys would've dared to use it on him; Dean was just too ferocious even for the older boys enrolled at the Brosigville Preparatory Academy, but Heine was a boy without fear.

Dean decided it wouldn't do any good to bash Heine. He knew perfectly well what the word meant. Every swearword, every obscenity in Spanish, German, and Standard English, the common languages spoken by the people of Wanderjahr, were known and used with great relish by the boys Dean played with; even the girls joined in. But every time Dean heard another boy use *that* word, he cringed. "They were too married," Dean replied at last. That had been his standard response before every fight.

"My dad says they weren't, that your dad screwed your mom in a tomato patch on your great-uncle's farm and then your dad went away with the Marines somewhere else and never came back, and then your great-grandma went to jail, where she died." Heine's father was one of the leading thule exporters on Wanderjahr, enormously rich and powerful although he supported Dean's mother, Hway Kuetgens, in her position as Chairman of the Wanderjahr Ruling Council.

Dean's mother had kept little of her past from her son, except for one very important detail. He did know that his great-grandmother, Lorelei Kuetgens, Oligarch of Morgenluft, had gone to prison for many crimes and died there. His mother, Hway, Lorelei's granddaughter, had become Oligarch of Morgenluft in her grandmother's stead and eventually been elected to the supreme political office on Wanderjahr, Chairman of the Ruling Council that sat in Brosigville, formerly the capital city of Arschland Staat, now the capital city of Wanderjahr. The tomato patch story he'd heard before but he didn't believe it.

"You'd better take that back about the tomato patch, Heine," Dean threatened. He knew with absolute certainty that with those words he'd crossed another Rubicon.

"I won't. My dad said it happened. You callin' my dad a liar?"

"I'm calling you a sonofabitch, Heine. Your dad fucked a dog and you popped out."

"You eat shit, Deany-beanie, and your mom got fucked in a tomato patch."

They went at it then. Heine was bigger than Dean but Dean was lean and quick with his fists. His first blow bloodied Heine's nose, then Heine grabbed Dean around the waist and threw him to the ground and they rolled in the dust. Neither boy said a word as they struggled.

Later, both boys stood before the headmaster's desk, heads bowed. Mr. Pablo Nguyen regarded the pair ominously. "Ever since you've been here, Mr. Kuetgens, you've had fights like this with other boys," he began. "Who started this one?"

"I-I struck the first blow, sir," Dean answered.

"Mr. Kurtz? Why'd he hit you, then?"

"Because—because I insulted his mother," Heine answered in a small voice.

Mr. Nguyen sighed. "Okay, boys, shake hands, make up. No more of this. The school nurse has pronounced you both physically fit to resume your short, brutal, academically undistinguished lives. I will be informing your parents of this incident, of course, and you'll both have to deal with that when you get home. That'll be nothing new for either of you, I'm very disappointed to say. Mr. Kurtz, you are dismissed." After Heine had departed, Mr. Nguyen silently regarded Dean for what seemed a very long time. "You've had a hard time of it, haven't you?" he said at last.

Dean began to cry.

Mr. Nguyen came around the desk, steered Dean into a chair, and then sat down beside him. "We say that a boy without a father is like a house without a roof," he said in a quiet voice. "But you *do* have a father, except he's very far away. Your mother's made no bones about it, Dean, but she's got a big job to do and she hasn't had the time to spend with you that most of our boys get from their parents, even those who have both of them living under the same roof. Are you mad at Heine?"

"No, sir," Dean sniffled. "He's really a good guy. He's honest."

"Well, so are you. That's something. And you're a good student. You know that since you've been with us you have received no privileges, no special treatment because of who your mother is. The students here are from the most important and influential families in our world, but we treat you all like what you are: boys and girls who every now and then need small adjustments applied to their backsides. Your father might call that an 'ass kicking.' " He smiled, remembering his own time in an army barracks when he was young. "Nevertheless, because of your special, um, status, I've recommended numerous times that your mother consider getting you a tutor, but she's refused. Do you know why?"

"N-no, sir."

"Because she doesn't want you to grow up alone, without boys—and girls—of your own age around. She's probably right, but it has been hard on you." He put an arm around Dean's shoulders. "Well, you whacked Heine a good one." He leaned around and looked closely at Dean. "And he bloused your eye, didn't he? You'll have some explaining to do when you get home."

"It won't be the first time, sir." Dean smiled.

Mr. Nguyen nodded. "I remember the Marines, how they came here to help us and how they changed things here. You know the form of government we have today would never have existed if it hadn't been for the intervention by the Confederation. I didn't know your father, Dean, but I bet there's quite a bit of him in you. All right." He got up. "Dry up, lad, and sally forth into the halls of learning, and sin no more—but remember, every time you get into a fight with someone the way you did today, it hurts your mother more than it does you." He laid a hand on Dean's shoulder. "Life is a struggle, Mr. Kuetgens, and fighting is inevitable. What we try to teach you here is, pick the right fight with the right enemy at the right time. And, of course, win."

Hway Kuetgens shook her head. "I talked to Heine Kurtz's father. Heine wouldn't say why you were fighting. I suppose it wouldn't do me any good to ask you why?"

Dean hung his head in silence. He would *never* repeat what Heine had said.

"I would like some kind of response, young man."

Dean mumbled something. Hway put a hand to her ear. "Speak up. I can't hear you."

"It was nothing, Mother."

"*Nothing?* You bloodied his nose and he blackened your eye just for *fun*? Son, I know why you were fighting. It was about your father and me. It always is. I may have been elected chief executive of Wanderjahr, son, but I'm not stupid. Well." She shook her head and smiled. "Thanks for defending my honor." She extended her hand and when he took it, she embraced him warmly. "I have news for you, Dean," she whispered into his hair. "Aunt Sonia's coming back."

"Aunt" Sonia, Sonia Motlaw, Hway Kuetgens's confidential assistant, was far more to her than just another staff member. Dean in fact had an eight-year-old's crush on Sonia, who, in addition to her official duties, was also his music teacher. He hated his piano lessons, but they were bearable because they brought him close to Ms. Motlaw, who was one of the very few persons he could really talk to, and who took him seriously when he did.

"And do you know what?" Hway continued. *"She has seen your father."*

At first Dean thought he had not heard his mother clearly. "Seen father?" he repeated. And then the words struck him like a thunderbolt. "Seen my father? *She has seen my father?*" he shouted.

"Yes. I have something to tell you."

"Mother, did he send me another letter?" Ever since Dean had been old enough to ask about his father, Hway had read him the letters he had written telling of his adventures and the exotic worlds he'd traveled to, the people he had met there, his fellow Marines, how much he loved his family and longed to be with them but couldn't because his mission as a Marine always had to come first, and ending always with the promise that one day soon he would return to Wanderjahr and be with them again. The letters had been written on flimsiplast with a composing machine, his mother explained, so Dean could read them better. The boy treasured them above all things and kept them neatly arranged in little stacks in chronological order. He read them over and over again with the greatest pleasure and as soon as he was old enough to write, he spent hours composing answers, which his mother dutifully posted for him. His greatest joy was receiving his father's responses, which always started off, "Dearest son, what a pleasure to receive your letter of—"

That night, after he had cried himself out and spent his rage breaking his things, Dean Kuetgens burned his father's letters, every last one of them. His mother had at last told him the truth, that until Ms. Motlaw visited him on Thorsfinni's World, his father did not even know his son existed. *She had written all those letters.*

Hway sat with Sonia Motlaw in her private office in the council chambers. "How's Ed?" Hway asked, meaning Eduardo Morelles, her ambassador to Thorsfinni's World.

"Healing up and as fierce as ever," Sonia laughed. "Christian sends his regards."

"Ah, Christian Mirelles, a gentleman of the old school." Hway smiled. "They don't make them like him anymore." She leaned forward across her desk. "Sonia, I told Dean about his father last night." She shrugged.

The news sent a small alarm, a breath of apprehension through Sonia Motlaw. "Oh. How'd he take it?"

"Not well. But you know how he feels about you, Sonia. You're more than just 'Auntie' to him. I think he'll be pleased to see you and he'll listen to you."

That meant he hadn't listened to his mother. Sonia knew how difficult Dean could be. "He's very mature for his age," she offered, hoping the words meant something.

"Let's go in and see him. He's waiting in the next room."

Hway and Sonia, smiling warmly, walked into the private sitting room just off Hway's office. Sonia, delighted to see the child, smiled broadly and held out her arms to him. "This is from your father," she said happily, offering him Joe Dean's letter.

"Goddamned fucking lying bitches!" Dean screamed. He snatched the letter from an astonished Sonia and tore at it ferociously, but it was of duraplast and so could neither be ripped nor burned. He threw it to the floor and rushed at Sonia Motlaw. He was screaming inarticulately and began beating and kicking her with his little fists and feet. Aghast, Sonia staggered backward. Hway had warned her, but this—*this* was totally unexpected. She had never seen the boy, *any* child, in such a rage. It was so unexpected because it was so unlike the boy she had come to love as much as if he'd been her own.

"Dean!" Hway screamed, but he was beyond listening, beyond control. The two women restrained him as best they could. A male aide rushed into the room and his face turned white when he saw the child on the floor. "Get Doctor Montez!" Hway ordered. "Quickly! Tell him my son has suffered a seizure!" The man rushed off while Hway and Sonia struggled to keep Dean from hurting himself. After a few moments he lay on the floor exhausted, panting, his rage spent, his eyes tightly closed.

"I've handled this badly," Hway whispered. "Badly, badly. I-I'm sorry, Sonia."

Dr. Felipe Montez, a short, spry old man, arrived shortly. He had treated the Kuetgens family members for so many years he was virtually one of them; he had delivered Dean *and* his mother and in her last illness he had attended Hway's grandmother in prison. "What? What? What do we have here?" he asked. He knelt beside Dean.

"He's had a seizure—"

"This is the healthiest boy I've ever seen. What's going on here?" He examined Dean carefully as the women stood by nervously. The aide stuck his head through the door but Hway waved him away. "Seizure my ass!" Dr. Montez announced. "The boy's had a temper tantrum." He shook a bony forefinger under Hway's nose. "What the hell brought this on?" He glared in turn at both women. Neither would answer.

"Will he be all right?" Sonia asked.

Dr. Montez shook his head in disgust, picked Dean up, and laid him gently on a nearby sofa. He turned and faced Hway. "You told him, didn't you? Sonia, what's your involvement in any of this?" Sonia briefly told him of her visit to Thorsfinni's World. "Good girl. At least *you* have some sense, and you were following orders, no matter how stupid, but *you,* young lady," he turned on Hway. "God*damn,* what scares me is we put the fate of our government into the hands of people like you! How can you manage Wanderjahr when you screw up with your only child like this? I *told* you that you'd have to be very careful about telling him." He shook his head in frustration. "The boy's vitals are normal. He hasn't ruptured or broken anything. Only time will tell what's happened inside his head, or *here.*" He tapped the left side of his chest.

Dr. Montez was one of those rare individuals who could, or thought he could, chew God out if he had to and get away with it. "All right, all right." He shook his head in perpetual wonder over the abysmal ignorance of the human species. "Matter at hand, matter at hand. What to do with this child? Here." He punched out a prescription on his writer. "Give him this tonight and call me in the goddamned morning." With that he gathered up his things, kissed each woman lightly on the cheek, muttered into Sonia's ear, "Ah, if only I were sixty years younger," and stalked out.

Hway looked at the prescription and smiled at Sonia. It read, "Tender loving care, Montez."

Hway Kuetgens had been raised to always hide her emotions. After her parents' death, her grandmother and guardian, Lorelei, Oligarch of Morgenluft Staat, had groomed Hway to be her successor as the ruler of the state. A calculating, scheming realist, Lorelei tried to instill her values in her granddaughter and had almost succeeded, until Joseph F. Dean came along with Thirty-fourth FIST and awakened something in the young woman. In the intervening years, after the Marines departed Wanderjahr, Hway had worked very hard to exercise coolheaded logic in all things and, since she had never experienced much affection growing up, it was not difficult for her to put Dean out of her mind, at least during the daytime. But while she loved her son, a constant reminder of their brief affair, more than anything in the world, it was difficult for her to express unfiltered, spontaneous affection toward anyone. Her son, in turn, could express rage but not the love he felt for his mother or the longing for his father. But now, after her son's reaction to Sonia's message from Corporal Joseph Dean, Hway realized it was time to break down the emotional barriers.

Dean Kuetgens was a precocious child in the sense that he could understand some things far beyond his years. He realized after he'd recovered his composure that the way he had reacted to Sonia Motlaw's message had been wrong. He loved Sonia as much as his mother and was profoundly disgusted with himself for having attacked her and for what he had said in anger to her and his mother. So, as he lay in bed the night of his rage, he realized he would have to make up for that somehow. As it turned out, he didn't have to, because his mother did it for him.

"Are you awake?" Hway asked as she came into her son's darkened room. Dean did not answer but lay stiffly in his bed, pretending to be asleep. He knew it was his chance, the opening he needed to jump up and embrace his mother and make up for what he had done, but he couldn't. He felt the mattress adjust to his mother's weight as she sat at one end of the bed. "It was all my fault, son," she began. "I should have told you about your father, but I couldn't. How do you explain to a child that his father does not even know him? What else could I do? I suppose I should have continued the lie until you were old enough to understand." She rested a hand gently on Dean's leg. "But I just could not do it." She began to weep. "I miss your father as much as you do," she confessed. Dean sat up suddenly and they embraced as if it were the first time either had ever done that with someone they loved.

Later, Dean said, "Please tell Auntie Sonia I'm sorry."

"She knows that already. But in a few minutes you can tell her yourself. Son, I have brought your father's letter. It's a real one this time." Hway smiled through her tears. "And I thought you might like to read it now." She flicked on a reading lamp in the headboard and handed Dean the duraplast sheet. "Read it. I'm going to get Aunt Sonia. When I come back we'll talk about many things and Aunt Sonia will tell you about your father."

"But it's late, Mother. I have school in the morning." Dean realized immediately that was the most ridiculous statement he'd ever made.

"No, you don't—and I am taking today off. Now read. I'll go fetch Aunt Sonia and then we'll make some plans. I promise you, son, great changes are about to happen around here."

At first Dean had to blink his eyes many times to clear his vision but then he read. The letter began, *"My dear son. I am writing this letter in a car in the snow on a world far, far away from where you live. An angel has just told me all about you. She's almost as beautiful as your mother."* When he wrote these words Joe Dean had glanced at Sonia Motlaw sitting there beside him and smiled, and that's when his fingers slipped on the keyboard.

But the boy knew his father must be referring to Auntie Sonia, not Euclid, because she *was* beautiful. The letter went on, the boy savoring every word. *"I can't come to see you now,"* Dean concluded, *"because I am needed here, but when this mission is over, I will come to Wanderjahr and the whole world will know I am your father and we are a family and we shall never be separated again. Joseph F. Dean, Corporal, CMC."*

Dean Kuetgens, the son of Joseph F. Dean, did not know what exactly a "corporal" was but he knew now, with absolute clarity, that when he grew up that is just what he was going to be.

CHAPTER
ELEVEN

"This heat! This terrible *heat*," Livy groaned, "is causing me to melt away. Is there no way, Auntie, we can convince this, this, *dreadful* general to put us up somewhere else on this godforsaken world? And the *food*! My God, Auntie, it's inedible! I shall lose forty precious kilos on this trip!"

"Auntie," or Senator Anteus Baibu Query, leader of the Confederation Senate Armed Services Committee fact-finding mission to Arsenault, smiled and applied a damp cloth to Senator Olivia ("Livy") Kancho Smedley-Kuso's lower left leg. They both sat naked on the bed in the quarters assigned to Senator Query upon his arrival at Task Force Aguinaldo's headquarters. Both did suffer in the heat since they carried more weight than was good in such a tropical environment, but General Anders Aguinaldo had made it clear to every member of the delegation that they would have to live as his troops did—and he himself did—while on their visit. "We are training for the invasion of the enemy's home world," he had explained, "so it's necessary to acclimate ourselves to what we believe is a very wet, warm environment."

"But the *food,* General, it's awful!" Senator Query complained. They had just tried to eat lunch in Aguinaldo's mess.

"Well, sir," Aguinaldo replied, "I want my staff to be lean and hard when they get to Haulover, so there are no luxuries in my mess. Just enough to keep body and soul together. The troops, they're different; they work off the calories. But I want you to see that it's no luxury to be a member of my staff in this task force. I want you to go back to Earth, Senator, and let everyone know that we are not living high out here, and I want our citizens to support us, as I know you do yourself, sir." He smiled warmly at the delegates, but behind that smile he was thinking, *You've come here to screw with me so the sooner you're gone the better for everyone.*

Livy sighed. "The old jarhead wants us gone, Auntie. Why not override him, have him put us up at that *wonderful* resort, you know, Jefferson and I stayed there some years ago. We could commute."

"Oceanside, Livy. It was ruined in an earthquake or something, remember? They haven't reopened it yet. More's the pity." He rubbed the cloth down Livy's sweaty leg and gently massaged her toes. "We'll be gone soon enough, my delicious little mountaintop. Just wait until Grimmer gets his glommers on Aguinaldo's short parts," he said with a chuckle. Grimmer had the reputation of doing hatchet jobs on generals and admirals, something he enjoyed since he'd been passed over for promotion in the Holloway Armed Forces and retired an embittered man. "And how *is* Jefferson?" Query asked with a grin.

"Oh, Auntie, why bring *him* up at this divine moment?" Livy drawled. She shrugged her massive shoulders, not at all pleased at the mention of her husband's name. "He's at home, doing what husbands do: porking the servants." She laughed lightly to cover her hatred of the man and her anger at Query for reminding her of him. "Or whatever," she concluded airily.

"Um, yeeesss, my delightful little snow cone," Auntie sighed. He wet the cloth and applied it to Livy's ample breasts. She groaned.

"Why have you never married?" Livy asked suddenly, propping herself up on one elbow. Her turn in the repartee.

"Well, my dear," Senator Anteus Baibu Query of Holloway's World answered, jiggling Livy's left breast playfully, "why ruin all my perfect relationships with marriage?" He leaned forward and brushed his lips gently over an enormous nipple. "And besides, you are now my mound of adipose, Livy, which I have hardly begun to consume."

"Well, be careful, Anteus," Senator Olivia Kancho Smedley-Kuso, of Wilkins's World, said in her most sharply senatorial voice, "that this 'mound of adipose' doesn't consume *you*."

"Promises, promises," Query sighed.

Major General Pradesh Cumberland, Task Force Aguinaldo Chief of Staff, set aside his spoon in disgust. "I don't know, Anders, this field ration gelatin is just too . . . too"—he shrugged— "*glutinous* for my taste."

General Anders Aguinaldo laughed. "You only have to eat it so long as those politicians are breathing down our necks." He shoveled a spoonful of the mass into his mouth. "Goddam, Praddy, reminds me of those lunches old Admiral Porter used to feed us in his mess back at the Heptagon." He laughed harder. "Something called 'macaroni' and, oh, yes, 'Jell-O.' Now that Jell-O stuff had the consistency of this but it tasted better."

"Christ on a rubber crutch, Anders, don't you think maybe you and I, in the dark of night, could rustle up something more, more, *edible* than this crap? I remember these rations from when I was a second lieutenant! I thought they were bad then! Now? Ugh! Do you think they'll catch on?"

"You mean that this stuff is twenty years out of date? Oh, yeah. And they know I want them gone. They may be venal, egotistical, self-serving swine, Praddy, but they're not stupid." Somehow Aguinaldo had found in storage somewhere on Arsenault a cache of field rations that hadn't been issued to anyone in nearly two decades. As soon as he learned he was to be the host for the Senate Armed Services Committee fact-finding delegation, he ordered the rations served exclusively in his private mess, where the delegation would eat most of their meals. The troops ate modern, Class A rations while in garrison and much more tasty field rations when on maneuvers. Aguinaldo saw no reason why *they* should suffer because of the senators' visit.

"This Colonel Grimmer." Cumberland shook his head. "I almost strangled him twice this morning. These rations would be ideal for that bastard." He was referring to Lieutenant Colonel, Retired, Sneedly Grimmer, Senator Query's senior military aide. Whiplash thin, Grimmer always wore a sour expression on a face accentuated by a sharp nose, and a mouth perpetually turned down at the corners as if he detected a foul odor in the air no one else was aware of.

"He's one of those aides who wears the senator's mantle like we wear our stars and novas, Praddy. Life's full of them. I checked his service record. He was a finance officer in the Holloway army. Never rose above the rank of light colonel." Aguinaldo shrugged. "Now he's got a blank check to wipe his feet on us. But he's dangerous because he does know something about the military, enough to cause trouble. Keep your eye on him at the briefing tomorrow." Aguinaldo had set up a commanders' briefing for the next morning where the senators would be given a full orientation on what TF Aguinaldo had accomplished and what the plan was for engaging the Skinks on Haulover. Then they would be taken around to visit the various troop units, talk to the personnel there, ask questions, dig into everything. And then, hopefully, go home.

"I wish Oceanside were up and running again," Cumberland said. "Then we could plant them there and they'd be out of our hair. Let them luxuriate on the beaches instead of bothering us."

"Yeah, if luck were with us, Praddy, maybe a tsunami would come in again and wash them all out to sea. Damn, did I actually say that?" Aguinaldo laughed.

"I guess we're fortunate old Haggel Kutmoi isn't out on this junket," Cumberland said. He reached into a cargo pocket and took out two cigars, which he clipped expertly. Aguinaldo took one and they lit up.

The mess personnel had been dismissed, since the two officers were dining alone that night, so Aguinaldo got up from the table and opened a cabinet. He took out a full bottle of Old Snort. "You know Colonel Raggers, Seventh MPs? He brought me this bottle of bourbon, best damned stuff I've ever tasted. They distill it back on Ravenette. They're famous for it. Since it's only you and me, Praddy, let's crack it over these cigars. We can afford to live dangerously for one night."

They sipped and smoked for a while. "Yeah, Kutmoi. You're right, we're lucky that sleazeball isn't along. Just ask Alistair Cazombi about that sack of shit. We're lucky he's running for president. But Praddy, if he wins . . ."

"I know." Cumberland blew a smoke ring. "Even money is saying he does."

"More than even, I hear." Aguinaldo leaned back and blew smoke toward the ceiling. "If the Old Girl loses the election we lose this war against the Skinks, this campaign, anyway. And then things will go disastrously wrong for humanity, until, in its own good time, mankind finally catches on, as it always does. So in the long run this senatorial junket is a fart in a whirlwind. Goddamned politicians," he said with feeling.

"But will they, Anders?"

"What?"

"Humanity. Catch on."

Aguinaldo finished his drink, poured some into Cumberland's glass, and refilled his own. He toasted Cumberland and sipped. "That, my friend, is the question."

The briefing for the senators, although conducted in the most professional military style, was a disaster—for the senators, that is. That was mainly because the auditorium where it was conducted was a hotbox. All the windows were open to admit even the slightest breeze. Flying insectlike creatures sizzled loudly in the protective screens over the windows, often distracting the senators and their staffers as they tried to concentrate on what the briefers were telling them.

Things were not made any easier for the senators by the briefers themselves, who had been told to concentrate on the most complicated aspects of their training and logistical preparations for combat on Haulover. Worst in this regard was the G4's presentation, which displayed an endless parade of charts and graphs, rows of figures on ammunition rates, short and long tons of supplies, replacement parts, all the sinews of war, vital statistics for commanders to know, but deadly boring stuff for the legislators slowly dehydrating in their seats.

The visitors and their retinue wilted visibly in the heat and humidity, that is, all but Sneedly Grimmer, who sat primly attentive throughout, whispering comments into Senator Query's ear. The senator was then expected to stand up and question the briefing officers, but after an hour he just sat there, virtually comatose in the heat, unable to respond. Smedley-Kuso couldn't help dozing. She had charged one of her young female aides to poke her in the ribs if she began nodding off. The military personnel in the huge auditorium found it difficult to suppress snickers as they watched the large woman's head bobbling on her fleshy shoulders, trying to look as if she were paying attention to what was being said.

But the military people, acclimated to Arsenault's tropical climate, were fresh, full of energy, confident, professional.

The very first briefer, a Colonel Hiram Brisque, a former instructor at the Confederation General Staff College on Arsenault, was anything but brisk. He was the chief planner in the Operations Section of Task Force Aguinaldo headquarters, and he'd been personally selected by General Aguinaldo to conduct the overview portion of the briefing. That was not just because he was a brilliant strategist but mainly because he was well-known for his droning lectures, which tended to put his students to sleep. He stood there, twenty kilos lighter than before he'd been assigned to the task force, his uniform hanging limply about his frame, waving his pointer at the vid charts like a saber. Regardless of how his words were received by his slowly slumping audience, Colonel Brisque was enjoying himself enormously.

"Ladies and gentlemen, the doctrine upon which Task Force Aguinaldo is basing its Haulover campaign derives from the classic treatise written by the Prussian general Carl Maria von

Clausewitz, who lived from 1780 to 1831. It is called *Vom Kriege,* or *On War.*

"The basic Clausewitzian principle we used in drawing up our war plan was that of *economy of force,* the principle of employing all available combat power in the most effective way possible, in an attempt to allocate a minimum of essential combat force to any secondary or ancillary efforts. Economy of force, then, is the judicious employment and distribution of forces toward the primary objective of the conflict. No part of a force should ever be left without purpose. The allocation of available combat power to such tasks as limited attacks, defense, delays, deception, or even retrograde operations is measured in order to achieve mass at decisive points elsewhere on the battlefield. In von Clausewitz's own words, 'Every unnecessary expenditure of time, every unnecessary detour, is a waste of power, and therefore contrary to the principles of strategy.'

"I trust you will find the following charts and graphs of particular interest and I direct your attention to this one, which demonstrates the ratio of available maneuver elements plus aggregate firepower of those elements that can be brought against the estimated enemy forces in the area of operations in the terrain to be expected on Haulover. Now, you will see that comparing this chart with the next one . . ."

The briefing went steadily downhill after that point. Much later that day, when he'd managed to pull General Aguinaldo aside for a moment, Senator Query asked, "General, for my constituents who don't understand military jargon, just what is your objective in this campaign? In plain Standard English?"

"Senator," Aguinaldo replied, "in 'plain Standard English' it is to find 'em, fix 'em, and fuck 'em."

"Um, General, ah, maybe that's a bit *too* plain?" Still, Query couldn't suppress a slight grin.

"Okay, Senator, we're going to squash the Skinks into a little spot on the floor and then wash them down the drain. You can announce that on the six o'clock news and everyone'll know *exactly* what we're going to do when we get all our forces deployed against these Skinks."

"But General, has anyone tried to contact these aliens, find out what they want, what motivates them? Negotiate with them? Could we perhaps coexist? I mean, from their first appearance in Human Space, their presence was kept secret from everyone, and all we've ever done is fight them. Chang-Sturdevant never got the backing of either the Congress or the voters to go to war with these creatures. She built no consensus on this matter. No alternatives to war with them have ever been tried, have they?"

Aguinaldo regarded Senator Query silently for a moment. "Senator, I was not consulted on the policy of keeping the existence of the Skinks a secret from you or the citizens of this Confederation. But I think the President got her 'consensus' when she announced the threat, laid everything out in public in her speech. I am convinced, sir, and so shall you be when you talk to men who've seen the Skinks up close and personal, that killing is their way of negotiating and that no, we cannot coexist with them."

Sneedly Grimmer perked up when Colonel Rene Raggel of the Seventh Military Police Battalion gave his presentation. Now here was something any politician could understand: military-civil relations. But by that time Senator Query was so far gone in REM sleep that Grimmer decided he'd reserve his comments for later, when his boss had had a chance to cool off and could pay attention. He made a note to talk to Raggel when they visited the units, which was scheduled for the afternoon. Meanwhile, as one briefer after the other droned on and on, Grimmer looked up Raggel's biography on his reader. All the visitors had been given these bios on the task force commanders as a courtesy and now Grimmer discovered how useful they could be. *"Traitor!"* he whispered into Query's ear. "The man's a traitor."

The three members of the Seventh MP Battalion about to receive their awards stood at attention before the senators and their retinue. Colonel Raggel had drawn up the entire battalion for the ceremony. Raggel turned to General Aguinaldo. "Sir, I'd like to request that Senator Smedley-Kuso come with me and do the honors. The men would appreciate it very much if a Confederation senator pinned on their decorations."

"Sure, Colonel, they're your men. Senator, it's a great honor to be asked to assist in the awards ceremony. Are you up to it?"

"Oh, General!" Olivia Smedley-Kuso perked up at these words, the fatigue of the long day disappearing instantly. One thing that revived her spirits more even than having her toes massaged was a photo opportunity. "Did they win them fighting anyone?"

"No, Senator," Colonel Raggel answered. "These are commendations for meritorious achievement, for the superb work they've done in getting the battalion ready for deployment to the theater of war. But they're important recognition of jobs well done and they'll mean a lot to these men."

"Well, yes," she cooed. "I'm honored!"

Sergeant Major Steiner called the battalion to attention. The battalion adjutant handed the medal boxes and award certificates to Colonel Raggel and then announced, "Attention to orders!" As the pair stood before each man the adjutant read the award certificate and Colonel Raggel handed Senator Smedley-Kuso the medal, which she awkwardly pinned on the flap of the man's tunic pocket. The first one was rather difficult for her, with her large, sweaty fingers, but by the second man she was getting the hang of it. Senator Smedley-Kuso, pinning medals on heroes! That was really going to look good to the voters back on Wilkins's World!

The third man turned into a disaster. Really enthusiastic now, Smedley-Kuso thrust the pin on the back of the medal so hard into the man's pocket flap that it went all the way through and stabbed him in the chest.

"Goddammit!" he shouted.

"Colonel! Did you hear what that man just *said*?" Senator Olivia Kancho Smedley-Kuso exclaimed, horrified.

"Oh, well, fuck'im if he doesn't want the goddamned thing,"

Raggel responded. He'd waited all his life for a moment like this.

"So, Colonel, I see by your bio that you were an aide to General Davis Lyons during the late unpleasantness on Ravenette," Sneedly Grimmer was saying. They'd just finished the disastrous awards ceremony and were sitting in the battalion mess for refreshments before leaving. They were drinking real, brewed coffee and eating cakes made from real flour and sugar, not the artificial stuff they'd been fed in Aguinaldo's mess. At the sight and smell of *real* food, Senator Olivia Kancho Smedley-Kuso had recovered her composure and was chatting gaily with General Aguinaldo at a nearby table, her recent embarrassment evidently forgotten, for the moment anyway.

"Uh, what was that, Colonel?" Raggel had been thinking about the awards ceremony. He was not at all worried that his offhand remark would be held against him, but he was really ashamed of himself for having embarrassed the soldier involved, even though the man, along with everyone within hearing, had burst out laughing.

"I said, I see where you were an aide to the traitor, General Davis Lyons."

"What?"

"You heard me." Grimmer's voice had taken on a hard edge now.

"General Lyons did his duty, as any soldier would. He was against the secession vote. And I might remind you, Grimmer, that General Cazombi, who is now the Chairman of the Combined Chiefs, recognized that fact when he signed the surrender agreement with General Lyons."

"Well, that was a very liberal set of terms. There are those who disagreed—"

"Excuse me for interrupting, Mr. Grimmer." Raggel held up a hand. "But the Congress upheld them and they were fair and honorable terms. Both General Lyons and I as well as every other man in our army swore loyalty oaths to the Confederation. And also let me remind you, sir, that we would never have gone to war against the Confederation if President Chang-Sturdevant's government had been more honest with us about the Skink threat. And she has very bravely and very publicly acknowledged that fact. So I don't want to hear any more of this shit from you or anyone else about Lyons being a 'traitor.'" Raggel's voice had risen, causing heads to turn in his direction. *I'm really putting my foot into it today,* he thought ruefully.

"Well, it just is, I find it intriguing how a man like you can just switch your loyalty so smoothly, fighting us one day, fighting *for* us the next," Grimmer said with a smirk.

Raggel said nothing for a long moment, then answered, "I am a soldier, Mr. Grimmer, as it is rumored you yourself once were. My loyalty is to my commander but, just to reassure you, after we were defeated on Ravenette and surrendered, I signed a loyalty oath to the Constitution of the Confederation of Human Worlds, which I am now prepared to defend with my life if necessary."

"A piece of paper, Colonel." Sneedly Grimmer sneered again.

Colonel Raggel's fist mashed Grimmer's nose in a full centimeter. Two days later the delegation left. Two days after that the XVIII Corps received its deployment orders. Someone convinced Sneedly Grimmer not to press charges.

CHAPTER
TWELVE

As soon as the *Grandar Bay* joined the still-assembling gator fleet in orbit around Haulover, Lieutenant General Patrice Carano, commander of the XVIII Corps, summoned Ensign Jak Daly of Fourth Force Reconnaissance Company. Daly was the commander of the two-squad Force Recon detachment that discovered the Skinks on Haulover. With Daly summoned, Carano contacted Brigadier Theodosius Sturgeon on the *Grandar Bay* and asked the brigadier to join him on the Crowe-class amphibious battle cruiser CNSS *Chapultepec*—and to bring the commander of Thirty-fourth FIST's reconnaissance squad.

Carano first met privately with Sturgeon. The tone was cool, but cordial. The army general didn't have anything against Marines, it was simply that Thirty-fourth FIST had been added to his corps *after* he left Arsenault and he knew neither the unit nor its commander. But considering that Thirty-fourth FIST had more contact with the Skinks than the rest of the Confederation military combined, he was glad to have those Marines with him.

After establishing Thirty-fourth FIST's position in the order of battle and Sturgeon's place in the chain of command—a component element of the corps and reporting directly to the corps CG respectively—Carano called Ensign Daly and Staff Sergeant Wu into his office. Daly's Force Recon detachment of eight Marines had suffered one dead and two too severely injured for fleet sick bays to deal with, so the badly wounded were still in stasis bags until they could reach a navy hospital. That left Daly with five Marines in his command, and three of them had been wounded in the actions with the Skinks. Carano had high regard for Force Recon, but he didn't think five, plus their commander, was enough to provide the eyes-on-the-ground he needed. That was why he wanted Sturgeon to bring the commander of his FIST recon squad; he intended to join the two units together under Daly's command, with Wu as his assistant, as XVIII Corps's primary ground reconnaissance element. He told them so. Daly seemed not fully comfortable with having FIST-level recon Marines attached to him but didn't object. Staff Sergeant Wu said he looked forward to working under Force Recon. Carano sent the two to his G3 to get the details of what they were to do when they went planetside.

A reinforced platoon went planetside with Ensign Daly and Staff Sergeant Wu. Its assigned mission was to provide security around Marine House in Sky City. Wu and his twelve recon Marines traveled with an army squad in one of the three Dragons the Essay carried. Daly elected to ride in the same Dragon as the army platoon leader—ostensibly to confer with him on how to provide security. He didn't get any conferring done; the army lieutenant had never made a combat assault landing before, and the straight-down plunge had him continually sick almost from the instant the gut-churning planetward dive began.

Corporals Ryn Jaschke and Harv Belinski, with two landcars, met Daly, Wu, and the other FIST recon Marines at Beach Spaceport. Daly introduced his men to Wu but held off on the rest of the introductions until they were at Marine House and the FIST recon Marines could meet all of the Force Recon Marines. Jaschke and Belinski followed Daly's lead and said just about nothing on the short drive through Sky City to the edge of the plateau that held the spaceport and Haulover's capital city, where the Force Recon Marines had their base of operations.

The main room of Marine House, which had felt so spacious when nine Marines met in it to plan their missions, debrief, or just relax, felt crowded with the thirteen FIST recon Marines and the remaining six from Fourth Force Recon. But nobody expected to be in the house long enough for sleeping accommodations to be a problem.

After quick introductions, Daly began the planning session by projecting his map onto the room's rear wall, between the corridor leading to the back door and the door to the shorter hallway to the second bath and two bedrooms; it was the largest open stretch of wall in the house. While studying the map and listening to Daly, the Marines ate a meal that Lance Corporals Hans Ellis, Santiago Rudd, and Elin Skripska had prepared while Jaschke and Belinski were picking up the others at the spaceport.

"This is where we are," Daly said, using a laser to indicate the location of Sky City, in the lower left-hand corner of the map. "And here's where we found the Skink base, a thousand klicks to the northeast." He pointed at an area in the northeast map corner. "The *Broward County* has found more signs of Skink bases here, here, and here, and we've confirmed those locations," he said. The bases were widely separated, but all were at about one thousand kilometers distance, in an arc that ran from north to east.

"Not everybody here has seen the Skinks," Daly said, looking at Wu and his men.

"Actually, Mr. Daly," Wu said, "we ran into them on Kingdom. We not only saw the same kind of Skinks you've been attacked by, but we saw them in their uniforms, and we fought their giants and their swordsmen, which, unless I was misinformed, you haven't."

Daly nodded at Wu. "You haven't been misinformed, but evidently I have. My apologies."

Wu waved off the apology. "No harm, no foul, sir."

"All right," Daly said, mentally kicking himself for assuming that he and his men were the only ones who'd fought the Skinks—he'd been told that Thirty-fourth FIST or its elements had already encountered them twice. "We all know what kind of creatures we're up against. Have you seen any of their underground facilities?" The last was directed at Wu.

"Yes, sir. We examined several Skink tunnels on Kingdom, and retrieved some of their materials for the scientists to study."

Daly nodded. "Did the tunnel systems you examined have multiple levels?"

Wu shook his head. "They were under what passed for high ground in a swampy area."

"Here, at least in the one we visited, they're in mountains and are multilayered." Daly turned off the map display and projected a 2-D vid onto the same wall. "Here are the highlights of what our minnie found in the first complex we examined." The low-grade vid went on for fifteen minutes, showing chambers that held war machines; smallish armored vehicles, artillery, and aircraft of types unfamiliar to the Marines; and what looked like maintenance depots for the equipment.

"We didn't see aircraft on Kingdom," Wu remarked. "What was your minnie disguised as?"

"Norway brown rat," Daly said. He smiled at Wu's surprise. "They stowed away on the colonization ships. They've got no natural predators on Haulover, and seem to thrive on the local grains and other seeds, so they proliferated wildly and are found throughout the continent. Sky City has an active rat eradication program," he said when he saw some of the Marines looking into corners and shadows of the room, "so there aren't many in the city."

The vid continued, showing chambers with stacks of munitions, fuel depots, and crates with indecipherable markings. Other chambers were filled with what appeared to be foodstuffs, located near food service facilities. There was a complete hospital. The vid showed barracks facilities sufficient to hold five thousand men. And there were tunnels leading off into areas the minnie hadn't gone into on its first visit.

"We've been back three more times," Daly said when the vid ended, "and took more minnies. Enough to get what we think is a complete map of the interior." He touched a button on his controller and a 3-D map of the cave and tunnel complex was projected above the low table in the middle of the room. The

FIST recon Marines studied it with a great deal of interest. "We found more of the same in later recons. I estimate that this one complex houses thirty to forty thousand Skinks."

There were a couple of low whistles.

"You said you've confirmed those other locations," Wu said.

Daly nodded. "We've sent minnies in, enough to confirm that they're complexes similar to the first one we reconned in detail. We didn't recon them as thoroughly as the first, but we think they're about the same in scope.

"What we're going to do now that you're here is check out some of the other locations where *Broward County* has detected possible Skink activity." He turned the tunnel map off and projected a new map on the wall, larger scale, and showing an area northwest of the first. Four areas were marked on it. "I will take a team consisting of Jaschke, Ellis, and Skripska to this area." He used his pointer to show which one he meant. "Staff Sergeant Wu, assign your teams to the other three. I'm going to be in the field, so I want you to stay here in command of our ops and comm center, with Corporal Belinski and Lance Corporal Rudd."

Daly looked at Belinski and Rudd, who clearly wanted to object to being left behind. "We've been over this already. You might be ninety-five percent recovered from your wounds, but you aren't one-hundred percent. We've got enough people now that I can afford to leave you behind until you're fully recovered."

Then to Wu, "If one of the teams gets into trouble and needs rescue, take that army security platoon outside to pull the team out."

Wu cocked an eyebrow at Daly. "On what authority will I give that doggie lieutenant marching orders?"

"You heard Lieutenant General Carano. If we need anything we don't have, call him and ask for it. It'll be ours."

"What about Brigadier Sturgeon? You know, my chain of command."

Daly shook his head. "You're part of my command now. You

aren't working for your FIST anymore—we work for the corps commander. If you need anything, go directly to him.

"The Haulover authorities have given us the use of a small aircraft. When we leave here, we will go to a location southwest of Sky City, using that aircraft and our landcars. We will rendezvous with an AstroGhost here." He projected another map and lasered the spot. "It will take us to drop points near our areas of operation." To Wu he said, "I'll have the AstroGhost come back here to stand by for you in case you need to come to anybody's rescue."

Wu's eyes lit up at that. Like all FIST-level recon Marines, he'd heard rumors about the highly stealthed, top secret AstroGhost shuttle that was capable of atmospheric as well as orbit-to-surface flight, and even beyond-orbit-to-surface, but he had never even seen one let alone ridden one. He almost hoped one of the teams would need extraction so he'd have the opportunity to ride the AstroGhost. Almost, but not quite; if one of the teams needed emergency extraction, it probably meant wounded or dead Marines. More than likely, *his* Marines. *That* wasn't worth a ride in an AstroGhost.

After that, nobody had further questions for Daly so he wrapped up the meeting with assignment of call signs. The Marines who were going got their weapons and equipment ready.

The AstroGhost dropped off second recon team a shade west of something more than eleven hundred kilometers due north of Sky City. The suspected Skink base the team was to recon was a bit less than eleven hundred klicks from the capital, but the four Marines would approach it from behind on the theory that security would be lighter in that direction.

The FIST recon Marines wore the same chameleons that the infantry did, not the superior ones that Force Recon had, so they had to move more cautiously than Force Recon teams did in order to avoid detection. But the FIST recon Marines' chameleons were impregnated with a neutralizer for the phosphoric acid mix shot by the Skinks' acid guns so they were safer from injury from the Skinks' primary infantry weapon.

Sergeant Saber, the team leader, didn't care that he and his Marines were relatively immune to the Skink acid; if they were detected their mission had failed. He didn't want the mission to fail. His men felt the same.

The AstroGhost dropped the four Marines a few klicks beyond the reverse slope of the mountain where the *Broward County* had detected Skink activity. The mountain wasn't high enough to project above what passed for a tree line on Haulover but had reasonably well-wooded slopes. It took the four Marines an hour to reach the mountain and another hour to scale it to a pass, but they didn't attempt to use the pass, opting instead to climb above it. That turned out to be a wise decision—they discovered a squad-size observation post covering the pass. Saber used his Universal Positionator Up-Downlink (UPUD) to report the observation post as soon as his team was in a defile and it was in no danger of detection.

They moved more slowly on the front side of the mountain. While they saw—and easily evaded—two small security patrols moving through the forest and saw signs of others, they didn't find any passive security devices.

And then they found a midsize clearing, about two hundred meters on its long axis and somewhat more than half that on the short axis, right where the string-of-pearls-guided you-are-here on Saber's heads-up display map said it was. The Marines backed up and took to the trees, climbing to about fifteen meters above the ground, high enough to let them look down into the clearing. Saber assigned Lance Corporal Hagen to watch the rear, which Hagen did by alternating through his magnifier and infra screens.

About fifty Skinks were evident in the clearing. Some of them were playing a sport that involved a ball being hit by a stick; it was slow-moving with occasional running around. Most of the rest of the Skinks were watching the game, some cheering, some groaning, having evidently picked sides. Many of the Skinks, including half the players, were shirtless, and many were barefoot. The lines of closed gill slits were visible on the sides of the shirtless ones. Few weapons of any sort were in evidence. The Marines watched for several minutes and saw numerous brown rats scurrying about the edges of the clearing, some even going in and out of the cave.

Saber checked with Hagen to verify that the rear was secure, then climbed down to the ground and input the final programming for two minnies, which he then released. Back in the tree, he watched as the minnies emerged from the forest and headed for the cave mouth.

His heart lurched when he saw a Skink throw something at a rat at the forest edge, then dart toward it with a cry of triumph. The Skink picked up the barely moving rat by its tail and held it aloft for its comrades to admire. Others gathered around the Skink and its trophy, cheering and pummeling its back. Then they began to chant. The rat must have been merely stunned by the blow, because it suddenly began squirming, struggling to get loose. The Skink holding it flipped it upward by its tail and bit its head off as its companions cheered lustily. Blood spurted from the rat's neck, and Saber felt relief; the rat wasn't one of his minnies. But he didn't relax fully, because he now knew the recon robots were in danger of detection by the Skinks. He had to report that to Staff Sergeant Wu, who would notify the other teams.

After a few more minutes, the Skinks returned to their game, although whether the same Skinks resumed play or some were replaced by others he couldn't say.

Motion at the forest edge caught his eye, and he turned his head as two rats slipped out from under the trees and scurried to the cave mouth, then disappeared inside it. He thought it pretty obvious that the two rats were his minnies. He prepared a report to Wu at Marine House in Sky City stating that his team had arrived at their objective and had it under observation, and on the Skink catching and killing the rat. He tight-beamed the report to the string-of-pearls, then settled down to watch and wait.

Over the course of the next five hours, the recon Marines observed several changes of Skinks outside the cave. Saber would have been exaggerating if he'd said the Skinks all looked alike to him, but he couldn't easily tell their faces apart, certainly not at the distance he was viewing them, even with his magnifier screen. But he could easily see that they didn't look like clones of one another, that there were subtle differences among the faces, just as there were among faces of the Marines in the recon squad. Their body types and skin coloration, though, were far more uniform than those of the Marines, which suggested to him that the Skinks were from a more homogeneous population. He wished his team had face-recognition equipment such as Force Recon had and, as far as he knew, hadn't used when they observed the Skinks before the arrival of Thirty-fourth FIST at Haulover.

Anyway, even without the means to identify individual faces, he was pretty certain that every replacement group of Skinks was a new group of individuals. Going by that, he and his men saw about three hundred different Skinks outside the cave.

He looked at the string-of-pearls map downloaded to his UPUD and saw that other, smaller clearings in the vicinity also had Skinks in them. He suspected they were from the same cave complex and that he was looking over what might be the primary entrance.

At intervals slightly longer than the rotation of Skinks into the open air, six or seven Skink patrols went out or returned to the cave. None of them came close enough to detect the Marines by whatever means it was that allowed the Skinks to spot chameleoned Marines.

After eight hours, with the sun lowering toward the western horizon, two rats came out of the cave mouth and skittered to the forest edge. Several minutes later, Saber heard scrabbling at the foot of his tree. It was the two minnies. He signaled his men, and they climbed down. He put one of the recon robots in his own pocket and gave the other to Corporal Soldatcu to carry. The Marines then headed toward their pickup location, reaching it an hour after sunset. The AstroGhost picked them up soon after, and in another hour they were back at Marine House along with the other recon teams. During the flight, Ensign Daly had had them upload their minnies' data to the string-of-pearls. At Marine House they began studying the recordings themselves.

The caves all seemed to be as massively developed and populated as the first one Force Recon had reconned.

"There must be a couple hundred thousand of them," someone murmured.

CHAPTER
THIRTEEN

"Gentlemen, I'll give you"—Gobels paused, pretending to think his offer over—"let's say, five hundred credits each to bring me the child."

Gooden Ashcake glanced sideways at his two friends and scuffed one foot in the dirt. As the spokesman for Adner Shackelford and Linney Liggons, he had to make the negotiations look good, but *five hundred credits*? Why, a man could live like a king for a whole year in Wellfordsville on that kind of money! "Ah dunno, sir," he answered, pulling on an ear. "Ah dunno," he repeated.

"We din't come all the way out here to Jack's Shop fer enny five hunnert credits, Mr. Gobbles," Linney said.

"Please," Gobels smiled pleadingly, "it's *Doctor Gobels*! I'm a pure scientist! I have academic degrees, you know."

"I knows pure corn likker, 'n thet's all!" Linney cackled, seeking approbation from his colleagues with a nudge. He thought that riposte unbelievably witty and that it put him one up on the fancy-doctor scientist. But Adner and Gooden remained unimpressed. Here he was, Linney Liggons, matching wits with a *scientist* fella and all those boys could do was dream about what five hundred would get them at Verne's place! *Damned hicks,* he thought, *went right over their heads.* "Well, what I mean, Mr. Doctor there, is thet woman's never wifout her shotgun, 'n ah don't hanker after gettin' shot fer no five hunnert."

"How well we know," Pensy Fogel muttered.

"Whazzat?" Gooden asked.

"Nothing, nothing, my good man," Gobels answered. He scratched his nose. "Well, the woman does go about armed with that ancient fowling piece—"

Linney nudged Adner and whispered, "Knowin' her, she keeps that scattergun clean as a whistle! No fouling on thet piece. Shows ya how much these city folks knows about us folks 'n our firearms."

"I'll tell you what, gentlemen, I'll give you a thousand apiece, five hundred each right this moment and the rest when you bring me the child. How's that?"

"I'll be a double-cunted cow pissin' on a flat rock!" Gooden shouted, slapping his thigh with one hand and extending the other to shake on it. "Thousand credits fer a night's work! Damn! You got yerself a deal, Mr. Doctor!"

Gobels smiled warmly as he shook hands all round. Pensy Fogel counted out the advance money. Back in Fargo five hundred credits would buy a decent supper in a second-class hash house.

Their plan was simple. Plan A: Linney would approach Treemonisha's cabin with a box saying it was supplies sent out from Wellfordsville by Tanner Hastings. When she opened the door they'd jump her and take the kid straight back to Jack's Shop and collect the remaining five hundred credits. Plan B: There was no Plan B and Plan A didn't quite work out.

Treemonisha's chickens gave them away before they were within fifty meters of the cabin door. It burst open and there she stood, shotgun leveled at the trio. "What you no-goods want here at this hour?" she thundered.

At first Linney was so startled he forgot his lines for a moment. "Well, Miz Giddin's, we is bringin' yew sum supplies from Tanner's place," he finally got out. He could plainly see the child peeking out from behind her skirts. *Damn,* he thought, *shore does look jist like a Shackelford, that kid!*

"What you grinnin' at, you damn fool?" Treemonisha shouted. "I ain't ordered no supplies! Now git th' hell off'n my property!"

Linney took several steps forward but stopped cold as Treemonisha cocked a hammer on her shotgun. "M-Miz Giddin's," he stammered, "no need fur thet! We is jist followin' Tanner's orders!" Linney squeaked.

Gooden Ashcake stepped forward, elbowing Linney aside. "Now see here, Treemonisha, quit this foolishness! We is jist helpin' Tanner out by deliverin' this here box o' goodies—"

"I ain't ordered no goodies," she replied, cocking the other hammer.

"Ah *said*, stop thet, woman! You is liable to git someone hurt!" Gooden snatched the box out of Linney's hands and advanced quickly to the steps. He thrust the box out at Treemonisha. He got then a good look at the kid. *Well, damn my eyes,* he thought, *thet thar kid is a gawdam Liggons if I ever saw one! Ol' Linney's been out here by his self fer sartin shore!*

He thrust the box upward suddenly and lunged forward. Both barrels of the shotgun discharged with a tremendous roar, blasting a big hole in the roof and leaving his ears ringing, but Treemonisha reeled backward, stumbled, and fell with a crash so hard she was momentarily stunned. In that instant Gooden stepped forward and snatched Moses by the back of his shirt. He whirled, holding a struggling Moses high in one hand, and shouting, *"Eeeeeehaaaawww!"* His two companions, startled at how quickly the action had unfolded, just stood there, transfixed.

Suddenly Adner's eyes grew large as saucers, his mouth fell open, and he pointed a shaking finger at the house. But it was too late. Treemonisha slammed into Gooden Ashcake so hard that Moses flew into the air and plopped down into the dust right at Linney Liggons's feet. But Gooden, with Treemonisha on top of him, slammed hard into the dust with a lung-bursting *"Ooofff!"*

"Run, Moses, run!" Treemonisha screamed as she banged Gooden's head into the dust.

"Gawdam!" Gooden shouted around a mouthful of dirt.

"Git 'im, git 'im!" Adner yelled. Linney scrambled after

Moses, but the little Skink was fast on his stubby legs. While Gooden struggled to get out from underneath Treemonisha, Adner and Linney chased Moses around the yard, raising a cloud of dust so thick they ran smack into each other. "Yew gawdam fool!" Linney raged, getting to his feet. "Th' lit'l bastard's gettin' away!"

"Faster 'n a gawdam chicken afore Sunday dinner!" Adner gasped.

"Gawdamit, git off'n me, yew tub o'—" Gooden yelled up at Treemonisha. The pair flailed away at each other in the dust.

"Run, Moses, run!" Treemonisha screamed, in spite of Gooden's hands around her neck. She was losing her grip on Gooden's greasy hair. In desperation he managed to roll her over. He spit out a broken tooth with a curse and smashed his fist into her nose. Blood spurted everywhere. Meanwhile, the chase after Moses had moved out into the road.

Gooden staggered to his feet and grabbed the empty shotgun. He slammed the stock onto the porch, snapping it off. "Yew ain't pointin' thet gawdam thang at ennyone agin," he wheezed. But at that moment Treemonisha slammed into him from behind, pushing him hard against one of the porch supports, which gave way, causing the roof to come crashing down on both of them. If either of them had been conscious after that event they'd have heard Linney and Adner shouting and cursing as they chased Moses down the country road.

"What in the world—?" Dr. Gobels exclaimed. The disheveled trio stood disconsolately in the gathering dusk outside his lab at Jack's Shop. "Wh-where is the child?" he asked.

"Well, we got 'im," Linney Liggons said, nodding his head vigorously.

"He in a safe place," Gooden Ashcake muttered, holding a hand to his busted lip. A dirty handkerchief wrapped around his head did not quite cover the gash left there where the roof fell on him.

"We wanna talk to you 'bout thet critter," Adner said.

"What's to talk about? Either you have him or you don't. And you don't. Not this moment," Pensy Fogel replied.

"Well, we got 'im." Linney nodded. "But ya see, it warn't no easy job to ketch thet little bastard 'n we suffered considerable damage in the process."

"You didn't kill that old lady, did you?" Fogel asked anxiously. Kidnapping and cheating the government was one thing, murder quite another.

"Hell no, asshole! She damn near kilt *us*! Lookit Gooden's haid! We jist laid 'er up a bit. Now see here, we want another thousan' afore we hand 'im over. We earned it!" Linney nodded his head again for emphasis.

"Well, gentlemen, I can hardly be expected to pay you such a huge amount without some proof that you have the, er, boy." Gobels smiled disarmingly. "Can I?"

"I s'pose not," Adner agreed. He pulled a red-and-black checkered shirt out of one overall pocket. "He wuz wearin' this when we caught 'im. See, it's the right size."

Gobels examined the tiny shirt and passed it to Fogel. "Could've come off any child," he said, tossing it back at Adner.

"Now see here, Mr. Doctor Gobbles," Linney said, his face turning red with anger. "Yew don't want th' kid, we kin always find someone else be interested. Thousan' credits more 'n we have us a deal, unnerstan'?"

"Oh, yes, yes. Quite. Um, Pensy, give them the money, all the money, the five hundred we promised and the thousand more they want to settle this business."

"Uh, you sure, Doctor?"

"Quite sure." Gobels smiled. "These are honorable gentlemen. I'm sure we can trust them. Count out the cash, my man, and let's get this over with."

Fogel slowly counted out the credits from a huge wad in his pocket. He handed each man a stack of bills. This part of the country was a barter and cash-and-carry economy where no one had heard of electronic banking in centuries, and the scientists had come prepared to buy their way with actual cash. The three men grinned as the money came into their outstretched paws. Even Gooden Ashcake. The gap in his front teeth may have been quite noticeable to him, but to Dr. Gobels it was hard to see among all the others.

A piercing white beam of light suddenly froze the small group and a godlike voice thundered from the sky, "Nobody move! This is the Confederation Ministry of Justice and you are all under arrest!"

"Meet at Yancy's still!" Adner Shackelford yelled and broke for the woods; the other two took off in different directions. They knew the woods from childhood. But Dr. Joseph Gobels and Dr. Pensy Fogel had nowhere to go.

"Goddamn, goddamn," Gobels muttered. "Well, Pensy, if I can't have it *nobody* can."

"No!" Fogel protested. "We can use your data to bargain with them! Don't do it!"

Gobels smiled and pressed a small device in his pocket. The resulting explosion destroyed his lab and all his research and pitched the two men to the ground.

"You goddamned fool!" Fogel shouted, around a mouthful of mud.

"Shouldn't talk with your mouth full, Pensy," Gobels said with a grin. "You don't know what I know and now nobody will. Nobody will!" He laughed.

For a long time after that evening at Jack's Shop, Gooden Ashcake, Linney Liggons, and Adner Shackelford lived high at Verne Driscoll's tavern. Late at night, surrounded by empty beer bottles, they'd sit with their heads together and chuckle about how they'd gotten one over so completely on the city slickers at Jack's Shop. They spent so much time at Verne's that their wives actually began to enjoy life a little.

But they made themselves scarce whenever Treemonisha Giddings visited town, although she never said a word about what had happened at her place. All she knew, and that made her feel good, was that Moses had escaped. It was enough for her that her baby had gotten away.

Men from faraway Fargo had come and interviewed everyone in Wellfordsville, but in the manner of country folk since the beginning of time, the locals told them nothing. For weeks the men from Justice combed the surrounding woods and drained ponds but in the end they'd gone away empty-handed.

Moses ran until his pursuers were left screaming and cursing far behind in the dust of the road. When darkness fell that first night he slept in the bushes by the roadside. In the morning he headed toward the rising sun and soon found himself in a marshy area that quickly turned into a swamp. He pulled off his remaining clothing and soaked in the warm, muddy waters. It felt inexpressibly good. He began to relax, to feel completely free.

Moses had always been good in the water. The Brattle boys had marveled at how long he could hold his breath. He'd never told anyone he didn't have to hold his breath under the water. His gill slits weren't vestigial; they actually worked and he could breathe in the water. He slipped beneath the scummy mass that morning and propelled himself along effortlessly. For the first time in his short life he *was* free!

Small, wiggling creatures—and some not so small—proved very edible and Moses happily gorged on them as he swam through the murky waters. He reflected on humankind. He was not quite sure what kind of creature he was himself, but he knew he was not human, or at least not completely. There had been times, though, when he'd felt kinship with the people around him. But who could possibly understand humans? The Brattles, Treemonisha, they were wonderful. Treemonisha especially. In fact he'd begun to feel real affection for the huge brown woman, stronger even than what he'd felt toward the Brattles. He supposed that was how people felt about their mothers.

But there were those *others*. How could anyone know if a human was kind and decent or cruel and evil?

Well, for now he would swim and eat and doze in the sun and enjoy life in the swamp. The swamp, that's where he belonged! But, maybe, in time, he'd go back for a visit with Treemonisha, eat some of her pancakes, sleep in a bed, play with the chickens. Now *that* had been real fun!

CHAPTER
FOURTEEN

"You don't want to send an advance party, Pat?" Vice Admiral Geoffrey Chandler raised an eyebrow in surprise. As fleet commander he was responsible for getting the army planetside.

"Naw, Jeff. I'll be the advance party." Lieutenant General Patrice Carano grinned. He knew what he'd just suggested violated military protocol. Commanders always sent advance parties to secure landing zones, liaise with the natives, do whatever was necessary to prepare for the follow-on forces in a deployment, but the commanding general himself was never the first on the ground. But General Carano was the kind of commander who liked to defy protocols. "The Marines have secured the landing zone, Jeff, so no need to send an army battalion down first." He drew on the Uvezian and gently expelled the smoke through his mouth. "Damned fine cigar, this."

"Well, Pat, if you think nine Force Recon Marines have secured the whole planet"—Admiral Chandler gestured with his own cigar—"be my guest. I'll have you on your way planetside in ten minutes."

"Thank you, Admiral." Carano winked at his chief of staff, Major General Donnie ("Doc") McKillan. "I'm takin' Doc here and Ted Sturgeon with me. I'd like an Essay and one Dragon, one of Ted Sturgeon's Dragons. That ought to be enough security." Since he'd arrived on Arsenault and on the flight to Haulover, General Carano had gotten to know Brigadier Sturgeon rather well and he respected the Marine's judgment and experience fighting Skinks.

"Pat, there could be a hundred thousand Skinks down there—"

"Probably are." Carano drew happily on his cigar. "Andy Aguinaldo and I discussed this operation at length with Ted—his Marines have seen more of the Skinks than anyone else—and we agree they've picked Haulover for a set-piece battle. They want us to land in force, secure a beachhead, and engage, so I'm starting the war out with one pinkie in the water, and this Ensign Daly is the man who knows the temperature and depth. Once I've talked to him, send the corps in per the landing schedule we developed on the way here: military police and engineers first with one battalion of infantry for perimeter security. I'll give the signal when I'm ready."

"We could bring Daly up here, Pat—"

Carano shook his head. "No. I go down there. Daly's a working man. He's got his command to look after. Best Mohammed goes to the mountain."

"The civilians down there are hopping mad, Pat. They resented our sending only a Force Recon detachment to begin with, and think we've taken too long to respond to the threat Daly identified."

"I know. I've read the messages they've been sending to God and everyone. I'll deal with them. I'm declaring martial law in Sky City and every other part of Haulover we control. That's why I want the MP battalion to go in first. Aguinaldo approved all of this before we left Arsenault, Jeff. You know that. You were at the conferences."

"I know, I know." Admiral Chandler waved his cigar in the air. "I'm just playing devil's advocate here, Pat. No sense ruffling the taxpayer's feathers if we can avoid it."

"I understand, but I want to meet this young Ensign Daly first, before I talk to them. I'd appreciate it if you'd let them know I'll be at Sky City to talk to them in a couple of hours. But first order of business, I want to personally thank Ensign Daly for a job well done."

* * *

Landing any military force from orbit is a demanding undertaking made more complicated and difficult by great size of the force, poor conditions on the ground where it is to be landed, or both. Such operations are rarely explained in novels or vids because it would be a crashing bore to anyone but a professional logistician. Instead, the onscreen admiral simply says, "Mr. Hawkins, land the landing force," and the action moves on.

Planning for landing the XVIII Corps on Haulover had begun weeks before the force left Arsenault. Task Force Aguinaldo's logisticians had spent many sleepless nights devising and revising the disembarkation plan. That is how they earned their pay. The task force's generals and admirals earned theirs by making the operation work according to the plan.

To make their work even more difficult, what the planners had to do for the XVIII Corps also had to accommodate the landing of the XXX Corps, which was to follow the XVIII into orbit around Haulover. That required the efficient and timely movement of tens of thousands of men and millions of metric tons of equipment and materiel.

Bottlenecks had to be anticipated and eliminated, landing schedules had to be coordinated to the second, ground accommodations had to be prepared in advance, and everyone involved had to remain alert and flexible because every plan develops glitches and when they happen they must be fixed immediately or backups begin, troops and materiel are not delivered on time, and, if the landing is opposed by an enemy, disaster can result. A task force commander cannot afford to have his troops languishing in orbit, waiting for ground clearance because things have stacked up on the surface and there is nowhere for them to deploy—or nothing to deploy with. Likewise, when they do land, they need to have *everything* required to live and fight in a hostile environment. It spells disaster to have sixty thousand men on the ground without their vehicles, fuel, spare parts, weapons, ammunition, rations, and the wherewithal they need to sustain themselves in a battle.

For instance, how much water would fully loaded combat infantrymen need to sustain themselves in heavy fighting in the kind of terrain and climate that prevailed on Haulover? All that water would have to come down with them and sustain them until engineers could discover natural sources and establish purification plants to sanitize the supply. All units carry with them a basic load of everything they would need to sustain themselves in battle, but how long would those loads hold out? What would the anticipated casualty rates be among the fighting units and how much medical support would they need to handle those casualties? What about replacements and reinforcements? They would have to be available and ready to fight when needed.

Military logisticians have ways to calculate all these apparently imponderable requirements with amazing accuracy.

But the initial landing is only the beginning of the military logistician's nightmare. Once on the ground, the force has to be kept supplied and the longer the fighting lasts, the more supplies the troops will need and *they* have to be unloaded quickly and efficiently and then distributed to the fighting units to be in their hands *before* they're needed. Often those units are hundreds of kilometers from the depots, so safe and efficient means have to be available to move them to the forward battle area where other depots are established, a very important and difficult task on a fluid battlefield. So, even if an initial landing is accomplished perfectly, keeping the force adequately supplied requires a tremendous effort. And bear in mind, resupply of the force must take place over a distance of *light-years*.

Military victories owe as much to the unsung rear-echelon logisticians and staff officers who plan them as to the heroes who fight them. But when something goes wrong with those plans, it's the common infantryman who has to make things work.

And the landing on Haulover was unopposed by the enemy who, with great patience and cunning, lurked silently in prepared positions for the right moment to strike.

* * *

"Whew, dusty out there!" General Carano exclaimed as he stepped into the prefabricated hut that was headquarters for the Fourteenth Air Wing at Naval Air Station George Gay. Captain Ronald Hahley was in command of the wing. A grizzled, no-nonsense officer, Hahley knew his business and he did not like to be interfered with in the transaction of that business. But out of respect for Brigadier Ted Sturgeon of Thirty-fourth FIST and Brigadier Jack Sparen of Twenty-sixth FIST, he had asked the corps commander to resolve a disagreement he had with the Marines.

Carano slapped dust off his tunic. "Never seen a landing go as smoothly as this one, gentlemen!" In two days the entire XVIII Corps had been landed on Haulover, bases and depots established, probes against the enemy initiated. "Hey, sit down, sit down." He laughed and waved the three officers back into their chairs. They had snapped to attention when he entered the hut. "No need for that here! What's up?"

The three were silent for a moment. Captain Hahley glanced at the two Marines, who nodded that he should proceed. "Well, sir, we disagree on the dispersal of our aircraft."

"So? You can't resolve that among yourselves?"

"No, we cannot, sir. Now I have ninety-six Raptors in my wing. As I understand the situation, the greatest threat we have here is from enemy ground attacks. I've seen all the vids and attended the briefings, just as all of us have, and I see the greatest threat to my aircraft coming from enemy infiltrators." He shrugged and glanced again at the two Marines. "So, I want to keep all my machines on the aprons where they can be guarded at all times against sabotage."

"Ted? Jack?"

"Sir—" Brigadier Sparen began.

"It's Pat, Jack. But please continue."

"Sir, as you know, each FIST has its organic air complement consisting of ten Raptors and ten hoppers. We Marines, well, we like to keep our toys close and under our control and we like to plan for everything to go wrong. We think Captain Hahley has a good point, but we prefer to protect our aircraft from *all* eventualities and therefore we want revetments constructed to accommodate our Raptors."

Sturgeon leaned forward. "Pat, we understand Captain Hahley's points, no disrespect intended toward him. He has almost one hundred aircraft to protect, and putting them all in revetments would require a tremendous engineering effort that might be used more effectively elsewhere. We understand that. Also, putting all his machines in one place makes security a lot easier to handle. But as Jack has pointed out, we Marines like to take all precautions. We only have forty aircraft in our respective inventories and if we can get the revetments built, we can guarantee their security without downgrading our own mission capability."

"Ron?" Carano turned to Captain Hahley.

The wing commander sighed and shrugged his shoulders. "If that's what they want . . ."

Carano turned to the Marines and said, "Then do it. I'll have the chief of engineers get with you two immediately. He can build your revetments by the end of the day." Carano slapped both knees, sending small clouds of dust into the air. "Okay, gentlemen, good work. I need to know right away when there are problems like this. You did good by not sitting on this one. I'll see you all at the 1700 briefing. I'm off now, fellas, to, to"—he laughed—"breathe another hundred grams of this goddamned dust!" He stood and stretched. "Or, as Grandma Carano used to say, 'We've all gotta eat a peck o' dirt before we die.'"

After making the introductions in his hastily established headquarters, General Carano asked Ensign Daly to walk with his party for a while, during which Daly gave the three flag officers a precise briefing on everything that had transpired on Haulover up to that time. "And, sir, let me say, are we *ever* glad to see you here now!"

"You put your finger on the problem, Ensign Daly." Carano

extended his hand. "Fine job! *Damned* fine job! Now, you mentioned some civilian dignitaries, Ensign. Tell me, are they going to be a problem?"

"Yes, sir, they are, but I think you have the, uh, horsepower to deal with them."

"They gave you a hard time, didn't they?"

"Yes, sir, but you have to understand, they're businessmen, and what's happened here is, well, not good for their business, and far beyond their ability to handle. They're concerned about what a major war on Haulover will cost them, has already cost them. Haulover's a rough place but many of these people have their families here with them, and they're understandably concerned about safety. A guy who's worried about his wife and kids may not think too clearly while he's waiting for the cavalry to arrive."

"Ensign, you look on both sides of the coin, don't you?" Carano said. His remark received agreeing nods from Sturgeon and McKillan. "I like that in a man. Before I send you back to the flagship and on to Camp Basilone, I want you to come with me on a little visit to these civilian dignitaries. Will you do that for me?"

"Yes, sir, absolutely! But, sir"—Daly looked imploringly at Sturgeon—"I think I'd like to stay here, until this is over. I'm speaking only for myself, of course, not the other men on the team. We were in at the start, and I want to be in at the finish."

Carano raised an eyebrow and glanced at Sturgeon, who nodded very slightly. He thought for a moment. "Well, you and your men have been through a rough time here, Ensign. Your job here is done, you know. I don't know." He rubbed his chin. "Okay, I'll find something for you to do. If nothing else, I may still need your level of recon." Daly broke into a big grin. "Now, Doc." Carano turned to General McKillan. "Return to the flagship and tell Admiral Chandler to commence landing the corps. I want the CO of that MP battalion to report to me as soon as he gets here. Ted, you and Ensign Daly jump into that Dragon with me and we'll go see our civilian counterparts and get some things straight around this place. Now tell us about the big cheeses who are in charge of things here. I've asked them to meet us at the planet administrator's office."

"That's Spilk Mullilee, sir. He's just that, an administrator. The real power here is Smelt Miner, who's running the mining and smelting operations, the main business on Haulover. Then there are Agro Herder, agribusiness; Rayl Rhodes, runs the rail system; and Manuel Factor, small-time manufacturer. They follow Miner's lead. Get any one of those guys by himself, though, and he can be a pretty easy person to deal with. Put Miner in his place and the others will cooperate with you."

"Excellent! Gentlemen, shall we mount out and eliminate the threat to our rear? While we're on our way over there, Ensign, let's discuss your future duties here on Haulover."

It was all General Carano could do to suppress a double-take when he saw Spilk Mullilee wearing a chartreuse suit, magenta shirt, and black suede calf-high boots.

"General! How *dee-lighted* we are to see you!" Mullilee virtually ran around the conference table, hand outstretched. The hand was damp and limp.

"It's about goddamned time!" a stout man rumbled. Carano knew from the files he'd read on the way from Arsenault that he was Smelt Miner, but he ignored the man, for the moment.

"Mr. Mullilee, pleased to meet you. This officer is Brigadier Ted Sturgeon, commanding Thirty-fourth Fleet Initial Strike Team. You already know Ensign Daly—"

"Izzat all you brought with you, General, a goddamned FIST?" Miner almost shouted.

"Sir, I have brought an entire corps, the XVIII, consisting of the Fifteenth Armored Division, the Twenty-fourth Medium Infantry Division, the Eighty-seventh Heavy Infantry Division, Twenty-sixth and Thirty-fourth FISTS, the Eighth and Fourteenth Air Wings—with ninety-six A8E Raptors to each wing—and all the naval vessels required to transport and support those units in combat. In addition, the XXX Corps is en route with the best weapon the Confederation has, that is, General Anders Aguinaldo. When he gets here he will assume overall command of this campaign. Until then, I am the senior Confederation officer in this quadrant of Human Space.

"Now, I have a lot to do. The XVIII Corps is landing as we speak and my time is short. Please be seated."

"Well, goddammit, General, tell us what you are going to *do*!" Miner bellowed, his fleshy cheeks swollen with outrage.

"That is why I am here, Mr. Miner. Please be seated." Miner's face registered surprise that Carano knew who he was, because he'd not yet introduced himself. "Now, gentlemen, here is the plan. To start, you and every civilian on this planet are now my responsibility. From this moment forward all of Haulover is declared to be under martial law—"

"Goddammit!" Miner roared while his colleagues blanched. "You can't do that!"

"Mr. Miner, do not presume to tell me my duty. From today until this campaign is over, every area on this planet that is under our control, starting with Sky City and Beach Spaceport, is under a dusk-to-dawn curfew."

"This is unprecedented, sir!" Mullilee gasped, his normally sallow complexion now ashen.

"This is an *outrage*!" Miner screamed. "I will not tolerate—"

"It is not without precedent, Mr. Planet Administrator. My judge advocate will be here shortly and he will explain the legalities of establishing and *enforcing* martial law.

"As for you, Mr. Miner, I want you to sit in that chair and keep your mouth shut. If you do not, I will have Ensign Daly place you under arrest, and I will transfer you to my flagship, where you will be interned until the campaign is over. Is that clear? That applies to every citizen, gentlemen. Right now, a battalion of military police is landing at Beach Spaceport. Their commanding officer will visit you soon. He will be responsible for establishing and enforcing military law as well as for the physical security of Sky City. He has the authority to arrest and detain anyone who violates the terms of the martial law I am now establishing." He dug into a cargo pocket and distributed crystals to the civilians. "Promulgate this information to everyone, gentlemen. I will hold you personally responsible for informing the citizens of the terms and conditions of this state of martial law."

The corps staff judge advocate and Civil Affairs officers had written the orders days ago. Miner looked as if he'd been poleaxed, puffing his cheeks in and out and breathing heavily.

"Are you all right, Mr. Miner?" Brigadier Sturgeon asked gently. Miner nodded.

"Now, gentlemen, within the limits established by my authority, you are free to pursue your ordinary business. But be aware of the fact that, to assist my troops in their mission, I have the authority to commandeer all equipment and personnel from your operations that I need. I have army engineers coming down from orbit even as we speak. Their officers will get with your engineers and arrange whatever support you can give them.

"Gentlemen, this world is in a state of emergency, a state of war." Carano emphasized each word carefully. "You should all know that by now. We must work together to defeat this enemy. The alternative is the complete destruction of you, your families, everything on this world that you have worked so hard to attain. You should all be familiar by now with what happened on the world known as Kingdom. Brigadier Sturgeon was there. He can tell you. You do not want what happened to the Kingdomites to happen to you. And let me tell you now, gentlemen, you have Ensign Daly and his men to thank for your hides, because they saw what was coming and called in the cavalry."

"S-sir?" Manuel Factor said. "Would you, can you, sir, tell us, um, what your plan is?"

"Mr. Factor, I'd be happy to do that, but briefly. First, I am going to secure Sky City and prepare accommodations for the XXX Corps. Next, I will deploy my maneuver elements to find and fix the enemy. By 'fixing' I mean establish a line of resistance and hold him where he is so that when XXX Corps arrives our combined forces can apply overwhelming military power and destroy him. Gentlemen, he is beatable. Brigadier Sturgeon can testify to that. And we're going to beat him again, this time for good.

"One final thing, gentlemen. You all know Ensign Daly here. You will get to know him much better in the future. He is my aide-de-camp, and henceforth when he speaks, he speaks with my authority." Carano had the authority to keep Daly on Haulover, Daly had seen the Skinks and knew the ground, and Carano wanted him close by at all times so he could take advantage of that knowledge.

After General Carano had left the civilian bosses, Miner recovered his composure enough to curse loudly and declare, "I'm contacting corporate headquarters! We have contacts at Fargo. By God, I'll burn the hide off that tin soldier—"

"Smelt!" Spilk Mullilee brushed a hand tiredly across his forehead. "Will you kindly *shut the fuck up*? You heard what the man said. Why do you have to always be such an asshole? If you oppose or obstruct General Carano in any way, Smelt, I swear, I'll get that military police commander to arrest you."

An aide rushed into the conference room. "Gentlemen! There are—" He was shoved aside by three soldiers in combat gear.

"Howdy, gentlemen. I'm Colonel Rene Raggel, Seventh Military Police Battalion. I want you to meet battalion Sergeant Major Steiner and Senior Sergeant Puella Queege, the best pistol shot in all of Human Space! We're here to enforce the law!"

CHAPTER
FIFTEEN

"All right, Mr. Daly, fill me in on the enemy situation," General Carano said when they reached his headquarters.

Ensign Daly withdrew a crystal from a pocket and held it up. "I have some visuals." A lieutenant colonel took the crystal from Daly and inserted it into a vid projector, then handed him a control clicker. "We inserted two minnies into each of the assigned underground complexes." He nodded to the 2-D display that came up. "Due to time constraints, we weren't able to examine the complexes as thoroughly as we did the first one we reconned, but we saw enough to be reasonably sure that each of them is similar in size and arrangement to the first." Daly clicked through images labeled with the coordinates of the complex being shown. A corner of each display also displayed a schematic of the complex, with a you-are-here icon to show where within the complex the images had been taken.

"Is all the data from the minnie recons on that crystal?" Carano asked.

"Yes, sir. It also has images from outside the complexes."

Carano gestured, *Show me.* On the third 2-D image, one of the staff officers gave out a quickly cut-off laugh.

"Yes, Colonel?" Carano asked, as everybody looked at the colonel.

"S-sir! Mr. Daly, could you play that sequence from the beginning again? I mean, the game."

"Yes, sir." Daly clicked back to the beginning of the image that the colonel had choked on.

This time the colonel didn't cut off his delighted laugh. "Sir, I guess this demonstrates that there are certain universalities among sentient species. That"—he nodded at the display—"looks almost exactly like baseball."

"Baseball?" Carano asked. He looked around. Blank looks everywhere.

"Baseball, sir. It was a popular sport on many parts of Earth during the centuries around the turn of the millennium."

Carano shook his head. "Baseball indeed." He nodded at Daly. "Proceed, Ensign."

"Thank you, sir. Sir, all the hard intelligence we gathered is on that crystal. I have only one thing to add; we estimate that there are no fewer than two hundred thousand Skinks located in those complexes."

A palpable hush fell over the room at those words.

"Two hundred thousand," Carano repeated.

"Or more. Yes, sir."

Carano twitched his eyebrows up and back down. "Those are long odds against us," he said. "But, on the other occasions Confederation forces have met the Skinks, they've gone against heavy odds, and come out the victors. If we plan right, and fight hard, I don't see any reason this time will turn out differently." He shot a look at Daly and added, "Don't say it."

"Say what, sir?" Daly asked blandly. There was no way that, in this company, he would say, *"But those other times, the Skinks faced Marines."*

Carano gave him a curt nod, and turned to the lieutenant colonel who had popped the crystal into the vid projector. "Make copies of that and distribute them. Then, gentlemen," he said to his staff at large, "get busy making plans. I'll have my commander's-intent for you shortly."

Lieutenant General Carano swore once he was alone. Then he began making his commander's-intent plans for offensive operations against the Skinks.

Estimate two hundred thousand plus enemy planetside, the Force Recon commander had said. The Surveillance and Radar

Division on the recently arrived CNSS *Grandar Bay,* which was reputed to have the best analysts in the surface surveillance business, said there were possibly more than the five known Skink cave complexes closer to Sky City.

And Carano's XVIII Corps only had five army divisions and four Marine FISTs. Fewer than ninety thousand troops—he was outnumbered by more than two to one. And military doctrine sanctified by centuries of repetition said an attacking force needed to outnumber dug-in defenders three to one to be able to carry the day.

Well, something better than four thousand of the troops of XVIII Corps were Marines. Unlike some army generals who had no use for them, Carano saw the Marines as force magnifiers; he estimated the four FISTs he had, even though they comprised little more than four thousand Marines, gave him fighting power equivalent to another medium infantry division of twenty thousand men, possibly more. But there was no way his force could mount a simultaneous assault on all the known Skink positions and expect to win more than one or two of them. He wasn't about to throw away his men's lives that way. But even attacking and clearing the Skink bases one at a time was a risky proposition with the number of troops he had. He'd have to maintain a sizeable reserve, and position sizeable blocking forces to stop a possible Skink counterattack mounted against his clearing operations.

Another advantage the XVIII Corps had over the Skinks was combat aircraft. Each of the FISTs had its own composite squadron, composed of Raptor fighter/attack aircraft, and hoppers that could be fitted as ground assault aircraft. And the navy had two aircraft carriers, each with an entire air wing. The Skinks didn't have combat aircraft. At least they hadn't used any in the contacts the Marines had had with them. In those contacts, the Skinks hadn't had aircraft of *any* sort, but on Haulover they *were* known to have some manner of airborne troop transport, so enemy combat airpower wasn't out of the question and needed to be planned for.

Carano gave his operations people his commander's-intent and one full day to draw up plans. Then he held a meeting of his major-element commanders: five division commanders, four FIST commanders, and two air wing commanders. The air wing commanders weren't actually elements of XVIII Corps, but Rear Admiral Worthog, the senior air commander, put navy air under Carano's command for the planetside operation. Carano also had his primary staff and Ensign Jak Daly, the Force Recon commander planetside, in attendance for the briefing. Daly probably had additional intelligence about the Skink positions—Daly had sent his recon teams back out a few hours after he filed his report, and they were gathering additional intelligence on the internal layouts of the underground Skink bases. With luck—or perhaps skill—they were also getting additional intelligence on the enemy order of battle.

"Gentlemen, I'll make this short," Carano began. "Everybody has been briefed on the enemy we're about to take on, but almost none of you has seen them. You've read the after-action reports filed by Twenty-sixth and Thirty-fourth FISTs, and the element of Thirty-fourth FIST that has had previous contact with the Skinks. Those contacts, and the recent encounters Force Recon had here on Haulover, are the only known occasions on which humanity has faced this implacable enemy. We do suspect, however, that the Skinks may be behind the disappearance of some human groups on isolated worlds.

"I just used the word *implacable.* It was quite deliberate; the first time the Marines encountered them, the Skinks fought until they were totally wiped out. On the second occasion, when two FISTs took on a force larger than a division, they fought until they were past the point where any human force would have surrendered to avoid further, needless casualties before they attempted to cut and run. On both occasions, individuals were seen to suicide when they were no longer able to continue fighting and were about to be captured. So, when you get planetside, you should expect and be prepared for the toughest fight you've ever been in. A *very* tough fight. Our best estimate at this time is that the Skinks planetside outnumber us by more than two to one, and it's possible they have an even larger advantage over us.

"Major General McKillan will give you the details, but in brief, what we are going to do is start with the easternmost enemy position and clear it. Once it's cleared, we'll move on to the next and clear it. We will continue moving and clearing until the Skink threat is fully removed from Haulover.

"General McKillan." Carano nodded at his chief of staff, and strode off the small stage.

"Atten-*tion*!" McKillan called out, and the assembled generals and staff officers jumped to their feet as their Corps commander exited the briefing room.

"Seats!" McKillan called out when the door closed behind Carano. McKillan pointed at the map that sprang into view on the wall behind him. "Here you see . . ."

CHAPTER
SIXTEEN

Among the lead elements of the gator fleet to arrive in orbit around Haulover was the construction starship CNSS *Wedge Donovan,* which immediately landed its construction battalion and their heavy equipment. The navy engineers selected land next to Beach Spaceport for an expeditionary airfield. Not that they had an easy time securing the land. Haulover Chairman of the Board Smelt Miner, the closest thing Haulover had to a head of state, wanted to charge top credit for the land, and refused to allow construction to begin until he was paid a sizeable deposit. Vice Admiral Geoffrey Chandler, the gator fleet commander, wasn't about to delay construction of the airfield just because some pipsqueak of a local dignitary let petty greed cloud his judgment. Chandler promptly ordered a light armored infantry battalion, one of the first ground combat elements to arrive with the fleet, planetside to convince the civilian authorities to let the construction begin even before proper negotiations on a lease began. Mr. Miner backed off as soon as he realized that the light armored infantry battalion was fully capable of defeating the entire military, such as it was, and police forces of Haulover without breaking a sweat. Miner was somewhat mollified when Chandler told him there was a chance that ownership of the airfield would revert to Haulover at the conclusion of anti-Skink operations.

Chandler didn't mention that it was at least equally possible that the airfield would form the core of a permanent Confederation military base on Haulover.

At any rate, the navy construction battalion had the airfield ready for use by the time Lieutenant General Carano briefed his major element commanders on the coming operation.

Within hours of the combat briefing, the Fourteenth Air Wing, off the carrier CNSS *Raymond A. Spruance,* landed at what the navy saw fit to name Naval Air Station George Gay, after a navy pilot of a twentieth-century war, and prepared for its first mission. The Twenty-fourth Infantry and Eighty-seventh Heavy Infantry Divisions were landed by waves of Essays two hundred kilometers east of the easternmost Skink base. The Essays had dropped from orbit south of Sky City, and flew nape-of-the-earth, to avoid detection by Skink observers, to their drop zones. The Twenty-fourth Infantry Division would be the assault element, with the Eighty-seventh in reserve. The Fifteenth Armored Division was dropped midway between the objective base and the next one to the left. Other Essays swung around to the east and landed Thirty-fourth FIST a hundred klicks northeast of the Skink base. The Essays that dropped the Twenty-fourth and Eighty-seventh Divisions turned about and retraced their routes to orbit, where they refueled and brought the Fifty-fourth Light Infantry and Twenty-seventh Medium Divisions, along with the remaining FISTs, to bivouac areas a short distance north of Sky City. The Eighth Air Wing, off the CNSS *Frank Fletcher,* followed to NAS Gay.

Even before the Fifteenth Armored Division was in position, the Twenty-fourth Infantry, mounted in armored personnel carriers, sped toward the Skink base. At that same time, the ninety-six Raptors of the Eighth Air Wing began launching and headed for the objective, intending to devastate the enemy forces taking their ease outside the cave and tunnel system.

The Eighth Air Wing passed over the advancing infantry division when they were still a hundred klicks away from their objective. Less than a minute later, they encountered a surprise such as Lieutenant General Carano had warned about.

"Magnum Lead," Ensign Jabarrah said in a voice that denied the excitement and adrenaline that suddenly surged through him, "I have bogeys at two o'clock low."

"Magnum Four," Lieutenant Deitz, Magnum Lead drawled, looking down and to his right front for the bogeys Jabarrah had alerted him to. He spotted them. "I have them."

"Buddha's blue balls!" Ensign Ghibson, Magnum Three, exclaimed when he spotted the bogeys. "How many of them are there?"

"Enough that not even you can miss," Lieutenant (jg) Hoot, Magnum Two came back.

"Can the chatter, people," Magnum Lead snapped. Then he said to the squadron commander, "Pistol, Magnum division has numerous bogeys approaching from two o'clock low. They have no IFF signal. I want to veer off to investigate."

"I have them, Magnum Lead," Pistol answered. He was Lieutenant Commander Pitz. "Check them out. Go red."

"Roger, Pistol. Going red. Magnum Division, arm air-to-airs, charge guns. Follow me." Magnum Lead turned his Raptor into a shallow dive to the right, heading for the middle of the approaching formation.

The pilots of the Eighth Air Wing were flying top-of-the-line fighter aircraft and were very highly trained. Many of them, including all of Magnum Division except Magnum Four, also had combat experience. So the pilots weren't unduly unsettled by unexpectedly encountering a sizeable force. After all, they'd won all of their air battles in the past. In fact, although the four pilots of Magnum Division seemed to be heading into combat against an entire sixteen-aircraft squadron, they were confident of coming out of the battle as undisputed victors.

Magnum Lead was closest when red flashes showed on the wings of four of the bogeys. Lieutenant Deitz didn't even have time to open his mouth to call a warning before half a dozen pellets struck his Raptor at a significant percent of the speed of light, disintegrating it and killing him. The other three Raptors of Magnum Division disintegrated less than a second later.

Pistol happened to be looking in Magnum's direction when the division was killed, and saw four of his aircraft get knocked into small bits, none of them as big as a human being. He was a good enough combat pilot that he didn't go into immediate shock at the inconceivably sudden deaths of four of his men and total destruction of their aircraft. Instead, he began immediately snapping orders to the remainder of his squadron to take evasive action.

Captain Mason Anderson, the Eighth Air Wing commander, had been monitoring that action and more, and knew that more squadrons were approaching his wing from various directions. He ordered his squadron commanders to have their pilots take evasive action, then counterattack what were obviously "bandits," bad guys, rather than just "bogeys," unknowns.

In seconds, the airspace occupied by the Eighth Air Wing was filled with Raptors flying in multiple directions, mostly in four aircraft divisions, but some flying in pairs or individually. A dozen bandit squadrons were rapidly approaching them from multiple directions, spreading out, spitting red flashes from their wings. More Raptors disintegrated. Some Confederation pilots tried to line up shots for their guns or to get solid locks for their missiles but most of those were killed before they could get their shots off. The rest of them began firing their guns and missiles as soon as they were anywhere near having a good shot or lock, trusting to luck. A few had that luck, but nowhere near enough of them. Most of their kills came when a bandit jinked to throw off someone's aim and accidentally put himself in the path of someone else's plasma bolts or missiles.

In minutes, the ninety-six aircraft of the Eighth Air Wing were reduced to thirty-seven, which turned tail and headed at maximum speed back to NAS Gay. Against their fifty-nine losses, they had scored twenty-three kills.

Unfortunately for them, the past air battles of the Confederation Navy had been against the air forces of planetary militaries, which were rarely a match for them. The Skink pilots, on the other hand, had turned out to be every bit as skilled as the pilots of the Eighth Air Wing. They had numbers on their side, and, although the Confederation forces didn't learn this until much later, the Skinks' guns were rail guns, which meant much greater destructive power. Every Raptor that got hit went down, mostly in rather small pieces.

The Skink aircraft then turned their attention to the still-advancing Twenty-fourth and Eighty-seventh Divisions.

At first, those soldiers of the Eighty-seventh Heavy Infantry Division who could see the fighting in the sky above cheered every time they saw the explosion of an aircraft being killed. Until they realized that those were *navy* Raptors, not Skink aircraft that were being pulverized. The cheers turned to groans and gasps, then silence when the surviving Raptors turned tail and ran.

The silence didn't last long. It was shattered by screams when the enemy aircraft turned their noses groundward and began firing their rail guns at the armored personnel carriers.

"Point those guns up!" shouted Captain Sparr, the commanding officer of Fox Troop, Seventh Heavy Infantry Battalion. His men were well enough trained that half of the swivel-mounted guns on his battalion's armored vehicles were already firing at the diving aircraft. It wasn't until the guns on all thirty-six of his vehicles were spraying bullets into the sky that they finally hit one of the attacking aircraft.

Fourteen aircraft began the run at the armored vehicles of Fox Troop, and eleven of them completed the run. But they killed seventeen of the armored personnel carriers—and more than 150 of the 170 soldiers in them.

Not every troop in the Eighty-seventh Heavy Infantry Division was attacked; each of the Skink squadrons struck at two troops, hitting twenty-four of the division's thirty-six troops. Not all of them were damaged as badly as Fox of the 505th, and only a few were hit harder. But by the time the Skink aircraft flew away, Major General Kocks, the division commander, had little choice but to turn his division around and head back toward the bivouac that was building just north of Sky City.

The Twenty-fourth Infantry and Fifteenth Armored Divisions, although uninjured, went with them; the initial offensive by the XVIII Corps died aborning.

Brigadier Sturgeon believed that the Skinks hadn't detected Thirty-fourth FIST, so he ordered his Marines to hunker down and hold their position until the army was ready to resume its offensive.

"Hurry up and wait," Lance Corporal Isadore Godenov grumbled. "Hurry up and goddamn wait!"

Corporal Joe Dean, his fire team leader, ignored him.

PFC John Three McGinty, still a bit uncertain of his position in the fire team, the squad, and the platoon, also didn't say anything, but he did stare at the complainer. Like Godenov, McGinty didn't understand why, after the rush to get all of the ground combat elements of Thirty-fourth FIST planetside a hundred klicks from their objective, and then onto Dragons and headed toward that objective, the FIST had suddenly stopped with orders to stay in place. So they sat, the third fire team, first squad, third platoon, Company L, in a hole in the ground where a large tree had toppled over and its root-ball had ripped free of the earth. Dean had put out a motion detector and was occupying himself by trying to figure out what local life forms made which signals on it. So far, all he'd positively identified was the platoon sergeant, Staff Sergeant Hyakowa, and a scaled animal twice the size of an Earth rabbit that hopped like a rabbit even though it didn't look like a rabbit at all.

"I don't like this one little bit," Godenov complained, swiping at some tiny, exoskeletoned beasties that were crawling across his legs. He looked at Dean. "You aren't listening to me, are you?" Dean continued to ignore him. "You're my fire team leader, Dean-o. You should be finding out why we're just sitting here letting these fire ants eat me up."

"That's *Corporal* Dean-o," Dean said absently.

Godenov snorted.

"If Sergeant Ratliff knew anything, I'm sure he'd tell us," McGinty offered.

Godenov gave him an "Are you really that dumb or do you have to work at it" look. "Triple John, you haven't been in Mother Corps long enough to realize that squad leaders don't tell their men anything. They get their rocks off by keeping their men in the dark."

"Rabbit will tell us when he knows something," Dean said, still not looking at Godenov. The local animal Dean had identified with his motion detector might not have looked like a rabbit, but Sergeant Ratliff did have a certain facial resemblance to a rabbit.

Godenov snorted again. "Can I at least get away from the bugs, honcho?"

Dean finally looked at him from where he lay against the side of the hole with his arms hooked over its top. Godenov was sitting in the bottom of the hole. "Move into a position where you'll be useful if any bad guys come looking for us. Like Triple John."

McGinty looked at his fire team leader, not sure that he wanted to be used as a good example for the more experienced lance corporal. Godenov slid his chameleon screen into place before glaring at Dean. Invisible, he scrabbled up the side of the hole and took a position on the other side of Dean from McGinty.

"See anything?" he asked.

"Not a thing, except those hopping things over there," Dean answered. "I wish somebody would tell us what's going on."

"That's what I've been saying," Godenov muttered.

"I could have sworn that Wolfman was still acting as runner for the boss," Dean said. "Nobody told me he was assigned to my fire team."

"What do you mean, 'Wolfman'!" Godenov squawked. "I'm not Wolfman."

"You're complaining like him."

Godenov's glare went unseen behind his chameleon screen, but he stopped complaining. Out loud, at least.

Thirty-fourth FIST was too far away from the sky battle and the aerial attack on the Eighty-seventh Heavy Infantry Division to have seen or heard it. The only people who knew why the FIST had stopped were Brigadier Sturgeon, his ground component commanders, and their respective staffs—and, for the moment, they weren't telling.

Brigadier Sturgeon knew what he wanted to do. He suspected that, following their breakup of the XVIII Corps's initial attack, the Skinks felt safe from an assault in the next few hours or even days. And he had an entire battalion of Marines who had fought the Skinks in their caves and tunnels on one or more occasions—fought them and severely beat them.

Brigadier Sturgeon was in his command post—the FIST's command Dragon—hidden under a canopy of chameleoned fabric. He was in intense conversation with his boss, Lieutenant General Carano, trying to convince the corps commander to let his infantry move ahead and tackle the caves with no more than the FIST's organic combat support units.

"That would be suicide, Brigadier," Lieutenant General Carano said. "I'm not going to throw away the lives of any of my people on a suicide mission." His voice cracked. He had almost said "any *more* of my people."

"General, we've got detailed maps of the tunnel system. We know they will only be able to fight us on narrow fronts. They won't be able to bring their superior numbers to bear—and our chameleons are impregnated with neutralizer for the Skinks' acid weapons. We can do it."

"Your uniforms aren't impregnated with a neutralizer for Skink rail guns!"

"Their rail guns are line-of-sight. Our chameleons make us effectively invisible. If they can't see us, that partly neutralizes their rail guns. Besides, we don't know that they can use their rail guns in the tunnels."

"That's a load of kwangduk shit and you know it, Brigadier!"

"Sir, the navy has orbit-to-surface weaponry. They can use their lasers and missiles to create a diversion by attacking the front door of the cave system while we slip in the back door. The orbital weapons can also fire into any reinforcing units coming from the other Skink bases."

"I'm surprised that I have to remind you that's a *gator* fleet in orbit, *Marine*!" Carano said, exasperated. "It's got *limited* orbit-to-surface weaponry!"

"The Skinks don't know that, sir. And they haven't been subjected to fleet weapons before. We start hitting them from orbit, and they won't know what to think."

"You *think* that they don't know that we only have a gator fleet in orbit. Are you willing to bet the lives of your Marines on an uneducated guess?" Before Sturgeon could reply, Carano shouted, *"Well, I'm not!"*

Sturgeon made a short mental count to give the corps commander time to regain control, then made another proposal. "Sir, then let me do this: I'll move forward, close enough to cover the back door, and insert my platoon that has the most experience fighting Skinks. That platoon, may I remind the general, has more experience than anybody else in fighting and defeating Skinks. It also happens to be led by my most experienced and best platoon commander.

"By moving my FIST forward, I'll have enough strength on hand to accomplish an extraction if the platoon needs to pull out in a hurry. And the navy can cover a withdrawal of the entire FIST should a withdrawal become necessary."

"What about the Skink aircraft? They caught us by surprise with that one."

"Yes, sir, they did catch us by surprise. And if they use the aircraft again, we can catch them by surprise in turn when our orbital weapons start knocking them out of the sky." Sturgeon waited for Carano to think about that.

Finally, having considered it, Carano said, "All right, Brigadier, I'll think about your proposal. Do not advance your FIST until I give you word to do so. Do you understand me? Hold your position until I give you orders to advance."

"Yes, sir, I understand. Thirty-fourth FIST will remain in position until I receive your order to advance."

"Carano out." The commander of XVIII Corps broke the connection with the Marine commander.

Brigadier Sturgeon smiled to himself. The way Lieutenant General Carano had worded his response to his final proposal, it sounded like only a matter of time before he gave the go-ahead. Sturgeon called his staff together and told them to begin making plans to send Company L's third platoon into the Skink cave and tunnel system.

The Grand Master sat at state in his hall. Four Large Ones were protectively arrayed to his rear. Their swords were in their hands, ready for use if need be; light rippled along the sides of the blades, attesting to the strength and flexibility of the weapons and the skill of their makers. Selected Leaders and Masters, armed with acid guns, were concealed behind the delicately decorated draperies that hid the rock walls of the chamber, ready to defend the Grand Master from any intruder into the hall—or from a traitor in their midst. A diminutive female knelt gracefully at the Grand Master's side, having already poured and tasted the steaming beverage in his cup.

The low tables arrayed on the mat-covered floor before the Grand Master's dais had been rearranged to allow the installation of a hologram display. The display was currently blank, the low tables untenanted. But in a short time, the Grand Master's staff and subordinate commanders would be seated at the low tables, served by more of the graceful, diminutive females. And then the hologram display would light up with its glorious images, giving the Grand Master and his major subordinates a magnificent view of the deadly surprise that the Emperor's soldiers under his command would be inflicting upon the Earthmen.

The Grand Master smiled, remembering the surprise his fighter craft had already inflicted on the Earthmen. His eyes closed in near ecstasy as he mentally reviewed the images of more than half of the Earthman fighter craft being annihilated. His smile grew wider when he thought of how few of his own craft had been lost in the splendid air battle. His smile widened yet again when he thought of the way his fighter craft had ravaged a lightly armored division that had been advancing toward his bases, and the subsequent, ignominious retreat of the Earthman attack forces.

The only blemish on the day's actions had been the failure of his aircraft to report that any of the enemy fighter craft or armored vehicles had the markings of the hated Earthman Marines.

No matter. The Grand Master knew the Earthman Marines were present on this world. Sooner or later, and more likely sooner, his forces would meet with the Earthman Marines. And when they did, *that* would be a victory most savory, a victory that would assure him a position just below all the Emperors' for eternity!

CHAPTER
SEVENTEEN

"Well." Colonel Rene Raggel, commanding officer, Seventh Independent Military Police Battalion, sighed and drummed his fingers on his desk. "Looks like we're in for the duration." He was talking to Sergeant Major Krampus Steiner, his battalion sergeant major, and Senior Sergeant Puella Queege, his chief clerk and reputedly the finest pistol shot in all of Human Space.

"I suppose so, sir," Queege replied. Colonel Raggel was referring to some recent events that affected him and Queege in particular. Raggel was an infantry officer, not an MP. He'd been given the job of battalion commander by General Aguinaldo because the battalion needed a firm leader to knock it into shape after its poor performance in the war on Ravenette, where every soul in the outfit had been captured without a shot. Every soul but Queege. She had been captured later.

"Top, wipe that smile off your face."

"I can't help it, Colonel," Steiner replied. "I don't want to take this unit into a combat theater with a new CO or without my gal Queege here, so I'm just pleased as punch you two will be going with us."

Raggel's name had come up on the brigadier general's list and he had been looking forward to commanding an infantry brigade in one of the divisions being sent to Haulover with the XVIII Corps. Queege had volunteered to be transferred to the Confederation Marine Corps even though that would mean a reduction in grade. She was fully qualified, single, no dependents, not too old, in good physical condition, and General Anders Aguinaldo, when he was still Commandant of the Marine Corps, had recommended her. But then Aguinaldo had frozen all transfers until the mission on Haulover was completed, and he had designated the Seventh MPs as the XVIII Corps Military Police Command, with responsibility for law enforcement and security in Sky City, the capital of Haulover, as well as control over all the other MP units assigned to XVIII Corps.

But one thing made the freeze on Queege's reassignment a bit more palatable for her: She'd stay close to Senior Sergeant Billy Oakley, the battalion S3 Operations NCO and her coach for the recently concluded pistol match, where she'd distinguished herself as a marksman. She'd really gotten to like Oakley during their time preparing for the match. That thought made her grin, too.

"What the hell you smirking about, Senior Sergeant Annie?" Colonel Raggel groused. He knew, of course, and broke into a smile himself. In the battalion, men had started referring to Queege as "Annie" after her performance in the shooting match. That was far better than what they had been calling her before Colonel Raggel took over the battalion, "Queege Old Squeege."

"Only thing I'm sayin', Colonel, is I'm damned happy to have you two around," Steiner said. "When do we pull out?"

"Two days, Top. General Carano says we're going in first, with the Engineers, and we're to take over the law enforcement functions for Sky City. Looks like we're stuck together until this war is over."

"You know what, sir, if your promotion comes through," Queege said with a lopsided grin, "you'll be a brigadier general in command of a battalion, a military police battalion. That's gotta be rare."

"Well, I don't care, Sergeant, as long as I'm the first in history to do it. Okay, children"—Raggel stood up—"get the company commanders and the special staff in here. We've got a lot of work to do to be ready to embark in two days' time. Oh, one more thing, children. General Carano says the civilians in charge on this Haulover place might not be easy to get along with so practice your smiley faces but keep your billy clubs handy."

Senior Sergeant Puella Queege did not know if she should be pleased or upset that her transfer to the Confederation Marine Corps had been placed on hold until after the Seventh MPs' mission on Haulover was completed. She'd had to agree to go through Marine boot camp, just like any other recruit, and take a demotion from senior sergeant to private and she wanted to get started on her new career as soon as possible. She had no doubt she'd make rank back once she had been assigned to the fleet, but she felt that giving up her status in the army was worth it if that's what was required for her to become a Marine. But what really upset her and on the flight to Haulover made her consider withdrawing her request was her growing affection for Sergeant Oakley. They probably would never see each other again after she left the battalion for Marine boot camp and she did not look forward to that.

All her life Puella Queege had had trouble deciding if she was a man or a woman. She couldn't help the way her body had developed, but nobody seemed able to accept her as a woman, so she'd been a tomboy in her girlhood and later, when she matured, she tried very hard to be one of the boys and that had led her, in the all-male company of army units, to booze and short-lived liaisons with men of the moment. She'd adopted the mannerisms of a hard-bitten military man because that's what she thought she wanted to be. Until, that is, she'd come under the influence of Colonel Rene Raggel, who gave her a chance to look at life sober for a change.

Puella had never felt toward any other man the way she did Billy Oakley. She thought she had liked her former first sergeant, and she certainly felt affection now toward Colonel Raggel and Sergeant Major Steiner for the way they had allowed her to grow as a soldier and straighten herself out as a person. But that affection was based on deep mutual respect. She respected Sergeant Oakley, too, at first, but that had gradually blossomed into something else. Puella thought she might be falling in love. But she just wasn't sure, and there was no one she could really talk to about the way she felt. All her life she'd kept her emotions bottled up and that might have been one reason why she liked drinking from bottles so much. But now, sober, she found it impossible to talk to anyone else about her feelings. But she knew Oakley liked her. And she had come to realize that she might, after so many years, really have "feelings."

So on the flight to Haulover she threw herself into her work, and there was plenty of that.

As a very senior colonel and the commander of one of the first units to be dropped on Haulover, Colonel Raggel had been given a compartment aboard the troopship, CNSS *PFC Ron Tate*, and that is where he established his battalion headquarters with Puella and Sergeant Major Steiner occupying workstations there and sleeping there when that was required, which it often was. One day near the end of the flight, the three were busy working on separate projects: Colonel Raggel was drawing up a plan to cover the interface between his battalion and the civilian law enforcement authorities on Haulover; Sergeant Major Steiner was absorbed in reviewing a series of disciplinary recommendations forwarded by the battalion's company commanders; and Puella was consolidating and verifying morning reports, a tedious but essential job that required her full attention.

Colonel Raggel liked to have music playing when he was absorbed in a project and that morning he was playing softly some ancient opera, when suddenly, and very unexpectedly, Puella burst into tears.

"Queege! What the—?" Sergeant Major Steiner started to his feet, regarding Puella with absolute horror. She could not have surprised him more if she'd given birth to a giant kwangduk right there in the compartment.

"Sergeant Queege, what in the world's wrong with you?" Colonel Raggel asked. Puella was the last person in his battalion Raggel would have suspected of some undiagnosed emotional problem.

"I-I d-don't know, sir," Puella sobbed. She wiped helplessly at the tears streaming down her cheeks.

"Queege, people don't burst into tears without knowing why," Colonel Raggel said gently. He walked over to Puella and laid a comforting hand on her shoulder. "You've been working too hard, Sergeant. I apologize for—"

She began crying even harder.

Raggel looked to Sergeant Major Steiner for support. "Well, shit, Colonel," Steiner growled, "Queege's been bustin' her tail ever since she came to work for us. Stretch out on the rack over there, Queege, and get some shut-eye, you'll feel better in—"

Puella began to cry even harder, her shoulders heaving as she sobbed. "I-I don't know why—" She made an effort to control herself. "Sure," she gasped. "I'll lie down for a while. Thank you, sir. Thank you."

Colonel Raggel helped her to a vacant bunk. "Look, Sergeant, you've been through a lot," he said. "Get it all out now. We're gonna have some hard times down on Haulover and I'm going to need you by my side, the same old, sturdy workhorse Top and I have come to rely on. Even the bravest men break down, but they get a grip and bounce back. You can do it. Rest for a while and you'll be as good as new." But he knew what her problem was. Everyone in the battalion did; he just didn't know what had brought on the crying jag at that moment.

Puella nodded her thanks and climbed into the bunk. "Sir? That music? What is it?" she asked as she lay back.

"Uh? Oh, Purcell, Henry Purcell, a very, very, old opera called *Dido and Aeneas*. Do you know the story? I'll tell you all about it sometime. Right now, you get some rest, Sergeant." He was surprised Queege had paid any attention to the music. She never had before when he played the baroque pieces he liked.

"N-no, sir. Just curious. I'll be better for a while, I promise." She turned her face to the bulkhead and closed her eyes. The music had set her off. Normally she paid no attention to the colonel's music. His taste did not match hers. She didn't care a fig about this "Deedo Anneus" or the guy who'd written the opera about him. But that one time, for some reason she heard the lyrics so clearly and powerfully they registered with her like a pulse from an M3 Bowman antiaircraft gun. What they said was something men in uniform have known from time immemorial:

"Come away, fellow sailors, your anchors be weighing.
Time and tide will admit no delaying.
Take a boozy short leave of your nymphs on the shore,
And silence their mourning
With vows of returning
But never intending to visit them more.
No never . . ."

And it was at that point, "never," that she broke down because she knew that once she left the battalion she'd never see Billy Oakley again. As soon as she was off duty today she'd go find him.

"I said, 'We're here to enforce the law,' gentlemen!" Colonel Raggel strode to the head of the conference table. "General Carano gave you copies of the martial law decree. I suggest you pop them into your readers and see just what 'martial law' means. Note that President Chang-Sturdevant has declared the world of Haulóver to be in a state of emergency that requires imposition of military law to ensure the safety of our military forces and the civilian population. That is my job, gentlemen. I am, in effect, *now* the mayor of Sky City; General Carano is the supreme authority on this world. General Aguinaldo, when he lands the XXX Corps, will assume that authority in his turn."

"Goddammit!" Smelt Miner shouted. "The fucking courts here are still in session! The civil authority can still act! The laws are running their free course on Haulover! You can't impose—"

"I can, and I am doing just that. Go ahead and disagree all you want but obey my orders or I shall arrest you, sir. Now. Mr. Mullilee? As you are the Confederation's Planetary Administrator, I wish to work through you to get things up and running here. I want to meet with your chief of security immediately. I have five hundred and one men—and one woman"—he nodded at Puella—"who will be responsible for keeping the thirty-five thousand citizens of—"

"I protest!" Miner shouted, rising to his feet.

"Mr. Miner, sit down, shut your trap, or Sergeant Queege here will place you under arrest. And for the remainder of the state of emergency, however long that lasts, you will be held in close confinement." Miner blanched but sat back down. "As I was saying, we will work with you to keep things running smoothly in the city. Now, call up a map of your city on that screen. I want to show you where I've decided to set up my headquarters and where I'll billet my men. I apologize for any inconvenience caused to the people currently occupying those facilities. You gentlemen are responsible for finding alternative accommodations for those displaced, but the Confederation will pay for any damages to their property and belongings. Come on, come on, let's get to work!"

Colonel Raggel established joint patrols throughout the city, his men with the local security officers; he set up surveillance equipment and manned checkpoints and put guards on critical facilities. He ensured that his men were spliced into the communications net that kept all the military security forces around Sky City, the naval air station, and the spaceport in constant touch. Since there was little real crime in Sky City, he let the civilian courts continue to operate, under his jurisdiction. He seldom disagreed with their dispositions. He saw no reason to interfere with the civil authorities if they could keep drunken brawls and other misdemeanor infractions under control. His enforcement was strict but humane and, aside from the dusk-to-dawn curfew, affected very few of the citizens of Sky City.

CHAPTER
EIGHTEEN

AC2 Jerri Wait had been on duty in the control tower at NAS George Gay since before midnight. There'd been little air traffic at the field since a flight of Raptors had returned some hours before from a short bombing mission at targets several hundred kilometers to the south of Sky City. She was almost dozing off at her console when a huge blip appeared on one screen. "Lieutenant!" She called out to Lieutenant (jg) Klinker, the control tower OIC, who'd been staring at her unobtrusively over the rim of his coffee cup as she bent over her console.

"Yeah, Jerri?" He liked the way she had gathered her hair into a bun at the nape of her neck. He also liked the way she fit into her pants.

"There's a lot of aircraft approaching from the southwest." She straightened up, fully awake now. "I mean a *lot* of them."

"Don't worry, honey, it's probably the Eighth Air Wing's birds. Come on, Jerri, wake up, you knew they were coming."

"Yes, sir, but—"

"They're supposed to be joining us here at"—he glanced at his watch—"hmmmm. They're early." His brow furrowed. They weren't supposed to be in until after he went off duty. "How long you been watching them?"

"Couple of minutes. Yeah, sir, I thought they were the Eighth, but, Lieutenant, they're moving so *fast*. And there really are a *lot* of them."

Klinker spun around slowly and opened his own screen. "Why the hell didn't anyone tell us there's been a change to the—goddamned typical military screwup." He gasped when he saw the readouts. There were more blips than there were Raptors in the Eighth Wing and they were moving very *fast*. And they were moving in *two* waves. "Oh, shit! Call the ready room!" he shouted.

Julie Holcom, forty-two, had worked for the Inkydo Mining Conglomerate on Haulover for ten years. This seventh-day morning (no holidays for mining company employees on Haulover) she was walking to the Shamhat Building, the Inkydo office-residential complex for senior executives, and she was worried she'd be late. But it was such a beautiful morning she couldn't drive herself to hurry. She was due in Mr. Miner's office at eight o'clock sharp. She'd gotten a late start because her fiancé, Josh Hardinat, had just gotten off his shift in Mine No. 3 and she just couldn't leave him without saying a long good-bye. She felt like whistling and there was a spring in her step that morning that wasn't usually there as she trudged to work. She glanced at her watch. She wouldn't be late. It was precisely 7:48.

She was startled by a sudden *popping* noise in the sky far above her. That was followed immediately by a whooshing roar as something, a hurtling black object, left her peripheral vision so fast she almost didn't see it. The object, which could only be some type of aircraft, left in its wake a large green cloud that slowly descended. Julie smiled. Must be some kind of aerial demonstration put on by the recently arrived Confederation forces to surprise and amuse the civilians. Boy, she thought, did Mr. Miner *hate* the military! That was all right by Julie. If her boss didn't like the military, she loved them! The green cloud began descending very fast as it neared the surface, coming down like a rainy mist. A drop plopped on her shoulder. Julie Holcom had just enough time left to emit a shriek of pain and terror before a mist of the greenish fluid settled on her, soaking her hair and clothes, melting the hair and flesh on her head, then liquefying her internal organs.

* * *

Smelt Miner and his wife, Shanna, occupied a penthouse apartment on the top floor of the Shamhat Building, as befitted the most senior executive. From their patio they had a 360-degree view of the countryside surrounding Sky City. On a clear day they could see for hundreds of kilometers in every direction. Miner took his breakfast on the patio when the weather permitted. That morning the day was perfectly clear. He sat in his nightclothes, sipping his coffee and enjoying the view. Julie would be there shortly but she could wait. Shanna liked Julie. He'd let the girls gab while he finished his coffee. Yesterday he'd let Julie handle promulgating General Carano's martial law orders while he sent screaming hot messages back to Earth via the company's FTL drones. He'd burn the hide off that ridiculous Carano. He smiled. He liked a good fight, especially a one-sided fight.

Something on the horizon to the southwest suddenly caught his eye. Slowly he lowered his coffee cup. After a few moments the object, moving very fast, resolved into many black objects. "Goddamned flyboys," he hissed. All day those jockeys from NAS George Gay flitted around in their toys. The approaching aircraft, he feared, were traveling faster than the speed of sound, so there'd be more of those thunderclaps as they passed over. "Goddamned adolescent tomfoolery," he muttered. He'd sure complain to Carano about this display.

Miner suddenly stiffened and his mouth fell open in amazement. Something was seriously wrong with the picture unfolding before his eyes. There were dozens, no, hundreds of aircraft rushing at him, bright lights winking, and they seemed to be using the Shamhat Building as their focal point.

The blast that tore apart his apartment, his wife, and forty years of their marriage, hurled Smelt Miner to the floor and knocked him unconscious.

Sergeant Dowling Hamsum, gun chief of No. 3 gun in Thirty-fourth FIST's antiaircraft platoon, knew he and the five men under him would have plenty of time to smoke and joke in their position on the north edge of NAS George Gay, where the engineers had built revetments for Thirty-fourth and Twenty-sixth FISTs' Raptors. But Hamsum was the type of NCO who believed Marines never received enough training and on this seventh-day morning, as soon as his Bowman M3A1 mobile, independent rapid-fire-control plasma cannon had been sighted and activated, he put his men in a "relaxed alert status," as he called it. The men were veterans, though, and knew their jobs. They'd all seen action on Ravenette and some had been on Kingdom and Diamunde before that. He'd never served with a better crew.

"This is bullshit, chief," Corporal Jack Newman, Hamsum's gunner, muttered as he lit a cigarillo. He offered the pack to Hamsum, who politely shook his head. "Best we can expect is a ground probe and I bet we don't even see that," he said, disgustedly. "Ol' Betsy here"—he patted the M3A1 affectionately—"ain't gonna get much action this deployment, is my bet." It was well known that the Skinks did not have effective close-air-support capability. On Kingdom the M3s had been employed in ground support roles, at which they proved very effective, adding tremendous firepower to the FISTs' artillery.

"You're probably right, Jack, but one more time, I want a double-check of all systems."

"Aw, Sarge!"

"Power module and umbilicals?"

"Firm contact, power up to max!" Corporal Renny Aldridge reported. As assistant gunner he was responsible for maintaining the Bowman's two-hundred-ampere independent power module, or the "plug-in" function, as the gunners called it.

"Target acquisition module?"

"Horizontal visuals out to a thousand meters. I can see a kwangduk shit if he's out there; radar, infras, all vectors and azimuths to the horizon. Vertical, all vectors, thirty thousand meters," Corporal Newman reported.

"Good. Tracking?"

"Standstill to Mach two," Aldridge replied. "Visual resolution, twenty/twenty."

"Sighting?"

"Ready!" Corporal Frank Rushin, the assistant gunner replied. "All registrations to all horizons recorded and on the screens."

"Vid recorders?"

"All recorders go," Rushin replied. For AA gun crews, video recordings of hits in a fast-moving, target-rich environment with many batteries engaging the enemy were essential to confirm a gun's accuracy. It was the vid record more than computerized scores that confirmed a gun's accuracy and resolved conflicting claims with other gun crews. Each destroyed target earned a gun a white band around its muzzle and that's how the team got its bragging rights. On Ravenette, Hamsum's gun had earned ten white bands, the highest in the platoon but four short of "Ace" classification.

Sergeant Hamsum went down the prefiring checklist list item by item until he was sure his gun was ready to go into action. "Okay, people, stand down but keep your positions and keep an eye on those screens. We'll rotate to chow beginning at eight hours." His mission was to keep his gun manned and ready 24/7. In a pinch three well-trained men could fire the M3 and his men were well trained.

"Geez, Dowly," Corporal Newman sighed. "You know the lieutenant told us we're to monitor ground activity, *primarily*. You sure—"

"Jack, this here is an *antiaircraft* gun and as long as I'm gun chief she'll be ready to perform in both modes, 24/7, 365. That's what we're paid to do when we're in a combat zone, and that's what we're in right now. Remember those guys on Kingdom who didn't give surveillance one hundred percent?"

"Um, yeah," Newman said. The entire crew was found sprayed with acid by a Skink infiltrator. Not much was left of the men to send home.

Each Marine FIST's squadron had its own antiaircraft gun

platoon. Each platoon, commanded by a lieutenant, had a battery of three gun teams consisting of a rapid-fire M3A1 Bowman plasma gun capable of hitting any target within line of sight. The guns could be used mounted on special-purpose vehicles or in static positions, which was how Hamsum's gun was mounted. Each gun with its ancillary equipment weighed 4,300 kilos.

The M3s could fire in bursts of ten, thirty, sixty, or one hundred "rounds," as the bolts were called, or sometimes "shells," harking back to the days of gunpowder weapons; or they could fire continuous bursts of one thousand rounds. Their fire control systems could be set up to operate independently or linked to a fire control center. Since the Bowmans were performing in a ground support role at NAS Gay, their fire control systems were rigged independently so the individual gunners could select targets of opportunity as they were identified. Men and vehicles move a lot slower than aircraft and are much easier to acquire. But in an antiaircraft role such as on Ravenette or in the war on Diamunde, the guns are linked to a central fire control module that is more effective in acquiring fast movers and coordinating fires of multiple weapons. In that mode, the gunners' main responsibility is to keep the weapon firing smoothly or fixing malfunctions when they occur. But a really good gunner with excellent reflexes operating in the independent mode could, theoretically, track and shoot down an aircraft moving faster than the speed of sound.

Each gun team has a sergeant as gun chief, a corporal gunner and assistant gunner, and a crew consisting of one more corporal and two privates first class. Brigadiers Sturgeon and Sparen had integrated their AA teams and set them up on the north end of NAS Gay in such a way that if there ever was an attack from the air they could put up a devastating umbrella of plasma bolts through which any enemy would have to maneuver. If the Skinks mounted a ground attack against the station, the Bowmans could be employed as deadly antipersonnel weapons in support of the infantrymen in their ground security role.

"Well," Hamsum drawled, "just hold your pants up, Jack. My

guess is once the XXX Corps gets here and we move against the Skinks, we'll mount up and go out with the infantry. We'll get into it, never you fear. Who knows, maybe the little bastards grew wings since we kicked their asses on Kingdom." He glanced at his watch. It was 7:48, almost time for chow. He yawned and stretched.

"Hey, Sarge," Corporal Rushin called from his radar console, "I've got a large blip comin' in from the south—damn, from the north, too!"

"Ain't the Twenty-sixth Wing due in today?" Newman asked, shifting his cigarillo to the opposite side of his mouth as he spoke. For some reason a cold chill raced up his backbone. He came alert now.

"That's *not* the Twenty-sixth!" Hamsum shouted. "Get the gun on line! Call the lieutenant! We're being attacked!"

In the next few minutes, NAS George Gay turned into a seething cauldron of fire and death as the field was raked from two directions by fast-moving attack aircraft, their onboard rail guns firing a devastating hail of pellets into the Fourteenth Wing's Raptors, all neatly parked and fully exposed on the apron; the maintenance facilities and fuel dumps also went up in greasy clouds of billowing fire. But the revetments Sturgeon and Sparen had ordered built by the army engineers worked. And the Skinks did not use acid.

The damage would have been far worse that morning if the Skink preattack reconnaissance had been up-to-date. Evidently they were not sure of the exact positions the XVIII Corps had established upon their landing, which had taken place only two days before the attack. So the waves of aircraft that struck that morning were after military targets of opportunity. Unfortunately, the Raptors of the Fourteenth Wing afforded them that opportunity.

When it was all over, the six men in Hamsum's team could only gaze with unbelieving eyes at the destruction. "We got some," Newman croaked. "The vids will confirm that, but we got some, Chief, we got some. We're Aces now, Marines." But there was no elation in his voice. The other men were too awed to say anything.

Hamsum stared at his assistant. His cigarillo had long since gone out, but throughout the fight it had clung stubbornly to the corner of his mouth, where it still dangled incongruously. That's the image of the raid on NAS Gay that stuck in his mind ever after. For his own part, Newman resolved never to question his gun chief again. "Yeah," he said at last. "The goddamned lizards wised up since we kicked their asses on Kingdom."

The attack had lasted less than ten minutes.

Unnoticed by the six Marines in their gun position, huge clouds of smoke and flames hung over Sky City on the horizon. Targets in the city had been carefully marked by Skink reconnaissance. Civilian casualties were very heavy.

CHAPTER
NINETEEN

Newly promoted Lieutenant Charlie Bass, Staff Sergeant Hyakowa, and third platoon's squad leaders joined Captain Conorado at Company L's command post when Commander Usner, Thirty-fourth FIST's F3 operations officer, came to brief them on their raid into the back door of the Skink base. Conorado sat on the ground next to Usner. Three sappers stood behind them. The five Marines from third platoon formed a semicircle in front of them. The Marines all had their helmets and gloves off and their sleeves rolled up so they could see one another in the visible.

"You need to know up front," Usner said, looking each of third platoon's leaders in the eye, "that Brigadier Sturgeon selected Lima Three for this mission. You have the most experience of anybody fighting Skinks and taking them down in their own caves. He absolutely did *not* choose you because you are in the least bit expendable. Got that?" He held each one's eye until he got a nod.

"Good. Now, the defile seems to be clear at this time. At any rate, the string-of-pearls doesn't show anybody in it." He showed them the live infrared satellite feed on his UPUD's display, a clear view of a cut in the mountainside where recon had discovered a back door to the underground complex. "Unless the Skinks have done more tunneling, we know their layout. This is the section we want to go into." He projected a hologram map onto the ground in the middle of their ellipse and oriented it so that the entrance faced Bass. "Captain Conorado already has a copy of this and he'll give it to you at the end of this briefing," he told them.

"This area is beans and bandages," he said, using a pointer to indicate a large cavern with an entrance two hundred meters inside the cave, beyond a dogleg turn. The cavern was perpendicular to the tunnel and ran deep under the mountain. The map didn't show any other entrances to it.

"We're more interested in this one." He pointed out a cavern on the other side of the tunnel. Its entrance was a hundred meters beyond the first. "It's filled with canister-on-packboard arrangements that we believe are compressed air and acid for the Skink small arms. We want a sample, and we want the weapons in the chamber destroyed—that's why these sappers are going with you. On the way out, if you have time, we also want the sappers to do some serious damage in the beans-and-bandages cavern.

"You've got your chameleons, so there shouldn't be any danger of you getting spotted—the back door was unguarded on both occasions recon was there, and the tunnel in that area seems to be lightly traveled except for a few Skinks occasionally taking an outside break. And if anybody does come along, the tunnels have crates along the walls; you can duck behind them. Given what's going on right now, the Skinks all seem to be staying in."

Usner noticed the quizzical looks he got, and explained what he meant. "Right, I guess you haven't heard. The Skinks are running waves of air attacks on Sky City and the XVIII Corps positions around the city. That's why the brigadier and the Corps CG think this is a good time to hit their base. The Skinks don't know that we're here, and all their attention is focused to the south. So this should be quick and easy."

Usner looked at the Marines from third platoon. "Questions?"

"Yes, sir," Bass said. "I see four entrances to that armory. How are they secured, or are they open?"

Usner rotated the hologram. "This entrance is on a higher level." He indicated one of two entrances on the far end of the cavern. "It has a secured hatch. The others are closed with simple wooden doors with primitive locking mechanisms. A firm kick should be all it takes to open any of them. But you'll only need to open this one." He indicated the nearer entrance off the tunnel.

"Anything else?" Nobody had further questions. "In that case, do this thing." Usner nodded at Conorado, collapsed the hologram, rose to his feet, and left.

"Stand by to receive," Conorado said when the F3 was gone. He transmitted the map of the operational area of the Skink complex to Bass's and Hyakowa's comps. They'd copy the map to the squad leaders and probably the fire team leaders as well. He checked the time and said, "Be ready to move out in thirty. Take the sappers with you."

"Aye aye, sir," Bass said. He signaled the sappers to come along, then turned and led the way back to third platoon's area. Along the way, he put his helmet on. Hyakowa and the squad leaders followed suit; they knew their boss wanted to discuss the upcoming mission privately.

"This mission isn't going to be the cakewalk the F3 implied," Bass said on the platoon command circuit. "If it was, he'd send a squad along with the sappers, not a whole platoon."

"He didn't mention passive security," Hyakowa said. "Vid cameras, motion detectors, sniffers, booby traps."

"I have trouble believing that we can just slip in, watch the sappers set their charges, and slip back out without anybody noticing," Sergeant Ratliff said. "We'll probably have to fight."

"Skinks don't show up very well in infra," Sergeant Kerr added. "We learned that on Society 437. We'll need to be on the lookout for them when we go into the defile."

"So we better be ready for anything," Sergeant Kelly said.

And then they were back where Lance Corporal Groth, the platoon comm man, and Lance Corporal "Wolfman" MacIlargie, acting as platoon runner, held down the command post in the platoon area.

"Fire team leaders, gun team leaders, up," Bass ordered on the platoon circuit. He took off his helmet and raised an arm to let his sleeve slide down his arm so the corporals could see where he was.

Hyakowa transmitted the map to the squad leaders' comps while they waited.

"Take a close look, memorize this," Bass said when the fire team and gun team leaders joined them; he projected the hologram map. "Here's what we're going to do . . ."

The "back door" of the underground Skink base wasn't on the reverse slope of the mountain; it was the easternmost entrance to the tunnel system. But it was small and situated in a narrow defile. The minnies sent into the cave and tunnel complex by recon hadn't found any tunnels or chambers east of the back door.

The defile was narrow and steep-sided, with a dry seasonal streambed in its bottom. Its sides were lightly wooded; it was too steep for trees of any size to hold on, though fallen trunks showed past attempts. Lesser bushes made up the vegetative deficit. The cave entrance was barely visible seven meters above the bottom of the defile, and it would have been difficult to spot had it not been for scuff marks left by the Skinks who used it to sun themselves in the defile.

The vegetation was thin enough that a few minutes of observation by Bass and the squad leaders was enough to reassure them that no Skinks lay in wait outside the cave mouth. It took them longer to be certain that there wasn't a post just inside the cave. They used all of their detectors to search for security devices but found none. That didn't mean there weren't any well-camouflaged passive detectors; truly passive detectors only *received* signs, they didn't emit any signals.

"All right, let's do it," Lieutenant Bass said on the squad leaders' circuit.

The four Marines slid back from the top of the wall and returned to their positions with the platoon. Sergeant Kelly took his guns to the top and set them up to cover the two blaster squads and the sappers on their approach to the cave mouth.

Lance Corporal Groth stayed with them. Sergeant Kerr and second squad went downhill before crossing into the defile, and approached the cave from the downstream end. Sergeant Ratliff led first squad, Bass, and the sappers uphill, then over and downstream. Once they were in the defile, the Marines used all their senses, natural and augmented, to look for passive detectors. Lance Corporal Schultz had the point of second squad, and even he didn't spot any.

"Doesn't mean," Schultz said on the squad circuit. He didn't feel the need to finish the sentence: "that there aren't any."

Schultz was also the first man up to the cave mouth; that was the way he wanted it. He believed he was the best able to spot danger, and the fastest to take the best action when he did—he always wanted to be in the position that was most likely to meet a threat first. Everybody else in Company L believed in Schultz, and they were always more confident when he held the most dangerous position anytime they were opposed by a live opponent.

Schultz had his ears turned all the way up when he reached the cave mouth and tilted his head to listen inside. All he got back was the hollow sound of empty space. He slid his light-gatherer screen into place and lifted his head above the lip of the narrow opening, just far enough to see inside with one eye. He made out a natural tunnel that had been enlarged and roughly finished. Crates of various sizes could be seen along its length. A light glowed dimly a hundred meters or so away, barely illuminating a blank wall where the tunnel made a sharp turn to the left.

"Clear," he murmured into the squad circuit. Then he slithered up and into the tunnel. He rose to a crouch and moved in a few meters to make space for Corporal Claypoole to join him. He would have crouched to make a smaller target of himself even if the lowness of the tunnel ceiling hadn't forced him to. Schultz was a big man, and the Skinks were smaller than an average human; the Skinks had enlarged the tunnel but only to their own dimensions.

Once Claypoole was in the tunnel, Schultz began to move forward. But something didn't feel right, starting with the fact that he didn't understand why the Skinks would leave an entry to their cave system unguarded. He reached the first crate along the side of the tunnel and stepped behind it. The crate was wide enough to cover him completely, and low enough to allow him space to look over its top. He left his ears turned up all the way but raised his helmet screens to look down the tunnel with his bare eyes. He saw even less than he had with the light gatherer, and nothing seemed out of place. He tried with his infra and nothing showed up.

"What do you have, Hammer?" Claypoole's voice came over the fire team circuit.

"Nothing." Schultz lowered his light gatherer before he stepped from behind the crate and resumed his slow movement down the tunnel. But something still didn't feel right.

The crates weren't all an equal size; some were almost too high to fit inside the tunnel, some were not quite knee-high, and others were in between. There was as much as ten meters between them, and an occasional stretch where several in a row were touching or almost touching. Schultz took time to quickly examine each before he passed it; they all seemed to be properly sealed—no one was hiding in them. Neither were there any sensors on the surfaces he could see, or wires leading into the crates, so he didn't think they were booby-trapped. But the sappers might find something when they took a closer look.

There was one other thing Schultz thought curious—the surface of the walls seemed to ripple. When he was concealed behind a crate, he removed a glove and ran his bare hand over the wall. It was smooth, with ripples that seemed to run down, almost like partly melted wax. He thought the walls must have been somehow heat-treated, so they were fused. That would explain why there was no visible shoring to keep parts of the ceiling and walls from falling. He didn't know if that was important, but it was interesting, so he reported the fused walls on the squad circuit. Sergeant Kerr agreed that it could be important, and passed the word to Lieutenant Bass. Schultz stopped paying attention to the walls and watched ahead. He moved forward.

He stopped and listened where the tunnel turned, watching the light on the walls where they met at the corner. He saw his own shadow in front of him, but no other variation in the dim light. The hollow absence of sound here was subtly different from what it had been in the entry tunnel, but nothing in it indicated anybody was near. He slid his chameleon screen into place and hunched himself up until the top of his helmet grazed the tunnel roof, then eased his head far enough to see around the corner with his right eye. A light burning where the ceiling met the walls at the next turn, and another midway between the turns, provided enough light to show that the hundred-meter tunnel leg was empty. There weren't even any crates lining the walls to provide potential hiding places.

Crouched again, Schultz ran on the balls of his feet to the next turn and listened and watched as he had at the first turn before lowering himself to peek around the corner next to the floor. The tunnel now ran straight as far as he could see. A few dim lights were visible at approximate fifty-meter intervals along the tunnel, at the junction of ceiling and wall. Something indistinct on the right wall caught his eye and he slid his magnifier screen into place. He studied the blemish for a moment; it appeared to be a door frame set in the wall. He slid the magnifier back up and resumed his advance. The long corridor didn't have as many crates along its sides as the entry corridor had. Schultz walked along the side of the corridor, taking as much advantage of the cover the crates offered as possible. At least so far, that stretch of tunnel didn't feel as *wrong* as the first section had.

Schultz took it slow and easy, constantly checking everything in sight or hearing, and letting his senses move out, seeking anything out of the ordinary that he might sense but not see or hear. Claypoole followed a few meters behind, watching beyond Schultz. Lance Corporal Ymenez came behind Claypoole, watching the display of the motion detector he carried. Sergeant Kerr inserted himself between his second and first fire teams, and Corporal Doyle's third fire team brought up the squad's rear. Then came the platoon's command group and the three sappers. First squad followed. The gun squad remained outside covering the back door.

Moving as cautiously as he was, it took Schultz several minutes to cover the hundred meters to the doorway on the right. As the Force Recon minnie had seen, the door looked fairly flimsy, as though it could easily be knocked open with a firm kick. He stopped and listened to the door; nothing sounded from inside.

"Check the lock," Kerr's voice said on the squad circuit.

Schultz tried the door. It gave slightly to pressure but didn't give way. "Locked," he reported.

"Keep moving forward," Kerr ordered.

Schultz didn't give the door another look, but continued toward the next doorway, which was dimly visible on the left side of the tunnel a hundred meters beyond. While he advanced, all senses alert for danger, he puzzled over the first stretch of tunnel. Why did he feel danger there, but not in this stretch, which was even deeper into the enemy complex? He found no answers.

Lieutenant Bass signaled the sappers to put a booby trap on the door to the beans-and-bandages chamber when they reached it—he didn't want to risk anybody's coming through the door after the platoon passed and surprising them from their rear.

When they were closer to the second door, Bass said over the all-hands circuit, "Second squad, keep going when you reach the door; get to that second doorway and set security. First squad, when the sappers have the first door open, you go in with them to provide security. Acknowledge."

"First squad," Sergeant Ratliff acknowledged. "We go in as soon as the sappers open the door. Check it out and provide security."

"Second squad, we have security beyond the doorway," Sergeant Kerr said.

Bass hadn't needed to remind the men of what to do; they all remembered the plan. But it never hurt to make sure.

Both blaster squads moved into position: first squad ready to rush into the chamber beyond the door as soon as the sappers opened it, second squad in positions beyond the doorway. Bass stood, crouching out of the way of the sappers. Like the previous door, this one gave slightly to pressure. The lock was simple, and the sappers were able to get through it without making much noise. The door slid into a recess in the wall with barely a rumble.

"Three, go!" Ratliff ordered, and Corporal Dean darted through the open doorway with Lance Corporal Godenov on his heels and PFC McGinty immediately behind Godenov.

"One, go!" Corporal Dornhofer and first fire team raced in behind third. Ratliff followed them and ordered "Two, go!" as he was moving through the doorway himself.

Inside the large, roughly square cavern, Dean led his fire team to the side wall with the two entrances. The three Marines scrambled up a stairway so steep it was almost a ladder to where a balcony wrapped around the room and along the wall to the door there. He put his helmet against the door with his ears turned all the way up and listened. He heard nothing outside the door. He took the motion detector from Godenov and positioned it to seek movement in the space beyond the door. He positioned his men to cover the door; they were ready to capture or kill anybody who opened it.

Corporal Pasquin led second fire team to the door on the lower level, below third fire team's door, and checked for enemy on the far side. Satisfied that nobody was there, he set his men to cover the door.

Corporal Dornhofer set his men in the middle of the chamber, in position to cover all entrances.

There were no stalagmites or stalactites in the cavern, though blemishes on the ceiling showed where stalactites had been removed. Dean discovered that the walls of the cavern were fused and rippled in the same manner as the tunnel walls.

As Commander Usner had said, the room was filled with racks holding the canister-on-packboard arrangements that the Marines who had been with third platoon on Society 437 or Kingdom well recognized. The weapons were stored on racks stacked as high as the Marines' chests, with three shelves of empty racks above them, awaiting more weapons. The racks were constructed of wood, with some sort of twine binding them together. Along the wall of the chamber near the lower door were stacks of lumber the same sizes as the risers and shelves that held the weapons and rolls of twine. It looked to Bass as though there was enough wood and twine to double the height of the existing racks.

Bass shook one of the racks and found it surprisingly stable. He climbed to the top of it and stood to look around the chamber. One thing he wanted to do was estimate how many weapons were in the room. First he counted the racks, then multiplied that by the average number of filled shelves in the nearby racks, and that by the average of weapons per shelf. He estimated the one cavern held enough of the weapons to arm two units the size of army brigades, with enough open shelves and parts for more shelves to hold the weapons for two full divisions.

How many Skinks are *there in this complex?* he wondered.

The three sappers hurried about, deciding where to place their charges to do the greatest damage; thermal charges that would burst in great balls of burning plasma, calculated to melt acid-containing canisters and explode canisters of compressed air. The sappers were careful to place their charges where they'd have the best chance of making the exploding canisters cause other canisters, beyond the reach of the plasma heat, to explode. Bass dropped off the racks and grabbed a packboard. While he was adjusting the straps to give him room to shrug into it, he had Lance Corporal MacIlargie also take a packboard. He didn't have MacIlargie try to wear the weapon.

On the all-hands circuit, Bass asked, "Has anybody seen the hose and nozzles for these things?" He swore when nobody had; the tank-and-packboard arrangement couldn't be used without the nozzle and the hose that connected it to the canisters. He didn't think just the tanks would be of much intelligence value.

It took the three sappers almost ten minutes to place their charges and set them to go off in twenty minutes. Then Bass ordered the platoon to withdraw from the chamber as far as the beans-and-bandages chamber, where the sappers could set their remaining charges.

None of the Marines noticed the tiny eye of a miniature camera tucked away in a corner of the ceiling.

CHAPTER
TWENTY

The Masters and Junior Masters who were supposed to be supervising the Leaders in the security chamber were riveted to the visuals coming back from the aircraft raiding the Earthman spaceport, military airfield, and city; they neglected to notice that the Leaders they were supervising were also glued to the visuals of the attacks, instead of to the monitors that showed various unguarded spaces within the tunnel and cavern complex. Even the Senior Master overseeing the Masters and Junior Masters was enthralled by the devastation being wrought on the Earthmen and their constructs. The Masters cheered every time a grounded Earthman aircraft was pulverized by a bolt from a rail gun, a building disintegrated after a burst of rail gun pellets, or Earthmen writhed on the ground in their death agonies after being sprayed by the acid from the aircrafts' missiles. The Leaders refrained from cheering—they knew better than to call their officers' attention to the fact that they were watching the action instead of their assigned monitors.

So it happened that by the time a Leader looked at his monitor and saw a door to the weapons storage chamber—to which he was supposed to be devoting his attention—as it closed, the door was closing behind the exiting Marines. The Leader, of course, didn't know that. He only knew that a door to a chamber under his watch was closing and that nobody was supposed to be there. With great trepidation, he got the attention of the Junior Master who was his supervisor and told him what he'd just seen.

Furious at the Leader's negligence, the Junior Master struck him across the head, hard enough to break the skin and draw blood. Harshly, the Junior Master demanded that the Leader replay what he had observed. The Junior Master watched while the door slid open for a short time, then closed again, seemingly on its own, as no one had entered or left the room while the door was open. Cursing at the Leader's stupidity and incompetence, the Junior Master ordered the Leader to play back in time and soon found the door opening and closing once more without anybody coming or going.

The Junior Master blinked at that. He played the image forward at double normal speed, and saw something that made his throat constrict and his gill covers tighten—one of the empty shelves suddenly sagged, as though an unseen weight sat on it. A couple of moments later, the shelf righted itself. This time, when the door opened and closed the second time, he saw something he hadn't seen before; it was just a flash and only partial, but he saw the corner of a packboard go through the doorway. Just a corner, as though something unseen was blocking his view. And he knew.

The Earthman Marines had penetrated the complex. He didn't think of the consequences to himself for his failure to properly supervise this Leader; proper supervision would have told him immediately that something was amiss. He called for the Senior Master in command of the security observation room. It was only as he was playing back the image for the Senior Master that the Junior Master realized that he was in as much trouble for dereliction as was the Leader under his supervision. It was no consolation to him when he realized that the Senior Master was in just as much jeopardy.

The Senior Master knew right away the punishment likely to be meted out to all in the observation room, and took immediate action. He swiftly drew his sword and chopped at the Leader's neck with enough force to nearly sever it. Then he spun at the Junior Master and, with one clean slice, disemboweled him. He copied the bubble that had recorded the opening and closings of the door onto his reader, and raced from the room without taking time to assign a Master to take charge, leaving everyone in the room wondering what had happened. By the time one of the Masters played back the moving images showing the visit of the invisible Earthman Marines, the Senior Master was in the Grand Master's hall, prostrate before his lord, showing him the image and explaining its meaning.

The Grand Master took a few seconds to order one of his Large One guards to decapitate the Senior Master, before he ordered an attendant Over Master to make haste with as large a force as he could quickly gather to the unguarded entrance to the complex.

A hundred meters back down the tunnel, second squad again took position to cover the platoon from deeper inside the Skink complex. The sappers opened the door to the beans-and-bandages cavern even more quickly than they had the weapons chamber. First squad entered and gave the chamber a quick going over to make sure it was unoccupied by enemy before the sappers went in to set their charges. While the sappers were doing their work of emplacing plasma charges, Lieutenant Bass had first squad break open a few crates and grab samples of their contents. They didn't have orders to take samples, but he thought S2 or G2 might learn something from them. He also thought, if they had enough time, that he'd have his men take samples from the crates in the leg of the tunnel leading outside.

Just as they'd had point coming into the Skink complex, second squad's third fire team would have rear point on their egress. Lance Corporal Schultz wouldn't have had it any other way. The three Marines took positions where they could guard the platoon's rear while first squad and the sappers were inside the beans-and-bandages cavern.

Corporal Claypoole was behind a crate, looking over it, with his ears turned up all the way, listening for anything he couldn't see. To his rear he heard the faint sounds that first squad and the sappers made returning to the tunnel. At the same time, he heard Schultz say into the fire team circuit, "Coming."

"I didn't tell you to come," Claypoole said an instant before he realized Schultz meant Skinks were coming. He switched to the squad command circuit. "The Hammer says the bad guys are coming," he said.

"Stand by," Sergeant Kerr replied. Seconds later Kerr was back on the squad circuit. "Second squad, listen up. Schultz says someone is coming. As soon as first squad reaches the dogleg, we're bugging out of here. Wait for the word."

The Marines of second squad waited for a tense minute while the rest of the platoon reached the turn and got around it.

"Second squad, on the double!" Kerr ordered.

"Go!" Claypoole ordered, and took a last look beyond Schultz. He didn't see anything before he twisted around and raced from shelter behind the crate. He heard Schultz coming with staggered steps—the big man kept twisting around to look to his rear.

Claypoole was only a few strides away from the corner when he heard the *crack-sizzle* of Schultz's blaster, immediately followed by the high-pitched whine of a rail gun, and saw bits of the wall he was running toward shatter and fly about with razor-sharp edges. At the same time he heard a distant explosion somewhere beyond the corner.

Claypoole dove to the floor and twisted about, slamming his infra screen into place. "Hammer, you okay?" he shouted into the fire team circuit. Schultz didn't answer with words, but instead with three spaced plasma bolts from his blaster. Claypoole's infra showed him that Schultz was prone, firing from behind a crate on the other side of the tunnel. At Schultz's firing, three red blotches almost three hundred meters distant flashed into a brilliance that blanked out Claypoole's infra screen for a moment. When he could see again, he didn't see anybody at the far end of the tunnel where Schultz had flared the three Skinks.

"Hammer, pull back," he ordered. "I've got you covered."

Schultz fired three more quick bolts, trying to angle them to ricochet around the far corner, then jumped up and bolted past Claypoole's position. "Rock, go," he shouted when he took a fresh position past Lance Corporal Ymenez.

Claypoole got up and sped past Ymenez and Schultz to the corner and dropped down where he could shoot down the length of the tunnel. "Ymenez, to me!" he ordered, and held his fire while Ymenez ran past Schultz, and then around the corner.

Schultz, meanwhile, kept a steady stream of spaced bolts going to prevent the Skinks' turning the corner. On Claypoole's command, he headed to his fire team leader's position and muscled him out of the way so he could continue keeping the Skinks away.

With both of his men out of the tunnel, Claypoole took the time to ask his squad leader about the explosion he'd heard when Schultz opened fire on the Skinks.

When first squad and the sappers had reached the dogleg of the tunnel, Lieutenant Bass ordered all but one fire team to wait for second squad to clear the long tunnel.

"Rabbit," he ordered, "send one fire team to get some samples from the crates in that tunnel. I'd like to see what the Skinks are storing there."

"Aye aye," Sergeant Ratliff had said. "Dean, go see what's in those crates. Get some samples for the boss."

"You got it, Rabbit." Dean switched to the fire team circuit. "Third team, we're going to collect some samples for the boss. Let's go get them."

Lance Corporal Godenov led the way around the corner, followed by Dean, with PFC McGinty bringing up the rear.

"Go halfway, Izzy," Dean had said. "Find a bunch together that look alike, then open one in the middle."

"Will do," Godenov had said back. He trotted down the tunnel toward the exit. Thirty meters down he found a line of six low crates stacked two high and stopped. He'd slung his blaster and drew his knife. He pounded the blade into a seam on the middle top crate and began levering the lid up. *"Oh, shit,"* he murmured when he heard a faint click from the lid. He let go of his knife and dove away.

An explosion caught Godenov and drove him into a corner where another large crate met the opposite wall. Three sharp splinters of wood, one almost the size of a man's wrist, shot into him; the point of one went all the way through his shoulder and imbedded itself in the crate he was against. Dean wasn't as close, so the blast only tumbled him backward—but two large splinters also found him and sunk in deeply. McGinty was far enough away that he was only knocked down by the force of the explosion.

"Dean, report!" Ratliff shouted into the squad circuit. When Dean didn't answer, he ordered, "Third fire team, sound off!"

"I-I'm all right," McGinty answered a moment later—he sounded dazed.

"Damn, damn—*damn!*" Ratliff swore. Then to Bass, who was demanding to know what was happening, he said, "I think I've got two men down. I'm on my way to check it out."

"Let me know as soon as you find out." Bass sent Lance Corporal MacIlargie to assist with the casualties.

"Will do." By then Ratliff had reached McGinty, who insisted he was all right. A few meters beyond him, he found Dean unconscious. Dean's uniform was trying to stanch the bleeding but was having trouble making a proper seal around the splinters. "I need a stasis bag," Ratliff said on the platoon command circuit. Then he reached Godenov and couldn't tell whether he was alive or not, because his bleeding had almost stopped, and Ratliff could see that Godenov's uniform hadn't made a seal around the splinters. "Make that *two* stasis bags. On the double!" To Bass he reported, "It looks like Izzy was opening a crate, but it was booby-trapped and went off on him. He might be dead; I'm not sure."

Just then a tossed stasis bag landed next to him. He flipped it open, then as gently as he could, drew the splinter in Godenov's shoulder out of the crate and put the lance corporal in the stasis bag. By then MacIlargie and McGinty had put Dean in another stasis bag.

"First squad," Bass ordered, "take your casualties and get out of here. Join guns on the ridge. Sappers, go with them. Second squad, pull back to the next corner."

"First fire team, pull back to the next bend," Sergeant Kerr ordered. "On the double. Third fire team, go when they're halfway there." Corporal Dornhofer and his men sprinted. Corporal Doyle got his men ready to move out. Even as his first fire team began moving, Kerr ran back up the tunnel to where Corporal Claypoole and his men were holding the corner. Using his infra screen, Kerr found PFC Ymenez kneeling a few meters from the corner, and Lance Corporal Schultz prone at the corner, aiming his blaster down its length. Claypoole was on hands and knees, watching over Schultz's shoulders.

"Move," Kerr said, grasping Claypoole's shoulder and pulling him back. With the corporal out of the way, Kerr leaned low over Schultz to look down the tunnel himself. "What have you seen?" he asked on the fire team circuit.

"Got four," Schultz answered. "Maybe five."

"Rock?" Kerr said, asking Claypoole to amplify Schultz's answer.

"The Hammer got at least one when they first showed up, then three more when they shot the rail gun. He's tried to ricochet bolts around the corner. I saw a flash of light, so he probably got another that we couldn't see."

Schultz fired two more plasma bolts while Claypoole was talking.

Kerr grunted at the report. "Rock, take Ymenez and join the rest of the squad. Hammer and I will cover you. Go."

Claypoole hesitated, but only for a second. "Aye aye." He turned and called to Ymenez, "Let's go. Double time." They sprinted, leaving Kerr and Schultz behind.

"Hold your fire, Hammer," Kerr said when they were gone. "I want to see how long it takes them to start coming again."

Schultz gave a disgusted snort but stopped firing.

While they waited for the Skinks to show themselves again, Kerr reported to Lieutenant Bass what he was doing.

"I'm moving the rest of your squad out of the tunnel now," Bass said. "If the Skinks aren't coming in two minutes, put some more fire downrange and pull out. Even if they do show, pull out in two minutes. Understood?"

"Pull out in two minutes, understood." Kerr checked the time.

A minute and a half later, the door to the chamber with the weapons slid open and a Skink tentatively poked his head out. Schultz fired at the head and the Skink flared up in the doorway. More light flashed from inside the chamber. Kerr thought another Skink had been too close to the looker and was killed by the heat of the first one's flame.

"Try to put a couple more in there, then let's get out of here," Kerr told Schultz.

Schultz rapid-fired six bolts at the doorway. One missed, hitting the wall just beyond the doorway, and pinballed down the length of the tunnel, but the others hit the far edge of the doorway, and at least two of them ricocheted into the cavern and hit Skinks. The two Marines got up and sprinted away. Just after they turned the corner to the last straightaway, muffled by walls, distance, and the corners, they heard the *cracks* of the plasma charges going off in the weapons cavern; some of the echoes may have been the hoped for secondary explosions. They were past the booby-trapped crate that had severely wounded Dean and maybe killed Godenov when they heard the charges in the beans-and-bandages chamber go off.

The Great Master who was the commander of the Over Master who went to kill the Earthman Marines who had penetrated the underground complex ground his teeth when he received the Over Master's first report. It was not a good report, but a report of pending failure. Duty and honor bound him to inform the Grand Master. Summoning his prime aides to accompany him, the Great Master headed for the Grand Master's hall; he devised a plan as he went.

In the Grand Master's hall, the Great Master prostrated himself and waited to be recognized. The Grand Master looked at him with some curiosity; it was uncommon for a Great Master to enter the Grand Master's presence without being summoned—or without having something of import to say. The Grand Master rasped a command and the Great Master rose from his prostration and sat back on his ankles. At another rasped command, the Great Master reported that the company sent to the side entrance had encountered Earthman Marines, but the Earthman Marines were somehow ready for them when they arrived and used their forever guns to great effect, killing a score or more of the Leaders and Fighters who exposed themselves to the hated Earthman Marines. They had even destroyed a light-fraction weapon. So far as the Over Master could tell, the Earthman Marines had suffered no casualties yet. Worse, they managed to destroy a weapons depository, and kill half the company that had gone after them. The food chamber was of too little import for him to mention. The remaining Fighters, and many of the Leaders, even some of the Junior Masters, were afraid to continue their pursuit of the Earthman Marines. On the orders of the Over Master, the Master commanding the company and his remaining Junior Masters were methodically killing all the cowards who refused to continue the pursuit.

Furious, the Grand Master roared out curses improper for so exalted a personage to speak, then demanded what the Great Master intended to do to rectify the failure.

The Great Master said that, with the Grand Master's permission, he was going to send a battalion outside the complex to annihilate the Earthman Marines when they attempted to exit the complex.

The Grand Master considered the proposed action for a brief moment, then nodded curtly, and rasped a warning that the Great Master's head might be forfeit if his plan failed.

The Great Master bowed low, showing that his neck was ready for the swordsman should his death be desired. At another rasped command, he rose and hurried back to his headquarters, giving orders to his prime aides as he went. But when the battalion, under the command of a different Over Master, reached the back door of the cave complex, the Earthman Marines had already left.

However, the clumsy Earthmen had left an easily followed trail.

CHAPTER
TWENTY-ONE

Third platoon made it back to the company area without further incident—the Marines all considered losing two of their own to be more than incident enough. Lieutenant Bass had radioed ahead with a preliminary report, so Commander Usner and the FIST F2 intelligence officer, Commander Daana, were waiting in the company command post to debrief the platoon's leaders. A Dragon was also there and took the casualties away as soon as they were loaded onto it.

"I don't know if they had a way of knowing we were there, or if we encountered a routine patrol," Bass said after he turned the samples over to Daana, "but they went into action so fast, they must have been expecting something." He then gave his estimate of how much was in the two caverns.

Bass, Sergeant Kerr, and Corporal Claypoole gave their accounts of the action in the tunnel—even Daana knew better than to attempt to get a detailed story out of Lance Corporal Schultz, so instead of continuing to the CP for the debriefing, Schultz had been allowed to stay with the rest of the platoon when it took its position on the perimeter. Bass, Sergeant Ratliff, PFC McGinty, and Lance Corporal MacIlargie told about the booby-trapped crate and the condition of the casualties when they were found.

"You're going to have to wait a bit for replacements," Usner told Bass. "It's too hazardous to try to integrate somebody new in the platoon while the FIST is in this exposed position."

"Thank you, sir," Bass replied. "I'd rather not get somebody new right now anyway. And I only need one replacement; I've been carrying an extra man since my last two men got out of the hospital back at Camp Ellis."

Usner cocked an eyebrow but didn't comment other than to say, "I'll inform Captain Shadeh that you only need one replacement." Shadeh was the FIST F1, personnel officer.

Satisfied with the debriefing, Usner said to Captain Conorado, "Help me get the samples loaded onto my Dragon, and Daana and I will get out of your hair."

They had just started loading the samples onto the Dragon when the forest's quiet was shattered by multiple *crack-sizzles* and the high-pitched whine of Skink rail guns.

Corporal Wilson, of first platoon, on the perimeter near where third platoon had come through on their return, was the first to see the pursuing Skinks.

"Heads up," he said onto the squad circuit. "Bad guys coming." As he switched to the platoon command circuit, he did a quick count of the Skinks he could see. "Bad company," he reported. "At least a platoon in three columns. Point is within one hundred meters. I see two rail guns."

Ensign Antoni, the commander of first platoon, answered Wilson's transmission immediately. "On my command, take out that gun." He switched to the platoon's all-hands circuit and said, "Bad guys, range one hundred. On my command, *fire*!"

"Get the rail gun!" Wilson shouted on his fire team circuit. His first bolt took out the Skink carrying the weapon; before he could aim at one of the gun's other crew members, his men took them out. A Skink who looked like a sergeant was yelling at others to get to the gun and put it in action. He shot the sergeant, then switched his aim to the rail gun itself and put several bolts into it in an attempt to disable it. In his concentration on the rail gun he didn't notice the whine of a second rail gun firing until its slugs ripped into the ground next to him. He yelped and rolled away—just in time to be missed by another burst. The incredibly fast slugs plowed into the ground where he'd been firing.

"Shoot and move!" Wilson yelled to his men. Putting action to words, he fired a bolt at another Skink and rolled without waiting to see if he'd hit his target.

"Someone find that rail gun and kill it!" Staff Sergeant Da-Costa yelled over the all-hands circuit. The Skinks might not be able to see the Marines in their chameleons but they could certainly see where their plasma bolts were coming from.

The other Skinks were maneuvering, trying to get within the fifty-meter range of their acid guns. Here and there and the other place, brilliant flashes flared as Skinks were hit, but more and more of them poured into the area, and by now second platoon, on the left side of the perimeter, was also fully engaged with the enemy. *Crack-sizzles* from farther away indicated that Kilo Company was also engaging the Skinks.

Third platoon, less Lieutenant Bass and the other five who had gone to the company command post for the debriefing, was holding down Thirty-fourth FIST's right flank. They didn't see any Skinks; neither did their motion detectors or other sensors pick up signs of the enemy to their front.

"That doesn't mean they aren't there, people," said Staff Sergeant Hyakowa, in command of the platoon in Bass's absence. "When we have them, be ready for volley fire."

"Allah's pointed teeth!" Sergeant Ratliff shouted. Like the others in the company CP, and those leaving it, he had his screens up and his voice carried through the air. He followed his shout with a shot from his blaster, and the light from a Skink vaporizing showed everybody nearby where to look—a mass of Skinks was racing toward them through the thin forest, getting close to the range of their acid guns.

"On line!" Captain Conorado shouted, taking command of the small group around the CP. He only had ten Marines with blasters. Another eight, including himself and the company's medical corpsmen, were armed with hand blasters.

Make that *ten* with sidearms.

"Where do you want us?" Commander Usner shouted.

"There!" Conorado pointed, and Usner and Commander Daana sped to the right end of the line, where they hit the dirt and began putting out aimed shots with their hand blasters.

The command Dragon that had brought Usner and Daana to Company L's CP was lightly armed but it maneuvered to bring its gun on the advancing Skinks as well. Its fire was effective, as a virtual wall of fire flared up along part of the line facing the Marines.

"Shoot and move, shoot and move!" Conorado shouted. The Skinks hadn't brought a rail gun into action against the CP yet, but he could hear at least two firing at other parts of the company's lines, so he knew they had some with them.

He looked at the display on his UPUD and saw the entire company was engaged in the fight. But the Skinks' heat signature was so faint he could barely make out where they were—he had no idea how large the force was that was attacking Company L, or how much of the rest of Thirty-fourth FIST was fighting.

"Kill those bastards!" Corporal Claypoole yelled into the fire team circuit. "Kill them, kill them, *kill them*!" Joe Dean was a friend of his, a damn good friend, a better friend than any of the other friends he'd lost to enemy fire over the years he'd been a Marine. And now the Skinks had seriously wounded him, maybe killed him. Izzy Godenov was also a friend, and he was probably dead. Claypoole wanted revenge; he wanted to kill every Skink in existence. But as furious as he was about the wounding of those two men, his fire was disciplined. He picked his targets and put every bolt into a Skink. The brilliant flashes of dying Skinks flaring up gladdened his heart.

When he finally saw movement through the trees that told him Skinks were passing third platoon's front, Staff Sergeant Hyakowa decided to engage them immediately even though they weren't coming toward the platoon.

"Third platoon," he said on the all-hands circuit, "two hundred meters, grazing volley fire. *Fire!*" He only had fourteen men with blasters available, what amounted to a reinforced squad, and neither of his guns was sited where it could put en-filading fire into the enemy. But the Skinks were two hundred meters distant and didn't have any rail guns so far as he could tell. When Sergeant Kelly told him he was moving the gun squad into position to support the rest of the platoon, Hyakowa told him how he wanted them used.

"First gun, traversing fire left to right," Kelly ordered a moment later. "Second gun, traversing fire right to left. Fire!"

"Squads, volley fire. *Fire!*" Hyakowa commanded. "Fire! Fire!"

With each command to fire, fourteen plasma bolts went downrange, where they struck the ground on a ragged line two hundred meters distant. Some of the bolts stuck and smoldered where they hit, while others fragmented and sent small streamers in different directions. But most ricocheted off the ground and continued in the same direction at no more than knee height. Many of the bolts—and even fragmented streamers—hit Skinks, even where the Skinks were out of sight of the Marines.

Reacting to commands from their officers, some of the passing Skinks dropped to the ground and began crawling toward the Marines, trying to stay below their lines of fire until they were close enough to engage with their own weapons. The rest retired deeper into the forest and continued their eastward movement.

Third platoon kept up its volley fire and traversing fire, adjusting range as needed to keep their plasma bolts striking the ground in front of the crawling Skinks and ricocheting into them.

"*Cease fire,* cease fire!" Captain Conorado shouted. In seconds, the *crack-sizzle* from the blasters and hand blasters of Company L's command post stopped; even Corporal Claypoole stopped when he had no more visible targets. "Did we get them all?" Conorado asked. "Does anybody see any more of them out there?" When nobody admitted to seeing any Skinks remaining to their front, he called for a casualty report. Nobody was injured;

the Skinks had only been able to get off a few ineffective spurts
from their acid guns before being beaten off. He turned his attention to his UPUD. *Damn, but the Skinks are hard to spot in the infra!* he thought. Conorado had no idea whether his CP was about
to get hit again. At least they seemed to have killed all the attackers without taking any casualties of their own.

"Wild Bill," Conorado ordered to his UAV team leader, "get
your birds in the air. I want to know if anybody else is coming
at us, and then let me know what the rest of the company is facing. Particularly third platoon on the right flank."

"Aye aye, Skipper," Sergeant Flett replied. He got up from
his fighting position and ran to the UAV control module. Corporal MacLeash was right behind him. They quickly got their
drones into the air and headed into the woods to the north. They
knew that, aside from needing to know if they had to prepare
for another attack, Conorado had to know if he could release
Lieutenant Bass and his five men to return to third platoon—
and how badly they were needed.

It only took a few minutes for the two UAVs, disguised as
something that vaguely resembled an archaeopteryx, to discover a hundred or so Skinks north of them and heading south,
almost straight at the company CP. And that company of Skinks
had at least one rail gun. Flett reported the discovery to Conorado, who told him to leave MacLeash watching over the approaching Skinks, and go himself to check on third platoon.

Conorado set about making better preparations for fighting
off the second wave of Skinks.

Two or three or five Skinks lit up with every volley the
shrunken third platoon fired. More Skinks turned to vapor with
every traverse of the guns. It appeared that none of the crawling Skinks would survive long enough to use their acid guns.

PFC Ymenez's fire was more ragged than Schultz's—or anybody else's in the platoon. He hadn't had as much practice at
volley fire. But he was close with every shot, and some of his
bolts flared Skinks. Enough that he felt queasy: His only other

combat experience was against the Coalition forces on
Ravenette. And there he'd shot at men who were shooting back.
But this, this was like shooting unarmed people, and that
simply felt wrong. Sure, he'd heard about the Skinks; how they
always fought to the death without any of them ever giving up,
that they never took prisoners—except that they captured Lieutenant Bass and turned him into a mindless slave. And he'd
heard about their weapons: the horrifying acid guns that ate
people whole and turned them to mush, their rail guns that shot
out pellets at 0.2c and utterly destroyed everything they hit.

But he hadn't seen the Skinks in action, hadn't faced their
weapons. Except for the brief action in the tunnel, in which he
hadn't done any shooting or even seen the Skinks for himself,
this was his first combat against them. And they weren't shooting back, they were simply flashing into vapor every time they
got hit. Still, even though it felt somehow *wrong,* he kept shooting and killing Skinks.

Most of the other Marines in the rump platoon *had* faced
Skinks before and had no compunction about shooting them
before they could shoot back.

"The skipper wants the range and azimuth on that rail gun,"
Corporal Escarpo said to Corporal MacLeash. "And he wants
the azimuth from the Dragon."

MacLeash whistled. "I'll see what I can do," he said.

"Yeah, the skipper said you might say that. He said to just
do it."

"Just do it. Right." MacLeash was maneuvering his false
gliding animal over the Skinks in the trees, trying to locate the
position of the rail gun Sergeant Flett had seen when the UAVs
first went into the forest and found the approaching Skinks. He
found it quickly enough and marked it on his monitor, then
worked an azimuth and the range from the Dragon to the rail
gun, and gave the numbers to Escarpo, who radioed them to
Captain Conorado.

"Have him spot for the Dragon," Conorado said. He gave the

azimuth and range to the Dragon commander and told him to use traversing and searching fire on the target—the Skinks weren't yet visible from the Marine CP. "Birdie Two will adjust," he finished.

"Aye aye," the Dragon commander replied. "Comm with Birdie Two already established."

Conorado signed off and went to the UAV control center to observe.

The Dragon opened fire. It may have been lightly armed for a Dragon, but its gun was more powerful than any of the personal weapons in the command post. The stream of plasma bolts burned their way through the foliage, seared off twigs and small branches, set fire to a few trees—and finally bored a hole through to where the Skinks carrying the rail gun were.

But the Skinks were advancing steadily and had already moved on from the Dragon's initial aiming point. MacLeash watched the Skinks moving and called corrections to the Dragon. Again, by the time the Dragon adjusted its fire and burned a hole through the forest, the Skink rail gun was no longer where the Dragon was shooting, but the bolts hit closer—and random bolts flared some Skinks. Once more, and yet again, MacLeash corrected the Dragon's fire, and still the Dragon missed.

But then the Skinks got almost in sight of the CP and the rail gun crew stopped to set up their weapon. MacLeash gave the Dragon the new numbers and its gun's next burst was on target, flaring the Skink crewmen just as they were opening fire.

"Hit it again," Conorado ordered. "Destroy that gun."

It took three long bursts but the rail gun was permanently silenced, along with a dozen Skinks.

Then a second rail gun, which hadn't been spotted by the UAVs, opened fire on the command post.

Some of the Skinks attacking third platoon finally worked their way close enough to use their acid guns and began spraying at the thin line of Marines. But the Marines shifted their positions after every shot so none of the greenish fluid struck close enough to hit. Every time a Skink shot he exposed his position and most were quickly flared before they could advance or fire again. Staff Sergeant Hyakowa canceled the volley fire and allowed the Marines to select targets and fire when ready.

Lance Corporal Schultz's fire was methodical, and he never missed. Now that the Skinks were shooting back, Ymenez stopped worrying that something was wrong about shooting at them and set to with a vengeance, readily killing every one he could. After all, a live, shooting Skink threatened the lives of him and his fellow Marines.

The firefight didn't last long after the few surviving Skinks had closed enough to return fire. And then there weren't *any* surviving Skinks facing third platoon.

When Thirty-fourth FIST had reached its location, the Marines expected to move out again on short order. They had dug no fighting holes, built no berms. All they had for defensive works was tree trunks and ripples in the ground. The Skink rail gun opened fire with a long burst at the command Dragon that had killed the other rail gun, pulverizing it and turning its crew into a rapidly dispersing cloud of red blood, flesh, and bone. Then it set to traversing fire, grazing fire that was low enough to kill any Marine not prone in a ripple in the ground and that moved side to side fast enough to keep any of them from rising up and taking more than one hastily aimed shot at the Skinks. Blood sprayed on its first traverse. The Marines in the Company L command post were fully pinned down, held in place until the Skinks with the acid guns could get within range of their weapons.

Sergeant Kerr, near the left flank of the thin defensive line, hugged the ground. Trembles shook his body and palsied his hands. His mind worked so rapidly that his thoughts became jumbled, almost chaotic. But his thoughts were of how to kill that rail gun before it killed Marines.

He lay with the right side of his helmet on the ground and examined the lay of the land to his left. It was almost flat, but almost isn't completely. Years of experience had taught him how to find low places and he saw a path that would take him beyond the rail gun's traverse. Keeping his helmet in contact with the ground he turned his head and looked to his right. He saw Corporal Claypoole, his helmet screens up, a few meters away.

"Rock, with me!" Kerr ordered. He began slithering to his left. He didn't look back; he knew that Claypoole would follow exactly in his path.

It took uncomfortably long for Kerr and Claypoole to low-crawl forty meters, long enough for the Skink infantry to get close enough to use their acid guns, but the two Marines were finally outside the area along which the Skink rail gun was firing. They raised their heads just enough to allow them to look into the woods from inches above the ground.

"This way," Kerr said, and he began crawling again. To their right the two Marines heard the flashing of Skinks and an occasional scream as a Marine was hit by streamers of acid.

Then the ground dropped and they were able to rise to hands and knees and make better time. When they finally stopped and looked over the edge of the shallow defile, they saw the Skink rail gun barely more than fifty meters away. It was tripod-mounted and had a crew of four: a gunner, a loader, a Skink who acted like a sergeant, and another whose job was probably ammunition carrier, but who now knelt ready with an acid gun in his hands.

Kerr touched helmets with Claypoole. "You get the gunner first, and I'll take out the sergeant. Then you disable the gun while I get the rest of the crew. Got it?" Claypoole said he did. "On three. One, two, three!"

Both Marines fired on the command, and the two Skinks they shot at flared up in all-consuming flame. Claypoole switched his aim to the gun and fired rapid bolts into it, concentrating on what he thought was the receiver, where pellets were taken from the ammunition drum into the weapon to be flung into the barrel and accelerated to 20 percent of the speed of light. Kerr flashed the other two crew members, then began looking beyond the gun for more Skinks—he needed to get them before any could begin spraying acid at Claypoole.

Bolt after bolt from Claypoole's blaster slammed into the rail gun, heating it to red, and then white, until the metal finally softened and began to sag. Claypoole kept firing at it until a gob of molten metal dropped off the gun.

"Got it," he said.

"Let's roll up their flank," Kerr said.

"Right. Sure thing. Are you fucking crazy?"

But Kerr was already on his feet, moving forward. Claypoole had little choice but to get up and advance with Kerr, to look for targets while hoping he took all of them before they could zero in on him.

Kerr's helmet comm couldn't transmit on the company command circuit but it could on the platoon circuit, so he switched to it and said, "Lima Three, the rail gun is dead. Friendlies are crossing your front. Make sure you don't shoot us!"

Lieutenant Bass got the message and immediately passed it on to Captain Conorado, who relayed it to the rest of the command post group. With the rail gun out of action, the defenders were able to rise up enough to take aimed shots at the Skinks.

The firefight at the Company L CP was soon over. And then it was time for the butcher's bill.

The Skinks' only previous contact with the Marines on Haulover was the Force Recon unit that had been on the planet for the past several months. Their only other ground contact with the "Earthmen" was when their air attacked the XVIII Corps and drove it back with heavy losses. When they discovered a small Marine unit inside one of their subterranean bases, they thought it was something similar to the Force Recon elements they'd already fought. So the Skink battalion that went in pursuit of third platoon was absolutely unprepared to run into the infantry battalion of a FIST.

Thanks to the alertness of Corporal Wilson of Company L's

first platoon, the Marines were able to begin fighting the Skinks well before the Skinks could begin to fight back. As a result, the Skinks were wiped out almost completely. The only casualties the Marines suffered were among the men in the Company L command post, which a Skink company had managed to outflank.

The entire three-man crew of the command Dragon was killed when the second rail gun opened up on it.

Commander Usner, Thirty-fourth FIST's longtime operations officer, was killed when a pellet from that second rail gun hit his helmet with devastating effect.

Sergeant Flett and Corporal MacLeash were both wounded by shrapnel when a short burst from the rail gun pulverized their UAV control center.

Commander Daana, the FIST intelligence officer, suffered a massive burn through his left wrist when a streamer of acid hit where he had carelessly left a gap between his sleeve and glove. HM2 Ronault could see that with a hole all the way through and sizeable pieces of muscle, bone, and nerve tissue eaten away, the injury was severe enough that Daana was probably going to require weeks of regeneration before his left hand would be functional again. Ronault used a pain blocker as well as a painkiller on the officer.

PFC McGinty was also wounded when a tiny drop of acid oozed through the improperly sealed chameleon screen on his helmet. The wound was painful but the regeneration treatment to prevent permanent disfiguration could wait until after the operations planetside, and he could return to duty without being evacuated.

The casualties would likely have been much worse had Sergeant Kerr and Corporal Claypoole not gone off to flank the rail gun on their own.

"Write them up," Daana said to Captain Conorado when the painkiller that HM3 Hough had given him took effect. "They deserve medals for what they did. I'll endorse your recommendations."

"Aye aye," Conorado answered. He agreed that Kerr and Claypoole deserved medals.

A Master, a Leader, and three Fighters were brought bound into the Grand Master's hall and roughly flung to the mats before his dais. The Grand Master glowered at the five for long moments before rasping out a demand to know if these five cowards were the only ones who had not properly died for the greater glory of the Emperor. The Great Master who commanded the division from which the destroyed battalion had come stood behind the five, legs akimbo, sword gripped hilt and blade in his hands, and affirmed that the others in the battalion had given their all for the Emperor. The Grand Master considered the groveling five for a few more moments before rasping out his desire to know what happened.

The bound Master struggled to get his knees underneath himself and rhythmically pounded his forehead on the matting while he recounted his story: that the hated Earthman Marines were present in much larger numbers than the Over Master commanding the pursuit battalion had imagined and that the Marines caught the battalion in an ambush from which there was no escape, and in which victory was impossible. The Master had no answer to give when the Grand Master demanded to know how, if there was no escape possible from the Earthman Marines' ambush, he and the other four had escaped. After a few more questions, the Grand Master concluded that an entire so-called FIST had been waiting for the pursuit. He snapped his fingers at a nearby Senior Master and gave him instructions on what to do with the five cowards before him: They were to be taken to a hillside exposed to the sun and then staked out with their gill covers cut off, and left to die.

He then turned his attention to the Great Master commanding the division that had dispatched the failed mission. He ordered the Great Master to hand over command of the division to his assistant division commander and order him to take the entire division after the Earthman Marine FIST. And when that transfer of command was done, to return to the hall and disembowel himself.

Of course, when the division reached the area where Thirty-fourth FIST had killed the Skink battalion, the Marines were no longer there and the division couldn't find them.

CHAPTER
TWENTY-TWO

A second gator fleet arrived in Haulover orbit and began landing XXX Corps. General Aguinaldo came down with the first wave and brought army engineers and Marine combat engineers and much of their equipment with him.

"General Aguinaldo, sir!"

Aguinaldo, stepping off the Dragon that carried him off the Essay that had brought him from orbit to planetside, instantly turned and strode toward the voice, extending his hand.

"General Carano," Aguinaldo said.

"Welcome to Beach Spaceport, Haulover, sir," Carano said. He added ironically, "And right over there is beautiful downtown Sky City." He waved at the battered cityscape of Haulover's capital.

Aguinaldo barely spared the city a glance and a quick, sympathetic shake of his head. "Show me your air base."

"This way, sir." Carano directed Aguinaldo to a waiting army Battle Car. The two generals climbed in and minutes later dismounted at Naval Air Station George Gay, where they were met by Captain Hahley, Fourteenth Air Wing's commanding officer. Hahley's face showed the strain of the past few days' one-sided combat.

"How bad is it, Captain?" Aguinaldo asked.

Hahley didn't know Aguinaldo personally but he did know him by reputation, and that reputation said that the former Commandant of the Marine Corps wanted the straight scoop, no matter how bad the news was.

"It's almost as bad as it could be, sir," Hahley said. "The only reason I have a few aircraft left is we managed to erect a few revetments on our first day planetside."

"How many aircraft do you still have?"

Hahley grimaced. "A baker's dozen." Thirteen surviving aircraft out of an initial force of ninety-six Raptors. "My mechanics are busting tail, cannibalizing aircraft to assemble as many more as they can and make them combat ready."

"Does your number include FIST aircraft?"

"No, sir." Hahley grinned wryly. "General Carano allowed the Marines to keep their aircraft—over my strenuous objections."

Aguinaldo looked at Carano for an explanation.

"Part of the strength of the Marines is their combined-arms organization. I wanted my best units to be able to operate at their peak abilities. That meant letting the Marines keep their aircraft—no matter what my planetside air commander wanted." He paused, then added, "The Marines have lost seven Raptors and five hoppers." Out of twenty of each. "I guess the Marines were more prepared for the Skink rail guns. At least some of the pilots had encountered ground-based versions of those weapons before."

"What about the Twenty-sixth Air Wing?" That was off the carrier CNSS *Jebediah S. Hawks.*

"Still in orbit, sir," Carano said. "I didn't want to risk them until I had proper air defenses in place." He gestured at the perimeter of NAS Gay. "I've got some antiair artillery in place now, but neither my corps nor the carriers have enough engineers or guns to properly protect the air station from as much airpower as the Skinks have."

"Well, you've got the engineers now," Aguinaldo said. "And more AA guns are being brought planetside by the next wave of Essays."

The Grand Master sat in his great hall, sipping a warm beverage from a delicate cup while he listened to the reports of his intelligence and air commanders, who knelt on the reed mats at the foot of his dais. The Earthmen were landing a second task force from another amphibious fleet. The first troops planetside appeared to be engineers and they were directing their heavy equipment to the Earthmen's military airfield. While the Earthman air forces had suffered better than 80 percent losses, there were now three carriers in orbit, with as many as three hundred additional aircraft aboard them—possibly more. It was only a matter of time, and a short time at that, before the additional aircraft were ferried planetside. If the observed engineers properly strengthened the airfield's defenses, and the three hundred additional aircraft made planetfall together, that could possibly turn the tide of the air battle.

The Grand Master listened and absorbed the information. When the reports were complete, he needed no time to deliberate. His voice rasped as he gave his orders:

All combat aircraft were to launch immediately.

Half would proceed to the Earthman military airfield, where they would slaughter the engineers.

The other half would attack and destroy the orbit-to-surface shuttle craft as they attempted to make planetfall, and thereby destroy the Earthmen's ability to land additional aircraft—or ground reinforcements.

The army engineers and Marine combat engineers of XXX Corps had barely started building revetments to shelter the aircraft coming from the carriers in orbit when sirens screamed and one hundred and fifty Skink aircraft attacked in three waves. The first wave launched acid at the workers, firing rockets that burst twenty meters in the air and spreading rapidly falling clouds of greenish droplets groundward. The engineers scattered, the Marines faster than the army engineers, heading for whatever cover they could find. Most of them made it.

Sergeant Regis Alfonse, Corps of Engineers, leaped out of his earthmover and dove under it when the Skinks began their first strafing run. He'd paid close attention when his company had been briefed on the Skinks and their weapons and he had no desire to be in the line of fire. He was sure, pretty sure, that his machine would shield him from the acid guns—the trids of injuries caused by Skink acid on some world he'd never heard of had been quite vivid, and he didn't want to be anywhere near that stuff without something tough between him and it. He'd quailed at the trids of armored vehicles that had been hit by the Skink rail guns, but was sure, pretty sure, that his earthmover was stronger and more massive than an armored vehicle, so it wouldn't get completely pulverized even by a direct burst and would effectively shield his very unarmored body.

He breathed a sigh of relief when the first Skink aircraft shrieked away, but his relief was very short-lived. They were only the lead planes of the first wave. Others followed quickly, staggered between the first, and their missiles sent sprays of acid where the leaders hadn't.

Sergeant Alfonse screamed when a dollop of acid from a missile that burst and dropped a stream of acid that splattered just shy of his earthmover struck the top of his right boot and began eating through it and into his leg. He remembered the briefing: The acid had to be dug out of a wound or it would continue eating at flesh and bone and sinew until there was nothing left to dissolve. He drew his utility knife and tried to twist around to get at his lower leg, but his machine was too low and there wasn't room for him to reach his injury and see what he was doing. No more aircraft seemed to be coming now, so he scrabbled into the open, where he was met by the sight and sound of men down on the ground, crying and screaming from their wounds, and army medics and navy corpsmen racing from one casualty to another, rendering aid and calling for litter bearers to take the wounded to the dispensary.

Despite his own pain, it seemed to Alfonse that the wounded being tended and the others waiting for assistance were more badly injured than he was, so he didn't immediately call for a medic. Instead, now that he could reach his lower leg and see what he was doing, he used his utility knife to cut away the top of his boot. He went faint when he saw the bubbling hole in the side of his leg right at the bottom of the calf, but he steeled himself and began cutting around the glowing greenish fluid in the bottom of the hole. He gritted his teeth when the point of his knife scraped against bone, flinched when the knife's edge nicked the tendon, and closed his eyes to the red blood that filled the hole when he flicked away the last of the greenish fluid. Seeing the blood flow into and over the hole made him faint again, but he retained enough composure to yank field dressings from the emergency medkit on his belt. He wrapped one dressing around the wound and then another when the first was quickly stained red. Only then did he remember the painkiller in the kit and stab himself with the injector. The severe pain quickly ebbed. He looked more dispassionately at his dressing and decided to apply the third and last dressing from his medkit.

The acid gone, the pain quelled, and the bleeding stanched, Alfonse looked around again to see if a medic or corpsman was available to see to him.

To the north he saw more aircraft approaching. They didn't look like Raptors in pursuit of the Skinks but instead seemed to be on a ground attack approach. He glanced quickly back at the wounded still being tended in the open and, without thinking about it, hoisted himself to his feet and gingerly clambered aboard his earthmover. Those wounded soldiers and Marines and the medics and corpsmen caring for them needed protection from more enemy fire, or they would all die!

Alfonse applied max power to his earthmover and drove it between the men in the open and the oncoming aircraft, digging into the ground, pushing a high line of earth into a long berm to give some cover to the men. He'd gone more than a hundred meters before the first rounds from the oncoming wave began impacting the air base, disintegrating buildings and knocking machinery into tiny pieces with their rail guns. Some of the rail gun pellets hit the berm behind Alfonse and raised such huge clouds of dust and dirt that he couldn't tell whether his hasty shelter held at all.

Without thinking, he turned back to build the berm anew.

One of the trailing aircraft fired at Alfonse's earthmover but it was inside the dust and dirt cloud and the Skink's aim was off. Still, the massive machine shuddered at the impact of the pellets moving at two-tenths of the speed of light—almost sixty thousand kilometers per second—and bits of metal flew off it before the last Skink flew over and away.

No more aircraft were coming at the airfield just then, but the sounds of aerial combat sounded to the north. Alfonse thought it was just a matter of time before more aircraft came to pound the base and kill men. He climbed awkwardly to the top of his cab and looked around, over the cloud of dust and dirt that was beginning to settle, looking for any place that could use a berm. Looking slightly downward, he could see that the berm he'd pushed up was largely still intact. Many of the wounded had been removed and most of those still in the open were about to be removed to safety—if there was any place safe on the base. He saw a small cluster of low buildings still intact and headed for them. Perhaps he could build a berm high enough to protect them when the next wave came in. He was sure, *very* sure that there would be another wave.

And there was, but it was much smaller than the first two and caused far less damage to the base. Still, the damage and injuries caused by the first two waves were very great.

When Alfonse finally drove to the dispensary, he needed help dismounting from his earthmover. His dressings hadn't held completely and he was pale from loss of blood. The medical personnel, and many of the wounded who had survived because of his actions, treated him like a hero. But he didn't care about that. He just wanted to sleep.

The crews of the few remaining antiaircraft guns had begun putting out a thin, painfully thin, wall of plasma bolts as soon as the first wave of Skink aircraft began their strafing run. Thirteen pilots scrambled from the ready room and raced for their aircraft, wanting to get into the sky before they, the base, or the Raptors killed. A few of them made it; not all of them who did found that their aircraft were still flight-ready. Four navy Raptors launched in jump mode, straight up from their reventmented shelters—and straight into the path of the oncoming second wave of fifty aircraft, coming fast with rail guns blazing. Most of the Skinks continued their strafing run, demolishing revetments, but a few briefly diverted to strike at the launching Raptors.

One Raptor made it to safety above the enemy attack wave. The pilot was about to turn tail up and dive on the attackers when he saw the third wave coming fast behind the second. Instead of going tail up, he went tail down and climbed for the clouds. Even a junior-grade lieutenant brave enough to make a solo attack on a fifty-aircraft formation isn't brave enough to take on two such waves simultaneously.

But one wave at a time . . .

Lieutenant (jg) Jon Trotte didn't stay in the clouds; he checked his radar and timed his dive to hit the Skink third wave from behind. His dive began while the lead aircraft of the wave were still slightly short of his position. Even though he was much farther above them than they were from directly below him, his diving speed was so much faster than their attack speed that he was on them before the last of the enemy had passed below. He lined up on one aircraft and opened fire with his plasma cannons. After a short burst he switched his aim to a second and gave that one a short burst. By then he had to hit his reverse engines and bounce out of his dive to avoid slamming through the attacking formation and into the ground below.

Back up at altitude, Trotte twisted his Raptor to a steep attack angle and closed on the rear of the formation from above and behind. He got off three bursts before he had to level off and come at the Skinks on their own level.

By this time, the Over Master who was the senior of the two squadron commanders in the Skinks' third wave realized that he had five aircraft fewer than he had when his strafing run began. He crisply ordered his wave to break into flights and scramble, to find whoever was killing his aircraft, and kill *him*. The forty-five-aircraft formation broke into a starburst as pairs scattered in different directions, with some looping up and over, heading back the way they'd come in search of whoever was hitting them from the rear.

Trotte was no dummy; he knew where the safest place for him was. He throttled back to keep from overflying the Skink starburst; if he could keep himself in the middle of the scattered enemy planes, they wouldn't fire on him out of fear of hitting their own.

Or so Trotte thought.

Three Skink pilots spotted Trotte's Raptor at almost the same instant and barked harsh words, telling the others to watch where their fire went. The first two didn't aim, just pointed in the general direction of the Raptor and fired. The third took the time to line his guns on the target. The three were in different parts of the sky, two almost directly in line with the Raptor, opposite each other. One of those two was the one who took the time to line up his shot. He never got it off because the burst fired by the Skink aircraft opposite him pulverized his aircraft, instantly sending him to the Emperor's ancestors.

Trotte, meanwhile, had lined up on another Skink and sent a short burst from his plasma cannons at him. The plasma didn't have quite the same velocity as the Skink rail guns but it wasn't much slower. It was fast enough that he barely had to lead his target. His reflexes were fast and he was already jinking and searching for another target by the time the plasma stream gave him his sixth kill of the fight.

When a Skink rail gun finally found and tore off the rear of Trotte's Raptor, he had killed nine of them—and in their eagerness to be the one to down the brave Earthman pilot, the Skinks had downed another five of their own.

Another 150 Skink aircraft orbited west of NAS Gay at thirty thousand meters, waiting for the next Essays to make planetfall. They intended to intercept that planetfall by killing the Essays before they spiraled to the ground.

But General Aguinaldo knew they were there through intelligence and the Marine had seen how Trotte had taken on a fifty-aircraft wave single-handedly. Based on those two things, Aguinaldo had issued an order to the fleets in orbit.

So the Essays scheduled to bring antiaircraft guns down in the lazy three-orbit spiral favored by nearly everybody other than the Marines, who came down in a combat assault landing. And they carried Raptors, prepared to take flight when they were still at fifty thousand meters.

As a side note, at the same time Aguinaldo issued that order, he put in strongly worded recommendations for the Confederation Medal of Heroism for the late Lieutenant (jg) Trotte and Corps of Engineers Sergeant Regis Alfonse—the highest decoration given by the armed forces of the Confederation of Human Worlds.

The three orbiting carriers launched sixteen Essays, which went into formations near their respective starships and held station while each carrier trundled another sixteen Essays into its well deck. Each of the Essays contained three Confederation Navy A8E Raptors. At the same time, each of the two gator starships carrying the additional FISTS for the operation launched four Essays carrying a total of twenty Marine A8E Raptors.

As soon as all 104 of the Essays were in their various formations, Rear Admiral Worthog, from his command center on the CNSS *Raymond A. Spruance,* commanded "Away All Boats" and the formations turned planetward, the Essays firing their engines in a carefully plotted sequence that would have all of them arriving twenty thousand meters above the orbiting Skink aircraft at the same time.

In a straight-down line, the plunge would take approximately seventeen and a half minutes from the fleets' thousand-kilometer orbiting altitude to the interface between the mesosphere and the stratosphere, where the Essays would commence braking maneuvers. But because none of the Essays were plunging straight down but rather at various acute angles, and they didn't all begin at the same time, almost twenty-five minutes passed before the Essays turned their noses up and began turning into the spirals that would eat their downward velocity.

That twenty-five minutes was more than enough time for the Skink intelligence operators watching the orbiting fleets to notice that the Essays were heading planetside in combat assault mode, and for the High Master who commanded the Skink air forces to alert his high-orbiting wings to change their tactics from attacking slow-moving shuttles to striking at fast-moving shuttles as they dove planetside, passing close to the wings waiting in ambush.

The Essays began their braking maneuvers in a much more tight timing sequence than the formations had begun their plunges; they were closer to one another at fifty kilometers altitude than they had been in orbit. As soon as their spirals stabilized, the Essays' crew chiefs pressed the levers that released the passenger Raptors from their firmholds. Firmholds released, the crew chiefs opened the ramps and the coxswains piloting the Essays tipped their noses planetward and fired their forward braking engines, then turned about, pointing their tails downward.

No longer locked in place, when the decks below them abruptly slowed and slanted down the Raptors slid over the open ramps and into the thin upper atmosphere to begin their own unpowered plunges. Seconds later the pilots ignited the solid fuel that allowed powered flight at high altitude and took control of their plummeting aircraft.

This was *not* a maneuver the Skinks were prepared for.

The approximate twenty seconds from the time they dropped from the Essays until they plunged through the scrambling Skink aircraft was barely enough time for the Raptor pilots with the fastest reflexes to gain control of their aircraft, acquire targets, and fire off brief bursts of plasma bolts. But with an advantage of more than two to one in aircraft, the navy and Marine air didn't need to have a terribly high proportion of their pilots get off aimed bursts to inflict serious damage on the enemy. So it was that approximately twenty seconds after the Raptors dropped from the Essays, the one hundred and fifty Skink aircraft were reduced to 107, and the 107 Skink pilots were monstrously confused; their ambush had somehow gone seriously awry.

Lieutenant Arby Doremus, leader of the four Raptors of "Walleye division," was one of the thirty-seven pilots who scored a kill on the first pass. Doremus's call sign was "Walleye" after a facial deformity he suffered when a piece of shrapnel fractured his eye socket during what should have been a routine flyover on some rinky-dink little peacekeeping mission—the powers that be thought the mere sight of the ten Raptors of the squadron of a Marine FIST would be enough to cow the belligerent parties into backing off from killing each other. The powers that be were wrong, and the rinky-dink little peacekeeping mission turned into an eleven-standard-month deployment that saw many more Marines than a junior pilot get wounded—and some get killed. Afterward, then-ensign Doremus refused reconstructive surgery on his eye socket—the deformity didn't affect his vision—because, he thought, the eye made him look more fearsomely warriorlike. Some insensitive pilots began calling him "Walleye." The nickname stuck and he came to wear the sobriquet with pride.

As soon as Walleye Doremus passed his kill he bounced, ignoring the bumps of debris rattling off his fuselage. His three divisionmates bounced with him and in seconds the four Marine Raptors were again above the scattering Skinks, flying level in a tight circle, ready for another dive. Doremus was no glory hound; he wanted his wingmen to get their fair share of kills. He scanned the Skinks and spotted half a dozen speeding in a northward climb that would shortly bring them to the same altitude as Walleye division.

"Walleye pups, this is the Walleye his own self. Azimuth, one-seven-two. Range, two-five and increasing. Six chicken-lickin's. Fricassee their tails!"

"Legs, breasts, and wings, too!" Lieutenant Robert Sandell, Walleye Three, said as the four Raptors peeled out of their circle and began pursuit.

"I want a drumstick!" Ensign Caleb Haynes, Walleye Four, came back.

"You and your drumsticks!" Ensign Albert Baumler, Walleye Two, said. "I'll stick with the tits."

"Gotta fricassee 'em first, pups," Doremus reminded his division. He increased throttle and the others began increasing their on-line intervals. They quickly closed the gap.

But the Skinks weren't fleeing the battlespace. Or they spotted their pursuit and decided to turn back on it—after all, they were six, and only four were chasing them. As one, the six Skinks whipped into a Cobra turn, flying straight up, then rolling as they turned back to dive at the Raptors.

Seeing the six enemy aircraft coming toward them and gaining speed, the Marine pilots executed barrel rolls to throw off the aim of their foes. The maneuver worked—all six Skinks fired rail guns, and all six missed.

Then the aircraft passed one another and the Marines went into wide horizontal turns, only to find the Skinks executing yet another Cobra turn. The Marines tightened their turns and slanted upward to come at the Skinks on an angle. As the Skinks adjusted their approach to put the Raptors directly to their front, the Marines changed their own arcs to prevent the enemy from getting a fix on them.

"Walleyes, turn before they reach us," Doremus commanded. "We'll weave on them." The other pilots aye-aye'd. "Now!" Doremus ordered when the two groups were still two kilometers apart. He and Baumler broke right and turned sharply; Sandell and Haynes broke left. The Skinks tried to get off aimed bursts from their rail guns but the Marines' maneuver was too fast and unexpected for them to get lined up.

But they tried. And when the Marines completed their turns and were headed back toward the north, a Skink was on the tail of each flight of Raptors; the other four Skinks had overshot and were climbing into a loop to drop back behind the Marines.

"Weave!" Doremus shouted into his radio as he began a wide

turn to his right. Baumler began swinging wide to his left; the Skink took an instant to decide which to follow and went after Baumler. Doremus quickly switched his right turn into the arc of a circle to his left and Baumler did the same to his right. In seconds they passed each other, each having drawn half a circle. They immediately turned in the opposite direction, describing the opposite sides of another circle. But Doremus throttled back slightly so that Baumler and the Skink on his tail would both pass in front of him. Doremus got a lock on the Skink and fired a burst from his plasma cannon. The Skink ran right into it and exploded. Doremus flipped his Raptor's nose up and bounced to get over the flame and debris from the disintegrating enemy aircraft.

Baumler quickly followed, shouting, "You got him, you got him!"

A few kilometers away, Sandell and Haynes executed the same maneuver, with Haynes getting the kill.

But there were still four Skinks, and the Skinks were now behind the Marines, maneuvering to line up their guns on them.

This time the Marines executed Cobra turns, whipping up and twisting around to dive on their opponents. They all fired, hoping the Skinks would fly through the streams of plasma their cannons spat out. Baumler got a kill but the others missed.

Then it was a scramble, with the seven aircraft all flying solo, trying as hard to avoid colliding with one another as they were to line up on targets.

Walleye Four was so intent on closing on a Skink's tail, ready to hit him with a stream of plasma, that he didn't see that another Skink, intently twisting to get a line on one of the other Raptors, was closing on him at a combined speed of close to Mach 2. Both pilots were so intent on the kills they thought they were about to score that neither noticed the other. Both were shocked when their wings clipped each other and their aircraft were thrown into uncontrollable spins.

Suddenly it was over, with another Skink shot down and the

lone survivor fleeing at top speed. Doremus took a last shot at him but the Skink jinked and the burst missed. Then three Marine Raptors turned back to where the main battle was ending.

Even though the Essays had continued to fall planetward after releasing the Raptors they carried, past the altitude at which the Skink aircraft waited to ambush them, and before they managed to stop their drops and began to return to orbit, none of them were lost. The Skinks had been too busy fighting the Raptors to molest their intended victims.

CHAPTER
TWENTY-THREE

The Grand Master sat on his low chair on his dais, glowering at the three in front of him. The four Large Ones flanking him also looked sternly at the trio. One of the three was the High Master commanding the air forces; he knelt, sitting on his heels. A long, sharp knife lay on the matting before his knees. To one side of him was the Over Master who had commanded the force that struck the Earthman air base. He was also kneeling, but his forehead was lowered to the matting before him. To the High Master's other side was the Over Master commanding the high air force charged with downing the Earthmen's orbit-to-surface shuttles when they made their next planetfall. He was likewise semi-prostrate. A Large One, sword drawn and held across his body, stood behind the High Master.

The Grand Master did not have a cup of steaming beverage at his side; the low table there was unadorned even by a single, perfect bloom. That lack of beverage and beauty clearly demonstrated his displeasure with the three officers before him.

The three commanders had already delivered their reports to the Grand Master, and now he demanded answers to questions.

First he demanded to know how *one* Earthman with *one* piece of heavy equipment could raise berms that protected Earthmen from the rail guns of the second wave, and then raise more berms that protected buildings from the rail guns of the third wave.

The High Master lowered himself to touch his forehead to the matting, then raised himself to support his upper body on his outstretched arms. He had no answer for the Grand Master.

Then the Grand Master demanded to know how *one—one!—* Earthman killer craft could be responsible for the deaths of fourteen killer craft of the People before being killed himself.

The High Master pounded his forehead three times on the matting before again raising himself halfway up. Once more he had no answer.

In a rasping bark, the Grand Master demanded answers to the same kinds of questions from the Over Master commanding the strike force. That Over Master raised his head far enough that the matting wouldn't muffle his voice. He had no more of an answer than had the High Master.

Then the Grand Master demanded to know how it was that the high force had not suspected that the Earthmen might be sending a responding strike force of killer craft to attack the high force when it was obvious from the way their shuttles plunged planetward that they were doing something unexpected.

This time, when the High Master raised his head from pounding it on the matting, it was marked with blood from the force of his pounding. He had no more answers than before.

Even surprised and outnumbered, the Grand Master demanded to know, how could the excellent pilots of the Emperor, in their nimble killer craft and with their superior weapons, have lost more than half their number while killing fewer than half that number of Earthmen?

The High Master pounded his forehead on the matting until most of his face was streaked by the blood that flowed from his brow. But he still had no answer for the Grand Master.

Neither did the Over Master in command of the high force when the Grand Master raspingly barked the same questions at him.

The Grand Master glowered silently at the three for long moments before finally giving a harsh command.

The High Master swallowed, then sat full up on his heels and picked up the long, sharp knife before his knees. He loosened his robes, baring his stomach. With a quick, sure stroke, he sliced his belly open so that his entrails tumbled out. The Large

One behind him shifted his grip on his sword and gave it a powerful swing at the High Master's neck. The High Master's head flew off and bounced at the foot of the Grand Master's dais. The Large One then beheaded the two Over Masters without according them the honor of first disemboweling themselves.

The Grand Master snapped his fingers, and his chief of staff glided from where he'd been hidden behind one of the draperies covering the walls of the hall. Using few words, the Grand Master instructed his chief of staff on appointments to fill the now-vacant leadership positions in the air force. He used even fewer words to direct that the mess before him be cleaned up.

He began to plan his next move.

It takes time for 308 aircraft to land on two airfields—Beach Spaceport's airfield was commandeered to assist in accepting the Confederation Raptors—especially when both runways still had damage suffered in the Skink air assaults. So much time, in fact, that the Essays on the gator starships carrying Thirteenth and Twenty-sixth FISTs, which hadn't launched until the air battle had been decided, made planetfall before all the Raptors were down. The Essays off the carriers didn't return home but went to the gator starships carrying the army divisions of XXX Corps to help ferry them planetside. The first of them were loaded and launched by the time the last Raptor from the Ninth Air Wing landed at NAS Gay.

With the Earthman navy and its circle of sky-eyes in orbit, the Grand Master knew that moving large numbers of his Fighters by aircraft was too great a risk. But his sky-gazers had plotted the positions of the satellites in the circle of sky-eyes, along with their likely fields of view. Those likely fields of view included, not unexpectedly, all of the bases in which the Emperor's army lay waiting for battle. But the Grand Master knew something the Earthmen didn't know: The Emperor's army had made good use of the lengthy time they had been on this world and had excavated extensive tunnels that extended far beyond the bases. All the way to within a few kilometers of the Earthman center at Sky City—and the Earthman air base and the bivouac area growing near the city and airfields.

With that in mind, the Grand Master dispatched two divisions into the long tunnels to attack the Earthman bivouac while it was still in the chaos of getting organized. Then he sat back and folded his hands over his belly to wait for reports from what was about to become the front lines.

"Move it! Move, move, movemove, *move*!" the sergeants shouted in the age-old cry of sergeants attempting to bring order to the chaos of large numbers of men attempting to get in formation, board vehicles, prepare camp, or advance to fire.

"You got lead in your pants, soldier? I said *move* it!"

"Your prom date ain't waiting up for you, sonny. You don't move any faster than that, Jodie's gonna get in her pants!"

"Your feeble old grannie can erect a mod faster than that, soldier! Move like you mean it!"

There was no scientific proof that yelling ever inspired soldiers to make camp any quicker or more efficiently. But it did keep them from thinking about what came next, or wherever else they'd prefer being, or whatever else they'd rather be doing. And using their voices gave the sergeants the feeling that they were actually doing something. Whether the yelling had a positive effect or not, the soldiers of the Second of the 502nd, Twenty-fifth Mobile Infantry Division had their bivouac, some eight kilometers northwest of Sky City and NAS Gay, up with all the mods properly aligned and streets laid out in less than three-quarters of an hour. The battalion commander was happy, which made the company commanders and platoon commanders happy, and gave the sergeants that warm and fuzzy feeling; their yelling had actually accomplished something. As for the troops, they were just glad that nobody was yelling at them for the moment and they could pause for a breather.

Then an order came down that set the troops to grumbling: "Weapons and ammo inspection in twenty minutes."

Nineteen minutes after the inspection order was passed, Sergeant First Class Rov Jaworski stood in front of his platoon, which had assembled in formation in front of its row of two-man modules, and gave them a quick eyeballing. He knew what the inspection would find; maybe not everybody's weapon was sparkly enough to pass a garrison-world inspection, but every weapon was clean and functional, and every needle tin filled and in its carrying harness pouch.

"Stand easy until the officers get here," he told his men. It was an admittedly feeble joke for the platoon sergeant of first platoon, Easy Company, but he always said it. It got the expected polite chuckles and mild groans.

Jaworski was a bit less confident about the blasters a quarter of his men carried. Major General Vermeil, the Twenty-fifth's division commander, was mightily impressed with the supposed one-shot-one-kill capability of the Marines' primary infantry weapon. Jaworski knew the Marines were crack troops but he'd been around long enough to know better than to believe everything they said about their combat prowess. Regardless of what a mere platoon sergeant thought might be the case, Vermeil had prevailed upon General Aguinaldo to issue him enough blasters for one man in every fire team to have one, and for every third machine gun to be replaced by a Marine assault gun, the automatic-fire plasma gun.

There was a sound of gunfire off to the left, in the direction of Howe Company, and Jaworski, fists jammed into his hips, turned to look toward it.

"What is it, Sarge?" somebody called out.

"Who's shooting, Sarge?" another asked.

"How the hell do I know?" Jaworski snapped. They were in a combat zone, and nobody had told him about any scheduled familiarity firing. As far as he was concerned, that only meant one thing.

"Lock and load!" he commanded, drawing his own sidearm to make sure it was loaded and its safety on. "Look alert while I try to find out what's happening." He got out his comm and tried to raise Lieutenant Murray, the platoon commander. Murray didn't respond, so Jaworski tried the company HQ, where he got a clerk. Dumbass clerk didn't know what was going on, only that the first sergeant and all the officers had gone to the battalion HQ as soon as the shooting started.

"So what the hell am I supposed to do?" Jaworski asked himself after signing off.

He figured it out in a hurry.

"Shit, Sarge!" a man in the platoon's front rank shouted, looking beyond Jaworski. The soldier raised his blaster to his shoulder and fired a plasma bolt that passed so close to Jaworski that the platoon sergeant clearly felt the heat from the passing star stuff.

Jaworski spun to see what the soldier had fired at and caught sight of the fading flare of a vaporizing Skink. He simultaneously saw fifty or more Skinks on line, coming out of the forest a hundred meters distant. They were carrying the tank-and-hose arrangements that the intelligence briefings said were acid weapons.

"Get on line and kill them before they get in range!" Jaworski screamed. The intelligence briefings had said the acid shooters had a range of fifty meters. But he'd been around long enough to know that intelligence briefings weren't necessarily accurate—he'd seen images of what that acid did to a human body, and he wanted those Skinks taken out before they got anywhere near his men.

First squad stayed in place and the soldiers began firing. Second squad ran to the left and third to the right. The entire platoon shifted formation faster than they'd moved when the sergeants were yelling at them to set up the bivouac. Jaworski had to hit the ground and crawl toward first squad to avoid getting hit by the flechette and plasma fire his men were pouring downrange. The fire was slackening a bit by the time he reached the squad and he was able to stand up and look over the ground between him and the forest's edge. He didn't see any Skinks.

"Cease fire!" he called out. "First platoon, cease fire!" There were a couple more *whirrs* of flechette fire and one *crack-sizzle* of a blaster and then the shooting was over. "Squad leaders, report!"

"First squad, no casualties."

"Second squad, we're all right."

"Third squad. Everyone's fine."

"Damn," somebody in first squad said. "Did you ever see anything go up in flame like those buggers did?" He hefted his blaster and looked at it admiringly.

"Flashed it righteously!" said the man next to him, clapping him on the shoulder.

"Hey, that one's faking!" a blaster-armed soldier in second squad shouted. He raised his blaster and shot at one of the crumpled bodies that had been torn up by flechette fire.

"That one, too!" called out a man in third squad. He fired his blaster at another of the Skinks. In seconds, every blaster-armed soldier in the platoon was firing plasma bolts at the downed Skinks.

"Hey, let me get one!" a flechette-rifle-armed soldier called out, and grabbed for a blaster.

" 'Toon, ten-*hut*!" Jaworski's bellowed command cracked over his men like a whip, and they stopped shooting and snapped to attention. "Get back in formation!" he yelled. He stepped in front of the reassembling platoon. "Squad leaders, watch the forest." He glowered at the men of his platoon and spoke in a low, ominous voice. "We are soldiers, not barbarians. We don't shoot the dead, or vaporize them just because we can. We treat the dead with *respect,* no matter how inhuman they—"

"Sarge, more coming!" the first squad leader shouted.

Jaworski jerked around. This time there wasn't any lousy fifty Skinks coming out of the forest, it was like the entire *forest* had come to life and was racing toward them.

"On line! Prone! Show them that the Second of the 502 is nobody to fuck with!"

Even faster than they had the first time, the twenty-seven men of first platoon got on line and began pouring fire into the mass of Skinks charging across the open. Skinks were falling all along the line, many flared up; some of the flaring Skinks ignited others running close by or already fallen.

Then a high-pitched *whirr* announced the arrival of the Skinks' other infantry weapon—the rail gun. The first long burst *whizzed* over the heads of the prone members of first platoon without hitting anybody.

"Take cover!" Jaworski screamed. He scrabbled behind a nearby mod. He covered his ears to block the cut-off screams of standing soldiers who didn't get under cover fast enough before the next burst tracked the line of first platoon's position. Still, most of them made it, either to ripples in the ground, or behind mods that gave them brief protection from the rail gun's pellets.

"Keep firing!" Jaworski shouted. "And change your position every time you do. Don't let that rail gun zero in on you!"

Behind the mod, the platoon sergeant couldn't see all of his men, but he could hear the *whirr* of flechette rifles and *crack-sizzle* of blasters, so he knew they were obeying at least part of his orders.

Then three pellets hit the mod he was hunkered down behind and splinters and dust sprayed over him. With the the side of his face pressed to the ground, he saw three more mods to his left get pulverized. He realized his platoon couldn't hold out for long with the rail gun shooting at them. He thought fast and remembered the instructions he'd been given earlier to zero in artillery. Well, he hadn't done the zeroing yet, but he had the orders on his comp. Fumbling, he got his comp out of his pocket and keyed it, looking for the artillery instructions. *There!* He found them.

He grabbed his comm and contacted the division's artillery fire control center. Once connected, he rattled off the coordinates for the zero check, gave his azimuth to the registry mark, and asked for three rounds to register.

Whoever was on comm at the fire control center told him to try again, to put his request in proper form.

Jaworski was in no mood for the petty shit. "We're under attack by a rail gun, goddammit! Let's get registered so I can guide you to the rail gun!"

After a few seconds of muffled voices, another voice came over the comm. "What's your situation, Easy-One-Five. Over?"

"We are about to be overrun by Skinks in the open, and a rail gun has us pinned down. Over."

The voice was muffled again for a moment, then Jaworski heard a distant booming over the comm, and the voice said, "Three spotter rounds coming downrange. Over."

"I'll adjust." Jaworski began counting off the seconds. The artillery park was ten kilometers to his rear, and the rounds traveled at better than Mach 4. A quick mental calculation told him it would take the spotter rounds about seven and a half seconds from muzzle to impact.

At the count of eight, three explosions impacted in the forest four hundred meters away.

"On my azimuth, down three-five-zero," Jaworski ordered into his comm. That would have the next rounds impacting a scant fifty meters away from his line—if the spotting was right. He hadn't made any adjustments to verify the registration.

"Three spotter rounds, on the way," the artillery voice came back a few seconds later. Then "Are you sure we were that far off?"

"I think you were right on. That adjustment was to get the Skinks that are about to overrun my position!"

"Holy mother of Buddha, I hope you got it right."

"So do I."

Less than eight seconds after the second three-round salvo was fired, a sharp whistling in the sky announced the arrival of three artillery rounds that impacted in front of first platoon, Easy Company. Shrapnel flew all about, shredding Skinks and thunking into the dirt. Jaworski heard a couple of screams from his men but couldn't let that affect him, not while they still had a battle to fight—and that rail gun was still out there.

He poked his head up, taking a risk, to see if he should call "fire for effect." Many Skinks were down but more were pouring out of the forest—and his men were still firing.

"Up fifty. Fire for effect!" Then he shouted to his men to shoot only the closest Skinks. Artillery rounds started exploding near the edge of the forest, some in the clear, some inside the trees. He remembered how the Skinks really did flare up when hit by plasma from the blasters, and how Skinks too close to their flaming comrades also burned. So he called in, "Use incendiaries!"

"My UPUD shows forest where we're firing for effect," the artilleryman replied. "Incendiaries will cause a forest fire."

"I don't give a damn. That forest is full of Skinks. The incendiaries will kill them faster than Hotel Echo will."

"It's your funeral pyre," the artilleryman said.

Seconds later, flames began erupting in the forest and just outside it. When Jaworski looked up he was relieved to see torches going up, the flashing of burning Skinks. In a few moments Skinks stopped flooding into the open. Only a few who made it through the barrage entered the open area, where the soldiers of first platoon shot them down.

The rail gun had stopped firing; Jaworski thought its crew must have been hit by artillery. Then no more Skink survivors made it into the clearing.

"Cease fire!" Jaworski shouted. "Cease fire!"

Most of his men obeyed the order fairly quickly, but the ones with blasters kept shooting, hitting the dead bodies, flaring them up.

"Cease fire, I said, goddammit! Stop firing!" He jumped up and started running along the line of his platoon, yanking blasters out of the hands of the soldiers who were shooting at the dead.

When the fire finally stopped, Jaworski called for the squad leaders to report. He'd started the battle with twenty-seven healthy, fit soldiers under him. Eight were dead and five more were seriously wounded—effectively 50 percent casualties. But when he looked out over the open ground leading up to the forest edge, and saw the scorch marks left by flashed Skinks, the ground dug up by the three artillery rounds he'd called almost on top of his position, and the fires burning in the forest, and re-alized that his men and the artillery he called in must have killed hundreds of Skinks, he was surprised that more than half of first platoon had survived the battle. And they all would have died, he was certain of that, if they hadn't been standing with weapons in hand and all ammo on hand, ready for an inspection, when the first Skinks charged at them.

He thought again of the platoon's casualties, and said softly, but with enough volume to carry to all the survivors, "Burn them." He watched with satisfaction as the blasters carried by his soldiers fired at the bodies in the open and flashed them all into vapor.

It's sometimes the small, unanticipated things that make all the difference in a battle. And so it was here. The Skinks had expected to assault a battalion in the midst of setting up their bivouac, with most of the men separated from their weapons. Instead, they hit when the soldiers of the Second of the 502nd all had their weapons in their hands and ammunition on their bodies, and were all assembled in their proper units. Thus it was that seven hundred soldiers were able to defeat an attack-ing force nearly four times their size while suffering relatively few casualties of their own.

CHAPTER
TWENTY-FOUR

"Sergeant Queege," Colonel Raggel announced one morning, "you are excused duty today. Get some sleep. You'll need it." He grinned. "Lieutenant Judy Bell here and I are going to spend the night on patrol. I'll need you to ride shotgun." Lieutenant Bell was the Sky City police department's liaison to the Seventh MPs. She grinned at Queege, whom she referred to as "PQ." In the short time they'd been together the two had developed a friendship. "Be back at dusk, booted, belted, and spurred."

"Well, what about you, sir?" Queege asked Raggel.

"I can sleep when I make brigadier general. Now scram until tonight."

During these nighttime patrols Colonel Raggel tried to visit every outpost in the city. These visits kept the men on their toes and him apprised of how things in his city—that's how he'd come to think of Sky City now, as "his"—were going. These were not inspection visits; he made them because a commander had to be seen by his troops, doing what they did, only doing it better. He insisted on driving with Lieutenant Bell riding shotgun and Queege in the back monitoring the onboard communications and sensor arrays. With the sophisticated communications system they had in the vehicle she could listen in on the chatter from the security outposts around NAS Gay and Beach Spaceport. While those activities were not within the Seventh MPs' area of responsibility, being patched into those networks was important in case those defenses were probed by the enemy. She also monitored the periodic line checks to the duty officer at the battalion tactical operations center made by the MP patrols and static security points, as did Colonel Raggel.

Suddenly Puella sat up in her seat. "Sir, someone out on the MSR—"

"What?"

"Someone out on the MSR is reporting—it's garbled but I think they were reporting activity along the highway out there— no, they've gone off the net." There was alarm in her voice. The main supply route to the forward units of the corps ran from Sky City down what they called Highway One to the southwest. Puella noted the time was three hours.

"We have a joint checkpoint on Townsend Bridge over the Tyber Creek," Lieutenant Bell reported. "That's right on the edge of the city where Highway One begins."

"Right," Colonel Raggel confirmed. "Six men: three of mine, three of yours. Sergeant Queege, what do they report?"

"Negative report, sir. All quiet."

"Tell them to be on their toes. Hold on, we're going over there. Queege, keep your ears open, see if Gay or Beach have anything. Inform the battalion TOC we're going over to Townsend. Tell them to wake up the quick reaction force. Who's in charge tonight?"

"Lieutenant Fearley, Fourth Company, sir," Puella answered, her voice an octave above its normal pitch; the atmosphere inside the car had suddenly gone very tense.

"All right, you two," Colonel Raggel said as he shifted the car into high gear, "get your infras on, lock and load. Be ready to deliver immediate fire." The tension had now shifted from eyeballs-bright to sphincter-tight.

Colonel Raggel turned off the lights and let the car roll to a stop a hundred meters up the road from the checkpoint. Through their infras the occupants could make out the gray-green images of the two fortified guard posts on the bridge, one on each side of the hundred-meter span. They could *not* make images of anyone inside them.

Colonel Raggel came onto the net and identified himself as Raggers Six. There was no response from the guard posts. "Scramble the reaction force," he told Puella. She felt a very uncomfortable sensation in her gut. "Okay, children. Judy, you take the right flank, Puella, the left, I'll be point. Shoot at anything that moves." Puella wanted to suggest they wait in the car until the reaction force arrived but her throat had gone so dry she couldn't form the words.

In the instant she stepped outside the car she caught, in the corner of her eye, movement in the bushes along the stream bank. She drew her weapon and fired. There was a scream. She went to one knee and began firing methodically at multiple targets emerging from along the stream bank. She fired her magazine empty and reloaded without even realizing she was doing it. She heard a horrible scream from somewhere and the reports of other weapons being fired. She could clearly hear liquid splashing across the hood of the car, hear the metal sizzling and smell the acrid odor of burning paint. Someone belly-flopped onto the pavement beside her. It was Colonel Raggel. "Holy shit!" he said, firing at targets advancing at them from the opposite side of the bridge. "They're *everywhere!*"

Puella saw her first Skink close up, its convex face and small size. It was coming straight at her out of the bushes along the water's edge, something like a fire hose clutched in its hands. Maybe all she really saw was a gray shape; maybe the clear images were just what she remembered from training classes and she only thought she could see the thing's face clearly in the darkness, but she was sure it was a Skink. She continued firing methodically but she knew that if the reaction force didn't get there soon . . .

Starbell's Coffee Shop, although it was right across the street from the Shamhat Building, had somehow escaped significant damage during the air raid. The front window had been smashed by a fragment of concrete from the exploding penthouse, but that was all, and it had been replaced by a piece of plywood until a glazier could be found to make the necessary repairs. Needless to say, glaziers, masons, all kinds of craftsmen were overworked just then at Sky City.

The few times Puella and Billy Oakley had found time to visit, the house coffee and the pastries were excellent. The latter were baked fresh each morning in the back of the shop. But they had not found much time to relax since the Seventh MPs had established themselves in Sky City, especially since Puella had spent some time in the hospital recovering from the wounds she'd sustained in the ambush at Townsend Bridge.

"Well, look at it this way, kid," Oakley was saying, regarding Puella over the rim of a steaming coffee cup. "You've got a wound badge to add to your collection of gongs. That'll give you five points on the civil service examination if you should ever decide to become a civil serpent. Bet yer growing hash marks, like an old soldier."

"Yeah." She flexed her right arm. It was almost back to normal where several drops of Skink acid had burned through the flesh. Colonel Raggel, who had come out of the fight unscathed, had dug them out with a knife before they burned all the way through her arm, and had done it under fire. But poor Lieutenant Bell, she'd caught a stream of acid right in her face and would need extensive surgery to repair what had been burned away. One good thing, if there was any, was that evidently the acids used by the Skink infiltrators had not been as potent as that fired from their aircraft. Puella had missed the air raid since she'd been reposing peacefully in a stasis unit in orbit when that occurred.

"And I wouldn't doubt you'll get an oak-leaf cluster to that Bronze Star medal of yours for what you did on Townsend Bridge that night. Guess my marksmanship training came in handy." He grinned.

"I hardly remember any of it, Billy. I just kept shooting at the targets, you know? Then that gun car from the reaction force showed up." She shrugged and sipped her coffee. "And that's the last I remember. Oh, I remember Colonel Raggers digging that shit out of my arm all right." Her face reddened. "But I switched hands and fired left-handed I was so intent on gettin' more Skinks before they got me. I was sure we were being overrun. But I don't even want to remember that much."

Oakley reached across the table and took her hand in his. "You did good, Annie. You've turned into one damned fine soldier."

Puella smiled. "Well, you know, I guess I found a home in the service, now, the colonel, Top, you . . ." Her face reddened again. Oakley squeezed her hand; he was slightly amused at how readily she showed her emotions. "My folks sorta threw me out when I said I was gonna join the army, you know? They wanted me to marry some asshole, have a batch of grandkids, the whole nine yards. I thought I was pretty hot shit when I got assigned to the Seventh MPs with their badass reputation. Then when the Marines captured me, I saw what a real army was like."

"How well I remember! I also remember that bet with the slimies, you and that fucking first sergeant of yours. Colonel Raggel canned his ass mighty quick."

"Well, he wasn't that bad, Billy, and we was both pretty drunk that night."

"But now you've found a home in the army."

"Well, not right away, not until after I come to Arsenault with the battalion, got to work for the colonel, met General Aguinaldo, uh, met you." She shrugged again.

"And now you're gonna leave us?"

"I been thinkin' 'bout that."

"I'll tell you what, Annie. I'm gonna miss ya, miss you a *lot*." He said that with feeling and now it was his face that flushed. "Yeah, I always thought you were a, well, a jerk, an airhead out of her depth, the kind of person the old Seventh MPs attracted like shit attracts flies, the kind of soldier who came to the Seventh because nobody else would take them. The only person I ever respected was Steiner, and I had my training schedules to keep me from thinkin' too much why they'd sent *me* to the Seventh MPs. But damn, when you sobered up and I got to know you better"—he gestured helplessly with one hand—"you sorta *grew* on me, know what I'm saying?"

"Yeah."

"And I'll miss you when all this is over."

"Yeah." She stuffed the remains of a doughnut into her mouth and said around it, "Let's go see the colonel."

"Yeah. Let's." They got up from the table.

"I want to see the general," Smelt Miner demanded.

"Well, it might be a long wait, sir," Ensign Jak Daly replied. He'd answered for the receptionist, a young corporal who obviously did not know how to handle the obstreperous Miner. Daly had just come out of the general's office after making a report on the attempted infiltration of Sky City by a Skink reconnaissance force and had been chatting up the pretty corporal when Miner barged into the anteroom.

"Ah, yes, Ensign Daly, isn't it?" Miner asked. Somehow he didn't look quite like the blustering executive Daly had come to know since his arrival on Haulover. He seemed more restrained. "Uh, I'll wait." *Well,* Daly thought, *that's different!*

"May we tell him what this is about, Mr. Miner?" Daly asked.

"Yes, I wish a few moments of his time. I, uh, want to discuss something with him in private, Ensign." Miner appeared embarrassed as he spoke.

There was something in Miner's attitude that registered with Daly. The Miner he'd come to know would've been demanding, pounding on the desk, to get into Carano's presence. But this version just sat quietly and said he'd wait?

"What, Mr. Miner? What do you wish to talk to him about? I can't get you in there, as busy as he is right now, without telling him what it is you want."

Miner cleared his throat. "Well, I want to—I—I want to offer him my—my *cooperation.*" The embarrassment in Miner's voice was evident.

Daly thought for a moment and then said, "Come on, Mr. Miner, let's go see the general."

"Mr. Miner, I'm very busy," General Carano said, lowering his feet to the floor, taking the cigar out of his mouth, and looking daggers at Daly for having interrupted him, especially by bringing the feather merchant unannounced into his sanctum. Daly only nodded, indicating the general should let Miner speak. "Well, what is it, goddammit?"

"General, I apologize to you, Ensign Daly, everyone, for being an asshole."

Carano's mouth fell open with surprise. From where he was standing Daly winked and let one side of his mouth curl in a smile. He *knew* there was something odd about the old boy this morning.

"You *what*?"

"Apologize, General. I apologize and promise to cooperate fully with your officers from now on."

General Carano stood up. "Well. Miner, you were injured in the air raid, weren't you?"

"Not seriously, a few bumps and scratches, but my wife was killed. So was my secretary, poor kid. She was engaged to be married." He paused to catch his breath. "So, I know this is all for real now. Your measures were necessary. We have to fight these bastards and I want to do everything I can to help you. And that was brilliant of you, sir, to build those revetments for the Marines." He shook his head in admiration. "Saved the day after the navy screwed up like that, leaving all their planes out in the open."

Now it was Carano whose face flushed slightly, but without missing a beat, he came barreling around his desk and stuck out a hand. "I am deeply sorry for your loss, sir. Apology accepted. Forget everything after 'hello.' We start a new slate as of right now."

Miner turned to Daly and held out his hand. "Same here," Daly replied, shaking the hand.

"And now, would you join Ensign Daly and me in a cigar?"

"Thanks, General, some other time, when we have the time.

But I really have to be off. I'm addressing my employees this
morning, telling them it's necessary we get behind you 150 percent. I really don't think that's necessary, not after the air raid,
but I want them to know where I stand. You'll have to excuse
me, sir." Miner turned at the door and faced the two. "But first
thing after I leave here is, I'm going to see your provost mar-
shal, Colonel Raggel, and give him my apology, too."

"Mary Baker Eddy's dried-up old dugs," Colonel Raggel exclaimed. "This has been a morning of surprises! Did you know
old Smelt Miner was just in here, *apologizing* for the way he's
acted, and promising me his full support? He even showed up in
General Carano's headquarters and apologized to *him*! We may
just win this war if this shit keeps up. And now you two—"

"I'll be dipped in shit!" Sergeant Major Steiner exclaimed,
shifting an unlit cigar from one corner of his mouth to the other.

"Well, sorry, sir, but we figured you should know."

"Yeah. Well, Sergeant Queege, you do know that your appli-
cation for transfer to the Marines will be automatically canceled."

"I'll be a monkey's uncle!" Steiner exclaimed.

"I know, sir," Queege replied. "I hate the thought of reneging
on General Aguinaldo, but I've thought this over for a long time
now."

"He'll understand."

"I'll be jerked off at the next battalion formation!" Sergeant
Major Steiner growled.

"Top!" Colonel Raggel turned to Steiner with a freezing look
on his face. *"Please!"* But the old sergeant major only grinned
broadly, chomping vigorously on his cigar. Raggel turned back
to the two standing before him. "Sergeant Oakley, what do you
say?"

"Best idea I ever heard."

"Tell me, Sergeant Queege, why now?"

"Um, well, sir . . ." Queege paused, so long the silence almost became embarrassing. "Well, sir, it just is, you see," she continued at last, "I—I don't want to be one of those 'nymphs on the shore' no more."

"All right," Colonel Raggel sighed, as he stood up and put on his cover. "Sergeant Major!"

"Yes, sir!" Steiner removed the cigar from his mouth.

"Get my shotgun! We're going over to see the chaplain and get these two fools married."

CHAPTER
TWENTY-FIVE

". . . and so, Madam President, in view of your blatant disregard for the Constitution of this Confederation, your running a secret war on the world known as Kingdom, expending the precious lives and treasure of our people, which was the direct result of a devastating conflict on the world called Ravenette, which you have promised to rebuild but so far have done nothing substantial toward fulfilling that promise, in view of these and your many other horrendous missteps, in view of your efforts to divert attention from your mistakes and malfeasance in office by creating a false hysteria over the so-called 'threat' posed by these alien entities hardly anyone but your minions have ever seen, would you please tell the people of this Confederation why, then, they should return you to the office of the presidency?"

Haggel Kutmoi had never made a finer speech. The applause echoed down the light-years, but there, in the Great Hall of the Confederation Congress, where the final presidential debate was taking place, it shook the rafters. Delegates and viewers began to chant "Haggel! Haggel! Haggel!" over and over again. It was the wrap-up of the long series of contentious debates, the concluding broadside, and it had been delivered in classical oratorical style. Kutmoi bowed toward Chang-Sturdevant, faced the audience, and raised his arms in victory. Even members of Chang-Sturdevant's own party joined in the applause. It was a moment of pure elation for Kutmoi, who saw an electoral landslide coming his way. He'd had "the old bitch," as he called the President in private, on the defense the whole time and now he had her on the ropes.

Chang-Sturdevant stood bracing herself against the podium, her face calm but haggard, waiting for the commotion to subside so she could speak. A strand of hair had somehow come loose from her coiffure and hung down one side of her face and a small rivulet of perspiration had started creeping down the other. It was fortunate she did not use makeup very heavily or it would have started running in the heat under the hot lights—and in the crushing verbal blows of Kutmoi's concluding remarks. Out of the corner of her eye she glanced over at him as he stood there, face flushed with victory, arms raised over his head, a grin splitting his face almost from ear to ear, and saw her defeat writ large in the ballot boxes.

The debate monitor, newscaster Dean Hollowhed, asked for order but the applause, chanting, shouting, and stomping continued for some time. Finally the hall grew quiet through sheer exhaustion. Hollowhed turned to the President and announced gravely, "Madam President, you have two minutes to respond."

Chang-Sturdevant stood there silently for a full ten seconds before saying anything. "When I first ran for this office I thought it was the noblest thing I'd ever done," she began. "Now I wish only to conclude the business I've begun and yes, leave the agony of this office behind me. Yes, I have made mistakes—"

This was met with a resounding chorus of boos from the chamber and shouts of "You bet you have!" and "Quit now, before we kick you out!"

"I have made mistakes," she repeated. "They are on my head and mine alone! *Anyone* who holds this office will make them. But I tell you this now, as long as I wear the mantle of this presidency, I shall *never* let my personal fate obscure my duty in the face of the grave and imminent threat to our species—"

"Yeah, yeah," people shouted, "we've heard all that before!"

"—that is now upon us, *that is now upon us,* to obscure my duty to fight this menace—"

At this point the audience went wild with shouts of derision

and calls for Chang-Sturdevant to step down from the podium.
The roar washed over her as she stood there and she knew that
she had just lost the debate, that she had just delivered the worst
speech of her career. *Well, okay,* she thought, *if I'm going to go
down, I'm going down in flames.* She nodded calmly at Hollowhed, who called again for order. The clock on her two minutes had stopped so she still had time to finish what she'd now
determined to say. She held out her arms and shouted, "Let me
speak! Let me speak!" but this time there was no hesitation in
her words, only calm resolution. Chang-Sturdevant smiled and
brushed the errant strand of hair away from her face. She stood
there patiently and gradually quiet was restored throughout the
Great Hall.

"Anyone among you who thinks that the war now being
waged on the world known as Haulover is a subterfuge I have
cooked up to divert attention from my mistakes, anyone who
does not think the invasion of Human Space by the aliens we
call Skinks is not the gravest threat to the existence of humanity in all of its history, anyone, my friends, who is not willing to
stand up and fight these things with every weapon at his disposal, *that person is either a goddamned fool or a goddamned
traitor!*" She turned and faced Haggel Kutmoi, extending a
rigid forefinger directly at him and said, in a calm, deliberate
tone of voice, "And the best I can say about you, Senator, is that
you are a goddamned fool."

The Great Hall erupted into pandemonium.

Sanguinious Cheatham, Haggel Kutmoi's campaign manager,
gave the senator a hearty thump on the back. "Brilliant! You've
got her! You destroyed her! The old hag is in your bag and so is
the fucking election!" Kutmoi had never seen Cheatham so
elated, probably because he realized now that his appointment to
the Supreme Court, along with Chang-Sturdevant and the election, was also in the bag.

Kutmoi mopped the perspiration off his face. Well, he had
delivered the coup de grâce to the old bitch, that's for sure.

"But damn, that last remark, calling me a goddamned . . ." He shook his head. "It was like someone walked over my grave."

Cheatham shook his head vigorously and waved a forefinger in front of Kutmoi's nose. "No, my dear Mr. President-elect, no, no, no! That was the *worst,* positively the worst thing she could have done! No politician in history who used the Lord's name in vain in a speech has ever survived and the old broad did it *three* times in *two* sentences! Delightful!" he chortled.

"Well . . ." Kutmoi agreed reluctantly.

"Cheer up, old man, cheer up! Your performance out there was spectacular tonight. We're on our way to the top!"

"Well, I'll tell you one thing, Sanguinious, we'd better make sure our skirts are clean or—"

Cheatham waved his hand dismissively. "Posh! Don't worry. Sure," he said with a shrug, "we've all had to cut a few corners in our time, but let me tell you, old boy, after her demonstration out there tonight, even if she could prove you'd committed murder and incest, and she can't, you'd still be untouchable after tonight." He laughed. "The public would see that as a mere peccadillo compared to her stumbling performance."

"I don't consider that very funny, 'old boy.'" Kutmoi was referring to "murder and incest." "And I'll tell you one thing and don't ever forget it, Mr. Campaign Manager, *never* write the Old Girl off. That old pussy has her nine lives and we would be fools to think she doesn't still have claws. Now I want you to be sure that any irregularities we might've committed during this campaign are brushed way, way under the rug. You understand what I'm saying?"

"Of course, Senator, of course," Cheatham said soothingly. "Not just under the rug but in the bag, deep in the bag. Trust me."

"Well, that was three *goddamn*s in two sentences spoken before all the citizens in Human Space, Suelee." Marcus Berentus sighed and shook his head. "Not to mention a personal attack on your political opponent that I believe makes your closing remarks unprecedented in the history of electioneering."

"Well, I meant what I said and said what I meant, Marcus, and *that* is also unprecedented in politics."

"How well we know."

Chang-Sturdevant took a big sip of Scotch. "And that bastard, Kutmoi!"

"Please, Suelee, whatever you do, don't add that word to your repertoire next time you make a speech!"

"He is going to destroy us all, Marcus. He is going to open the gates to the barbarians."

Marcus was quiet for a long interval. "Yes, you're right," he agreed at last. "And we have to do everything we can to stop the sonofabitch."

"I hope," Chang-Sturdevant said with a laugh, "*that* word doesn't slip out, too."

"Knowing you, love, it just might," Berentus laughed. "But name calling won't stop this man. We've got to expose him for what he really is and prove to the *voters* that electing him spells their doom."

"Easier said than done, Marcus." She stared into the bottom of her glass. "I could always have him assassinated," she mused.

"Oh, for Christ's sake!"

"Just joking, Marcus, just joking." She toyed with that loose strand of hair. "I can't use an instrumentality of my government to dig into Kutmoi's shady past and his current dealings," she mused. "If I did, everyone would think I abused the taxpayers' money to keep myself in office and whatever we dug up would be suspect."

"Yes, then what you need is a 'consultant,' a private investigator or an investigative reporter, and I have just the man." He snapped his fingers.

"And who might that be?"

"Jack Wintchell."

In the fifty years Jack Wintchell had been digging dirt for the Confederated News Network, he had learned that when searching for corruption, you follow the money. That had made him a top-notch muckraker. Usually he worked several stories at one time. He had been interested in Haggel Kutmoi for quite a while before Chang-Sturdevant's now very unusual exchange, but the note from Marcus Berentus had whetted his journalistic scalpel. Wintchell had ruined many reputations in his time but now he saw a chance to derail a sure-thing presidential candidate. He had also been working on several juicy stories exposing Chang-Sturdevant, which he now abandoned in favor of this lead.

Jack Wintchell did not particularly care for Chang-Sturdevant or her presidency. His personal opinion of her was that she was a bumbling fool who badly needed retirement. But he respected Marcus Berentus, whom he knew from a short stint as a person-nel officer in the wing where Berentus was a fighter pilot during the Third Silvasian War. He had come to respect Berentus for his valor and his total lack of pretension. All the man wanted to do in those days was fly. The tougher the mission the more he liked it. But when back on the ground he displayed none of the disdain aviators usually show toward nonrated officers, especially those in personnel. After one long, boozy night in the officers' club, the two had become unlikely friends, and that friendship had lasted through the years as each rose in his career.

Now Berentus was married to "that ditzy broad," as Wintchell called her, who had been left squirming at the end of her debate with Kutmoi. If she squirmed, Berentus squirmed, too. Jack Wintchell was a past master at destroying the reputations of prominent people but he never stepped on his victims once they were down, and Chang-Sturdevant was all but out with the trash of her administration. And on top of everything else, on top of Jack's disdain for her, Chang-Sturdevant was a veteran and he could never extinguish that tiny spark of recognition he felt for anyone who'd worn a uniform and shared his own experience of serving, however briefly but honorably, something besides their own self-interest.

The note from Berentus read: *"Jack, you might be interested in fund-raising activities, particularly involving the Tabernacle Rock of Ages True Light Christian Church, and certain contrac-*

tors involved in rebuilding Ravenette's infrastructure. Tally ho, Marcus."

Jack Wintchell went to work, and the report that CNN broadcast was a masterpiece. His technique was simple: visuals of his evidence accompanied by a dispassionate voice-over explaining their significance, concluding with a close-up of Wintchell himself asking the key rhetorical questions—never accusing, but asking his viewers if the evidence supported the allegations, and his famous tagline, "And so, Mr. and Mrs. Taxpayer and all the ships in space, this is Jack Wintchell reporting." His reports would be weeks old by the time they reached outlying worlds, where their effect was still impressive, but in Fargo, the center of government, where *everyone* watched his show, they were damning.

That night his report began with close-ups of various documents, a government contract awarding thirty billion credits to the Highjump Construction Company for rebuilding of public utilities in the city of Ashburtonville on Ravenette, of which only three hundred million had been spent to date. "This contract," Wintchell announced, "was awarded under the competitive bidding process established by the government. Highjump submitted the lowest bid for the work requested, all very aboveboard." Next appeared a list of the board of directors of Highjump Construction with one name highlighted: *Viktoria Culbobble;* a list of the shareholders showing that this Viktoria Culbobble owned 51 percent of the company's stock; and Wintchell intoning, "Viktoria Culbobble's maiden name was Kutmoi." This revelation was followed by a close-up of Viktoria rushing into a stockholder's meeting.

The vid then segued to the Tabernacle Rock of Ages True Light Christian Church in downtown Fargo. The congregation of the megachurch consisted of the missing preacher Jimmy Jasper's followers, who still maintained their prophet would return and welcome them to the Millennium. Viktoria Culbobble was shown entering the church and participating in the charismatic service, gesticulating, screaming Jasper's name, tears streaming down her cheeks. Then a canceled check appeared before the rapt viewers. It was made out to the Tabernacle Rock of Ages Church for twenty-five million credits and signed by Viktoria Culbobble. "This check," intoned the Reverend Strachey Starling, his enormous jowls jiggling, the thin veneer of perspiration shining on his forehead, "was writ by the Finger of God!"

"It may have been 'writ by the Finger of God,'" Wintchell said, "but He signed Viktoria Culbobble's name to it." Pregnant pause. "It has been alleged," Wintchell continued, "that the late Reverend Jasper was an agent of the alien Skinks who are even now ravaging the remote world known as Haulover. But Mrs. Culbobble is to be commended for her generosity to the Reverend Jasper's church."

Now a familiar face flashed before Wintchell's viewers: a grinning Sanguinious Cheatham, caught on a hidden camera accepting a large packet from the Reverend Strachey Starling, the pastor of the Tabernacle Rock of Ages Church. "Here is a list of the contributors to Senator Haggel Kutmoi's campaign, a campaign managed by none other than Mr. Cheatham." A long list of names unfolded on the vid screen and, as they appeared, certain ones jumped into a sidebar with the amounts of their contributions, along with the donors' employment. "These fourteen individuals," Wintchell announced, "contributed a total of twenty-five million credits to Senator Kutmoi's campaign. Our investigation has revealed no evidence that the fourteen people listed here ever gave any of this money to Senator Kutmoi's campaign and in fact they could not have, not in the sums listed, because they do not have that kind of money." The vid zoomed in on one name. "This lady is a chambermaid here in Fargo but she allegedly contributed six million credits to the senator's campaign." The other thirteen names, with their contributions and employment, scrolled out before the viewers. "All fourteen contributors are members of the Reverend Starling's Tabernacle Rock of Ages Church. Is this something the Confederation Election Commission should look into? Does this imperil the Tabernacle Rock of Ages tax-exempt status? The commission should start with the Highjump Construction Company, Mrs. Culbobble, Senator Kutmoi's sister, the Rock of Ages Church, and these fourteen campaign contributors." Very pregnant pause. "And so, Mr. and Mrs. Taxpayer and all the ships in space, this is Jack Wintchell reporting."

Five months later. Election night on Earth was almost over. Although all the returns would not be in for another two months, until the votes from the outlying worlds could be counted and verified, Chang-Sturdevant and her entourage sat glued to the vid screens because often as Earth went, so went the entire Confederation.

"Not only did you nail his teats to the shithouse wall when you called him a 'goddamned fool,' Madam President," Huygens Long, the Confederation Attorney General, chortled, "Old Jack Wintchell tacked his balls up there beside them."

"Please, AG." Chang-Sturdevant grimaced and sighed. "It'll be a close one, though."

"The military services are all solidly behind you, ma'am," General Cazombi said, nodding his head in confirmation.

"Ma'am." Marcus Berentus set his drink on a sideboard. "You can unpack your bags; you're in for another term." He gestured at the screen with his cigar. The board that had been giving a running count of the votes all night long now stood at 7,564,493,223 for Chang-Sturdevant to 6,345,321,587 for Haggel Kutmoi. "Not a landslide," Berentus announced, "but if the rest of the Confederation goes the way Earth has, you've won. And it *will,* Madam President, it will."

Cazombi permitted himself a very slight twitch to the right corner of his mouth (which passed for a grin with him), because it amused him that Marcus persisted, when in company, in addressing his wife so formally. But he knew Marcus Berentus was an old soldier and believed in protocol.

"And on that note," Berentus announced suddenly, striding over to where the President was sitting, "I congratulate you." He placed a huge, wet kiss right on her lips.

And for the first time in many, many years, General Alistair Cazombi laughed outright.

"You stupid shit!" Haggel Kutmoi shouted at his campaign manager. "You had to go and let that bastard get you on camera! I thought you were a *lawyer*," he sneered.

"You set it up, old man," Cheatham replied calmly. "And, if you remember, I warned you in the first place against getting that sister of yours involved in your fund-raising efforts. I could've gotten millionaires to distribute the money for you but no, you followed her advice and got chambermaids, housewives, auto mechanics!" He snorted and shook his head.

"My election campaign is ruined!" Kutmoi shouted. "My career in the Senate is ruined!"

"Yeah, well, my heart pumps for you, old boy, but I'll never be a Supreme Court justice now, and I'll be lucky not to get disbarred. Next time I try to subvert the rules I'll do it with another lawyer." He stood up, put on his mantle, and walked to the door.

"What am I going to do, Cheatham?" Kutmoi whined. "You're my fucking *lawyer*! Tell me what am I going to *do*?"

Cheatham paused, his forefinger resting on the door pad. "I was never your *lawyer*, Haggel. I was only your campaign manager. But"—he paused as if thinking—"I'll tell you, as a lawyer, what I think you should do." He smiled at Kutmoi sitting slouched, crushed down in his armchair. "Do what Jason Billie did. Get a pistol, put the muzzle in your mouth, and pull the trigger. Good evening, Senator."

CHAPTER
TWENTY-SIX

The Grand Master sat in solitary state. The four Large Ones with drawn swords who protected him on his dais were the only persons in attendance. Not even the graceful, diminutive female who served and tasted his steaming beverage was present. The small, low table at his side was bare, lacking even the delicate vase that usually held a single, perfect bloom. The Masters and Leaders, behind the draperies to provide full protection for the Grand Master, were out of sight and therefore did not alter the Grand Master's solitude.

The Grand Master pondered the failed assault against the Earthman army unit to the northwest of the Earthman city and airfield. It was fortunate that the High Master who led the assault died in his miserable attempt; there was no need to make an example of him.

But, the Grand Master smiled grimly, one positive thing had come of the failed assault, a positive that would allow the Emperor's Fighters to reach victory against the Earthman army, and then the much-desired victory over the hated Earthman Marines.

It was obvious that the Earthmen didn't know about the tunnel mouths that were so near to the defensive lines they were establishing. His scouts had told him how many Earthman soldiers were there, and he knew his own Fighters greatly outnumbered them. Yes, he could send his Masters, Leaders, and Fighters through the tunnels to attack the thin Earthman lines, and defeat them. The Grand Master's smile changed from grim to anticipatory. He clapped his hands, signaling the female to serve him.

*   *   *

So it happened that the Second of the 502nd wasn't the only unit the Skinks attacked. They also came up from tunnels near the positions of the Fifty-fourth Light Infantry Division's regiments. In twenty minutes of hard fighting, supported by rail guns, they overran the 227th Infantry. The 138th Infantry managed to hold, with heavy casualties. But the 499th was barely hanging on after three-quarters of an hour—the Skinks who had overrun the 227th were flanking the 499th.

Lieutenant General Carano called on his experienced Skink fighters to save the 499th.

"We have to plan this on the fly." Brigadier Theodosius Sturgeon looked pointedly at Captain Chriss, the FIST's assistant operations officer who was filling in for the late Commander Usner. Chriss had done a good job as assistant, but this was the first operation on which he'd acted as the F3; it was going to be a tough baptism. "Here's what we know about the situation." Sturgeon projected an overlay onto the map table that filled the center of Thirty-fourth FIST's operations center. The overlay showed the position of each of the 499th Infantry's squads, and the known positions of Skink units, along with icons representing their weapons and lines of movement. An uncomfortable number of icons indicated rail guns. Other icons indicated the positions of probable survivors of the 227th Infantry.

"We will go in through the 227th's positions. If possible, link up with the survivors and have them join when we hit the Skinks from the rear. But don't waste time if the soldiers are too shocked. Kilo and Lima will be the main force, with Mike in reserve. General Carano is providing us with Battle Cars for transportation and support." He turned to Commander Wolfe, the squadron commander. "Arm your hoppers for ground attack. Work with Captain Chriss to form an air-support plan, but keep your aircraft out of line of sight of the rail guns to the greatest extent consistent with providing close air support to the infantry units."

"Aye aye, sir," Wolfe said.

He checked his UPUD. "The Battle Cars should be here in less than one-zero. I want the companies to begin mounting them and our own Dragons as soon as they arrive. Do it."

"Third herd, saddle up!" Staff Sergeant Hyakowa called out. "Form on me." In little more than a minute, the Marines of Company L's third platoon had their weapons and gear and were assembled in front of their platoon sergeant, helmets and gloves off and sleeves rolled up. Hyakowa gave them a quick once-over, then looked on approvingly as the squad leaders and fire team leaders checked and double-checked their men.

"Listen up," he said when the squad and fire team leaders finished. "Doggie Battle Cars are on their way to pick us up. From here we go to rescue a doggie regiment or two that are getting chewed up by the Skinks. That's all I have for now, so don't ask any questions. Lieutenant Bass is at the company CP. I'm sure he'll have some more information when he joins us."

After the fight in and near the back door of the Skink complex, the platoon had done a bit of reorganizing. PFC Gilbert H. Johnson came from Whiskey Company, the FIST's replacement pool. Bass and Hyakowa had assigned him to second squad's third fire team as Corporal Doyle was their best junior NCO at breaking in new men. They assigned Lance Corporal Longfellow as a temporary replacement for the badly wounded Corporal Dean in first squad's third fire team, and transferred Lance Corporal Francisco Ymenez to Longfellow's fire team, which freed Lance Corporal MacIlargie to rejoin Corporal Claypoole and Lance Corporal Schultz. PFC John Three McGinty stayed where he was.

A rumble of tires on dirt announced the approach of the Battle Cars. The Marines looked at them with curiosity; most of them had never seen the army armored personnel carriers up close before. They were significantly smaller than the Marine Dragons, had wheels instead of air cushions, and didn't seem to be nearly as heavily armored or armed. Three of them pulled up in front of third platoon, and an army officer with single blackened bars on his shirt collars stepped out of one of them. If the lieutenant was at all startled by the display of disembodied heads and arms, he didn't show it. He introduced himself to Hyakowa, asked him a couple of questions, and turned to the platoon.

"Listen up, you Marines!" the army lieutenant called out. "These Battle Cars are designed to carry one nine-man army squad each, so you might be a little bit crowded with your heavy weapons. But we don't have to go far, so you won't be cooped up for long." He turned to Hyakowa. "Sergeant, board your men."

"By squads," Hyakowa ordered. "First, second, guns." He pointed at a different Battle Car as he called out each of the squads.

Lieutenant Charlie Bass arrived from the company command post as the last of the platoon boarded.

"Lieutenant," the two officers greeted each other.

"You'll ride in the command car with me," the army lieutenant said to Bass. "Your sergeant can ride in the driver's compartment of the second Battle Car, and your communications man in the third." Bass and Hyakowa flicked their eyes at each other when the lieutenant referred to Hyakowa as "your sergeant." But neither commented. They boarded the Battle Cars and drove off to a fight.

It would have taken two Dragons to carry the platoon, and they wouldn't have been as crowded.

"Listen up, third platoon," Lieutenant Bass said on the platoon all-hands circuit; the Marines had put on their helmets and gloves and rolled their sleeves down when they entered the Battle Cars. "The 499th Infantry regiment is in danger of being overrun by Skinks to their front and flank. Those Skinks are supported by rail guns in the forest. Kilo Company is going after the flanking Skinks to hit them from the rear. Company L is going after the rail guns in front of the 499th. When we stop and dismount, squad leaders on me so I can give you overlays and orders. That is all."

The Battle Cars went at their top overland speed, ignoring the possibility of ambush, and in less than fifteen minutes stopped just east of the former position of the 227th Infantry. Their doors popped open and the Marines poured out and automatically set a defensive perimeter facing to the north and west. Bass raised an exposed arm for the three squad leaders to guide on.

"Here we are," he said when they joined him. He transmitted the overlay to their comps; there was a "you are here" clearly marked on the overlays, and a "here they are." Icons showed the locations of a dozen Skink rail guns; the nearest was three-quarters of a kilometer to their northwest.

Sergeant Ratliff whistled. "We're supposed to take out twelve rail guns without assistance?" he asked.

"We're Marines," Bass answered. "I don't see any reason we can't."

Sergeant Kelly elbowed Ratliff in the ribs. "You heard the lieutenant; we're Marines, we do the impossible."

Ratliff grunted.

"One other thing you need to know before we set out: You've probably noticed that I didn't have a corpsman with me when I came back from company. The skipper's keeping them all with the command unit. He gave me stasis bags in case we have casualties. Here." He handed one to each of the squad leaders. "I'm keeping a fourth myself. We shouldn't need them."

None of the squad leaders commented on the lack of a corpsman, or the stasis bags, but Bass saw concern in their faces. He chose not to comment about it.

"Now, here's how we're going to do it . . ." Bass said.

Second squad, naturally, was given the job of taking out the first rail gun. Second squad's second fire team had the point on the mission—Lance Corporal Hammer Schultz wouldn't have it any other way.

The forest was thinner than Schultz would have preferred for a stealthy approach, scattered trees and low, scraggly undergrowth, but he knew better than to be put off by the less than optimal. The Skinks were going down and Schultz was going to see to it that as many of the Marines as possible were going to survive.

The squad was on line moving through the forest, and it wasn't Schultz, but PFC Gilbert Johnson, the platoon's newest member, who spotted the first Skink.

"Corporal Doyle, bad guys," Johnson said on the fire team circuit, from his position on the squad's right flank. "Thirty, thirty-five meters, my right front."

Sergeant Kerr, listening in on all the fire team circuits, heard, and said, "Second squad, freeze." Then, to his third team, "What do you have, Doyle."

"I, ah, I—. There they are. I c-can make out seven. Oh hell, they've spotted us! Summers, Johnson, back up! Fire as you go!"

Kerr heard the *crack-sizzle* of blasters from his right and saw the flashes as two Skinks were hit and flared into incandescence. Before he could give commands to the rest of his squad, Schultz came on the squad circuit:

"Second team, flanking them."

"Wait up, Hammer," Corporal Claypoole shouted on the fire team circuit. "Who told you to—"

A rapid series of *crack-sizzles* from Schultz's blaster cut off Claypoole's words. Shouts and conflicting orders came over the radio on all of second squad's circuits: "There they are!" "Get down!" "There's a dozen of them!" "Fall back!" "Over here!" "Aim your shots!" "They're all around us!" "Volley fire!" "Where's the rail gun?" Until Sergeant Kerr's voice managed to cut over the others:

"Second squad! Second fire team, pull back, firing as you go. Third fire team, swing to your right, pivot on first fire team. First fire team, pick targets and flare them!"

The confused shouting stopped and the Marines' fire became

more disciplined. Flashes flared up in the forest where the Marines were firing.

"Cease fire!" Kerr commanded after a moment. "Fire team leaders report!"

The fire team leaders reported none of them had casualties.

"Is anybody else moving out there?" Kerr asked when the reports were in. Nobody saw sign of Skinks to their front. Kerr reported to Lieutenant Bass.

Bass looked beyond second squad's line, toward the rail guns that were the platoon's objective. And at just that second, the nearest rail gun turned and began firing in the direction of third platoon.

"Down!" Bass screamed into the all-hands circuit. They were still about half a kilometer from the rail gun, and the gunner was shooting a little bit high, so the rail gun's pellets zipped harmlessly overhead. But Bass knew that state wasn't likely to last. What Bass didn't know—and wasn't anxious to find out the hard way—was what the extremely high-speed pellets from the rail guns did when they hit the ground in front of a prone man.

Lance Corporal Schultz wasn't concerned about what the pellets flying at two-tenths the speed of light did when they hit the ground in front of a prone man—he wasn't prone. As soon as he'd let Corporal Claypoole know he was all right and there weren't any living Skinks to the squad's front, he crouched and began trotting to his right front. He knew the brief firefight was going to attract attention, and part of that attention was likely to be from the nearest rail gun. He'd only gone a few paces when he was proved right and the rail gun began firing in third platoon's direction. Schultz kept moving, with only part of his attention on the rail gun; it was shooting more toward the left side of the platoon than in his direction—and his route was taking him even farther from its likely cone of fire.

Movement to his right front made Schultz pause in his advance, frozen immobile for a moment. He turned up his ears and rotated through his helmet screens. Seven Skinks, armed with the acid guns, were running through the forest, headed toward second squad's position. He radioed a warning to Sergeant Kerr, then began moving again, ignoring Kerr's and Claypoole's demands to know where he was, and their orders to return to his position.

Schultz had seen enough of the Skink rail guns in action on Kingdom to know how they were set up and that he didn't need to close on one in order to kill it. When he'd increased his lateral position relative to the gun by a hundred meters, he began moving straight on a perpendicular path that would lead him to a position a hundred and fifty meters to the gun's left. Behind him, he heard the *crack-sizzle* of blaster fire, and the *whooshes* of flaring Skinks.

Little more than two minutes after leaving his position, Schultz was where he wanted to be. Now he was thankful for the thin forest—he had a clear line of sight to the Skink rail gun crew. But that same line of sight gave him a clear view of a platoon of Skinks heading on an angle to flank third platoon. Most of them were carrying the acid shooters but one team bore a rail gun. The nearest of them were within the fifty-meter range of the acid guns.

Schultz smiled.

Halfway down the platoon line, a small group of Skinks, maybe half a dozen, advanced closely together. Schultz carefully lowered himself to a prone position and sighted on the farthest Skink in that group, aimed, and pressed his blaster's firing lever. Instantly, he shifted his aim to the middle of the group and fired again. Once more he shifted aim and shot the nearest. The Skinks in that group were bunched so close together that each hit ignited at least one other Skink. Then Schultz turned his attention to the Skinks closest to himself. They had been confused by the unexpected fire, but their sergeants and officers quickly began shouting orders, and they were dropping to the ground to return fire. But Schultz had moved after he shot the three closest Skinks. It was less than fifteen seconds since he'd fired his first bolt and already the Skink platoon had lost more than a squad.

Schultz looked to where he'd seen the crew carrying the rail gun and saw they had gotten it set up and were about to begin firing. He snapped off three quick bolts, and, on toes and elbows, changed his position, five meters to his right and ten back just as streamers of acid splashed the area he'd vacated. He looked through the thin undergrowth but couldn't make out prone Skinks through it. He'd have to wait for them to fire again and give away their positions. The rail gun crew was gone, likely vaporized when he shot them. But as Schultz looked, he saw three more Skinks running to crew the weapon. Three quick shots took them out. He moved again, then sent several bolts into its barrel, heating it enough to bend and thus rendering it useless.

Once more he moved and this time marked the positions from which Skinks had returned fire. He fired several quick bolts into the undergrowth a few meters short of where he'd seen the acid streamers begin their arching flights and was rewarded by three or four flashes of flame as plasma bolts skittered along the ground and struck home.

The original forty-Skink platoon was down to half strength. But Schultz hadn't yet taken out his primary target—the rail gun that had third platoon pinned down. Or rather, *had* had the platoon pinned. That rail gun was now shooting over the heads of the Skink platoon, fishing for Schultz.

And coming close.

Schultz raised his shoulders, propped himself on his elbows, and sighted in on the rail gun. He took out the gunner, then fired three more bolts at the weapon—it didn't matter if the rest of the crew survived, they were no threat if the weapon was useless. But he couldn't finish the job.

Officers screamed and sergeants barked and the remaining Skinks jumped to their feet and charged, spraying a wall of acid as they came. Schultz pushed himself up and rapidly backed away, firing as he went. Nearly every bolt hit home. Some of the bolts must have hit the officers and sergeants because suddenly nobody was yelling orders, and the few remaining Skinks broke and ran.

Schultz let them go. He didn't care whether they lived or died, but alive, after so many of their comrades had been killed by one Marine, they could spread uncertainty and fear among the ranks. That uncertainty and fear would reduce their fighting ability, and that would save the lives of Marines. Besides, he still had to render the rail gun useless. He knelt and aimed at it, pouring plasma bolt after plasma bolt into it until its receiver glowed red, then white, and started to sag.

Satisfied, Schultz turned and began trotting back to where third platoon was beginning to advance again.

"Schultz." Lieutenant Bass's angry voice came over Schultz's helmet comm. "I want to see you. With your squad and fire team leaders. Right fucking now!"

When Lance Corporal Schultz reached Bass, the lieutenant sent the rest of the platoon on under Staff Sergeant Hyakowa. Bass stood, bare arms akimbo, fists jammed into his invisible hips, helmet dangling from one wrist. Sergeant Kerr stood to Bass's left, bare arms folded over his chest, also helmetless. Both were glowering at Schultz, who raised his helmet screens to show his coppery face. Corporal Claypoole was also there, to the left of Kerr, bare-armed and bare-headed and with an expression of *Why, gods? Why one of my men?* on his face.

"Lance Corporal." Bass's voice was a growl that began somewhere deep in his chest and grew louder as he spoke. "Who told you to go off on that flanking movement by yourself? I'm waiting for an answer, Lance Corporal!" He did his best to tower over Schultz but failed, since Schultz was taller and not about to be intimidated by anybody, not even the one officer he respected above all others.

Schultz looked back at Bass laconically, and didn't bother to answer—he figured the question was rhetorical.

"Are you trying to get yourself killed, Schultz?" Bass's voice rose as he asked the question.

"Two rail guns. Twenty Skinks, maybe more" was all Schultz had to say.

"I *know* what you accomplished out there, dammit!" Bass shouted. "But you could have gotten yourself *killed,* pulling a stunt like that. Don't you realize that?"

Schultz gave an almost imperceptible shrug.

Bass shook his head. "You're fucking impossible, Schultz. If you hadn't done so well, I swear I'd have your ass in front of Commander van Winkle for disobeying orders and insubordination. And endangering government property! A Marine *is* government property—you do understand that, don't you?"

Schultz gave another minor shrug. He knew that Bass wasn't going to do anything to him, that he was just upset because Schultz had gone off on his own and might have gotten killed. Except, Schultz knew he wouldn't have gotten killed. The fact that he came back without a scratch was all the proof he needed.

"Corporal Claypoole," Bass snapped, making Claypoole jump, "keep better control over your people in the future. Now take him and rejoin your squad."

"B-but how am I—I mean," Claypoole stammered, "this is the Hammer we're talking about. *Nobody* can control him!" But he was leading Schultz back to the rest of the squad as he voiced his objection. He rolled his sleeves down and donned his helmet as he went.

"What do you think?" Bass asked Kerr in a much calmer and quieter voice when Claypoole and Schultz were far enough away not to overhear. "A Gold Nova?" The second-highest decoration given out by the Confederation Marine Corps.

Kerr considered the question for a few seconds before saying, "If it was anybody else, I'd say the Confederation Medal of Heroism. Or at least the Marine Heroism Medal. But for Hammer Schultz? Yeah, the Gold Nova sounds about right. That was ballsy even for him."

Bass nodded. "I'll put him in for the Marine Heroism Medal.

That way, if higher-higher wants to knock it down, he'll still get what he deserves." He looked in the direction the platoon had gone. "Let's catch up."

Kerr headed for his squad and Bass went to where Hyakowa had moved, behind the center of the platoon.

CHAPTER
TWENTY-SEVEN

Third platoon, Lance Corporal Schultz actually, had killed two
of the rail guns that were raking the front of the 499th Infantry
Regiment. But six more of the weapons were in the platoon's
area, along with an unknown number of foot soldiers. Lieutenant
Bass had the platoon shift a hundred meters to the north along
their west-to-east axis of movement. The angle of movement
of the Skink platoon that Schultz had encountered suggested that
the bulk of the Skinks were either on line with the rail guns or
slightly in front of them. By shifting north, Bass hoped to reduce
the chances of running straight into moving Skinks. He somehow doubted that the enemy was building up in depth.

Bass stopped the platoon a hundred meters beyond Schultz's
one-man assault on the first Skink rail gun. The platoon should
have been directly behind the second gun on their assigned list.
But he didn't hear it firing.

"One, on me, bring your second fire team," Bass ordered on
the all-hands circuit. "Five, put the rest of the platoon in a defensive perimeter."

Sergeant Ratliff and Staff Sergeant Hyakowa rogered. A
moment later, Ratliff and Corporal Pasquin, along with
Pasquin's men, reached Bass.

Bass got right to it. "There should be a rail gun about one-fifty
meters south of us, but I don't hear one firing. It could be that it
was the one with the platoon that Schultz took out, but I don't
know. Pasquin, you're former recon. Get close, see if that gun's
still there, and if not, what the Skink disposition is. Questions?"

Pasquin looked at his men, Lance Corporal Quick and PFC Shoup. Both were good men and had fought Skinks on Kingdom but neither man had recon experience. Could they snoop and poop well enough this close to the enemy? He knew they knew how to move close to enemy positions. If he was careful about guiding them, and did not let them get close enough to alert the Skinks' sixth sense . . . Yeah, under his leadership, they'd do all right. "No questions," he said. Except for the obvious one: Why was Bass giving the job to him instead of to Hammer Schultz? He decided that, as former recon, he knew how *not* to fight, but Schultz only knew how *to* fight.

"Keep in close touch with your squad leader."

"Aye aye."

"Do it."

Pasquin took the point and led his men south. Quick was staggered to the right, Shoup to the left, and all three could shoot straight to the front without danger of shooting one another.

Pasquin turned his ears all the way up and he used the light-gatherer screen on his helmet; it wasn't very dark under the thin canopy but he knew from experience that the Skinks' skin and uniform colors allowed them to blend in with their surroundings if there was some shadowing; the light gatherer should make them stand out. He heard rail guns fire along a line to his right front but not to his front or left. The *whizz* of army flechette rifles came from farther ahead. At the moment he wasn't concerned about getting hit by friendly fire; flechette darts were so fast they quickly burned up in atmosphere. He and his men were beyond flechette range anyway.

Seventy-five meters from where the nearest Skinks should be, Pasquin halted his patrol. He still hadn't heard or seen sign of the enemy to his immediate front, only to his right front, and the nearest sounds he heard there were more than a hundred meters to the right. He considered his options, then called Quick and Shoup to join him. When they did, he drew them close and touched helmets, to communicate through direct conduction rather than via helmet comm, which could be intercepted by the Skinks.

"Stay here, back to back," he told them. "I'm going forward on my own until I find where they are. As soon as I locate their positions, I'll be back. Got it?"

"Are you sure you want to go alone?" Quick asked. "Wouldn't it be safer if we went with you?"

Unseen inside his helmet, Pasquin shook his head. "One man is quieter than three," he said. "Plus, I've got more training and experience in the kind of movement that'll get me close undetected. You two stay here."

"I don't like it," Quick murmured.

"You don't have to like it, Marine," Pasquin said harshly. "Just do it."

Quick shrugged. "Whatever you say, Corporal."

Satisfied that his men were going to do as he said, Pasquin broke contact and headed farther south by himself. He didn't bother to check that Quick and Shoup went back to back as he'd told them; he was confident that they'd do as he said without close supervision.

Weaving cautiously, avoiding contact with the undergrowth as much as he could, and keeping behind trees where he could, Pasquin advanced toward what he thought should be the Skink line. He reached it without seeing anything more than traces of past movement.

And then he was right where the Skink rail gun had been. Examining the ground, he saw where the crew had picked up the gun and headed west. Looking more, he found where what must have been an entire platoon, maybe more, had gone with the rail gun—this was evidently the markings of the platoon and rail gun that Schultz had encountered. Pasquin wondered where the survivors of that platoon had gone. He resumed moving south but turned back after he'd gone two hundred meters without seeing more signs. What convinced him to turn back then, though, was the *whizz* of a flechette dart that spit past him; he was within the extreme range of the army's shoulder weapons.

Pasquin followed a track fifty meters west of his original route on the way back to his men. Standard procedure: Never return along the same route you came out on. The enemy might discover your movement out and set an ambush to catch you on your way back. Because of his changed route, he came across signs of movement that he wouldn't have otherwise seen: traces of large numbers of troops moving at an angle to the Skink main line. He checked his position and turned off his route to follow the Skink marks—they might lead to the transport the Skinks had used to get from their underground bases to the positions of the Fifty-fourth Light Infantry Division.

He found what he sought but it wasn't what he was expecting. Instead of vehicles, he found the entrance to a tunnel, a long ramp dug into the ground, well enough camouflaged that it wouldn't be spotted from orbit or by an air patrol. Faint sounds from inside suggested vehicles and a ventilation system. He wondered if the tunnel ran all the way to the underground bases—and whether there were more such tunnels. He shook his head in marvel. *Just how long had the Skinks been on Haulover?* he wondered.

Pasquin hurried back to where he'd left his men. The three Marines followed a different track returning to the rest of the platoon.

"I wish I could tell you more, sir," Corporal Pasquin said when he completed his report to Lieutenant Bass.

"You told me plenty, Corporal," Bass said. "I'm going to get this to the skipper ASAP. Return to your squad, but be ready to be called in to report higher up the chain of command."

"Aye aye, sir." Pasquin looked to Staff Sergeant Hyakowa for directions to the rest of first squad.

As soon as Pasquin left, Bass had Lance Corporal Groth contact the company command unit on his comm then reported Pasquin's discovery to Captain Conorado.

"Well, that's very interesting," Conorado said. "I'll report it to battalion. There are probably more tunnels out there; it would have taken too long for so many Skinks to come out of one tunnel. Carry on, and keep me apprised of what's happening."

"Aye aye, Skipper," Bass replied.

Half an hour later, third platoon had killed another Skink rail gun and was closing in on yet another. Lance Corporal Schultz, as was his habit, was on the platoon's right flank as it moved on line through the forest; the position most exposed to the enemy. This time, the Skinks were waiting for them.

The Skinks may have been ready *this* time, but Hammer Schultz was ready *all* the time.

"Bad guys, sixty," Schultz said into the squad circuit.

"Second squad, halt," Sergeant Kerr said into the squad circuit, then into the platoon command circuit, "Schultz reports bad guys sixty meters ahead."

"Third platoon, hold in position," Lieutenant Bass ordered when he got Kerr's message. Then to Kerr, he said, "Have they seen us?"

Kerr was already asking Schultz the same question. Schultz grunted in reply; if the Skinks had detected the Marines, he would have already been firing at them.

"Negative," Kerr told Bass.

"Third platoon, take a knee," Bass ordered. Sixty meters was a pretty extreme range for the Skink acid shooters, but he was concerned about the rail gun; the Marines didn't know what its range was, guesses ranged all the way up to interstellar, if the pellets didn't burn out in the atmosphere before they escaped a planet's gravity well. "Does anybody have a fix on the rail gun?" he asked.

All through the platoon, the fire team and gun team leaders asked their men, then reported negatives back to their squad leaders. Nobody in the platoon saw the rail gun to their front but they could all hear it—and more of them reported seeing Skinks to their front, Skinks facing in their direction. While Bass waited for the squad leaders to report, he contacted Captain Conorado and informed him.

Bass considered his options. He had an approximate position for the rail gun, but the reading on his UPUD from the string-of-pearls wasn't capable of giving him any more accurate a location than he would get by triangulating on what his Marines could hear. Anyway, if he had everybody fire where they thought the rail gun was, the other Skinks would be able to see where the Marines were and could quickly close to effective range. Even though the chameleons his men wore were impregnated with an acid repellent, the acid could still cause casualties. His other option was to fire on the closer Skinks and try to take them all out, and then shift fire before the rail gun could turn. He didn't like either option, but the latter was probably the better one.

"Listen up, everybody," Bass said into his all-hands circuit. "We've got to clean out those Skinks right in front of us before we can go after the rail gun. Don't fire until I give the command. If you have targets, on my command burn them. If you don't have targets, then fire into the dirt fifty meters to your front, and make those rounds skitter along the ground. Gun one, sweeping fire from left flank to center, gun two, sweeping fire from right flank to center. I'll tell you when to shift your fire to the rail gun. Squad leaders, report when all your men understand."

All along the platoon line, fire team leaders checked their men to make sure they understood the orders, then reported to their squad leaders, who in turn checked that the fire team leaders had it right.

After the three squad leaders reported to Bass, he said, "Stand by to do it. One, two, *fire!*"

The Skinks, as Bass had hoped, were caught off guard—all along the Marine front Skinks flared up as they were hit by plasma bolts. But there were a lot more Skinks than Bass had suspected. Hordes of them—maybe an entire battalion of Skinks—suddenly rose up and raced forward to get in easy range of their acid shooters. There were so many that, even if every plasma bolt the Marines fired flamed a Skink, there were too many Skinks to get them all.

Suddenly, after charging forward thirty meters, the Skinks

dove for the ground, and the rail gun that had been third platoon's objective turned and began firing. Not all of the Skinks got down fast enough, and some of them virtually exploded when the rail gun's pellets hit them.

Acid streamers, hundreds of them, began arching at the Marines.

"Down!" Bass screamed, "everybody get down!"

Everybody was already down; they'd gone prone when the rail gun opened fire. With the Skinks in front of them also down, most of the Marines could see their targets only by noting where the acid arcs started.

"Volley fire," Bass ordered. "Twenty meters. Pull back between volleys! Fire!" A volley of twenty bolts *crack-sizzled* from the two blaster squads, striking the ground along a line twenty meters in front of the Marines. The bolts skittered forward, spreading as they went; some fragmented and continued on as though they were multiple shots. Skinks flared into brilliant flame as the Marines shifted positions, moving slightly to one side or the other, and a few meters to the rear.

The rail gun's fire swept back and forth, across the width of third platoon's position and beyond, but the fire was ineffective—the gunner had to shoot high enough to avoid hitting the Skinks who were so close in front of the Marines, and so the bursts sped harmlessly over the Marines' heads as long as they remained prone.

"Fire!" Twenty more bolts flew at the Skinks, immolating more of them. The guns continued sweeping fire, left and right to center, their bolts striking the ground along the same line as those from the blasters. The Marines moved again, and acid streamers struck the ground all around where they had fired from, some splashing far enough for Marines to be struck by drops of acid.

"Shift aim, up five meters," Bass ordered. "Fire!" The Skinks were dying by the dozens, yet the rate of their acid streams didn't ebb.

"Fire!" Bass heard shouts to his right front and left front and looked to where the cries mounted in frequency and intensity.

He saw the flanks of the Skink mass rising and running to the left and right.

"Fire!" Bass continued to watch the Skink flanks while his men fired volleys into the massive formation in front of them, and then shifted position, further increasing the distance between themselves and the acid shooters. Another volley and the Marines would be far enough back to shift their aiming point again.

"Fire!" Now Bass saw the Skinks on the flanks turn forward—they were moving to close on third platoon from both flanks!

"Blaster squads, continue volley fire front," Bass commanded. "Guns, turn to your flanks. They're trying to flank us in both directions!"

The volume of fire to the front was sharply reduced as the guns shifted their fire to the flanking elements. But still Skinks flared up in front of the platoon. Then Skinks began flashing into vapor on the flanks as well.

Lance Corporal Schultz noticed, here and there along the front, that when a plasma bolt struck right at the base of a bush or other bit of the undergrowth, the vegetation hit began burning, though the fire generally went out in a few seconds. Vegetation struck a glancing blow, or through its leaves, didn't burn. He experimented; the next time Bass called "Fire!" Schultz shot three quick bolts into the base of a bush, right where he saw its stem emerge from the ground.

The bush started burning. It was still burning two volleys later, far longer than any of the bushes that had been hit by one bolt had.

"Rock," he said into the fire team circuit. "Watch." He fired another three rapid bolts into the base of a bush.

Claypoole saw the bush go up in flames that didn't look like they were in any hurry to die out. Beyond that bush, he saw the one Schultz had fired at before; not only was it still burning, the fire was beginning to spread to other bushes.

"Mohammed's pointy teeth," he murmured. He switched to the squad circuit. "Honcho, three hits at the base of a bush sets it on fire. If we zap enough of them, we can make a wall of flame between us and the Skinks, maybe drive them back."

Sergeant Kerr looked at the bushes Schultz had lit up. "You may be right," he said. Then he switched to the platoon command circuit and reported Schultz's finding to Lieutenant Bass.

"Claypoole said that?" Bass asked. "Doesn't he remember what happened on Maugham's Station?" Third platoon had been caught in a forest fire, started when the Marines' fire had ignited some volatile brush. None of the Marines were killed in the fire, but Claypoole was one of several who had to be evacuated and treated for smoke inhalation.

"Fire!" Whatever reports Bass was getting from his squad leaders, the platoon still had a battle to fight. He consulted his UPUD, checking the meteorological report for the area third platoon was in. The prevailing ground wind was from the northwest but midlevel currents could shift the ground current to the east shortly.

"Fire!" Still, he liked the idea of making a wall of fire between the platoon and the Skink battalion. If the shift in wind direction held off for a little while, the ground wind could sweep a fire toward the Skinks to the platoon's front—and maybe even go far enough to get the rail gun.

As soon as the volley was fired, Bass said into the platoon circuit, "Blaster squads, listen up! For the next volley, fire three rapid bolts into the base of the closest bush to where the Skinks are. Gun squad, continue your fire on the flanks. Fire!"

A dozen bushes between third platoon and the Skinks to their front ignited.

"Do it again, *fire*!" More bushes ignited and the fire was beginning to spread.

"Again, *fire*!" Then he asked Sergeant Kelly, "Guns, which gun is on our left flank?"

"First gun team," the gun squad leader answered.

"You know what the blaster squads just did?"

"Affirmative."

"Have first gun team do the same. Second gun team is *not* to fire at the base of the bushes. Got it."

"Gun one, light up the bushes. Gun two, do *not,*" Kelly said.

"Do it." Then to the blaster squads, "Fire!"

The Skinks in front of third platoon had been slowly crawling toward the Marines, not allowing them to increase the distance between them as fast as they wanted to. But burning bushes began to block them and the Skinks' forward progress was broken up. Some were able to continue but others stopped and were unable to see where the Marines were firing from. A few jumped up to run from flames that were beginning to advance on them, and in their panic some of them were killed by the rail gun that was still firing over their prone companions.

Bass had Hyakowa take control of the volley fire while he contacted Captain Conorado to update him on the action—and inform him about the fires the platoon was starting in the underbrush.

Conorado checked his UPUD's real-time map. The Skinks were hard to detect, but it looked as though a huge mass of them was closing on the front of the 499th Infantry, which Company L was trying to relieve with its attacks on the Skink rail guns. A fire coming at the Skinks from behind could break up the assault. The fire in front of third platoon showed clearly in infrared and was becoming visible in visible light. Moreover, it seemed to be spreading farther. He checked the location of the tunnel entrance that Corporal Pasquin had found and thought it was a good time to move third platoon, or even the entire company, to the tunnel mouth to set an ambush for Skinks who might retreat to it.

"All right, Charlie, I want you to run a fighting withdrawal, get away from the fire you started. Then swing back east and set an ambush at the tunnel mouth. I'm going to check with battalion, see if I can get permission to move the entire company."

"Aye aye, sir." They signed off.

"Fire!" Hyakowa called, for the sixth time since Bass gave over control to him.

The attackers on the left flank stopped their advance in the face of the growing wall of fire, a wall that the northeast wind was beginning to push in their direction. The only Skinks still making a serious attempt to get to the Marines were the company or more coming from the right flank. However, that group was no longer a company or more; second gun team had reduced its number by nearly half. Still, fifty or seventy-five Skinks were now within acid range of the gun team, and the gun wasn't able to maneuver as agilely as blastermen. The three Marines of second gun team were getting hit, hard enough that the acid retardant on their chameleons was in danger of becoming overwhelmed.

"Two," Bass ordered between orders to fire a volley, "turn one fire team to assist gun two."

"Second fire team," Kerr snapped, "wheel right, assist gun two. Lay down enough fire for them to withdraw."

"Three men, enough fire to hold down that many Skinks," Claypoole grumbled, as he and his men slithered to the right flank to assist the gun team. "Right." They began firing past second gun team, and enough extra Skinks flared up that the rest of them hesitated.

"Let's move!" Corporal Taylor ordered, and his men picked up the gun and its tripod and pulled back, out of range of the Skink acid shooters.

"Honcho, we've got to get out of these chameleons soon," Taylor reported to Kelly. "Mine are starting to steam. I think they're pretty close to being eaten through."

"Did you get that, boss?" Kelly asked Bass, and repeated Taylor's report when Bass hadn't.

Bass looked to the front and the left flank. The Skink advances in those directions had stopped and the Skinks were withdrawing. It seemed like a good time for the platoon to break contact. But first . . .

"Everybody not involved in the fight on the right flank, listen up. Estimate where that rail gun is and put everything you've got into it. *Fire!*"

One gun and seventeen blasters opened up on the estimated position of the rail gun. Some of the bolts must have struck their intended targets, because the rail gun abruptly fell silent.

"Second squad, assist gun two to break contact," Bass ordered.

"You heard the man," Kerr shouted. "Let's do it!"

First and third gun teams jumped to their feet and ran to the flanks of second fire team, adding their fire to what was already flying at the Skinks. In less than a minute the few surviving Skinks ran.

"Third platoon, let's bug," Bass ordered. "Second squad, guns, first squad. I'm with guns."

The platoon began to move at a trot away from the Skink lines. Bass checked on second gun team as they went.

"Damn!" he said when he saw the state of their uniforms. "I'm surprised your chameleons held out this long." And he *did* see the chameleons—they had been coated by so much acid they were visible to the naked eye.

CHAPTER
TWENTY-EIGHT

Second Lieutenant Steven Moreau's fourth platoon, George Company, Second Battalion, 499th Light Infantry, held the regiment's right flank, where it linked with the left flank of the 227th Light Infantry, Fifty-fourth Light Infantry Division. Moreau couldn't remember for the life of him which company of the 227th was on his right—or was supposed to be there. All he knew was that all the devils in hell were coming straight at the front of his platoon, and an equal number were trying to get at his platoon's flank through the remnants of the 227th. At least that's how he saw the Skinks.

He'd called Captain Grady Riggan, the George Company commander, and asked for artillery support, but the CO couldn't get any for him. The captain had said he'd tried already, but all of the division's artillery was busy supporting the 138th, which was in imminent danger of being overrun.

"Well, so the hell are we, Captain!" Moreau had just about screamed into his comm.

"The whole damn division is in danger of being overrun, Lieutenant!" Riggan shouted back. "Now fight your platoon and try to kill those Skinks before they *can* overrun your position! George Six-Actual out."

Fight my platoon, sure, Moreau thought. *Fight my platoon?* Sure, a platoon commander's weapon was his platoon, but Sergeant First Class Smith Downes, the platoon sergeant, and the squad leaders seemed to be doing well enough on their own without his meddling. Moreau risked raising his head far enough to look along the line of his platoon from its left, where it linked with third platoon, to its right, where one fire team had turned to meet the threat from the flank. Yeah, everything seemed about the same as it had the last time he'd looked. The Skinks with the acid shooters were pinned down beyond the range of their weapons, in the cleared stretch of ground between the division's hastily prepared defenses; and every time a Skink stood up to dash forward a few meters, one or more of the soldiers of fourth platoon zeroed in on him and the Skink went down hard, shredded by flechettes.

Speaking of flechettes, his men were putting out a horrendous amount of fire. How was their ammo holding up? *That* was something he could do something about. But before he could, a lengthy *whirr* made him duck back down below the lip of the hole he was in—a Skink rail gun seemed to be devoting its entire attention to the platoon. He didn't have a recent count, but he knew the platoon had already suffered several casualties with devastating wounds.

The rail gun's fire moved on, and Moreau got on his comm and asked his squad leaders about their ammo. All of them were getting low.

Not the report Moreau had been hoping for, it meant he was going to have to expose himself. Sure, he could send a runner to get fresh ammo boxes and distribute them, but he was in charge and it was incumbent upon him to take care of his men. That meant that going for more ammo was on him. That didn't mean he couldn't take his runner with him—the two of them could carry twice as many needle boxes.

"Yancy," he said, "come with me, we're getting more ammo."

Private Yancy looked at his platoon commander with horror. Get out of the bottom of their hole and expose himself to the rail gun? Was the LT out of his mind? Yancy listened, heard the whine of the rail gun's pellets way off to the side somewhere, and decided it was safe enough for the moment. He poked up like a prairie dog and looked toward the company's supply point, where the ammo dump was, some two hundred meters away. He saw three piles of thrown-up dirt that indicated hidey-holes along the way.

"Right after you, sir," Yancy said.

"Good man." Moreau vaulted out of the hole and ran, zigging and zagging, toward the supply point. Yancy followed five meters behind him. They only had to go to ground once along the way, but it was close; Moreau's helmet got sideswiped by a high-velocity pellet from the rail gun. When he took it off and looked at the damage—a fist-size chunk was missing from the helmet's rear—he thought it was a miracle that his head hadn't been shattered at the same time. He'd have to get a new helmet—if the supply dump had any.

The supply dump wasn't out in the open, it was in an interconnected maze of bunkers that had been dug by heavy equipment. Two soldiers Moreau didn't recognize were in the trench, guarding the entrances to the bunker.

"Whadaya need, Joe?" one of the soldiers asked when Moreau and Yancy dropped into the tunnel.

"I'm looking for Sergeant Grubley," Moreau answered.

The stranger shook his head. "Grubley got took out by the damn Skinks," he said. "He looked above the trench when the rail gun was firing this way. Took his head off."

" 'Cept we couldn't find his head afterward," the other stranger said with a snort.

"Then who's in charge here?"

"I am," the first soldier said. "Sergeant Constable. Battalion sent me down to replace Grubley. Who the fuck're you?"

"Lieutenant Moreau, fourth platoon. We need more ammo." Moreau decided to ignore the noncom's insubordinate attitude for now.

"Ammo. You got it," Constable said. "As much as you two can carry?"

"Every bit of that."

"This way." Constable turned to the entrance to one of the

bunkers and motioned for Moreau and Yancy to follow. In about a minute, Constable had the two loaded so heavily with needle boxes they could barely stand.

"Where's your helmet, LT?" Constable asked.

"Got whanged by a rail gun."

"Were you wearing it at the time?" Constable's eyes opened wide when Moreau acknowledged that he had been. "You're damn lucky you're still alive. Here, take this one, you need it more than I do." He yanked his own helmet off and plunked it on the officer's head. "I'll scrounge up another one for myself. Now let's get you back to your platoon." He led the way out of the bunker, to the ladder that climbed out of the trench.

"Wait one." Constable held up a hand as he listened to the fighting. "Now!" he shouted when the rail gun whine sounded farthest away. He and the other soldier gave Moreau and Yancy a boost, and the two were on their way back to fourth platoon.

Their progress on the return was much slower than it had been on the outgo; Moreau and Yancy didn't so much zig and zag as they staggered and stumbled. And they had to go to ground twice—deliberately. But at last they made it back to the hole Moreau had begun thinking of as home, sweet home. They dropped into the hole, drenched with sweat and heaving for breath, but otherwise unscathed.

Moreau quickly divided the needle boxes into six approximately equal piles. Pointing at one of them, he said to Yancy, "Take that to third squad." They were on the right of the platoon line.

"Yes, sir," Yancy gasped. Having made it to the supply dump and back without undue incident, he was perhaps feeling a touch invincible. He slung the needle boxes over his shoulders and clambered out of the hole.

Moreau scooped up the second pile and scampered to the platoon sergeant. He reached him and got down just as the rail gun came back.

"Get this to second squad," he said without too much gasping;

he'd almost regained his breath. "I'm going back for more for first squad."

"Don't take so long this time," SFC Downes said. "They're dangerously low."

Moreau shook his head. "I only have to go back to my CP; Yancy and I brought back two full loads for the entire platoon."

Downes looked at the young lieutenant with new respect; he knew how much two full loads for the platoon weighed—and they'd hauled it under fire. "Will do, LT." Downes waited for the rail gun to pass them by, then jumped up and ran for second squad's position. Moreau headed for first squad at the same time and made it back to his hole before the rail gun returned.

A few minutes later, when he looked up after another pass by the rail gun, he saw the most peculiar thing he'd ever seen on a battlefield.

Streamers of fire were coming out of the forest, arching over the prone Skinks, who were still pinned down by the fire from fourth platoon. The fire moved back and forth on the killing ground where so many Skinks had flared while trying to get in range of their weapons, and every time a streamer hit one of the bodies, the body blazed up in brilliant, vaporizing fire. When the flashes cleared, the Skinks were retreating into the forest. The rail gun had gone silent.

"Get them!" SFC Downes's voice rang out, and the soldiers of fourth platoon increased their rate of fire into the retreating Skinks. As soon as most of the Skinks were far enough into the trees, the flaming streamers began arching again, incinerating the dead and wounded left behind.

Moreau reached for his comm to report to the company commander, but Captain Riggan beat him to it:

"George Company," the CO ordered, "this is Six-Actual. Cease fire! Repeat, cease fire!"

The command was repeated all along George Company's line, and the fire quickly died out.

"Is anybody still engaged?" Riggan asked.

All four platoons reported that the enemy had broken contact and that they were no longer receiving fire from the rail guns.

"Casualty report!"

Moreau called for a squad leaders' report, and waited for the squad leaders to get back to him. The news was bad, but his voice was calm when he gave the casualty report to the company commander.

"Fourth platoon. Six dead, four major wounds. No minor wounds."

Ten casualties in a platoon that an hour earlier had been thirty-five men strong. Moreau was sick; he'd never had that many casualties before. He didn't think SFC Downes ever had, either. He wasn't at all consoled by the thought that the 227th was hurt even worse; some of its platoons had been wiped out.

There was a brief pause after all the platoons delivered their casualty reports, then the CO came back. "I just got word from battalion," he said. "The Marines hit the Skinks from behind, that's what broke their attack on us. The Marines are pursuing the Skinks. We sit tight and tend to our wounded."

After a hundred meters, Bass stopped the platoon for a moment.

"Roll on the ground," he ordered the Marines of second gun team. "Maybe the dirt will sop up some of that acid and keep it from eating through your chameleons until we can replace them." It didn't stop their disintegration altogether. The platoon hadn't been on the move for very long when Lance Corporal Dickson stifled a scream and tore off his shirt.

"Shit!" Corporal Taylor swore, only in part because one of his men was suddenly visible. Dickson's shoulders and torso were speckled with tiny greenish dots.

"Get him on the ground!" Sergeant Kelly yelled. "Roll him, try to get that shit off him."

Taylor and PFC Rolf Dias knocked Lance Corporal Dickson off his feet and began rolling him in the dirt.

Dickson gritted his teeth to keep from screaming as the

droplets of acid nibbled away at his skin. Some of the acid was absorbed and drawn away from Dickson by the dirt he was rolled in, but most of it remained on his skin, eating away at him under the dirt that now coated his body.

Kelly stripped the leaves off a bush branch and shoved them at Taylor. "Wipe off the dirt," he snapped. "That should get rid of more of the acid."

Taylor snatched the leaves from Kelly and began wiping. Kelly stripped more handfuls of leaves, gave one to Dias, and held the other ready to give to Taylor when he tossed the first.

In moments they had most of the acid off Dickson, but some continued to eat at his flesh.

"Start cutting," Kelly ordered. He bumped Dias aside and knelt on the opposite side of Dickson from Taylor. He drew his fighting knife and began scraping acid from Dickson's body, wiping the blade in the dirt between swipes. Then he began digging the point of his knife into the holes the acid had eaten into Dickson's body, flicking away the mix of acid, blood, and flesh that he dug out. Taylor did the same. When Kelly thought they had cleaned Dickson's chest and belly well enough, he flipped him over and set to on his back.

An occasional whimper passed Dickson's lips, but he never cried out again, despite what must have been excruciating pain.

Lieutenant Bass had been on the comm with Captain Conorado and the other platoon commanders while the platoon was stopped. He checked with Kelly when he had the platoon's new orders.

"Put him in your stasis bag," Bass ordered when Kelly told him the extent of Dickson's injuries. "Is anybody else in similar danger?"

"Taylor and Dias."

"Damn. Is it visible on the surface, can you wipe any of it off?"

"That's an affirmative—both times."

"Do it, and listen up while you do." Bass switched to the platoon circuit. "Listen up, everybody. Battalion reports that the

Skinks the company was hitting are retreating in the direction of the tunnel mouth that Pasquin found. We've got the go-ahead to set up an ambush for them. Kelly, let me know when you've got Dickson on a litter and are ready to move out."

"No litter, boss," Kelly replied. "Tischler's carrying him. We're ready to go whenever you say."

Bass nodded. Lance Corporal Tischler, the gunner of first gun team, was a big man, easily capable of carrying Dickson by himself.

"All right, third platoon, move out. Same order as before. Hammer, here's the route." Bass transmitted a hastily drawn overlay to Lance Corporal Schultz and to Sergeant Kerr and Corporal Claypoole.

The platoon resumed its movement, on a sharp tangent to the direction it had been going before Dickson tore off his shirt.

Company L had severely mauled the Skinks attacking the 499th Infantry's front, and Kilo Company had done equally well against the Skinks advancing on the 499th through the position of the 227th Infantry. The remnants of both Skink units were in hasty retreat, though not all were heading for the tunnel Corporal Pasquin had found. Kilo Company was engaged in a running firefight with its Skink unit. Company L's first platoon harried the Skinks who had been in front of them as the Skinks attempted to get out from between the Marines and the army. Second and third platoons, along with the assault platoon, raced to the tunnel mouth to set their ambush. Mike Company was moving to assist.

There was no good location for an ambush near the tunnel mouth; no low rise the ambushers could hunker behind, no dry rill they could use as a trench line. There weren't even enough trees big enough to give a man adequate protection from the Skinks' acid shooters.

But even though they were ambushing a much larger unit, the Marines had two major factors in their favor: the element of surprise, and range. They set up far enough outside the maximum range of the Skink acid shooters that the Skinks had little chance of getting close enough to return fire before most of them were flashed—if the Skinks attempted to charge into and through the ambushers.

The only thing the Marines had to worry about was the Skink rail guns, and they'd killed enough of them during their counterattack from the Skinks' rear that the rail gun threat wasn't what it would have been earlier.

Third platoon, being closer to the tunnel mouth to begin with, got into position first. The Skinks were already pouring into the tunnel.

"Hold your fire," Lieutenant Bass ordered as his Marines began dropping into firing positions two hundred meters away from the fleeing Skinks.

"Right there," Lance Corporal Schultz grumbled, caressing his blaster's firing lever.

Schultz hadn't said it into his comm, but he may as well have—Bass knew his men well enough to know what Schultz was most likely thinking.

"Don't sweat it, Hammer," Bass said into the private circuit. "There's plenty more where they came from. The skipper wants everybody in position before we hit them."

Schultz grunted. It was an acknowledgment; even though he didn't like the order, he'd hold his fire.

The Skinks continued to stream into the tunnel, unmolested by the Marines watching them. Hundreds of Skinks, perhaps as many as a thousand, ran into the tunnel while third platoon watched and waited for second platoon to get into position.

Corporal Doyle carefully kept his hand away from his blaster's firing lever—he was afraid that if his fingers got close to it, he would accidentally fire a bolt, setting off the ambush before everybody was in position.

He'd never seen so many Skinks at one time, even if right then he wasn't seeing all of them at once, but rather in a steady stream. The rational part of his mind rejected that idea and tried to think back to the war the Marines had fought against the Skinks on Kingdom. But the frightened part of his mind insisted that there hadn't been so many Skinks on all of Kingdom during that entire war. So many Skinks were going past third platoon that if they suddenly detected the Marines, they could turn and charge, and the Marines would have no chance to win against them—they'd all die!

Doyle realized he needed to distract himself. He slid his infra into place and looked to his sides. The red blurs representing PFCs Summers and Johnson were visible in position right where he expected them to be. The rational part of his mind told him the shaking he saw in them was an illusion, that they seemed to be shaking only because his own trembling distorted his view. The frightened part of his mind insisted that his men were as nervous as he was about the hundreds of Skinks passing so close to their front.

He swallowed. He had to steady his men and reassure himself that they were all right, that they weren't as frightened as he was. If they were as frightened as he was, then he would have to steady himself so he could calm them. If they weren't, then he needed to show them that he also wasn't frightened.

He looked to his left and said into his fire team circuit, "Summers, are you all right?"

"Maintaining, Corporal Doyle," PFC Summers answered. "Just waiting for the word to burn some Skinks."

Doyle nodded to himself. Summers sounded relaxed. He took a deep breath, and said, "Be patient, it'll happen." He turned to his right. "Johnson, you?"

"I'm cool, Corporal Doyle." Johnson didn't sound as calm as Summers; there was a slight tremor in his voice. Doyle thought he could use some bucking up.

"Hang in there, Johnson. It'll happen any minute now."

"Right. Thanks, Corporal Doyle."

There was a moment of silence, then, "Corporal Doyle?"

"Yes, Johnson?"

"I was nervous before. Hearing your voice helped."

"You're not nervous now?"

"Not so much, no."

Doyle didn't say anything else. He turned off his comm and breathed a deep sigh of relief. The rational part of his mind told him he'd done exactly the right thing in checking on his men. The frightened part of his mind was still there, it just didn't have anything to say on the matter. He turned on his comm.

It felt a lot longer to most of the Marines of third platoon than it actually was, but the second and assault platoons finally got into position. Captain Conorado was with them and took a position behind the middle of his company's line.

"Company L," Conorado said into the all-hands circuit, "get ready. On my command, *fire*!"

Almost as one, the blasters and guns of two platoons, and the heavier guns of the assault platoon, all opened fire.

The stream of Skinks flowing into the tunnel mouth lit up in gaudy flashes of pyrotechnics. Hundreds of the enemy were vaporized in less than a minute. Those who weren't immediately incinerated ran, trying to reach the safety of the tunnel mouth. Very few of them made it. If any of them attempted to turn toward the Marines and charge to within range of their own weapons, they didn't get far enough for anybody to notice what they were trying to do.

It was a slaughter. The Skinks in the open never had a chance.

The firefight was so one-sided that after a few bolts, Lance Corporal Schultz kept shooting only because his company commander had told him to open fire, and nobody had told him he could stop shooting yet.

"Cease fire!" Conorado shouted into his all-hands. "Cease fire!"

The company commander looked and listened, but saw no more Skinks approaching the tunnel mouth, or lying prone in the thin brush that partly covered the scorched killing ground where so many of them had just died.

Corporal Doyle kept shooting until the cease-fire order came, then flung all of his screens back and violently threw up. He wasn't the only Marine sickened by the massive killing; both of his men were as well, and Doyle heard retching from beyond their positions.

"Second and third platoons, on line," Conorado ordered. "We're going to sweep through the area. If any of them think they can hide from us, we're going to show them just how wrong they are. On your feet. Watch your dress. Let's move out!"

They found no living Skinks, only scorch marks where the enemy soldiers had burned so hot and briefly.

CHAPTER
TWENTY-NINE

Lieutenant (jg) McPherson listened to the orders he was receiving from the Combat Information Center, aye-aye'd, and hung up his talker. "Chief," he said, loudly enough for the two petty officers at their stations in front of Chief Petty Officer Nome to hear, "the jarheads planetside found something and Fleet wants us to find out if it's the only one."

Chief Nome's jaw moved side to side as he shifted the stub of a one-inch hemp cable clamped between his teeth from one side of his mouth to the other. "What and where is it, and where should we look for more?"

The Surveillance and Radar Division commander diddled buttons on the arm of his chair and changed the scale of the large display showing the current area of operations planetside, to focus more tightly on the section where the Skinks were attacking the Fifty-fourth Light Infantry Division and the Marines were counterattacking the Skinks from their rear. The positions of the soldiers on the line showed clear in infra; the Marines' chameleons had limited infrared damping effect, so they were less clear—but the plasma bolts from their weapons showed up exceedingly bright. The Skinks barely showed; the main indicator of where they were was the flickering strobes made by the pellets thrown out by their rail guns.

"The Marines found a tunnel mouth here," McPherson said. He touched buttons that put an icon where Corporal Pasquin had discovered the Skink tunnel. "Fleet wants us to find out if there are any other tunnel mouths in the area."

SRA2 Hummfree broke discipline and swiveled around in his chair to face his division commander.

"Sir, you realize, of course, that Fleet's asking the impossible. I mean, unless there are more tunnel mouths and lots of Skinks start pouring in or out of them."

Chief Nome removed the stub of rope from his mouth, preparatory to reaming Hummfree a new one for speaking out of line, but McPherson spoke first.

"Yes, Hummfree, I *do* realize that. And that's why I'm assigning the two best surveillance and radar analysts in the entire navy to the job."

Hummfree's mouth pursed as he looked at the officer. Then he glanced at SRA2 Auperson in the chair next to his, and shook his head as he swiveled back to his displays. He could hardly protest being asked to do the near impossible after publicly being called one of the two best SRAs in the entire navy. *But if,* Hummfree thought, *I'm one of the two best, how come I'm still a second—*

His musing was interrupted by McPherson adding, "You know, Hummfree, that the skipper has put you in for first class. If you find what Fleet wants, that'll almost guarantee a meritorious promotion."

He hadn't known, but if it was true . . .

The first thing Hummfree did was focus on the discovered tunnel mouth and examine the image in all frequencies so he'd know the signs that would help him find what he was looking for. He had SRA2 Auperson, the other of the two best SRAs, do the same thing.

Chief Nome stuck the stub of hemp back in his mouth and leaned back in his chair with his arms folded across his massive chest to watch the two work their magic.

It took some time, because the tunnel mouths were very well camouflaged to prevent detection from orbit, but SRA2s Hummfree and Auperson found three more tunnel mouths before the Marines broke the Skink attack. Then they switched to following the faint traces of the retreating Skinks and found where they disappeared into two more hidden tunnels.

"Chief?" Auperson suddenly said.

Chief Nome grunted permission for Auperson to speak, and rolled the stub of hemp rope to another place in his teeth.

"Something just occurred to me, Chief."

Nome snarled something that might have meant "Stop wasting my time, Auperson. Spit it out!"

"Right, Chief. Like I said, it just occurred to me—"

Nome removed the rope from his mouth and growled, "Yeah, I know something just occurred to you. You've said that. Now what was it?" He chomped back on his rope.

Auperson swallowed. "Well, Chief, it's this." He rushed on before Nome could get on him again for repeating himself instead of getting where he was going. "Those places we spotted earlier, you know, the ones we thought might be smaller Skink bases close to NAS Gay? I think some of these might be some of the same places."

Hummfree hadn't been paying much attention to the exchange between his fellow SRA and Chief Nome, but he caught that last. He jerked and felt like kicking himself for not noticing what Auperson had. His fingers danced over the controls on his panel, and an overlay came up, showing the suspect locations that had been found earlier. Five of the nine matched one of the tunnel mouths the two of them had found over the past few hours. It was a matter of minutes before he matched another to a known tunnel mouth.

"Check the rest of 'em," Nome growled around his rope stub.

In less than ten minutes, all nine of the suspect locations were matched.

"Keep looking, gentlemen," Lieutenant (jg) McPherson told them. "I have a feeling there are a lot more of those hidden tunnel mouths."

Hummfree straightened in his chair and stretched side to side to work the kinks out of his back, then settled in to search some more. Auperson aped him and moved his search to a different area. They kept to it long enough for McPherson and Chief Nome to take turns leaving for mess and for McPherson to go out for a division commanders' call. They worked not only through their entire shifts but halfway through the next shift before McPherson called a break.

"Grab a meal, a shower, and a few hours' sleep," he told them. "You did damn good."

As they had—they'd found another dozen hidden tunnel mouths. Fleet was quite pleased with what they had done. The ground commander was even more pleased.

"The navy's really come through for us, Doc," General Anders Aguinaldo said to Major General Donnie McKillan, his chief of staff.

McKillan nodded. "It's that SRA off the *Fairfax County,* the one Ted Sturgeon recommended."

"SRA2 Hummfree," Aguinaldo agreed. "I'll drop a not-so-subtle hint to Admiral Chandler to give him an 'attaboy.' "

McKillan chuckled. The army and navy gave medals for exemplary duty performance. The Marines *expected* exemplary duty performance, so they didn't award meritorious service medals, and referred to those given by the other services by the derogatory "attaboy." "So what are we going to do with the information Hummfree got for us?"

"Assemble my staff, and round up Generals Carano and Almond with their senior commanders and staff. By the time everybody's together, I should know."

"Aye aye, sir." McKillan left to do his boss's bidding.

As soon as his chief of staff was gone, the overall Confederation commander contacted Ensign Jak Daly, the army's recon commander, and gave him instructions.

It was a couple of hours before all the commanders and staff officers General Aguinaldo had called for were able to assemble in Aguinaldo's headquarters, which gave Ensign Daly's recon people time to get a good start on fulfilling Aguinaldo's orders.

"Gentlemen," Aguinaldo began without preamble, "at this moment, recon minnies disguised as Norway brown rats are in the tunnels, following them to wherever they go. In the normal course of events, we wouldn't know what they find until they exit the tunnels back into direct control of the recon units that deployed them. But they are being followed into the tunnels by recon Marines, who are in contact with the minnies and are emplacing comm repeaters along their route so we can receive real-time intelligence from them. Look at this."

Aguinaldo nodded to Lieutenant Quaticatl, who turned on a 2-D display. The image was grainy, and bounced about, but it was clearly the light-amplified view of a tunnel along which the source of the image was moving. A window in the lower left corner of the display showed a series of numbers, detailing the speed of the minnie, its distance from the tunnel entrance, and environmental data. The image was accompanied by susurration that sounded like a ventilation system. There may have been an undercurrent of rushing water in the sound, but at the moment the ventilator susurration masked it too much.

Aguinaldo nodded at his aide again, and the image changed to a surface map. The known tunnel mouths were marked, and paths indicated, showing the routes taken by the minnies inside the tunnels. All paths led generally to the north.

"Based on this very preliminary intelligence, I believe that the tunnels lead all the way to the underground Skink complexes a thousand klicks north of Sky City. Unfortunately, given the speed of the minnies, it'd take about ten days for them to go that far. We shouldn't give the Skinks ten days to recuperate from the defeat they suffered in the pincer between the Fifty-fourth Division and the Marines—or allow them that time to prepare and launch another assault. Instead, I want to strike back at them as quickly as possible.

"Between the two corps, we've got ten divisions. I want two divisions to station themselves outside each of the five known Skink complexes and be prepared to enter and clear those complexes. I want the Marines to break down into companies and enter twelve of the tunnel complexes and follow them to their end in Dragons and Battle Cars. There are more tunnels than Marine companies, so the Corps of Engineers and the combat engineers will enter the remaining tunnels and collapse them to a depth of one kilometer. Draw up your plans and have them for my review by ten hours tomorrow."

Major General McKillan called all present to attention when Aguinaldo stepped away from the dais to exit the room. When the top commander was gone, he looked at the two corps commanders and said, "Gentlemen, you have limited time. Dismissed." The assembled commanders and staff scrambled.

Company L was in positions covering the mouth of the tunnel where they'd ambushed the Skinks. If the Skinks tried to come back out, they would be met by the full firepower of a Marine company. None of the Marines thought the Skinks stood a chance if they tried it.

The command came down, and the Marines boarded Dragons and Battle Cars. The three stronger, heavily armed Dragons entered the tunnel, followed by the Battle Cars. The Dragons carried third platoon, one section of the assault platoon, and the company command element.

The column was three kilometers in when an order came from Battalion to halt. Commander van Winkle spoke to all of his company commanders on his comm.

"Recon reports that all tunnels are flooded," van Winkle said, "beginning about eleven kilometers in. The flooding is nothing that the Dragons can't handle, but the water's too deep for the Battle Cars. So Corps has scrapped the idea of a Marine assault at the northern termini of the tunnels. But we still need to know where they go. So here are your new orders.

"Return all Battle Cars to the surface immediately. I say again: return all Battle Cars to the surface immediately. The Dragons will proceed to where the tunnels are flooded. Once they reach the water, two Dragons will return to the surface. One, I say again, *one* Dragon will pick up the recon element it will meet at the water's edge and proceed at top speed to the terminus of the tunnel. Recon will drop comm repeaters at appropriate intervals so that contact can be maintained. Upon reaching the tunnel terminus, the Dragon will report what it finds. The Dragon and the Marines it carries are not, I say again, are *not* to initiate contact with the enemy. Do you understand?"

One by one, the company commanders replied that they understood their orders.

"One more thing," van Winkle said. "Company commanders are not to go with the Dragon heading deeper. You will remain with the bulk of your company outside the tunnel mouth. Understood?"

Again the company commanders replied that they understood—but there was a certain reluctance in their voices.

"All right, then, do it." Van Winkle signed off.

Captain Conorado, from his position in the second Dragon, gnawed over the orders. He didn't like them, neither the part about sending twenty of his Marines a thousand klicks into unknown territory, nor the part about not going with them. He was their company commander. If he was sending them into harm's way, he should go with them! But his orders were clear, and he had acknowledged them; he had no choice but to obey them. He got onto the company command circuit and spoke to the company's officers and senior NCOs.

"Listen up. The tunnel is flooded up ahead. The Dragons can handle the water, but the Battle Cars can't. When I give the order, everybody but the lead Dragon will reverse and head for the surface. The lead Dragon will continue on to the water, where it will pick up the recon element, and continue to whatever is there and report back. That one Dragon and its Marines are *not* to initiate contact with the enemy. Questions?"

"Sir," Lieutenant Bass, whose men were in the lead Dragon, said, "do you realize that if the tunnel goes all the way to the enemy complexes that we know about, it'll take almost eleven hours for us to get there?"

Conorado nodded. He hadn't made the calculation himself,

but he'd understood from the time he'd gotten the original orders to enter the tunnel that it would be a long ride if they went all the way north. "I know that, Lieutenant. I also know that these orders came from Corps. And when a lieutenant general gives orders—"

"Captains and lieutenants obey," Bass completed. "I understand our orders, sir. Will do upon your command."

"All right, then," Conorado said. "Let's do these things."

Before he departed, Conorado had one last thing to say to Bass—on the private circuit. "Good hunting, Charlie."

"Thanks, Skipper."

The Battle Cars and the Dragons leaving the tunnel reversed and headed for sunlight. A lone Dragon moved out.

Before they headed onward, Bass had shifted people around to put himself, second squad, and one gun team in the Dragon heading deeper into the tunnel. He picked second squad over first partly because first squad had an inexperienced fire team leader, Lance Corporal Longfellow, who was leading a thrown-together fire team that couldn't be expected to function as well as one that had trained together. And second squad had Lance Corporal Schultz. Going to an unknown location, into an unknown situation, the one Marine whom Bass wanted at his side more than any other was Hammer Schultz. Four Marines from the FIST's recon squad were waiting for them at the water's edge. Bass got out to examine the area. There was no light; the Dragon had to turn on its floodlights for him to see by.

Bass also let his Marines out to stretch their legs for the last time in what might be many hours. The tunnel widened slightly here. Its floor started sloping downward a few meters before it met the water, and the water met the floor across the entire width of the tunnel.

"How deep is it?" Bass asked Sergeant Steffan, the recon ream leader.

"The ramp continues to slope at the same angle until the water's a bit more than a meter and a half deep." He shrugged.

"We don't have any underwater gear, so I couldn't check it any farther than that."

Bass grunted; a sheen on Steffan's chameleons showed that he'd recently gone into the water to shoulder depth. "Deep enough to float a boat."

Steffan nodded.

"Where's your minnie?"

"I sent it ahead. Minnies don't swim well. We lost contact with it after a hundred meters or so. It probably drowned."

Bass peered down the tunnel; he could see a few hundred meters. It was water all the way, and no ripples. He looked at the overhead and felt the faint breeze on his face. The susurration of ventilators provided a background noise.

"What have you found out about the ventilation?" he asked.

"There's large fans in the overhead every quarter klick. One blows up, the next down. None of them are at high speed, just enough to keep fresh air flowing. They're concealed from topside somehow. At any rate we couldn't see through them to the surface."

"All right. Let's go. Marines, saddle up!"

In seconds they were on the way again, leaving a rooster tail that rose high enough to splash against the overhead.

It was crowded in the Dragon. Even though the Dragon could carry twenty fully outfitted Marine blastermen and it only had eighteen, it also had a gun, which took up one space. And they were going a very long way; there was little room to stretch muscles that, after several hours, would threaten to cramp.

Every few hundred meters, Sergeant Steffan dropped another comm relay in a flotation device so they could maintain contact with the rest of the company where it waited outside the tunnel. A hundred kilometers into the tunnel, Steffan told Bass he was out of relays. Bass ordered a halt and contacted Captain Conorado to ask for instructions. It only took a couple of minutes for Conorado to come back with "Continue the mission."

So they continued on, unable to contact anybody on the surface, going an unknown distance, into an unknown situation.

Six hours in, Bass called a halt and had Corporal Duguid, the Dragon's crew chief, lower the ramp so the Marines could stretch the kinks out of their muscles and void their bladders into the water. After ten minutes they moved on.

They reached the end of the tunnel. It emptied into a cavern, large enough that the Dragon's lamps couldn't fill it with light. A gravel beach bordered the cavern, and hundreds of boats were pulled onto the beach or lashed to pilings sticking out of the water. The ceiling of the cavern was high enough that they had to be under the mountains—which jibed with the inertial positioning shown on the platoon's UPUD.

Bass ordered Corporal Duguid to drive onto the beach and turn parallel to the wall. The ramp dropped and the Marines piled out, automatically setting a defensive perimeter around the Dragon. They paid little overt attention to the boats that had been crushed by the Dragon passing over them to gain the beach.

"Where the hell's the door?" Bass asked over the platoon circuit, into which he'd patched the recon team. The only egress he could see from the cavern was the tunnel by which they'd entered. Nobody else could see one, either. The exit was very skillfully hidden or it was underwater.

"By fire teams, piss break," Bass ordered.

Bass took his break with the Dragon team. Most of the Marines used uncrushed boats as the receptacles for their bodily wastes. While he pondered what to do next, Bass gave his Marines a fifteen-minute meal break. Then he huddled with Sergeant Kerr, Sergeant Steffan, and Corporal Duguid to discuss what he wanted to do next.

"Did anybody find entrances or exits that I don't know about?" Bass asked.

The three NCOs exchanged glances and shook their heads.

Bass looked at the quiet, boat-filled pool. "Must be underwater," he said. "Remember Society 437?" he asked Kerr.

Kerr nodded. "Yeah, they had a tunnel that led from the lake into their caves. Probably the same thing here."

Bass looked at the boats again. "I'm not going to look for any tunnels here, but we can't leave the boats for the Skinks to use to come after us. We'll burn them, then get back in our Dragon and take off."

"Aye aye," the NCOs agreed, grinning at the prospect.

"Let's do this thing."

Finished with the leaders' meeting, Bass had the boats set afire. Then the Marines reboarded the Dragon and headed back the way they'd come. A growing fire blazed behind them.

Good, Bass thought. *Now they won't be able to follow us.*

Fifty kilometers down the tunnel, the Dragon stopped under an up-drawing fan set. Lieutenant Bass and Sergeant Steffan climbed on top of the Dragon and examined the fans. The overhead was low, and even when they kneeled their helmet tops brushed stone. The fan was large, its blades more than two meters in diameter, and it moved slowly, but the strong breeze being drawn implied there were more fans above it. Bass shined a light between the blades and saw another fan the same size two meters higher, which was also moving slowly. He was pretty sure he could make out another fan above that.

"Do you think you can climb between the blades?" Bass asked the recon team leader.

"It'd be a lot easier if I could stop them," Steffan answered as he examined the fan's mechanism.

Suddenly a disembodied hand shot upward and plunged a metal rod into the hub of the fan. The blades screamed to a stop.

Bass looked where the hand came from and saw Lance Corporal Schultz through his raised helmet screens. Schultz looked a question at Bass. Bass considered, and nodded.

Schultz stood between two now-immobile fan blades and reached up to jam another metal rod into its workings. The fan shrieked as it came to a halt. He climbed up, standing on the bases of two blades, then pulled himself up onto the next fan. Bass heard the screech of another fan. And then another. That was followed by the sounds of a body moving away from them, and then silence for a few minutes. Then they heard the moving body again, and a moment later Schultz dropped back onto the top of the Dragon.

"Good camouflage," Schultz said. "I pinged the string-of-pearls."

"Good man," Bass said, punching at where he thought Schultz's shoulder was. He didn't miss by much. "I'm going topside and report." He began scrambling to the surface. Steffan and Schultz followed.

Lieutenant Bass quickly located the string-of-pearls and bounced his comm off it to contact Captain Conorado.

"I'm glad to hear from you, Charlie," Conorado said when he came on. "What did you find?" He listened while Bass described the boat chamber and its lack of visible exits; he chuckled grimly when Bass told him about burning the boats. "All right, I've got a fix on your location now." While listening, Conorado had Corporal Escarpo, his comm man, use the UPUD to locate Bass's position. "Get all of your people topside. A few hours ago we got the word to move up. The army needs some help. We'll rendezvous with you. Stand by for more. I'll be in touch as soon as I have further instructions. Lima Six-Actual out."

In fifteen minutes, all the Marines except for the Dragon crew were on the ground above the well-camouflaged ventilation fan set. Soon after that, Conorado called.

"Bring the Dragon crew up. The engineers are blowing the mouth of your tunnel. We should be at your location in an hour. It'll be a little tight getting you in the rest of the vehicles, but we won't have far to go."

Before heading for the surface, the Dragon crew set their main plasma supply to erupt. They gave themselves a ten-minute window to get clear.

CHAPTER THIRTY

The Dragons and Battle Cars were crowded, just as Captain Conorado predicted, but, as he'd said, the ride wasn't far. As for the help the army needed . . .

First platoon, Easy Company, Second of the 502nd, heading north at high speed in its Battle Cars, was the first element of the Twenty-fifth Mobile Infantry to encounter the Skinks, four kilometers south of the underground complex the division was headed for. The platoon's earlier losses, when the Skinks had attacked the forming main line outside Sky City, had been replaced, which didn't exactly thrill Sergeant First Class Jaworski. Not that he wasn't glad to have the platoon back up to strength. The problem as he saw it, and it was a problem, was that the new men hadn't trained with the platoon's survivors—or even with one another. So he knew there were going to be problems when the fighting started. He hoped Lieutenant Murray, the platoon commander, wouldn't expect the platoon to act like the well-oiled machine it had been before getting hit so hard.

First platoon was in four Battle Cars rather than its normal three because Jaworski had managed—don't ask how—to score a Marine plasma gun, and extra soldiers to man it. That first battle had convinced him of the value of plasma weapons—at least against the Skinks. He only wished he'd been able to come up with more blasters so his entire platoon could be armed with them. But the plasma gun, that would go a long way toward giving first platoon the firepower—he chuckled at *fire,* it was so literal now—it needed to defeat this enemy.

Jaworski was riding in the second Battle Car with second squad, mulling over how to keep the LT from expecting too much of the platoon once the shooting started so he had a ringside seat when a rail gun shredded the lead Battle Car.

"Sharp right!" Jaworski yelled at his Battle Car's driver. "Hard right!" The vehicle yawed wildly, almost tipping over, before the driver got control. It barely got out of the way of the next rail gun burst, which took off a rear corner of the troop compartment.

"Is everybody all right back there?" Jaworski yelled into the comm.

"No casualties," Staff Sergeant Wynn, the squad leader, shouted back.

Jaworski looked and saw a thick clump of trees just ahead. "Pull behind those trees and open up," he ordered the driver. "We're about to stop and open up," Jaworski told Wynn. "Everybody out and take cover." Only then did he get on the comm to Lieutenant Murray.

"The LT's hit bad," Staff Sergeant Cunningham, third squad leader, answered. "Looks like you're in command."

Jaworski swore, then asked about other casualties; Murray was the only one in the third Battle Car who was hit. "Get your people out, under cover, and start returning fire," he ordered. Then he contacted the fourth Battle Car, but those soldiers were already dismounted and were trying to get their unfamiliar weapon set up to return fire at the rail gun.

Swearing under his breath, Jaworski skittered, then bent over far enough that he had to use one hand to keep from falling on his face, to where the gun crew was. The crew got it up and firing a few seconds before he reached it.

"Move that thing!" the platoon sergeant ordered. He could see it wasn't firing at where the rail gun was, and knew the Skinks would try to take it out right away. He plowed into the crew when they didn't move fast enough and grabbed the gun to bear it out of the likely rail gun fire. He made it just in time, but only two soldiers from its crew came with him—the third was killed by the burst that had been meant for the gun.

Jaworski swore again; one hand had partly gripped the barrel of the gun and he suffered second-degree burns before he managed to shift his grip. "Follow me," he snarled at the two remaining crewmen, then headed at a crouch back to where he'd left second squad. Wynn had the squad on line, firing into the forest to their front. So far, the only fire that had come their way was from the rail gun, and they hadn't seen any Skinks yet.

"Just keep moving!" Jaworski told Wynn. "Don't let that lizard zero in on you." He ran to the far end of the squad's line and set up the gun, faster than the assigned crew had. The rail gun didn't give out a blazing trail, like the blasters did, nor did the gun smoke or steam. But he'd figured out how to find it when first platoon came under attack the first time. The rail gun was shooting through the undergrowth; he watched for the green fuzz of leaves being blown away by passing pellets, and followed the track back to where the pellets came from. *There!* He had them! He aimed and squeezed the firing lever, and a solid bar of plasma shot out from the muzzle of the gun to where he believed the rail gun was located.

He must have been right, because he saw a brilliant flash that wasn't plasma, and the enemy stopped firing.

Only then did he become aware of the voice calling on his comm. It was the company commander wanting a report. He gave it: the LT down, first squad gone, one other soldier killed in action, one Battle Car destroyed. One rail gun taken out, no other enemy sighted.

"Stand by. The rest of the company has dismounted. We'll advance to your position on line. The entire battalion is going to move forward on line to attack whoever else is in front of us."

In ten minutes, the entire Second of the 502nd was advancing on line, laying down a steady, light fire to their front. No flashes of vaporizing Skinks met any of their blaster bolts, and no one returned fire. Not at first.

But they knew it would happen.

And when it did, they were ready for it.

An opening *whirr* of rail gun fire splattered a few soldiers over the forest green, but most of the troopers hit the ground and were down by the time more rail guns opened up. Streamers of greenish fluid arced out of the trees toward the soldiers—and expended themselves against foliage or fell short.

Sergeant First Class Jaworski grinned; it was obvious to him that a nervous rail gunner had opened fire too soon, before the soldiers were in range of the acid shooters.

The soldiers of the 502 put up a wall of flechette and blaster fire. Flares went off in the forest to their front, almost one every time a blaster bolt flew at the Skinks.

Gods in heaven, Jaworski thought, *they must be shoulder to shoulder!*

He still had the gun and got it set up. He found where one rail gun must be to his left and looked for another to his right. When he found it, he began firing a long traverse, from one gun to the other. A row of brief torches lit up along the traverse, and the soldiers of first platoon cheered. The volume of fire coming at them dropped precipitously. They didn't need any urging to increase the rate of their own fire, and soon nobody was shooting at them anymore.

The Twenty-fifth Mobile Infantry Division resumed its advance, along with the rest of the XXX Corps and the XVIII Corps. The soldiers and their commanders didn't know it, but they had inflicted severe casualties on the Skinks.

The help the army needed wasn't to avoid being overrun, but to finish off the Skinks fast.

The mood in the Grand Master's hall was somber. The Grand Master himself was a study in stone, his face so totally expressionless that it might have been carved from the same granite from which was hewn the battlements of the Emperor's High Castle. He wore armor. Not shiny ceremonial armor, but battle-scarred armor, riveted where bands had been broken by enemy swords. He held a sword across his knees. The sword had the slight, graceful curve of all proper swords, but it wasn't a graceful thing that he held; even a casual glance revealed it as a killing tool.

No delicate flower stood graceful in the delicate vase on the low table at the Grand Master's side. The diminutive female who served him and tasted his beverage huddled in sackcloth. The cup on the table was made from crudely thrown clay and was unglazed. The beverage it held did not steam. It was not a soothing drink; it was a clear, distilled beverage that increased strength and aggressiveness.

No females knelt gracefully between the Great Masters, High Masters, and Over Masters who sat on their ankles before the Grand Master. Instead they were grouped together behind the dais, overseen by a Large One. The tables between them were barren. In formal settings, each of these ranking Masters had an assigned mat on which to sit. Many of the assigned mats were unoccupied, especially those of the Over Masters, though several of the High Masters, and even one of the Great Masters, were missing. The missing had gone before the living to join their ancestors—should they be allowed to join them after they reported their failure to the spirits of the Emperors past.

The Grand Master spoke, his voice rasping because of his dry, atrophied gill slits. He told the assembled commanders and senior staff what they already knew or suspected: that the Earthman Army had just inflicted such severe casualties on the Emperor's army on this planet that the latter was no longer capable of fulfilling its mission. He told the assemblage that he had prepared a message, that the message was even then being loaded into all the drones the corps had. The drones would all be launched at once, with the expectation that at least one of them would get through the cordon of the orbiting Earthman fleet and find its way to Home.

Then he told them what they were going to do.

When the Grand Master finished talking, he raised his unglazed cup in salute to the Emperor, and barked one word. The assembled commanders and staff withdrew flasks from within their garments. The Grand Master quaffed the contents of his cup; the commanders and staff drank deeply from their flasks. The Grand Master stood without another word and marched from the great hall. His guardian Large Ones marched at his side. The assembled Great Master, High Masters, and Over Masters rose and marched behind them. The Masters and Leaders who provided true security in the hall stepped from behind the draperies and joined the parade. After the last of them entered the tunnel that would lead the procession to the surface, and glory at the hands of the Earthmen, a fire flared briefly in the hall as the remaining Large One immolated himself and the females.

Commander van Winkle assigned Company L to cover the back entrance to one of the underground complexes—the same back entrance that third platoon had entered a few days earlier. The company didn't quite get there in time.

Lance Corporal Schultz, on the company point, froze half a klick from the company's assigned position. "Skinks," he said into his helmet comm.

"Where?" Sergeant Kerr asked, rushing forward from his position between second and first fire teams. He used his infra to locate Schultz and found the point man down on one knee, pointing his blaster in an arc to his front.

"Mohammed's pointy teeth," Kerr murmured when he looked where Schultz indicated. He got on the platoon command circuit. "Skinks, hundreds of them, one-fifty to our front. Moving right to left."

"Roger," Lieutenant Bass answered. He then called Captain Conorado on the company command circuit to pass the word to him.

"Everybody, line on third platoon," Conorado ordered on the

all-hands circuit. "Double time; the bad guys are crossing our front. Hold your fire until I give the word."

The forest through which Company L moved was thin enough that the Marines moved in two columns fifty meters apart, and thick enough that they were closed to six-meter intervals instead of ten or more. It took a bit more than three minutes for the entire company to get on line. Skinks, many deep, continued to flow past the company's front, fleetingly visible one hundred and fifty meters away. Lieutenant Rokmonov, the assault platoon commander, positioned his assault guns, one behind each blaster squad. One hundred and twenty-four Marines—and four corpsmen—tensely awaited the company commander's order.

Captain Conorado used his infra and magnifier screens to look at the streaming Skinks. It was just as Bass had told him: hundreds of them. He thought there might be a thousand or more, and he didn't know how far to his right they extended. Still, Hammer Schultz held the right end of the company's line, and Schultz would know if anybody attempted to flank them.

He took a deep breath and shouted into the all hands circuit, *"Fire!"*

As one, all the blasters, guns, and assault guns of the company opened up on the Skinks. The forest one hundred and fifty meters in front of them blazed in fierce fire as hundreds of Skinks flashed into vapor; the forest filled with sudden smoke. Screams and wild cries came from left and right of the burned area, and from beyond it as well.

Skinks burst through the smoke in front of the company, hundreds of them, screaming war cries. Some of the war cries were intelligible; they sounded like "Marine, you die!" and "Die, Earthman pigs!" and "I fuck your mother!"

The Marines paid no attention to the cries, except perhaps to use them to help pick their targets as they continued to pour fire into the charging Skinks, vaporizing the implacable enemy. And then there were no more Skinks coming through the smoke, nor did any cries come from that direction. But the shouts and screams from the right front and left front were closer.

"Third platoon, pivot right," Conorado ordered. "First platoon, pivot left. Second platoon, hold your position!"

Third and first platoons, on the ends of the company line, swung to face the Skinks coming from the right and the left; the assault guns placed behind their squads shifted with them. Second platoon remained in place, in case more Skinks came from the front.

The move came just in time—the nearest Skinks were already within a hundred meters of the company's flanks.

"Third platoon, fire!" Lieutenant Bass shouted into his comm. But his command wasn't necessary. His Marines were already firing into the mass of Skinks coming at them.

"How many of them are there?" Corporal Doyle squealed. He'd already used up one full four-hundred-shot charge on his blaster and was well into a second, and the Skinks were still charging, screaming, "You die today, Marine!" There seemed to be an endless supply of them.

"Don't sweat it, Doyle," Kerr said into the private circuit.

Doyle flinched. He hadn't known he'd asked his question into his comm.

"We won't run out of ammo before they run out of Skinks," Kerr said. "Now calm down, you're scaring your men." Kerr wondered where the rail guns were.

That may or may not have been true as far as Doyle was concerned, but Sergeant Souavi, the company supply sergeant, and the two company clerks were already distributing more ammunition from the supply they'd carried on two of the Battle Cars and one Dragon.

Twenty meters to Doyle's right, Schultz methodically shifted his aim from one target to another, flashing Skink after Skink. On his left, Corporal Claypoole wasn't quite as methodical, but still flashed one after another. Between them, the mass of Skinks weren't getting any closer to the platoon's line. But far to Doyle's left, on the platoon's other flank, where Lance Corporal Longfellow, Lance Corporal Ymenez, and PFC McGinty held the line, the Skinks were almost within range with their acid shooters.

"We need some help here, Rabbit," Longfellow said into the squad circuit.

Sergeant Ratliff looked and saw the Skinks already firing at his squad's left flank—and the streamers of greenish fluid were getting close. He turned around and saw the assault gun supporting his squad firing straight ahead and to the right side of the squad's line. He low-crawled to the gun and grabbed the team leader's sleeve.

"Put your fire over there," he said, and pointed with a bare arm. "My flank is about to get overrun."

"Ah, shit," the gun team leader swore. "Sorry," he murmured as he redirected his gun's fire.

The Skinks closing on Longfellow's fire team were torched until none were closer than a hundred meters. Then the assault gun had to return its attention to the center and right of the squad, because the Skinks had closed the gap there.

Sergeant Ratliff wondered where the Skink rail guns were.

Where the Skink rail guns were was two kilometers to the west, in front of the Fifty-fourth Light Infantry Division. More specifically, in front of George Company, Second Battalion, 499th Light Infantry, Fifty-fourth Light Infantry Division.

Second Lieutenant Steven Moreau of fourth platoon hunkered down and watched his two sharpshooters. His platoon sergeant, Sergeant First Class Smith Downes, had somehow managed to get his hands on two Marine plasma shooters and given them to the two best marksmen in the platoon. Moreau didn't know where or how Downes had gotten the weapons, and figured both he and the platoon sergeant were better off if he didn't. By then, everybody in both corps knew that the plasma shooters were the most effective weapons to use against the Skinks. He was glad there were some Marines to the right of his platoon; they kept the Skinks from attempting to flank his position.

Moreau watched the sharpshooters. They'd both found dips in the ground that were deep enough to keep them below grazing fire from the Skink rail guns. They were using a piece of obsolete equipment, also found by Downes, to locate their targets—periscopes. Where the hell had Downes found periscopes? He could have probably stolen the plasma shooters from the Marines, but periscopes? He shook his head. It didn't matter where or how Downes had gotten them; the periscopes were exactly what the sharpshooters needed. The two soldiers stayed low, scanning the area to their front, watching for the signs that would tell them where the rail guns were. When they located one, they'd watch until none of the super-high-speed weapons were firing in their direction, and pop up long enough to fire several shots. Their efforts were often met by the flashes of Skinks being vaporized.

But they never managed to kill the rail guns themselves; the Skinks always managed to come up with new crews.

The other Skinks, the ones with the acid shooters, were kept at bay by the rest of the platoon. The soldiers fired the most expedient way when pinned down; they stayed below the grazing fire and exposed only their rifles and machine guns, firing blindly. They were well enough trained and disciplined that not too much of their fire went high.

And the steady artillery fire helped a great deal, although Moreau thought it was a shame that George Company was in the forest with the Skinks. Because of the risk of forest fire, the artillery couldn't fire the incendiary rounds that would literally burn out the Skinks.

If only there weren't really the inexhaustible supply of Skinks that there seemed to be.

The supply of Skinks wasn't inexhaustible, as third platoon found out soon enough. The Skinks stopped charging, no more Skinks flared up, no more screams and war cries came their way.

"Cease fire!" Captain Conorado ordered. "Cease fire!" He

listened; everybody listened and watched. There was no more sign of Skinks threatening Company L's position. But there was plenty of sound to their left. Battalion called.

"Lima Six-Actual," Conorado answered.

Battalion wanted to know if there was any enemy activity in the company's area. When Conorado said no, Commander van Winkle ordered: "The rest of the battalion and army are holding the Skinks two klicks west of your position. The Skinks are in a good position to be flanked. Go two platoons abreast; keep one platoon in reserve and to guard your rear. Put your left flank one hundred meters north of where you are now. Questions?"

"No, sir."

"Do it."

"Aye aye," Conorado said into a broken connection. He got his platoon commanders and platoon sergeants on the comm and told them what they were going to do. Company L got on line and moved west, one hundred meters closer to the mountains.

The Marines slammed into the flank of the Skinks just as the Skinks were rising to move to where they could attempt to flank the Marines of Mike Company. The Skinks were already demoralized because they'd been unable to advance in the face of massive casualties, and meeting Company L head-on was devastating to them. Many of them chose to use the tiny incendiaries they carried to suicide rather than be killed by the Marines. Company L was already in front of the 499th Light Infantry when they encountered the most remarkable sight any of them had ever seen outside a historical action vid.

A small horde of screaming Skinks, fifty or sixty of them, came charging through the forest at the army lines. They were unmolested by the army, as both George Company and the company on its far side had ceased fire to avoid hitting the Marines crossing their front. So it was up to Company L to stop this last charge.

And this suicidal charge simply *had* to be the Skinks' last hurrah. Nothing else made any sense—as if any of what the Marines saw made sense.

The Skinks weren't in uniforms and didn't carry acid shooters or rail guns. They wore what looked for all the world like aged leather-and-metal armor, and they carried swords.

As surprised as they were by the incongruous sight, the Marines wasted no time in flashing the charging sword bearers.

That signaled the end of the battle. All along the line, the remaining Skinks suicided into brilliant vapor.

Corporal Claypoole looked up bewildered from the helmet he held in his hands. It was something that looked and felt like leather, and had metal rectangles riveted onto it. It was somewhat conical in shape, flattened a bit from front to back; it didn't rise to a point, but curved abruptly before it reached its peak, and had two horns jutting above. The leather fell in an apron in back, and the apron had wings that could wrap around to protect the neck from the front. Short wooden dowels held by loops of leather secured the wings of the apron.

"What's this supposed to protect you from?" he asked nobody in particular.

"Th-this, probably," Corporal Doyle said. He was turning a sword around in his hands. The blade of the sword was nearly a meter long and gently curved. Its surface rippled under the changing light of its movement. The sword's hilt seemed to be strips of wood tightly bound with a leather strap, and the pommel was a simple metal ovoid with elaborate engravings on the blade side.

Sergeant Kerr held a leather-and-metal tunic, scorched by the fire that had vaporized its wearer. Old repairs in the tunic showed that it had actually seen use, that it wasn't a ceremonial garment. "They've got real weapons," he said. "When would they fight like this? And *why*?"

Lieutenant Bass stood nearby, examining another sword. "They're alien," he said. "We may never understand them."

What everybody *did* understand was the war against the Skinks on Haulover was over. But the war against the Skinks was probably not. Over the next few days, the elements of the XVIII and XXX Corps that were permanent parts of Task Force Aguinaldo began heading back to Arsenault. The other units returned to their home bases.

CHAPTER
THIRTY-ONE

"Mr. Brackle, I am Special Agent Don Rittenhouse of the Ministry of Justice." The man held out his credentials. "And this is Special Agent Trace Keen." Keen held out his credentials. "We'd like to talk to you."

"It's 'Brattle,' gentlemen," Zechariah Brattle interrupted Rittenhouse.

"What? Oh. Excuse me, Mr. Brattle. Sorry. We'd like to talk to you about—"

"That letter I sent to Ensign Bass on Thorsfinni's World?" Zechariah asked eagerly.

Rittenhouse glanced at Keen. "Uh, yes, Mr. Brattle, that letter, the effect it had, and our search for the Skink you call Moses—"

"Thank the Lord!" Zechariah exclaimed. He got up from his desk, came around, and shook hands vigorously with the two agents. "I *knew* Charlie'd come through! You've found him, then? Moses? Thank God, thank God!"

"No, we have not found this Moses, Mr. Brattle," Special Agent Keen said. "We've arrested Dr. Gobels and his assistant, Pensy Fogel."

"Devious and untrustworthy charlatans," Zechariah said, nodding.

"We've questioned everyone at a place called Wellfordsville, on Earth, a small town on the eastern seaboard of what used to be the United States. Near there was where this Gobels had his clandestine laboratory. But Moses," he said with a shrug, "has got away and we have not been able to find him."

Zechariah offered the two agents chairs and resumed his own seat. Rittenhouse briefly explained the raid on Dr. Gobels's lab outside Wellfordsville, how the two renegade scientists had been apprehended as well as, eventually, his three accomplices, three local ne'er-do-wells. "A lady named Treemonisha Giddings had been harboring Moses, Mr. Brattle, but he fled into the wilderness. We have this Ms. Giddings, a fine old Christian woman, to thank for saving Moses. But he's gone, sir, disappeared into the vast swamplands somewhere north of this Wellfordsville place and we have not been able to find him."

Zechariah was silent for a moment, regarding the two agents. Rittenhouse was tall and spare, Keen short and round. "Then you will never find him," Zechariah pronounced at last. "Water is his element. He's like a fish when he gets into it. But no net, no hooks, no weir will ever snare that boy. He's as intelligent as we are, and his instinct will override whatever civilization we've been able to breed into him."

"Winter's coming on back there, Mr. Brattle. How will your Moses survive when the swamp water freezes over? He has never had to fend for himself in nature, and there is not much time for him to learn. We know enough about Skinks to know they thrive in warm, wet climates. How will he fare when it gets really cold? Can he hibernate? We were hoping to find out these things. This Dr. Gobels, he ran extensive tests on Moses, but he has refused to divulge what he knows, and his laboratory, along with all his records, burned." Rittenhouse shrugged. "You know how important Moses can be to us in our war with the Skinks. We've come to ask for your help, Mr. Brattle."

Zechariah looked from one man to the other. "How? How can I help?"

"We think it's a good bet that since Moses lived with you and your family, he'll trust you," Keen said. "To him you may be a father figure."

"That's right, Mr. Brattle. You can come back to Earth with us and we'll take you into the swamps and you will proclaim the name of Moses throughout the land, and lead *him* to the promised land." Rittenhouse smiled.

"I can hardly wait," Zechariah replied dryly. "I hope it doesn't take forty years," he added, and then laughed. "When do we leave?"

"Right now," Rittenhouse replied.

They made the trip to Earth in the luxury of a BOMARC 37A starship, a great improvement on the earlier, 36V corporate starships. This, Rittenhouse explained, was the attorney general's personal starship.

Once at the Fargo spaceport they were chauffeured directly to the Ministry of Justice, where Huygens Long, the Confederation's attorney general, awaited. On the long ride into the city Zechariah gawked at the huge buildings. He had thought Haven and Interstellar City were the epitome of urban sprawl, but Fargo took his breath away.

"Mr. Brickle, I've heard a lot about you, sir," Long said as Rittenhouse and Keen escorted Zechariah into his office.

"He hasn't learned to pronounce my name," Zechariah muttered to Rittenhouse.

"It's *Brattle,* sir, Zechariah Brattle," Rittenhouse corrected Long.

"Well, Mr. Brattle, I'm not attorney general 'cause I'm the smartest guy in this government, I'm AG 'cause I'm an old cop and I always get my man. I don't practice law, Mr. Brattle, never have. Please accept my apologies. Please be seated."

Immediately Zechariah took a liking to the bluff, plainspoken, portly official. "Sir," he said, "the Skinks killed my only son, Samuel, and I killed Skinks." His face colored and his eyes took on a brightness. "True justice is the Lord's business, but until He prescribes, I'll do what I can to help our fight against these alien monsters."

"Well, Mr. Brattle, maybe our fight is the Lord's way of meting out justice."

Zechariah shook his head. "We of the City of God believe that will only come on Judgment Day. Our jurisdiction is only over their bodies, not their souls. I'll do whatever I can to help you destroy those bodies."

"Does your Moses have a soul, Mr. Brattle?"

"You bet, Mr. Long, and he's living proof they all aren't bad."

Long smiled. "It's almost time for lunch, Mr. Brattle. You have been invited to a special luncheon elsewhere in the city. Shall we go?"

"Will there be cold beer?"

"You bet, Mr. Brattle!" Huygens Long in his own turn had taken an instant liking to the straightforward Zechariah. They left the office in close conversation, Long's massive arm draped over Zechariah's thin shoulders.

Zechariah had the surprise of his life when ushered into a private dining room somewhere in the innards of Government Center (he'd become completely lost as they negotiated the vast complex) to find that their host was none other than Cynthia Chang-Sturdevant, the President of the Confederation of Human Worlds.

"Mr. Brattle," she said, rising from the immaculately set luncheon table and extending her hand, "how very pleased I am to meet you!" Her hand was smooth, dry, and warm.

Zechariah had seen vids of Chang-Sturdevant but he never realized she looked so charming, so handsome in real life. He could only stand there, his mouth hanging half open. He glanced accusingly at Long as if to say, "Why didn't you *tell* me who our host was?" Long only grinned and helped Chang-Sturdevant back into her chair, after which he excused himself and left them alone to dine and talk. All Zechariah could say as he took his own place was "Why, thank you, ma'am."

They made small talk throughout the luncheon. Chang-Sturdevant asked many questions about Kingdom and the

Brattles, and Zechariah had the distinct impression she found his responses genuinely interesting. He found her an easy person to talk to and he found himself warming to her; he felt comfortable and at ease in her company. She had the effect on people of relaxing them with easy, friendly conversation about everyday things and a genuine interest in their personal lives.

"This beer is excellent!" Zechariah exclaimed at one point.

"It's Reindeer Ale, Mr. Brattle."

"Ah! The Marines drink Reindeer Ale!" Zechariah replied. "They really like it."

"I do too, sir. And I like my Marines."

After the dishes had been cleared away, Chang-Sturdevant leaned forward and said, "Mr. Brattle, I want you to know how important it is we find your Moses. He's a frightened child, alone in a strange world and he's been hunted like an animal. Those renegade scientists are both in custody, but as you probably already know, their laboratory and records were destroyed. Gobels is not talking, and his assistant doesn't know as much as Gobels does, although he's been cooperative, the AG tells me. But Moses is wandering now in the wilderness, wandering out there by himself and we must bring him in. You've seen the Skinks. I know what they did to you. You know how vicious they can be. But Moses may be our only link to understanding them so we must bring him in, we must find out all we can about these"—she almost said "people"—"these creatures. We think you can help us in this. Will you help us, sir?"

"Will we get him back when this is all over?"

"Yes, I promise you that."

"Then even if it takes me forty years," he said smiling, "I'll wander out there until I find him."

At that point, on some hidden signal, Huygens Long came back into the room and assisted Chang-Sturdevant from her chair. "Mr. Brattle, very soon I'll have my own child," she announced. "Yes! At my age! My first one, can you imagine that? Mr. Brattle, I want that child to grow up in a world where he isn't threatened by Skinks. We're all counting on you. Thank you for coming." She walked around the table, kissed Zechariah on the cheek, and walked out of the room.

"I never got one of those!" Long exclaimed, joking. "Well, Zechariah, let's get a move on. You and my boys are headed for Wellfordsville in the morning. We can't waste much time. Winter's coming on."

Dr. Joseph Gobels sat primly at the small table in the interrogation booth, his hands free but his feet in shackles. "You are treating me like a common criminal," he told the young woman sitting opposite him.

"I assure you, Doctor, you are not at all *common,*" she replied evenly. "You are a very rare and unusual specimen of the so-called criminal mind." She smiled briefly. She said her name was Quyen; she was about forty years old, judging from her appearance. She had been interrogating Gobels for several days now. "Things will go much easier on you, Doctor, if you will tell us all you know about the baby Skink, Moses."

Gobels smiled. "Sure. I'll tell you everything about him. For one million credits and immunity from prosecution. Oh, and one thousand Davidoff cigars. I've already made that very clear, young lady."

"I've discussed your proposal with the attorney general's office, Doctor. We may be able to come to an agreement here. But first we need something, something to assure us that you will cooperate. I need a carrot before we can give you an apple. If you do not cooperate, you will go on trial for treason, you will be convicted, and you will spend the rest of your life behind bars. But time is short, Doctor. The season is rapidly turning colder. We know he can't survive the winter." She reached into a pocket and produced a Davidoff. "An Anniversario Number Two." She handed it to Gobels. It had already been cut.

"You know, we can always go to Dr. Fogel. He is cooperating fully with us."

Gobels laughed pleasantly. "Pensy? Yes, he knows a thing or two, but not what I do. For the real dope on Skinks you have to come to me, I'm afraid." Quyen lit the cigar for him. He sat back and sucked in the delicious smoke and regarded her carefully through the blue-gray cloud that billowed between them. "Excellent," he sighed. In a way, Quyen was very attractive. He rolled the cigar between his fingers and said, "They are watching us, every moment, aren't they? They are recording my every word, aren't they?" He glanced up at the corners of the room and grinned into the hidden devices.

"Yes, they are."

Gobels nodded affably. "I will give you something important, now, this moment, then. Let the cameras roll!" he shouted happily.

"Yes?" She leaned forward expectantly.

Gobels smiled. "Skinks are homeothermic, not ectothermic."

"That means?"

"That means they maintain a stable internal body temperature regardless of external influence. My study of Skink thermophysiology has proved they are, well, like us, Miss Quyen." He grinned. "They have a large number of mitochondria per cell, which enables them to generate heat by increasing the metabolic rate at which they burn fats and sugars. They have deep layers of fat under their skin that act as insulation in cold weather, and veins close to their arteries that extract heat from them and carry it back into the trunk. Skinks are omnivorous creatures. In the swamp where your Skink has escaped is an endless supply of food, so that even in the coldest weather he will be able to eat enough to keep his metabolic rate at the proper level to ensure survival."

"Then he won't die in the cold?"

"Of course not," Gobels snorted. "Now, Miss Quyen, that is my gesture of goodwill and cooperation for today. But when you have agreed to my terms for release, I will then tell you things about these Skinks that will, well, raise the beautiful hairs on the back of your pretty little head." He laughed, leaned back, and playfully blew a huge cloud of cigar smoke at the ceiling.

* * *

Moses knew the season was changing. He could feel the lower temperatures in the mornings and he noticed the leaves on the trees turning beautiful colors. But he was happy where he was. In the weeks he had been free he had come to love the vast swamp that he had almost to himself. Occasionally men would come through on vehicles that roared and sputtered and threw up waves of vegetation and mud. They laughed and shouted and fired guns into the water but none came near where he lay, carefully submerged in the muck. But he was growing bigger. He ate his fill, consuming small swimming creatures, and animals he found hiding in the mud beneath the water, and succulent plants with delicious roots.

Moses was also growing more conscious of his environment, conscious of *himself.* He knew now that he was not a man-child but, as he swam and hunted and ate and basked in the waning sunlight, he wondered *what* he was. The natural maturity that came with growth, together with experience, was changing him. The Brattles and Treemonisha, whom he remembered with fondness, had treated him as a human being, but he knew now that he was not of their kind. He knew also that he belonged in the swampland. And he knew that many men were looking for him. Once he encountered a creature as big as himself and he spoke to it but it fled, splashing and shrieking and, for the first time, Moses knew what it felt like to frighten something else, a power he did not know he had up until that moment.

Moses realized that soon he would need shelter. He could see in his mind's eye very clearly the route he had taken to get where he was. How he could do this he did not know. He considered going back to Treemonisha's house and living there again with her. But that would never do. Those men who had hurt him would come back. So carefully, meticulously, he dragged branches and twigs out of the surrounding forest, entwined them, covered them with mud and leaves, and built himself a hut in the water that could only be entered by swimming up through a submerged entrance hole. From the surface the hut looked like a mound of jetsam accumulated in an eddy. But inside it was dry and comfortable and he could sleep and live there in perfect safety.

And then one morning, when the first thin layers of ice had formed in the places where the water lay quietly, Moses heard a familiar voice.

The suborbital flight from Fargo to Falls Church in the former state of Virginia took about two hours. Zechariah was accompanied by Special Agents Rittenhouse and Keen. Once on the ground again, they boarded a Ministry of Justice hopper for an hourlong flight to Wellfordsville in the southeastern part of the region known as Virginia.

"Since the war," Rittenhouse explained, and he meant the Second American Civil War, "the region from Falls Church south down into what used to be called the state of North Carolina has reverted to a primeval condition. If you look below us you'll see one vast stretch of forest and swampland that has consumed what used to be the thriving metropolises such as Richmond, Norfolk, and so on. Your Moses has disappeared into this wilderness."

"Then no wonder you haven't been able to find him," Zechariah said.

"You are our last hope, Mr. Brattle," Special Agent Keen said. "Our plan is a simple one. We'll send your voice into and over the wilds using a special broadcasting system through which you can call Moses out to show himself and come to us. We're hoping he'll recognize your voice and respond. We've had hundreds of men searching for more than a month now with no success."

"There is a reward for Moses, Mr. Brattle," Rittenhouse confessed rather sheepishly. "One hundred thousand credits. It's caused a virtual gold rush down there. I'm afraid, with the locals jumping in and muddying the waters, that someone will get hurt, possibly Moses. It was not my idea, sir, but the local people know these woods and swamps and it was thought . . ." He shrugged helplessly.

"What we got was a riot," Keen added. "Vigilantes competing with each other for the bounty. There *have* been casualties."

"We've pretty much got things under control now," Rittenhouse continued. "We'll start your search from Wellfordsville, where we've set up a command post. We want you to meet someone down there first and then tomorrow at dawn you'll commence your first overflight."

That someone was Treemonisha Giddings. "You that boy's father?" she asked, standing on the rickety porch of her cabin.

"No," Zechariah answered. "My boys found him down in a stream near our home back on Kingdom and we took him in. That's why we named him Moses."

"As in the Bible?"

"Yes."

"Then you did the Lord's bidding, Mr. Brattle." Treemonisha stepped down off the porch and extended her big hand.

"Yep." Zechariah took the hand in his. It was strong and warm.

"Those scientists did terrible things to that boy. They come here to take him back and we had a fight, yes, sir, we shore did." Treemonisha emitted a rumbling laugh as she remembered the struggle with the three rubes. "Knocked my porch down. Never have had time to fix it back up." She laughed again. "And that's how the boy escaped, in the confusion, and we ain't seen hide nor hair o' him since." She nodded her head in affirmation. "Nobody been able to find that boy, not these gents here"—she nodded at the two special agents—"'n 'specially not them rednecks who been out there shootin' themselves up." She laughed derisively.

"Well, we're gonna find him now," Rittenhouse promised.

Zechariah turned to Rittenhouse. "Don, what do you say, if Ms. Giddings here is free, maybe she'd come along with us tomorrow? You harbored Moses, gave him succor, Ms. Giddings. Maybe between the two of us we can get him to show himself. What do you say?"

Treemonisha thought about that for a moment and said with finality, "Does a bear shit in the woods?" and laughed that deep, rumbling laugh again. Zechariah Brattle knew he would enjoy the company of the big woman very much.

For a week they flew low over swamps and forests, taking turns calling Moses's name until they were hoarse. During that time Zechariah got to know Treemonisha Giddings very well. He found out that she was more than a century old, give or take. Births were not accurately recorded when she was born so she was not sure how old she was. Her husband was long dead and her children, those who had survived, had all moved far away and never came to see her. "I think they's all passed on," she confessed. "It's a terrible thing, Zach, when you outlive your own youngins." Zechariah in turn told her all about his family and life back on Kingdom.

At the beginning of the second week, Zechariah had an idea, which he discussed with Don Rittenhouse. "Give us one of those swamp boats and let us go alone into the wilds, Don. This airborne search is not working. I want to get down on the water and call him in my own, natural voice, not over some speaker system. We'd frighten the shit out of a kwangduk the way we've been doing this."

"It could be dangerous, Zach. The locals have mostly given up on the search but there are hunters out there, wild, dangerous men who consider outsiders poachers and trespassers."

"Give me and Ms. Giddings a brace of shot rifles, Don, and we'll take care of ourselves."

Rittenhouse considered. "All right, but we'll fly an escort hopper nearby and if anything happens you *can't* handle, you can call us for support. But remember, Zach, if anything were to happen to you two, it'd be my ass."

"Give your ass a rest, Don, and it'll be all right." Zechariah laughed.

For several days Zechariah and Treemonisha cruised along in the powerful air-cushioned Swamp Runner with no success. At night they shut the engines down and slept in the small cabin.

Several times each day they performed a radio check with the hopper escort maintaining its position just over the horizon as it followed their progress.

"Don said they once called this place the Great Dismal Swamp," he remarked one afternoon as they rested by a huge mound of flotsam.

"Thass right, Zach. I don't know where the name *dismal* come from. You live here long enough and this place sorta grows on you, becomes part of you."

"Even this late in the year the place is still beautiful. It's like we're the first people ever to come to this spot."

"Mebbe we are."

"How cold does it get here in the winter?"

"Colder than a well digger's ass." Treemonisha laughed.

"I've *never* head that one before." Zechariah grinned.

"It's just the way we talk about these parts. Why, sheeyit, you shoulda heard my husband when he got fired up." Remembering, she bellowed that enormous laugh out over the waters.

"Pappy, momma!" Moses shouted, sticking his head up over the gunwale.

Zechariah was so surprised he jumped to his feet, spilling his soup. "My little baby!" Treemonisha exclaimed, tears in her eyes. She reached out and hauled the Skink into the Swamp Runner.

"I heard you," Moses said. "I knew it was you," he added.

Treemonisha embraced Moses warmly and rocked him back and forth. "We thought you was dead." She was crying now.

Zechariah knelt on the deck. "You've grown big," he observed. "And you are talking distinctly. How in the world—?"

Moses shrugged. "I don't know, Pappy. I just do it."

Zechariah noticed with growing amazement that Moses's voice sounded exactly like that of his two stepsons. "We've come to take you with us," Zechariah announced.

"No!" Moses exclaimed. He had grown big enough and strong enough that he was able to push Treemonisha away. He stood up. "Those men—" he began.

"No, no, Moses, we won't let anyone hurt you!" Zechariah protested.

"Two men *hurt* me Pappy. Other men have come here, bad men. I live here now. I stay here."

"No, Moses, you *must* come with us, we *need* you!" Zechariah insisted.

"Leave him alone!" Treemonisha demanded. She put her arm around Moses and held him tightly.

"Pappy, Momma Hannah said we have to obey God's will." Zechariah was astonished. His wife, Hannah, had often said that when faced with problems she couldn't overcome. But he never realized Moses was listening or even understood what she said. "It is God's will I remain here, Pappy. God made me to live here. I am *not* going with you." He broke Treemonisha's grip and slid over the side of the boat into the water before Zechariah could stop him. Zechariah watched helplessly as Moses disappeared beneath the murky water.

A few meters out, Moses surfaced again. "I love you both!" he shouted. Zechariah found he could not speak.

"Baby! Come see ol' Treemonisha one day! Promise me!"

"I will! Pappy, give my love to Hannah, Samuel, and Joab! Good-bye, good-bye," and he submerged, leaving only a small eddy on the surface of the murky water.

Zechariah found his voice at last. "I've gotta report this!" He reached for the radio.

Treemonisha laid a hand on his shoulder. *"Don't,* Zach, don't."

Zechariah hesitated. "But the fate of the entire human race may depend on our bringing Moses back with us," he protested.

Treemonisha shook her head. "Listen to me, Zach. The fate of the human race has depended on many things, but it's still here, 'n that boy ain't gonna make a bit of difference to humanity's survival. Let him go. Set that radio down 'n let our Moses go, Zach. Besides, now he's back in the water we ain't never gonna find him again. They'll think he's dead, and we—you and I—we can keep a secret, can't we?" She said that with absolute confidence—and joy.

Slowly, Zechariah Brattle put the radio set down. A few days later, news of the great victory on Haulover came to them and the search for Moses the Skink was called off. Zechariah never told anyone what happened that day in the swamp and he never lost any sleep over it, either.

Dr. Joseph Gobels, however, lost many years' sleep. Because with the victory on Haulover, his information about the Skinks suddenly became merely academic. The attorney general refused to make a deal with him, he was convicted on several felony counts, and given a very long prison sentence. He was still there when Pensy Fogel won a pardon.

A long, long time later, when Moses had learned how to clothe himself in the skins of furry animals, he returned to Wellfordsville to visit Treemonisha. It was an arduous trek made endurable by the soaring anticipation he felt that soon he'd see the big black woman again, eat her delicious cooking, and lay his weary head upon her capacious breast. Many times he lay hidden in the forest to avoid travelers and hunters but he knew they were no longer looking for him. And if they found him, if they threatened him in any way, he could defend himself. He possessed the strength and maturity and agility of an experienced hunter who knew how to kill swiftly and silently with hands and snares and the sturdy, sharpened cudgel he'd made from a supple pine branch, hardened in the fires he built to cook the prey that roamed *his* swamp.

As he emerged from the woods his heart skipped a beat. Treemonisha's home did not look at all as he remembered it. The chicken coop was reduced to an overgrown pile of brambles. A large blacksnake slithered through the weeds that choked her front yard. He suppressed a desire to kill it and feast, for he was hungry, but he could always catch something, and the dried meat he had brought with him still hung heavily in the deerskin pouch slung over one massive shoulder.

He stopped and stared in fearful wonder. Treemonisha's neat little house lay in ruins, the roof open to the sky. Bushes and weeds had grown up around the place and the windows were empty, staring sockets that revealed a dark, weather-ravaged interior.

Moses the Skink sank down into the grass and wept. His howls of grief echoed in the surrounding forest, for he realized that Treemonisha Giddings was no more. He was now truly alone in the world.

CHAPTER
THIRTY-TWO

The day after they returned from Haulover, Thirty-fourth Fleet Initial Strike Team assembled on the parade ground of Camp Major Pete Ellis, the companies marching in from various directions to gain their places in the FIST formation, the Marines resplendent in their dress reds. Families, friends, local dignitaries, and others who wanted to welcome the Marines home gathered in the bleachers to the left and right of the reviewing stand. Despite the larger than normal number of people in the stands, the parade ground and its surroundings were quiet, save for the *tramp-tramp-tramp* of marching feet. At length the last of the units to arrive halted in its assigned place in the formation, with a loud stomp of feet coming to a halt, and a swish as they faced left to present to the reviewing stand.

There were holes in the formation. Some of those holes marked the positions of Marines still in the hospital, recovering from serious wounds. A few holes, among the pilots of the squadron, were the positions of pilots who had died in combat and not yet been replaced; the dead among the ground troops had been replaced by transfers from Whiskey Company. But there were twenty-seven other holes; the Marines who normally would have stood in those positions were present, standing in one line on a broad platform erected between the reviewing stand and the ranks of the formation.

When all were present, Brigadier Sturgeon stepped front and center on the reviewing stand, gave greetings to the Marines and visitors, and introduced Rear Admiral Blankenboort, the commander of the naval supply depot on Thorsfinni's World and the Confederation military's highest-ranking officer on the world. The admiral took Sturgeon's place front and center and delivered a speech that bordered on long and boring, giving praise to the Marines of Thirty-fourth FIST and honoring the families, friends, local dignitaries, and others who thought enough of the Marines to come and welcome them home on this auspicious occasion. He volubly noted that there were an un-usually large number of decorations to be given out for heroism in the face of the enemy. "After all, Marines who perform heroic acts are normally considered to simply be doing their jobs. But sometimes they do things that are heroic even for Marines."

Blankenboort then turned his attention to the twenty-seven Marines on the platform in front of the reviewing stand.

"And here stand the heroes," he said solemnly. "Marines who took the extra measure, went the extra distance, went beyond anything that could be asked of them. And lived to tell of it. There were others who went the extra distance and gave their lives that others could live. They are also heroes, and, like the twenty-seven standing here today, shall be honored."

He turned to Brigadier Sturgeon and nodded.

Sturgeon stepped forward as Blankenboort moved aside. He called Commander Wolfe, the squadron commander, and Mike Company's Captain Boonstra forward. After they arrived and had exchanged salutes with the brigadier and the admiral, Sturgeon read the citations for the Marine Heroism Medal earned by a pilot and a squad leader and presented the medals to the commanders—neither Marine had family on Thorsfinni's World to accept the decorations. Wolfe and Boonstra would hold the medals for a brief period before returning them to Sturgeon, who would send them to the two Marines' next of kin.

After Wolfe and Boonstra returned to their positions in the formation, Sturgeon looked over the formation, and finally the twenty-seven Marines in front of him.

"It is with great pleasure"—and he did sound pleased—"that I now have the honor of assisting Rear Admiral Blankenboort in presenting decorations for heroism in combat to these brave Marines." He followed the admiral off the reviewing stand and onto the platform. Sturgeon's aide, Lieutenant Quaticatl, and Sergeant Major Shiro, the FIST's senior enlisted man, accompanied them. Quaticatl carried the citations and Shiro the medals about to be awarded.

The Marines being awarded medals were lined up by unit, and within unit by where they stood in that unit. Kilo Company was first, and Dragon Company last. As the flag officers stepped in front of each Marine, Quaticatl handed the citation to Brigadier Sturgeon, who read it, his voice amplified so everyone could hear, and Shiro handed the medal to Rear Admiral Blankenboort, who pinned it on the Marine's tunic and congratulated him.

After Kilo Company, the awards party came to a particular three Marines from Company L. Brigadier Sturgeon absently accepted the first citation from Lieutenant Quaticatl, while he studied the three Marines. He shook his head wonderingly.

"This is most unusual," he said. "Three Marines from one squad receiving decorations at the same time. But they are well earned." He cut his amplification to speak privately to the three. "I guess it shows how right I was to promote Charlie Bass before Haulover." Then back to allowing everybody to hear, he read the Silver Nebula citation for Sergeant Kerr, the Bronze Star citation for Corporal Claypoole, and the Gold Nova citation for Lance Corporal Schultz. Rear Admiral Blankenboort pinned each medal on as Sturgeon read the citation.

Before they moved on, Sturgeon cut his amplification again and said to Schultz, "It's damn well time you got a decoration, Lance Corporal. Well done, Marine!"

"Doing my job, sir," Schultz said.

But Sturgeon thought Schultz was standing a little straighter with that medal, the highest General Aguinaldo could award on his own authority, pinned to his chest. And later, after the rest of the FIST passed in review and the awardees were dismissed, Hammer Schultz was noticed walking with a strut in his step.

*   *   *

While he stood at parade rest, and then at attention on the platform, Corporal Claypoole swiveled his eyes right and left, looking for Jente in the stands, but he didn't see her. That didn't mean she wasn't there, or so he told himself. After all, he couldn't see everybody, standing with his head straight forward. He continued looking as the Marines from Company L marched back to the barracks, but didn't see her then, either. He sighed softly and thought the scene she made when he boarded the Essay to head for Haulover hadn't meant anything, not really. She wasn't waiting for him outside the barracks, either.

Before the medal recipients could go into the barracks, they were mobbed by the rest of the company, all of whom wanted to congratulate them, pound their backs, shake their hands, and admire their medals. It was a good twenty minutes before they could get inside and change out of their dress reds. Then came pay call. They hadn't received their pay during the deployment to Haulover, and having all those creds in their cards felt good. Now they only needed a way to spend it. Right before evening chow, liberty call sounded, Brigadier Sturgeon gave them five days before they had to report back for morning formation. Most of the company was pretty lively as they headed for the liberty buses that would carry them into Bronnoysund, some then heading for points more distant. Most, but not all.

Corporal Claypoole joined Sergeant Ratliff, Lance Corporal Longfellow, and PFC McGinty, all in their liberty civvies, heading for the hospital to visit Corporal Dean. Along the way they encountered Lieutenant Bass and Staff Sergeant Hyakowa, off on the same errand. Dean's room was crowded with the six visitors.

"Well, where is it?" Dean demanded of Claypoole as soon as the hellos were done. "I want to see it."

"Where's what?" Claypoole asked, feigning confusion.

"Your hero medal, dumbass. Come on, fork it over."

Claypoole indicated his clothes. "But I'm not in dress reds. I'm not wearing it."

"I can see that. Doesn't mean you don't have it in your pocket."

Claypoole just looked at him.

"Come on. I know you're not going to leave it in the barracks. You're going to sleep with it, and probably shower with it. Now let me see." Dean gestured to hand it over.

A grin slowly spread over Claypoole's face. "You're right." He chuckled as he reached into his shirt pocket and withdrew the presentation case the medal was in and opened it. He gazed at the Bronze Star for a moment before handing it to Dean.

"Damn," Dean murmured. He reverently turned the star that hung from the ribbon over and read the name and date inscribed on the back. "You did something with Sergeant Kerr, and he got a Silver Nebula for it?"

Claypoole nodded, chewing on his lower lip.

"Too bad I wasn't there. I would have liked to have seen it."

Claypoole didn't know whether Dean meant the action that won the two Marines their medals, or the awards ceremony when they got them. He chose to believe the former. "It was pretty hairy. You were better off where you were." He hesitated, then added, "We lost Commander Usner then."

Dean shook his head, then straightened the medal in its case and handed it back. "Staff officers," he murmured. Everybody understood the rest without him saying it. "They aren't supposed to get killed."

Bass took control before everybody started getting morbid. "I talked to your doctor earlier. He said you will be released tomorrow, or the day after."

"You'll be free to join the rest of us on liberty," Ratliff added.

That perked Dean up. After his injuries, he said, he was looking forward to a big, juicy reindeer steak and a few pitchers of Reindeer Ale. And getting hold of Carlala again.

Longfellow assured him his fire team was in good hands and would be returned to him in good condition; McGinty agreed.

After that, their talk ranged widely until the nurses chased the visitors out after an hour's stay.

*   *   *

When the latecomers arrived, the din at Big Barb's sounded louder than any of the firefights third platoon had engaged in on Haulover. The Marines of third platoon occupied a cluster of tables in a corner of the big common room, celebrating their return in high style. Sergeant Kerr, with Frida on one knee, feeding him slices of reindeer steak, and Gotta on the other, lifted his mug of Reindeer Ale to his lips between bites. Erika snuggled with Corporal Pasquin, who managed to eat and drink steadily without ever removing both hands from her. Sigfreid cupped her breasts for Corporal Chan to fill with ale, into which he dipped cuts of steak before wolfing them down. Klauda straddled Corporal Dornhofer's lap and draped her arms over his shoulders, leaning back to give him room to feed himself. Meisge was tucked under Lance Corporal MacIlargie's left arm, holding his mug, while he fed himself with his right hand. Lance Corporal Zumwald bounced Skoge on his knee and fed her tidbits of reindeer steak when he wasn't shoving bigger pieces into his own mouth. Stulka, the youngest of Big Barb's girls, hovered about, not sure which of the Marines to attach herself to. Asara, Hildegard, and Vinnie busied themselves serving the tables.

"Take over for me, Stulka," Asara shouted, as she squeezed between the table and Lance Corporal Quick's chest to sit on his lap. She picked up his mug and took a sip before holding it to his mouth. Quick grinned and took a gulp.

"Talulah, over here!" Vinnie called. She wanted to squeeze in with Corporal Doyle. Some of the other Marines looked at her oddly when they saw, but nobody said anything about it. Hey, some of them were even willing to accept that Doyle was almost a real Marine.

Lance Corporal Schultz was nowhere to be seen, and the quality of the food coming from the kitchen dropped noticeably shortly after the big man disappeared into it.

That was the situation into which Sergeant Ratliff, Corporal Claypoole, Lance Corporal Longfellow, and PFC McGinty entered.

Stulka saw McGinty, squealed, almost dropped the tray she was carrying before managing to put it on a table, and ran to him.

Ratliff twisted around when a low voice behind him said, "Hey, sailor, buy a girl a drink?" It was Kona.

Ratliff grinned and said, "I'd love to, but you gotta stop calling me a damn squid!" He had to struggle to maintain his balance when she threw herself into his arms.

Claypoole and Longfellow exchanged looks, then headed for the tables that held the rest of the platoon—Longfellow eagerly, Claypoole less so. He didn't expect to see Jente here and couldn't for the life of him remember whom he'd paired off with after she'd kicked him out before the last deployment—or if there'd been more than one; he thought there might have been at least two, maybe three women. Not that it much mattered whom he'd paired off with; she wasn't Jente.

It was well into the evening and every Marine was fed, a sheet or two to the wind, and with a woman—except for Sergeant Kerr, who had two women, and Corporal Claypoole, who had none. Big Barb had done her wailing act about wanting her Cholly and insisting that a skinny woman like Katie wasn't enough woman for him, then had gone back to tallying the day's take. The locals, many of whom had to go out on fishing boats early the next morning, were drifting away, well enough fed and far enough drunk.

The door opened, with considerably less exuberance than it normally did, and a figure slipped quietly inside. She stepped aside once she was through the door and looked around. She saw the man she was looking for and sighed with relief—that he was back, seemingly whole, and not encumbered. She wasn't sure how she would have reacted had he been with someone. She softly stepped toward him. She moved so quietly and smoothly that she was almost there before anybody noticed her; Sergeant Kerr raised an eyebrow but didn't say anything.

She reached the man she'd come for, placed her hands gently on his shoulders, and bent to kiss the top of his head. She found herself standing face-to-face with him, with his arms wrapped tightly around her and his mouth crushing hers.

"Oh, Rock," she murmured when they broke apart enough to take a breath.

"Jente," he murmured back.

"I'm so sorry," she whispered.

"I missed you," he rasped.

"Let's go," she said, almost too quietly to hear.

He picked her up and started toward the stairs to the second floor.

She slapped at him playfully and giggled. "Not here, silly. Let's go home."

"Home?" he croaked.

"Home."

He looked into her eyes, searching. He didn't find any sign of the woman who had angrily thrown him out of her house. "Live in sin?"

She bit her lower lip and nodded. "Live in sin."

"Home," he agreed, and carried her to the entrance and outside, without a word to, or even a glance at, the other Marines.

Silence reigned when the door closed behind them, but not for long. The Marines hooted and shouted comments. The women cheered and clapped their hands delightedly.

"Way to go, Rock!"

"Claypoole's got it bad!"

"I didn't spot the ring through his nose until it was too late to save him!"

Some of the women looked speculatively at their Marines. The Marines were men, and they were . . . well, they were women.

EPILOGUE

From time immemorial, network news, in its endless competition for audiences and ratings, has relied more on appearance than substance. For hundreds of years the "sound bite" has delivered the news to trillions of viewers—thirty seconds of words intermixed with short vid segments and a voice-over delivered by a newscaster more meticulous about his or her personal appearance than the facts of the news being reported.

What sticks in the minds of viewers is not the news itself but the *image* of trustworthy Dan, or Katie or Hugh or whomever, as the photogenic news personality of the hour, carefully groomed talking heads, who become so adored by their audiences that every word they utter is taken as gospel. They, not events, come to determine what is the news. Network executives love that because if people are drawn to their coverage because of trust in the newscaster, ratings go up and so does advertising revenue, and that is the all-important factor in keeping them solvent. So packaging is and always has been more important than product in the news business.

The Confederated News Network was no different in that dog-eat-dog world than any of the other networks, although CNN, more than its competitors, did strive for accurate and objective reporting much of the time. And the icon for that sort of old-fashioned news reporting was Jack Wintchell, because Jack was a news *reporter,* while all the other personalities in the business were merely news *readers*.

Jack Wintchell had been investigating and reporting stories for half a century. He had a well-deserved reputation for meticulous honesty. That is why Marcus Berentus, the Confederation Minister of War, had turned to him for help in reporting the machinations of Haggel Kutmoi. It was Jack's story on Kutmoi's illegal fund-raising that had helped swing the recent presidential election in favor of Cynthia Chang-Sturdevant. Possibly his influence alone had done the job, so highly regarded was Jack among the countless viewers who hung on his every word.

Now, tonight, he was preparing to deliver possibly the most important newscast of his long, respectable, and influential career. He sat patiently in his dressing room at CNN headquarters in Fargo. A hair stylist was putting the finishing touches to his trademark coiffure: chestnut hair that looked as if he'd just come in out of the wind. His shirt, wrinkled, open at the collar, sleeves rolled up past the wrists, made him look as if he'd just rushed into the studio to deliver the hottest and freshest news anyone had ever heard. That and his rapid-fire delivery, as if what he had to report was too important to wait one more second, were a good part of his appeal.

Other news personalities dressed to the nines when on camera and flew into rages if one strand of hair wound up out of place. They never seemed able to catch on to the simple fact that Jack Wintchell's disheveled appearance, although as meticulously planned and groomed as their own sartorial splendor, lent immediacy and authenticity to his reporting. He looked as sweaty and hardworking as Joe and Jane Citizen, just back from a hard day, their feet up, a drink in one hand, eyes glued to the vid screen, anxious to find out what the rest of humanity was up to. And Joe and Jane loved him for it.

"Jackie, m'boy," Collard Simperson, CNN's news director, enthused, rubbing his hands together excitedly. "You'll knock 'em dead tonight, knock 'em dead!"

"I always do, Collie," Wintchell drawled. He regarded his carefully dirtied fingernails as the stylist put a finishing touch to his hair.

"Ah," the stylist said at last, "you are *perfect,* Mr. Wintchell!

Perfect! I've never seen you so, so, *Jack* as you are right now, sir!"

"Thank you, Henri." Wintchell held out his hand and Henri obligingly assisted him to his feet. "Collie, old boy, let us proceed," he said, and together they marched boldly into the studio.

"Tonight," Jack intoned at the start of his report, "we commence a historic new beginning." These words shot into the homes, offices, stadiums, bars, clubs, and bistros, on hundreds of worlds spread out over the vast reaches of human space; many did not hear them until two weeks after they had been spoken, but because it was *Jack Wintchell* talking directly to them straight out of their vid screens, his words had the immediacy of live broadcasting.

"My friends, the alien menace known as the Skinks has at last been eliminated. Our brave forces have achieved total victory in the campaign against them on the world we know as Haulover. I ask you this: Can't we now beat our swords into plowshares? Can't we now get on with the business of business and return without fear to the peaceful pursuits of our lives? Yes! Go to your representatives in government and tell them that we no longer need to live in fear that every light in the nighttime sky presages death and destruction. Tell them: The future is *ours* and we must seize it. Tell them: The trillions we have earmarked for war can now be spent on peace! Tell them: *No more war!*

"I pray now, tonight, before you all, that we take the road to peace and prosperity and leave war behind us forever."

Jack paused at this point and gazed earnestly into the camera. He looked as he always did, a haggard fighter, a man of principle and truth, everyone's Uncle Jack, telling them straight, telling it like it is. Tears of joy ran down the cheeks of countless viewers over Jack's memorable words in that memorable speech on that memorable night.

"Friends," Jack continued sonorously, "Madam Chang-Sturdevant has been reelected our president. I am proud to have had a hand in that process. May God grant her the wisdom to lead us into this new Golden Age of Humanity that is now dawning. She has her work cut out for her. She has much to do to clean up her administration, reorganize our military forces, get this Confederation at last back on track. But she can do it, with our help and with God's loving kindness."

Jack paused again. He fixed those trillions of eyes with his own, gazing soulfully out at them from their vid screens. "This is my last broadcast," he announced solemnly. "Tonight I am concluding my fifty years in the news business. It has been a good run and I have loved every minute of it. But it is time to say 'Good night' one final time. And so, Mr. and Mrs. Taxpayer and all the ships in space, this is Jack Wintchell saying good night and good-bye." Real tears sparkled in Jack's eyes as he spoke.

It was the greatest speech of Jack Wintchell's long career. It was also the worst advice anyone had ever given the human race.

The Prime Master sat at the small desk in his tiny office, through which anyone seeking audience with the Emperor must pass. Few who sought it were allowed passage; the Prime Master tightly controlled who might disturb the Emperor. Nearly everything that others thought should be brought to the attention of the living god could be disposed of by the Prime Master.

So when two drones, launched by the Grand Master commanding the corps on the world the Earthmen called "Haulover," reached orbit around Home and their messages were downloaded, the messages, still sealed, were brought immediately to the tiny office and handed to the Prime Master.

The Prime Master broke the seals and read both messages, only to find that they were identical. The messages included the information that twenty-seven drones had been dispatched with the exact same message. The Prime Master dismissed the High Master who had brought him the messages, giving him instructions to bring him instantly any other messages that might come from Haulover, regardless of the hour. If he was in session with the Emperor when a message came, the High Master was to wait in the tiny office until the Prime Master finished with the living god.

The High Master bowed himself out of the Prime Master's presence.

The Prime Master destroyed one copy of the message, and sat for a long time, reading, rereading, and pondering the preserved copy.

An entire corps had been destroyed by the Earthmen. While that corps had inflicted significant casualties on the two Earthman Army corps that had annihilated it, it had inflicted little damage on the Earthman Marines who had assisted the Earthman Army in the destruction of the corps.

It didn't take the Prime Master long to decide that the Emperor didn't need to be bothered with knowledge of the fate of the corps, any more than the Emperor had needed to know of its existence on the Earthman world of Haulover to begin with. Should the name of the Grand Master who had died in his failure ever cross the mind of the Emperor, and the Emperor inquire after him, he could always be told the Grand Master in question had died in a hunting accident. Such accidents were not unknown, whether they had happened in fact or not.

The Prime Master read the message again. This time, by the time he finished reading, he smiled beatifically. The message included a great deal of information about the Earthman Army and airpower and their tactics. That was intelligence that would serve the Emperor's army well when it next encountered the Earthman Army. As it most assuredly would.

Read on for a sneak peek at the next book in the series:

STARFIST:
Double Jeopardy

"Does the Mother bless this?" Hind Claw asked.

Mercury flicked a hand at Hind Claw's face, barely nicking the side of his snout. "You know the Naked Ones keep the men and women in separate camps," he snarled. "The Mother doesn't know about it."

"Then what does the Father say?" Hind Claw asked, not to be dissuaded in his search for proper authorization.

This time Bobtail smacked Hind Claw on the back of his head. "You know the Father is kept caged and guarded by the Naked Ones, so none can approach him."

Hind Claw slowly bobbed his head up and down on its long neck. "So," he said, "there is no authority for what you propose doing."

Mercury leaned forward with his knuckles on the ground and his head stretched out, his whiskers close enough to tickle the side of Hind Claw's face where he'd nicked it: the classic intimidation stance. "Proper authority or not," he said softly but threateningly, "it needs to be done."

"If we fail?" Hind Claw asked, unfazed by the threat.

"Then we are dead."

"And if we succeed?"

"Then we have freed the people of our clan," Ares said.

Hind Claw nodded again. "And we gain status in our clan." He looked into Mercury's eyes. "And you could challenge for the

Father. I would like to be allied to the Father." He drew back far enough that Mercury's whiskers no longer tickled the side of his snout. He raised his head high, baring his neck in submission. Hind Claw had been the last of the six to be persuaded. They were ready now.

They took turns napping until the early moon set, then squeezed through the bars of the aboveground cage where they were kept at night.

"Where are you going?" a sleep-slurred voice asked, someone awakened by the sounds of their squeezing between bars that were more symbolic of imprisonment than intended to keep them in.

"We'll be back," Dewclaw whispered. "Go back to sleep." He heard a faint rustle as the questioner resettled himself next to his mates.

Hunched over, their narrow shoulders blending into long necks, the six slipped through the prison camp until they reached its edge. Mercury had scouted the way on several nights and he knew where the perimeter sentries were stationed. He also knew that the sentries would not be alert, that they weren't afraid of other, still-free clans launching a night attack. Besides, the sentries were positioned to watch out, not in.

They found the hidden armory that Mercury remembered preparing during the war against the Moon Flower Clan, a war that was interrupted by the arrival of the Naked Ones and their rapid subjugation of both the Moon Flowers and Mercury's own Bright Sun Clan.

The armory was well camouflaged; the Naked Ones had not found it, even though tracks on the ground made it clear that their vehicles had come by many times during the year they'd held the Bright Sun and Moon Flower clans in slavery and increased their sphere of control to include all the clans of Bright Sun's Brilliant Coalition and Moon Flower's Starwarmth Union. For all Mercury knew, the Naked Ones had conquered part or even all of the world beyond those two nations.

The Naked Ones had come from the sky, roaring down in flaming sky vehicles such as none of the people had ever seen and only the most imaginative had ever conceived of. Their weapons were terrible, advanced far beyond the rifles and artillery of the people, and that, combined with the surprise and speed of their attack, had allowed them to conquer all the clans of two nations quickly and decisively. No one had been able to resist them for long, and none had been able yet to rise against the Naked Ones. At least not so far as Mercury had heard.

But the Naked Ones had become complacent, and Mercury believed it was time to strike at them, to begin to free his people. But to do that they needed weapons.

Getting into the hidden armory was harder than finding it. But get into it they did. They loaded themselves; each took two rifles and four hundred rounds. One carried a mortar tube and another a baseplate. The other four each took two of the canisters displaying the red skull, the mark of weapons that dispensed a lingering death. Each also carried four rounds for the mortar. They also each took four grenades. By the time they were finished, each was carrying his own weight in weapons and ammunition.

They would have liked to rest before the long run back to the prison camp, but there was too great a chance that the Naked Ones would notice they were missing in the morning. So, heavily laden, they ran until they were within half a kilometer of the camp, where they hid the weapons and ammunition in a place Mercury and Hind Claw had prepared over the previous several nights.

They only had an hour's sleep before the Naked Ones roused the camp for the day's labor in the mines.

After the night's exertions, the day was difficult for Mercury and his small team. But they took every opportunity they could to dig into the roof of the tunnel for grubs, worms, tubers, and anything else they could eat to give themselves energy; tonight would be just as difficult as last, even if they wouldn't have to run for hours carrying their own weight in weapons and ammunition.

Last night they would have died if they had been caught; tonight they might die regardless.

Mercury already knew who the other eight he wanted to recruit were. Over the previous several weeks he'd listened carefully to the guarded grumblings of his fellow prisoners and sounded out those who seemed most realistic about what they'd do if the opportunity arose. The eight were also males alongside whom he'd fought the Moon Flowers or other clans with whom the Bright Sun Clan had been in conflict. During the day he and Hind Claw approached each of the eight and told them to slip from their cages after moon fall and meet at a specific location.

The two did not tell the eight why.

It was half an hour after the moon set before all fourteen were assembled. Even then, Mercury didn't tell them why—although their restrained excitement showed that they were sure of what was up.

"Follow me," Mercury whispered to his squad. "Keep your tails low until you see mine go up, then run as fast as you can to keep up with me." Mercury was well named; he was a very speedy runner.

Without another word, they followed their leader at a safe distance past a drowsy guard post, dropped to all fours to lope through the scrub, then galloped tails high when Mercury began his sprint.

It wasn't a long sprint; the weapons cache was only a half kilometer from the ill-guarded camp. Mercury whispered orders while he distributed the weapons and ammunition. The eight newcomers who joined Mercury's original half dozen grinned while they armed themselves and listened, memorizing their parts in the upcoming action.

Fourteen males. Not many to free an entire clan. But they would strike with speed and surprise, as had the Naked Ones when they first attacked. And the Naked Ones had become overly confident; they'd recently reduced the size of the force

guarding the twin camps, one for the males and one for the females, in which they'd imprisoned the Bright Sun Clan.

The Naked Ones would pay dearly for that complacency.

Armed and with their instructions committed to memory, the
fourteen spread out, going in pairs to their assigned attack positions, six of the positions within two hundred meters of a guard
post. The mortar team remained farther out; its weapon had
greater range and was to take out the camp office and the guard
barracks.

None of them had a timepiece; those were among the personal items confiscated when they were interned in the camps.
But everyone in the squad had put in his army time, and they
were familiar with the heavens. The planet the Naked Ones
called Opal was high in the night sky. When it entered the constellation of the Two-step Asp they were to listen for the mortar
team to fire the shot that would launch the attack. Then they
would fire on the guards in their stations and charge to kill them
or drive them from their posts into the trenches they'd forced the
people to dig as protection for the Naked Ones in the event of an
attack. That was when the canisters marked with the red skull of
the weapons of lingering death would come into play.

Mercury wasn't his real name. That was what he was called by
the Naked Ones—at least by the Naked Ones who could tell the
People apart. And Naked Ones was an ironic name, since they were
not naked: They wore garments that covered all of their bodies except their heads and forearms. They were called the Naked Ones
because they had no fur other than a short, thick thatch on the top
of the head. Some of the Naked Ones had hair too thin to be called
fur elsewhere on their bodies, as Mercury had discovered once
when he saw some of them bathing. They also had a thick patch of
fur at the groin, an area where the People had little or no fur. While
the People wore swatches of animal skin or plant-fiber fabric for
decoration or as symbols of rank, their languages and philosophies
lacked the concept of modesty, so their hairy bodies had no need
for clothing in the hot, arid climate in which they lived.

* * *

All the members of the squad watched the wandering star Opal as it moved through the sky nearer and nearer to the sinuous line of stars that formed the image of the deadly Two-Step Asp. Mercury bared his teeth in a smile, thinking of how that night the constellation did augur death—the death of the Naked Ones who'd imprisoned his people.

Opal never moved rapidly against the starry background, and not nearly as fast as the moon. But on that night, with tension high, it seemed to move even more slowly than usual. Still, Opal did move, and eventually entered the constellation.

Karumph came the muffled sound of the distant mortar bomb being launched.

Mercury tensed and tried to imagine what the Naked Ones in their guard posts might make of the unexpected sound. Did they know it was the opening shot of an attack? Did they think it was distant thunder? Were they even awake and aware enough to recognize the sound as the launching of a mortar bomb?

Seconds later, there could no longer be any question that it was the beginning of an attack; the mortar impacted in the middle of the camp, near the Naked Ones' barracks. By the time it hit, a second mortar bomb was on its way, and then a third and a fourth and a fifth. The mortar team shifted aim slightly between rounds; a millimeter change in the angle of the mortar tube could make a change of meters in the striking point of the bomb.

Under and between the explosions in the middle of the camp, Mercury could make out the faint screams of wounded or frightened guards. A fire suddenly blazed where the mortars were striking; one had hit a fuel dump.

Now, with light to see by, Mercury made out an officer who was shouting orders and hastening the guards out of the area under bombardment, organizing them to go out of the camp in search of the mortar. Closer to him he saw, silhouetted against the flames, the two Naked Ones in the guard post directly in front of him. Instead of facing out, watching for an attack on their position, they were standing erect and looking into the camp at the bursting bombs and burning fuel.

Mercury reached out to touch the neck of Furball, with whom he was partnered, and told him what he wanted to do. Furball answered with a grin that was all teeth. The two took aim and shot at the standing guards. They were already loading fresh rounds into their rifles by the time the bullets they'd fired had hit their targets, and the standing guards dropped out of sight. The guards didn't rise again or return fire.

Mercury heard two more pairs of shots at other places around the perimeter and laughed to himself, certain that more guards had met the Two-step Asp, paying for taking the Bright Sun Clan into captivity.

By then the Naked Ones officer had his males organized and led them at a run toward the nearest gate through the fence. Mercury aimed at the officer, unsteadily seen through the flickering light of the burning fuel, led him, and fired. He rapidly reloaded and fired again. In the increasing darkness as the officer raced from the fire, Mercury couldn't judge his aim well enough; both shots missed. He stopped firing to preserve his ammunition. Besides, he had given away his position. He touched the back of Furball's neck and the two left their position for another, from which they could better intercept the guards who were exiting the camp. Mercury had no way to be sure, but he was confident that at least two other pairs from his squad were also moving to intercept the guard force.

Mercury had been right about the wisdom of changing position; he saw half a dozen of the guards peel off and head, crouched, toward where he and Furball had been. But by the time those Naked Ones reached his former position, he and Furball would be on the other side of the guards who were heading for the mortar's position.

And they were. Mercury sniffed the air and picked up the scent of Ajax and Midnight moving in some fifty meters to his left as he faced the path of the approaching Naked Ones.

Good! Hind Claw and Junior were probably also approaching. Listening, watching, and sniffing, Mercury observed the Naked Ones as they neared his front. He hoped the other pairs would wait for him to fire first, but even if one of the others fired the first shot, his rifle would bark almost immediately. He did his best to aim at one of the guards and waited until the Naked One was almost directly to his front. He fired.

The others had obviously been waiting for him, as five more shots rang out almost simultaneously. The Naked Ones weren't far away, only seventy-five meters or so. From the cries and thuds, Mercury thought that at least three of them had been killed or wounded by the opening shots. As he reloaded he heard shots ring out in the distance as the other three pairs attacked their assigned guard posts.

Before him the Naked Ones had dropped to the ground and were manically returning fire. But they made little attempt to aim, and the shots that didn't strike the ground between Mercury and his males flew harmlessly overhead. *Flechettes,* Mercury had heard the Naked Ones' bullets called. He knew the flechettes were slender, needlelike, and that a flechette rifle seldom needed to be reloaded, unlike the rifles of the People, which had to be reloaded after every shot. Perhaps, Mercury thought, that was why the Naked Ones didn't aim as carefully as the People; if they put out enough fire, they believed that something had to hit. But only being able to fire one time before having to reload, the soldiers of the clans had to aim carefully. Besides, spending much of their lives in tunnels as the People did, they had excellent night vision, far better than the Naked Ones did. And the Naked Ones had almost no sense of smell at all.

So Mercury was confident that he and his five males could take on three times their own number in this night fight and win. Especially after the mortar team stopped firing at the middle of the camp and began dropping its bombs near the Naked Ones. Not long after that, the fire from the guards stopped.

Mercury called out for his own fighters to cease fire. He spent a long moment looking, listening, and sniffing. When the mortar stopped firing, Mercury called out instructions, and he and Furball slung their rifles across their bodies and loped, tails down, toward the end of the line of Naked Ones.

The Naked Ones were all dead or badly wounded. Mercury and Furball collected the Naked Ones' weapons and ammunition and moved them far enough away that the wounded couldn't easily reach them. He called for the rest of his men to come forward. Then he looked, listened, and sniffed for sign of the six guards who had peeled away from the main group and headed for the position he and Furball had originally held.

He smelled blood and fear. Moments later, he and Furball found two Naked Ones, one dead and the other critically wounded. They disarmed the two and returned to the other fighters.

There was still sporadic gunfire from inside the camp, but the boom of the clan's rifles outnumbered the sharper crack of flechette rifles. With all the Naked Ones' weapons and ammunition gathered, Mercury led his fighters into the camp. The fighting was over by the time they got inside. The six who had entered the camp earlier had already collected the enemy's weapons and ammunition and were opening the cages in which the People were held during the night.

The Father had been one of the first to be freed. Mercury hurried to him to report and was shocked by the condition of the clan's dominant male.

The Father didn't want all of the details, not now. He was too weak and in too much pain from the maltreatment he had suffered at the hands of the Naked Ones. After learning that all of the guards were dead or wounded, and satisfied that the wounded guards had not been executed—it was good that there were survivors to tell what had happened—the Father told Mercury to remain in command until he had freed the Mother and the rest of the females and then do as the Mother instructed as though she were the Father.

Murmuring that he wasn't worthy, but not truly believing it, Mercury went to where the gate in the fence between the males' camp and the females' had been breached and sought out the Mother.

The Mother was also weak and in pain. She was even less interested in the details of how Mercury and his squad had accomplished what they did and quickly told him to continue in charge, to free all the members of the clan and lead them to safety.

It didn't take long to gather everybody; fewer than three hundred members of the Bright Sun Clan remained. The Mother and the Father weren't the only ones who had to be carried on litters, but there were enough others sound enough in body that carrying them wasn't an undue burden. They also took all of the Naked Ones' weapons and ammunition that they could find.

Before leaving, Mercury and two of his males took the eight canisters marked with the red skull of lingering death and put them in the tunnels in which the People had been harvesting stones for the Naked Ones. They put four of the canisters deep in the tunnels, set to spew their contents in a short while, after the males exited. The other four canisters they hid near entrances and other places in the tunnels, and attached hidden trip-wires to them so that the next person to pass by would unleash the lingering death they contained. It was a horrible weapon, but most likely Naked Ones would be the next to enter the tunnels.

Naked Ones were the next to enter the tunnels and several of them died horrible, lingering deaths before the decision was made to abandon and seal the tunnels.

In the fullness of time, individual Naked Ones completed their contracts and left the world their kind called Ishtar. And quite naturally, some of them told tales of the lingering death in bars and other gathering places elsewhere in Human Space. Once told, those tales of a killing gas eventually reached the ears of people who knew about an implacable enemy who used weapons that fired a horrible acid, and made a perhaps understandable connection between the horrible killing gas and the horrible killing acid.